MURDER BECOMES MAYFAIR

MURDER BECOMES MAYFAIR

A DALTON LEE MYSTERY

JEFFREY EATON

www.jeffreyeaton.com

Book Three of the *Murder Becomes* series
www.murderbecomes.com

Dedications

This book is dedicated to:

Betsy Baldwin Sunstrom

Kate Coleman

Steve DeWolf

Terry Gallion

Linda Grimes

Ronald Kinney

Russ Munsch

Orvind White

Acknowledgments

The following individuals provided invaluable insights that shaped the content of this novel, and they have my most profound gratitude:

Kathy Biehl

Sandy Chapman

Brandon Conway

Gloria Walker

Randall White

Sharon Wilson

"We never learn. We've been here before.
Why are we always stuck and running from
the bullets, the bullets?"

— Harry Styles

1

"Yes. I now have the target in my sights. But . . ."

"But what?"

"It's not a clean shot. The target keeps swaying. And, depending on which way he leans, the window frame gets in the way."

"Well, give it a minute."

A long pause.

"Okay, I've got him in my sights again. Here we go. Three . . . two . . . oh, bugger!"

"What is it *now*?"

"He's leaning forward. One of the others is in the way."

"You don't have much time. You have to take the shot."

"I know that. I'm just letting you know I'm not very confident about how this is all going to turn out."

"You *need* to be confident. You need to be *very* confident. And *very* precise. You're called a *sharpshooter* for a reason."

"I'm not a sharpshooter, I'm a sniper. There's a difference."

"Oh, bleedin' hell! Are you gormless? This is no time to worry over names. Are you going to go through with this, or do we need to put someone else up there?"

"Okay, okay, he's back where I need him. "Ready to fire. However . . ."

"No, 'however!' Just take the bloody shot.
"NOW!"

Two weeks earlier

2

"We have finally reached that moment in the proceedings when we spotlight the finalists for this year's Metzger Prize and announce the name of the firm that has been chosen to receive it."

Dalton Lee straightened in his chair, arched his shoulders back. For some reason, he felt a need to tug his right pant leg toward his knee, place both shoes firmly on the carpeting.

He had no reason to play coy, really. He wasn't in the least bit ashamed to say that he wanted this award. He wasn't ashamed to say that he wanted it *a lot*.

"Every year," the speaker continued, "the North American Institute of Architecture reviews a portfolio of outstanding designs that, over the past twelve months, evolved from speculative drawings on someone's computer screen to completed buildings that amaze and inspire us."

The woman at the microphone was Felicity Beck, a woman he had worked with several times and for whom he had the highest regard. Her short, upswept hair was now closer to silver than the blonde it had been since birth; she wore a simple, but elegant, black cocktail dress accented with a brooch that shimmered aquamarine.

The fact that Felicity was the one announcing this year's Metzger Prize recipient only made Dalton want the award *that much more*.

"Over the past few weeks, we received more than forty nominations for the prize," she continued. "The projects submitted included everything from a five-star hotel constructed on Vancouver's waterfront, to a cutting-edge library on a college campus in Tennessee, to a cluster of innovative housing pods that homeless people in Detroit now reside in rent-free as they strive to transition to a more conventional lifestyle." A smattering of applause interrupted her; she glanced up from the lectern, smiled, and nodded back at the audience in acknowledgment. "Our esteemed selection committee spent many hours, I promise you, poring over all of the proposals received, studying not just the engineering and architectural challenges each one faced but also the tangible benefits the projects brought to their respective communities. That committee then narrowed the field to . . ." She bowed her head and stepped away from the lectern. ". . . Our three finalists, whom we are delighted to showcase now in this brief video."

The lights lowered, a screen descended from the ceiling, and a bold, red square appeared upon it. Through the stereo speakers, a rock-guitar riff blared, causing several in the audience to duck and cover their ears. Felicity Beck darted back to the microphone.

"Um, could someone please lower the volume?" she asked, but her request had been fulfilled before she had finished her sentence.

Surrounded at the table by his team at The Lee Group, Dalton Lee took two shallow breaths, pressed his lower spine against the back of his chair, and implored the universe to help him somehow endure the presentation with grace. He always loathed these presentations and he had good reason to believe this one would be especially difficult to sit through.

And, sure enough, the first finalist showcased was the new convention center serving northern San Diego County, just a few miles down the freeway from where the awards banquet was taking place. Having been raised in San Diego, Lee had hoped his firm would win that project, would have the chance to produce a "crowned jewel" of a convention center that could serve as a legacy to his beloved hometown. Instead, the contract had gone to the Los Angeles firm of Schraeder, Lofland and Kim. It was a firm bursting with what Lee perceived to be self-possessed "star-chitects" in training, egos each more committed than the next to creating designs that flouted the boundaries of good taste, as well as the laws of applied physics.

It didn't help that, at a coincidental meet-up the previous year at a roulette table in Monte Carlo, the firm's lead principal, Evan Schraeder, raked in more than twelve thousand dollars in less than an hour while Lee bled fifty-dollar chips.

As the images showed each angle of the half-bulbous, half-spiky, convention center, Lee's expression turned from miffed to sour. Every section of the building, he felt, was out of proportion with the other; to him, its goal was not so much making an arena of inspiration for its occupants but making a dramatic spectacle of itself instead.

A warm palm descended upon his left wrist. It belonged to Lara, his second-in-command. She squeezed his wrist firmly, raised both eyebrows, and gave him an outrageously artificial smile. Lee knew she was sending him a signal, and he contemplated whether to ignore it or cooperate. He chose the latter. Taking in a deep breath, he steeled himself and smiled back, his countenance even more counterfeit than hers.

As discreetly as he could, he leaned in her direction and silently mouthed the word "bleh."

The second finalist was the new Museum of Indigenous Art in Ottawa. Lee felt more kindly toward this project and its design firm, Tremblay and Potts. He and Nick Tremblay, the firm's principal, had been interns together at an architectural firm in Toronto before Nick had drifted off on some six-month adventure in the jungles of Indonesia. Also, he felt the designs delivered by Tremblay's team were at least respectable, if somewhat staid.

I do love the Canadians, Lee thought as he took a sip from his water glass. *They are such ... pleasant people. But I have to wonder if at times, all that civility gets in the way of their ingenuity.*

An "ahh" went up from the assembly as a shot of one of the museum's galleries appeared. From a trapezoidal skylight above, an almost blue-yellow light bathed the gallery's dove-gray walls, adding a soft iridescence to the paintings and artifacts on display.

Lee had to agree that the angle at which the firm had directed the natural light was pure genius. *Still,* he thought, *I would have positioned the interior walls at more unusual angles.*

That's when the microphone on the side of the lectern took a nosedive from the brace that had been holding it, causing a painful reverberation that ricocheted throughout the room. Conference volunteers–bent at their waists as if they suffered from severe osteoporosis–darted toward the lectern from both sides of the dais. In so doing, they jostled the screen, causing the heralded museum to suddenly look as if it were on a boat that was navigating choppy seas.

Lee glanced to the far right of the room where conference organizer Wendy McCambridge stood against a sturdy partition, the tips of two fingers pressed heavily against the bridge of her nose. He tapped Lara's forearm and nodded toward the anguished architect.

"I think you should volunteer to manage next year's event," he whispered. "If you were riding herd on this group, things like this would never happen."

She looked back at him, the faintest of smirks crinkling the side of her mouth.

"Not in a million years," she replied, with the tone of someone asked to swallow a rattlesnake.

Eventually, the chaos subsided, and the presentation resumed. It was time for The Lee Group's project to get its due.

Under consideration was the mixed-use complex along Biscayne Bay they had been commissioned to design after their assignment in Miami two years earlier. It housed a striking condo tower equipped with the latest technologies, a retail village occupied solely by locally owned businesses, and a combination charter school/research hub where children from the neighborhood could explore how to build an app for the latest smart phones, or program a robot to accomplish complex tasks. The project was already considered a rousing success, with 97 percent of the residences and 91 percent of the business spaces occupied. More important, it had been heralded worldwide for the creative ways The Lee Group had lessened the complex's impact on the environment.

The narration accompanying the slides began. But Lee's mind drifted to the people around his table, the architects and designers who had not only guided 3 Biscayne Tower to its completion, but had also locked arms with him, joined forces with him, in ways no one else in the room could possibly imagine.

On his right sat Warren Jackson, the senior architect he could most rely upon to deliver stellar designs and innovative thinking about how to make projects desirable and sustainable. And, when the need for crucial evidence required it, to clamber up the side of a building, or scale a towering wall.

Warren provided the team with a balm of Caribbean cool that had steadied it through many a chaotic turn, a nonchalance Lee assumed his employee had acquired during his early years in Barbados. Lee sighed silently as he thought of Warren's two young children and how close they had come to losing their father in Manhattan.

We must rescue his wife from those barbarians, Lee told himself. *I can live without my parents. Those kids need their mother.*

On the other side of Warren was Bree Westerman. For someone who always seemed to be in motion, whose hands always had to be toying with, fumbling with, *something,* Bree seemed uncharacteristically focused at the moment. She wasn't twisting her napkin into a knot, wasn't manipulating the knitting needles that usually came with her. It seemed she had wrestled to the ground whatever demon it was that, for so many years, had caused her to lash out at her boss, at Warren, at most any male she came into contact with. And, he was pleased that she had become more engaged in their projects of late and had contributed several smart tweaks to the complex being showcased at that very moment.

Lee hoped that someday, they could also rescue Bree's long-time friend and confidante, Carole. If they ever received verifiable information as to Carole's whereabouts, he would move the earth *and* sun to get her out of captivity for Bree.

Liam was in the chair beyond Bree, and what a stir he had caused when they all sauntered into the ballroom. The perpetual surfie— usually adorned in torn jeans, a t-shirt, a puka-shell necklace, and flip-flops—stunned the room in his designer tuxedo and glistening cufflinks. Somehow, Liam seemed to have suddenly added an inch to his height, to have broadened his shoulders by a couple more. And then there were *those eyelashes.*

The head of The Lee Group couldn't help feeling somewhat envious of the young Aussie. Prior to Liam joining the firm, Lee was the one everyone would smile at and coo over whenever The Lee Group attended a public function. Lee was still handsome, but he knew he was now a day or two past his sell-by date. So, he felt no guilt whatsoever at employing a "face boy" like Liam to help restore the firm's sex appeal. Plus, Liam had proved his value to the firm time and again with his superior knowledge of all things technological.

He thought of the young man's older sister, being held bound and gagged in some jungle, tundra, warehouse, or cave. Forced to eat who-knows-what. *If* she were being fed at all. Lee narrowed his gaze at Liam, nodded once in his direction and silently said, *Glad you're on OUR team, not theirs, mate.*

The architect was distracted by a crescendo of applause. A slide showing the interior of the innovative day-care center they had designed for 3 Biscayne Tower had flashed upon the screen, and it was being met with a chorus of "ohs" and "wows". The purple and orange and silver walls were bedecked with large placards that showed how several words were pronounced in the Mandarin language, or how to form the most common hand gestures used in American Sign Language. One entire wall was an interactive tablet computer providing students access to educational apps and touch-screen navigation. And the center's fitness corner featured flooring made of recycled cork.

Lara leaned into him.

"I swear," she whispered, "if the judges weren't impressed by the fact that every bolt, rivet, and beam in that project is eco-friendly *and* was manufactured in an American factory, then *I give up.*"

Lee nodded but returned his attention not to the screen but to those seated around him. He studied Roberto, directly across from him, who was fidgeting the way Bree normally would. Some might stereotypically attribute the young man's high-strung behavior to his Puerto Rican background. Lee just assumed that as the project's chief designer, Roberto was probably more nervous about the award than anyone else at the table.

Or, more likely, he thought, *he's still frantic over Isabela's condition. Brothers are protective enough as it is. BIG brothers take it to a whole different level.*

What Lee was witnessing was the designer drumming his fingers on the tabletop and bouncing one leg almost maniacally. What he tried to visualize, instead, was the designer embracing his adolescent sister, a look of joy and relief on his face.

That left Lara, who was now engrossed in how the presentation was going and how others in the room were responding to it. She was his rock, but he would never let her know that. She kept the firm anchored, humming, united, every minute of every day of every week of every year. And, thanks to the legacy of award-winning projects designed by her father, the Järvinen name resonated in development circles far beyond her native Finland and probably attracted business The Lee Group wouldn't otherwise receive.

She had seemed to withdraw that night in Miami when he showed her the engagement ring he hoped to offer a betrothed one day. However, her iciness had thawed as quickly as it had appeared. He just chalked her attitude up, as he always did, to her constant battle with the fact her father now seemed committed to assisting The Organization, a defection he was horrified to learn his own father was about to make (if he were to believe what his secret contact had told him in Miami).

How did a cult inspired by a popular science-fiction novel evolve into such a venal group of human beings? he wondered. Lee had read the book *Wayward Colony*—not once, but three times. Had come to appreciate some of the literary wordplay it offered. Had even understood, at a certain level, the exasperation of the colonists who lived on one of Saturn's moons, yet suffered under the rule imposed upon them by those on the mother planet.

The architect chewed the inside of one cheek, then shook his head. The book was great reading, but it was still *fiction. Most people in the world today have more freedoms than ever,* he told himself. And yet, The Organization continued to attract hundreds (maybe thousands) of acolytes every year—disenfranchised people, who had fallen behind educationally, emotionally, financially, or all the above. People certain that, if the world would just let everyone do whatever they wanted, whenever they wanted, everything would be ideal. What was the phrase they used to describe it . . . *living flawless lives in a very flawed world?*

And yet, to achieve those ends, The Organization had murdered several innocent people, kidnapped scores more, and practically instituted martial law when they were on the cusp of controlling some city or country. *Do they not see the hypocrisy of their actions?* he asked himself. *Or are they aware of their duplicity and just don't care?*

Lee was jolted from his daydream by thunderous applause. The video detailing the finalists for the award had come to an end and Felicity Beck was returning to the lectern, her face beaming with joy.

"Well, I do believe all of you will agree with me when I say this year's finalists for the Metzger Prize embody our industry's most demanding standards and encourage us all to seek out novel pathways to making the buildings we work, play, live, and assemble in even more rich, and more resonant, than those created by our predecessors."

Another round of applause echoed throughout the room. The emcee carefully tilted the top of the microphone so she'd be speaking more directly into it and allowed a more serious look to replace her smile.

"It is now my privilege to announce the recipient of this year's Metzger Prize, our industry's highest honor." She looked down and started to unseal an envelope hidden by the lectern. "The Metzger Prize this year is awarded to . . ." She appeared to fumble some with the contents of the envelope, but then suddenly erupted in an almost schoolgirl grin.

Everyone at Dalton's table sat in suspended animation, their focus locked on the front of the room. Everyone, that is, except Dalton, who was blinking non-stop, studying the busboy in the right back corner, and wondering where the young man had gotten such a terrific haircut.

"To Tremblay and Potts, and their Museum of Indigenous Art in Ottawa!"

It was as if someone at Lee's table had simultaneously let go of six party balloons, the necks of which had never been tied. The representatives of The Lee Group applauded sincerely but not enthusiastically. The worst part for Lee was having to watch all his employees swivel in their chairs and send him a downcast look.

Lee started to carve once more into the mystery chicken on his plate, but quickly replaced his utensils when Lara shot him a disapproving look.

At that moment, a server stepped up to the right of Dalton Lee's elbow.

"Excuse me, Mr. Lee?"

The architect turned slowly. Dressed in the obligatory white shirt, dark slacks, and black bow tie, this server stood out from the others only because of his towering height and shiny, shaved head. In his hand was a simple white card, folded in half.

"Yes?" Lee said, his voice taking on a wisp of worry.

"For you, sir," was all the giant said. "I was instructed to tell you that it's urgent." Lee's colleagues stopped accumulating their belongings and bolted their attention upon the head of the firm.

Lee nodded, and the server retreated. The architect opened the card and began to absorb its message, his lips parting ever so imperceptibly as he did. When he had finished reading, he carefully closed the card. Set it on the table. Took as long as he possibly could before he returned the looks of his employees.

Who waited.

Finally, he twisted his lips into a half-smile, half-grimace. Arched his eyebrows dramatically. Then gave them one brief but definitive nod.

Collectively, the architects and designers sitting around the table sighed, shut their eyes, and lowered their heads in perfect unison.

3

Their flight to London seemed endless. And the landing at Heathrow was anything but gentle, waking Lee from what had been a fitful slumber.

As a result, by the time everyone had collected their luggage and trudged their way through customs, the head of The Lee Group was cranky.

"I've never liked the design of this airport," he announced with a sniff. The others glanced around the terminal lobby, looking for obvious verification of their boss's verdict. But they weren't sure what they should be looking for.

"I mean, Terminal One was *abysmal*. Thank heavens they've demolished that. And we can't really say these newer terminals light a fire in anyone's soul, can we?" Lee continued.

Bree looked at Roberto, who squinted at Liam, who turned toward Lara, who raised her eyebrows at Warren, who dropped his gaze to the floor for a few moments, then looked directly at his superior.

"You know, Dalton, you're absolutely right. There is *so* much more they could have done with this terminal alone." Warren paused, swiveled to his left. "Take that bank of windows over there. That's the best they could do with a bank of windows? Seriously?"

Everyone swiveled in the direction Warren was gesturing, provided vague murmurs of half-hearted support.

"Precisely," Lee replied. "Look at those windows. Just *look* at them! I mean, *really!*"

Warren turned and headed for the exit, winking at Lara as he did so.

They wheeled their luggage through the bustling baggage claim area to the even more crowded passenger pick-up area. On their right, they spotted a young woman in dark slacks and a crisp, white short-sleeved shirt who was holding a placard that read "THE LEE GROUP."

"Mr. Lee?" she asked, extending one hand and flashing a bright smile. "I'm Anisa. I'll be taking you and your group to headquarters. I hope you had a pleasant flight?"

Instantly charmed by the young woman, Lee decided to be cordial rather than truthful.

"Yes, it was quite . . . relaxing," he replied, flashing a grin in return. "I was watching an action-adventure film, so that helped make the time speed by."

Everyone slowly filed toward the exit. Since all of them would be traveling in one shuttle van, Roberto elected to join them, on the grounds the carbon footprint he'd be leaving wouldn't be *that* much larger than the one he'd create if he used the Underground. Besides, he had no idea where they were headed.

Lara sidled up next to Lee, nudged his elbow.

"You know you slept off and on almost the entire flight." She looked at him like a teacher admonishing a student who has just offered an outlandish excuse for not having his homework. "And when you did watch a movie, it was one of those silly – what do you Americans call them? – romcoms."

Lee shrugged his shoulders, allowed one side of his mouth to crinkle in delight.

Once they were all inside the van, Anisa spent much of her time looking at the team through the rearview mirror as she commandeered the steering wheel. Lee was impressed with how she could simultaneously manage an intelligent conversation and London's congestion.

"C. J. was hoping to brief you this afternoon," she told them, "but she's had a personal issue come up that prevents that. Besides, you probably will have some meaningful jet lag for the next day or so. I know I always did after my flights here from Amman. And, I think, even with a stopover, that's a much shorter trip than your flight from LA." She presented the idea as a statement rather than a question.

Roberto nudged Liam and raised his eyebrows to indicate how impressed he was with their driver's knowledge of the world.

"So, C. J. thought it best that I just take you directly to the residence you'll be staying in for the length of the investigation, and let you get some rest," she went on. "She told me to tell you she'll be prepared to brief you first thing tomorrow morning."

Lee nodded, folded his hands in front of him. The traffic came to a sudden halt, hurling everyone forward in the van. Anisa twice hit the horn sharply with the bottom of her palm.

"Sorry about that, everyone," she said with a slight frown. "Looks like there's quite a smash-up on the M4. Fortunately, I know a way around, but I'm afraid it will add several minutes to the trip." She edged the van forward to the next intersection, swung the wheel to the right, and headed them down a narrow side street. Once she had cleared the gridlock that had been in front of them, she glanced into the rearview mirror. "In the meantime, Mr. Lee, I'm happy to answer any questions you might have about the case."

"Excuse me?" the architect replied, his reverie broken. "You are . . . you can . . . what?"

Anisa captured his gaze in the rearview mirror and flashed another broad smile. *Really, she is quite beautiful,* the architect thought. *Stunning eyes. Amazing cheekbones.*

"Oh, I see. You thought I was just your driver." She returned her attention to the vehicles ahead and her smile became more self-knowing. "Sorry I didn't properly introduce myself back at Heathrow. My name's Anisa. Anisa Nassir. Inspector at Scotland Yard. Pleasure to meet all of you."

With that, everyone shifted in their seats, improved their posture. This time, it was Liam who nudged Roberto.

"And you *drive the shuttle van?*" Lee asked, chuckling.

Her wide smile was back. "Only for our most prestigious visitors," she answered.

After a few beats, Lee decided to get things underway.

"So, who is our victim this time, Anisa?"

Her attention was back on the cars and trucks around them; her tone became more businesslike.

"His name was Antonio Tinti. Late forties. A tailor. A tailor on Savile Row, actually. Widower. His wife died of cancer about five years back. Lost his only child, a son, just a few weeks ago in an automobile accident. No known connections to organized crime . . ." She hesitated, looked back at Lee through the rearview mirror. "No known connection *to them.*" Lee nodded, and she returned her view to the panorama outside the van's windshield.

"Perfectly average person in every way, as best we can tell. Unassuming. Mostly kept to himself. We're still gathering intel about his recent whereabouts, close associates, things like that."

Lee nodded again, peered out the window at a gaggle of Chinese tourists taking selfies beside the Royal Botanic Gardens, Kew.

"How was he murdered? And where?" he asked.

The van slowed to a crawl again, but Anisa kept her gaze in front of her. "He was shot with a Glock G19 equipped with a silencer. Three or four times, at point blank range. Landscapers found his body behind some hedges in a secluded corner of Hanover Square, in Mayfair. Seems to me a rather odd place for them to kill someone, it being such a prominent location." She carefully guided the van into the next lane.

"We haven't found anyone who admits they saw or heard anything. Which I also find a bit peculiar. The park closes at four in the afternoon, but even though it's a quiet area, there can be people milling about the area well into the night. And the medical examiner says Tinti was killed within an hour or so of midnight. You'd think someone might have noticed somebody inside the park that late."

"How did they get into the park?"

Anisa's eyes caught Lee's in the rearview mirror.

"That's another good question," was her reply.

A somber quiet enveloped the van for several seconds. Eventually, Lee cleared his throat. "And they left their . . . calling card?"

Once again, Anisa used the rearview mirror to capture his attention. She flashed a smile, but it was more pained than pleasant. "Unfortunately, yes. It was found on his chest. A blank page sliced from a first-edition copy of *Wayward Planet,* folded neatly into a small square. With the words, *Griff Davis Did It* written across it. Their standard procedure."

Lee set his lips firm; nodded over and over. In the book, Griff Davis was a poet and raconteur the rebels imprisoned for running afoul of their local customs. The mention of a character from the novel was the definitive sign the murder had been engineered by The Organization.

He chewed the inside of one cheek for a time, shook his head back and forth once. Finally, he softly uttered, "Well, I guess that ties everything up in a neat little bow, doesn't it?"

4

They sat at the back of one of the subway cars, side by side, silent. To the disinterested observer, it would appear they were traveling together, and to a certain degree, they were. But they had entered the car at completely different tube stops and had not spoken a word during the entire trip.

Until now.

"I love to ride the Underground late at night," one said to the gentleman nearby. "I love how quiet it gets, especially this far out." They were on the District line, passing through Hornchurch on their way to Upminster, the line's final stop. The cars traveled above ground here, but most of the scenery was obliterated by darkness outside the windows and grime upon them. Only one other person was in their car, a young black male with a vaguely Rastafarian air, who sat several seats in front of them, eyes closed. He was slumped against the window, listening to music through a pair of grimy earbuds. He had paid them no notice for as long as they'd been in the car.

"Now that the tailor is no longer a problem, I assume I'm free to . . ."

The other person turned his head to peer out the window.

"Yes, thanks to you, we do have one less person standing in the way," he said. "We are truly grateful for the service you provided. However, we need for you to stay a bit longer."

The interruption had been swift, but gentle. Still, the comment came across more as a declaration than a request.

"How much longer?"

A long sigh exited his nostrils. The car jostled some as it banked a curve, the rhythmic clack of the wheels against the rails took up the temporary void.

"Not long. A week, maybe two. We need to keep you close by for a while. It's standard operating procedure at this stage of The Transformation."

Headlights from a nearby motorway flashed throughout the carriage as it raced past the automobiles and lorries; the car swayed once again, before settling onto a smooth straightaway.

"Would everything remain the same? I mean, my benefits, my fee?"

"Of course. Absolutely. Same as it has been. Low key, undercover. Again, it should only be for a week or two. Three at the most."
The conversation ended. The subway car began to brake; soon it would be arriving at the Upminster stop.

"Oh, sorry," he added. "There is one thing that will be different." His companion turned and was surprised by the grave expression the speaker exhibited.

"The phase of the project you executed for us in Hanover Square was – how should I say it – very *strategic*. Very *precise*. Very *clean*." The speaker plunged one hand into a jacket pocket, extracted a Malteser, and tucked it underneath his tongue. Slurped on it quietly for a couple of moments then resumed the conversation.

"The next phase, however, will be more . . . *tactical*. It will be *anything but* clean. It will be . . . gruesome . . . really. You're likely to witness great devastation, horrific carnage." He stopped to suck some more on the candy.

"Are you up for that?"

The passenger near the front of the car stirred some, then fell back against the window. Suddenly, the brakes screeched, and the car jerked, as it began to enter the line's last station.

"I am willing to do whatever it takes to overthrow the powers that be," came the reply. It was issued softly, as if it were an incantation being recited before candles. "I have said it before and I will say it again. Power to the cause."

The train was grinding to a slow lurch. The glaring lights from the station platforms began to appear up ahead.

The person in the jacket swallowed the malted milk ball in one quick gulp, flashed a forced smile in the other's direction.

"Yes," he replied. "Most certainly. Power to the cause, indeed."

5

Most of Lee's team slept luxuriously, uninterruptedly. Slept a dense, invigorating sleep beneath majestic comforters and sheets that felt like their thread count was in the thousands. A sleep they bounded from with energy to spare.

The rejuvenation came to everyone on the team . . . except for Lee. His afternoon and night were not really fitful, but neither had they been restful. For an hour he had sat wide awake in an armchair, working through the questions he wanted to ask at the briefing. Then, for the next two (maybe three) hours, he would be heavy-lidded and slouching, dreaming either of red-leather wrist cuffs, or his Maicoletta scooter (which he hoped would arrive from California in a day or two).

As a result, while the others rose just before five and devoured a full English breakfast prepared for them by the housekeeper he'd hired after their adventure in Miami, the head of the firm padded into the dining room a full hour and twenty minutes later. At that point, only Bree and Lara remained at the table, sipping breakfast tea and skimming the pages of the *Times*.

"Dalton, I think there are some *huge* advantages to all of us staying in a townhouse like this," Bree chirped as she set the paper down to take a large gulp of coffee.

"Really?" he replied, buttering a piece of toast. "And, by the way, where *is* everyone else?"

"They're here, somewhere," Bree replied, lifting two fingers to her lower lip so an errant scrap of egg wouldn't tumble from her mouth. "And, see, that's one advantage right there. Having everyone in the same place means we're less likely to be out doing . . . you know . . . touristy things." Lee and Lara looked at one another, smiled discreetly.

"This feels more like a home, with common areas, so I think we'll probably strategize and collaborate more frequently than we would in some impersonal hotel. Plus, this townhouse has *so much* character! It can't help but make us feel more . . . British. I know I'm going to think more like an Englishwoman, better understand the English psyche, by being here."

Lara looked across the table at Bree, stone-faced. "Are you, now?" the older woman said, chewing discreetly on a bite of scone. "Do tell, when precisely can we expect your transformation into the perfect English rose to occur?" Bree tilted her head, unsure what to think of that, but soon chuckled when she saw her colleague's mouth relax into a wry smile.

Lara shifted her attention toward her superior.

"To answer your question, Dalton, everyone else is getting ready for the briefing. What time are we to be there?"

Lee shifted his wrist to see the face of his watch and jolted.

"Nine, sharp," he replied, now devouring the scrambled eggs on the plate in front of him.

***

The vestibule outside the commander's office was cramped. It had one less seat than Lee had team members.

So Roberto slumped against a tall metal file cabinet, playing on his phone. *He's probably hoping to get a message from his little sister that's probably never going to arrive,* Lee thought. Lara was casually flipping through the pages of some forensics magazine that he knew she couldn't possibly be interested in. Bree, of course, had brought her knitting, the red ball of yarn almost invisible against her maroon skirt.

Warren sat placidly in his chair, his eyes narrow, sleepy slits. Liam had taken the seat next to Warren when they first arrived, but after a while, he jumped up, strode over beside Roberto, and peeked over his co-worker's shoulder to watch whatever the designer had up on his screen.

Lee tilted his head upward. *Please don't let them be watching porn,* he beseeched the universe.

Somewhere nearby, a wall clock was ticking, a sound Lee thought had vanished years ago. From the vestibule, he could see the department's other employees milling from one cubicle to the next. At one metal desk nearby, a young blonde resembling a bit player in a 1940s-era movie studied a computer screen intently, occasionally pushing an errant lock of hair back over one ear.

"This C. J., the one's who's heading the investigation, what do you think?" Liam whispered to Roberto. "Catherine Janelle? Courtney Jeanine?" A mildly lascivious sneer was on the young Aussie's face.

Roberto smiled, shrugged slightly. "I dunno." He used an index finger to scroll through the content on his phone. Then he turned and tilted his head toward Liam. "You know, it could also be Camila Juanita or Catalina Jimena." His colleague nodded, dug an elbow into Roberto's rib cage.

"I bet it's Caitlyn Janette," the Aussie said with total conviction.

Her name was Clara Josephine Digby, and after having some difficulty opening the door to her office, she stumbled into the vestibule with all the grace of a Bulgarian weightlifter approaching the mat. Her cocoa-brown pantsuit pulled taut against her lumpy frame; underneath it she wore a light blue blouse with a collar that jutted out over the jacket's lapels like the wings of some contemporary fighter jet. Bree first spotted how thick the woman's ankles were; Lara noticed instantly that C. J.'s hands resembled oven mitts.

The men, however, were instantly drawn to (or was it repelled by?) another of her features.

"That *hair,*" Liam whispered into Roberto's ear as discreetly as possible. "Did someone just drop a colander over her head and start hacking around the bottom of it?"

"Dalton Lee!" the commander blared, one mitt extended. "C. J. Digby. Welcome. A pleasure to finally meet you, I do say. I trust you and your team are all set in the townhouse we secured for you? Do you find the accommodations to your liking?"

Lee found the grin she offered disarming, for it made her come across like that friendly, freckle-faced kid who always got picked next-to-last for the softball team.

"Yes, everything is awesome . . . I mean, it's lovely," the architect replied, shaking her hand.

"Brilliant," she responded, clapping her mitts in front of her as if they held blackboard erasers that needed cleaning. "And not to worry, Dalton, here in London we allow California speak." She crossed her hands in front of her abdomen, widened both her grin and her eyes at him.

"In moderation, of course."

She ushered them into her tiny office, encouraging them to stand or sit wherever they could find a place they could squeeze into. Sickly plants occupied much of the space in front of the windows; in one chair rested a battered satchel, its clasp slightly askew. Stacks of journals and periodicals cluttered the floor, and the room had a vaguely medicinal smell, as if a small bottle of camphor were sitting open in some corner.

Overall, the room reeked bland, save for a vibrantly colored poster behind C. J.'s desk promoting a concert by a local saxophonist.

"Sorry about the . . . disarray," C. J. said, waving her right arm throughout the air. "In their most recent round of budget cuts, my superiors insisted I relinquish my workspace at Windsor Castle." She ended her commentary with another goofy grin to let them know the castle reference was a joke, then plopped herself into the large wooden chair behind her desk. She leaned to one side and, like a bear snaring a trout from a river, scooped up a bulging file folder and dragged it toward her. She exhaled once and flipped open the file.

"I believe all of you met my very capable assistant, Inspector Nassir," she said as she rifled through the sheets of paper inside the folder. "I was going to have her join us this morning but thought she best gather some additional background about our victim instead. And I do apologize for not being able to brief you yesterday, but some sort of belt or hose or cable under the bonnet of my sedan decided it was time to meet its heavenly reward." She methodically turned over each page in the file, mouthing the words on each as she read.

She stopped and peered up at them.

"Mr. Lee, I want to impress upon you that we have nothing but the highest regard for your expertise as it pertains to The Organization, their *modus operandi*, and the like. At the same time, although I know you have some familiarity with our fair city, we probably are the experts when it comes to the local angles of this case.

"That said, *do not hesitate* to ask us for whatever resources you need. You and your team members are welcome to join us to gather your own insights and evidence on whatever reconnaissance missions we go on. *Comprende?*"

Roberto did a double take, impressed not only that she knew Spanish, but also that she had pronounced the word almost perfectly. The rest of the team looked at one another and nodded in reply to her question.

"All right, then. I'm assuming you want to visit the *scène du crime* as soon as possible?"

Bree and Liam gave their boss a baffled look, but he dipped his head once and replied, "Yes, commander, I would appreciate the opportunity to see with my own eyes where the victim's body was found."

She dipped her head in return.

"Fine, we'll arrange for that to take place this afternoon. But two things. First, everyone here is to call me C. J. No need for silly protocol among us. I never attended a boarding school, and although I'm grateful you have respect for my position, the fact is, you probably have a lot more respect for it than I do."

Some on Lee's team exchanged humorous glances on the sly, but Lee remained laser-focused on the woman behind the desk.

"Second, I should probably fill you in on what we know so far, which is not much." She returned to the pile of papers she had taken out of the folder and flipped the first two over to read from the back.

"I believe Inspector Nassir provided the few details we have about the victim. According to the medical examiner, Mr. Tinti met his demise sometime between eleven in the evening and one in the morning. We know a pistol was used, but we haven't yet located it. The poor chap was found on his back, and it appears he was shot at very close range, which means he likely knew his assailant."

Lee raised one eyebrow. *"Our* victims always *know* their assailant," he said with solemnity. C. J. turned to him and nodded that she both understood, and agreed with, his point. "However," Lee continued, "what's interesting to me is both the proximity of the killing *and* its remote location in the park. That tells me we have a killer who probably didn't act as a sniper, but instead, confronted Mr. Tinti within–or perhaps even accompanied him to–the square before shooting him. Would you agree?"

"I do," the commander replied. "And the answer is 'accompanied to.' Or at the very least, 'met him at.'"

Lee cocked his head.

"How do we know that?"

C. J. smiled, reached behind her to scratch a spot on her upper back.

"As I said a moment ago, the examiner says Mr. Tinti was murdered sometime between eleven and one," she replied. "However, I believe Inspector Nassir informed you that the gates to Hanover Square are locked at around four p.m." She flashed another quick smile to make her point.

Lee squinted. "And we don't have any indication as to how Mr. Tinti and his killer got into the park around midnight."

The commander cocked her head and raised both eyebrows. "I am sorry to say we do not."

Bree gripped the ball of yarn in her lap with her left hand, raised her right palm tentatively.

"Is it possible he was . . . murdered elsewhere? And then his body was taken to the park and left there?"

C. J. issued a scowl, then quickly righted it into another tight smile.

"Not likely, milady," she answered. The commander pushed her head forward. "Bree, is it? Like the cheese?"

Bree tilted her head to one side and began, "Well, no . . ."

"Yes, Bree, such a *lovely* name, it is," C. J. interrupted. "Well, Bree, that's a good thought you had there, a very good thought indeed, however . . . well, you see, the fence surrounding Hanover Square is not terribly tall, but it does have quite a bit of foliage right up against it for much of the length around. So it would have required someone with the strength of Samson, I think, to heave over the fence and beyond the shrubbery a body that was likely well along with rigor mortis. Also, the odds of our victim landing perfectly on his back after such a heave are . . . well . . . astronomical, aren't they?"

C. J. sent a friendly smile Bree's way.

"And then, of course, there is the circumstance of The Organization's calling card. Even if it had been placed in Mr. Tinti's shirt pocket, which it was not, a toss like that probably would have sent that piece of paper sailing well into the north of Scotland if not the North Sea itself, now, wouldn't it?"

Bree grinned meekly at the commander and returned her attention to her ball of yarn.

"So, when all is said and done, it appears what we have is a killer who gained Mr. Tinti's trust, lured him to the park somehow, shot him there, and then, skedaddled."

Lee clasped his hands in front of him.

"Well, a quick review of the texts or voice mails sent to his phone should tell us who lured him there, correct?" The commander frowned.

"You're right, Mr. Lee, it *should*. However, we've not located the victim's mobile. Oddly enough, it was not on his body inside the park. And, fairly thorough inspections of his flat and automobile have not revealed its whereabouts."

"Are there any surveillance videos that would show the movement of people around the park that night?" Lara asked.

C. J. was nodding, when she stopped, thrust her head toward a precise point on her desktop, squinted some, and then flicked onto the floor what had either been a dead fly or a crust of food. After a moment, she pulled her head back and returned her attention to Lara.

"I'm sorry, what was that?"

Lara looked uncertainly at Lee, who couldn't hide a smirk as he nodded to her to proceed.

"Videos. I was wondering if there might be any surveillance videos."

"Oh, right, videos. Well, possibly. That's one angle I was hoping someone on your team might be able to help us with, Mr. Lee. Track down with the borough and the city what footage might be out there and then help us obtain it. Staff shortages truly are hampering us these days, I must say."

"We'd be happy to," he replied. "And please, call me Dalton."

C. J. sighed heavily and pushed herself back in the chair, causing it to roll away from the desk. "Obviously, Dalton, I'm quite dispirited by Mr. Tinti's demise," she said softly. "But what I am more concerned about is what his murder *portends*. What exactly is it a . . . harbinger of." She stopped, looked at Lee gravely. "What The Organization has in store for us now that Mr. Tinti has . . . bought the farm."

She extended both arms, gripped the front of her desk and rolled the chair back to its original location. She placed both palms horizontally on the top of her workspace, elbows out, and pressed firmly against the desktop, like a child struggling to keep a bunch of rambunctious puppies inside a cardboard box.

"And as for that," the commander continued, "we haven't a single clue."

6

Lee was able to enjoy a reasonable catnap before it became time to head off to Hanover Square and explore where Tinti had been murdered.

Upon exiting the townhouse, he was delighted to see that, for early autumn, the weather was unusually crisp and exceptionally bright. So Lee chose to walk that afternoon rather than take the Tube or a car. The fresh air would help clear his head, he believed, and the exercise would give him a chance to enjoy London at street level.

His route took him through the heart of Belgravia, the uber-wealthy residential district Lee had admired since his school days at Cambridge. Developed in the 1820s, the district exuded a grand yet understated dignity one would not easily find in other cities around the world. Expansive terraces of white-stuccoed structures, with balconies sporting flags or potted trees, stretched out seemingly in every direction. Behind many of the stolid façades were second homes owned by some emir based in Dubai or a petrocrat living in Russia.

It was the neighborhood once occupied by Mozart and Chopin, by actress Vivien Leigh and Beatles' manager Brian Epstein. The father of Prime Minister Winston Churchill had been born here, former prime minister Neville Chamberlain once lived in Belgravia, and former prime minister Margaret Thatcher had retired here.

More to Lee's liking, however, was the fact that Belgravia had been the home of not only James Bond's creator, Ian Fleming, but also two actors who had portrayed the intelligence officer 007—Sean Connery and Sir Roger Moore.

Lee had to admit he was probably most keen on the area because its developer, Richard Grosvenor, had been an enthusiastic patron of many of the best architects of the day, from William Burn of Scotland, to John Douglas of Chester (who had designed more than five hundred buildings before his career came to an end). Lee tried to calculate how many structures he himself had created but stopped when he realized it wasn't even one-third that many.

In time, his route took him alongside Chesham Place, a dignified manse composed of a 20,000-square-foot grand house and three large apartments. *How anyone can afford to purchase such an estate these days, much less maintain it, is beyond me,* he silently exclaimed. As he always did, Lee looked across the road to see what views the residence enjoyed and discovered they were of the gardens of Eaton Square, named for the Grosvenor family's estate outside Liverpool.

Before World War Two, the square had been a second-tier address. But since then, many of the tonier buildings in Belgravia and Mayfair had gone commercial, evolving into premier office space or boutique hotels. As a result, Eaton Square had surged to the top of the list of places to live in London, with each flat costing several million pounds.

He loved their classical profile—three bays across and four (or five) stories tall, augmented by an attic, a basement, and a mews house in back. *They have such an elegant order about them,* he thought.

He loved the square's architecture but did not love its name.

Eaton, he sniffed to himself. *Never have liked the sound of that. It sounds so . . . curt . . . so brusque . . . so . . . . BARBARIC.*

He felt a stirring and was tempted to pop into a nearby pub, The Antelope, and order some battered cod and a pint of London Pride ale. But he'd already had lunch, and work was calling, so he forced himself to move on toward his appointment.

Lee turned north on Chesham Street and headed toward its intersection with Lowndes Street next to the Egyptian Consulate. He now had to resist an urge to run into the Pierre Hermé shop for one of its milk-chocolate-and-passion-fruit macaroons, or its tarte made with vanillas from Tahiti, Mexico, and Madagascar. The temptation was strong, but he knew either treat would destroy the calorie burn his stroll was affording him.

He glanced at his watch, and in so doing almost stumbled headlong into a baby stroller being navigated by a young woman wearing a charcoal-gray hijab.

"Sorry," he blurted out, reverting to the linguistic patterns he had acquired while attending Cambridge. The woman pushing the pram looked at him as if he were a museum curiosity. She reminded him of Inspector Nassir, only without the relaxed accessibility of the Scotland Yard detective. Or her breezy sensuality.

He had gone only a few steps down the street when a soft click and the rustle of fabric behind him made him wheel around. The mother wearing the hijab was holding a phone in the air and pressing a button on its side. It appeared to Lee she was taking several photos of him; nonetheless he turned around to see what interesting attraction might have grabbed her attention.

But there was nothing unusual, ornate or photogenic for her phone to capture. "Hey, you!" he called out, but she was already at the end of the block, careening the pram around the corner.

Come to think of it, he asked himself, *did I even see an infant in that stroller?*

He set off on a dash, almost toppling an elderly couple in his haste to catch up with the woman. "Wait!" he called out, although she had already rounded the corner.

When Lee careered around the building at the corner, however, the woman was nowhere to be seen. A few steps ahead sat the pram the woman had been pushing, a dark wig splayed across its mattress. He picked up the hairpiece but dropped it back into the stroller when a young woman walking a Jack Russell terrier began to eye him with concern.

He was now almost ten minutes late for his appointment, so he decided to accelerate his walk to Hanover Square. At Knightsbridge, he veered right, and the atmosphere suddenly became more hectic, as the pedestrians, bicycles, and small motorcars were replaced by industrial lorries and double-decker tourist buses. Adding to the sudden bustle was a sense of construction *everywhere.* On his left, two young men in grimy smocks hammered a piece of plywood to a storefront that had recently lost a plate glass window; across the way on his right, the steady clang of metal and the shriek of electric saws cascaded from scaffolding that rose five stories above the street.

This city, he told himself, *is nothing like I remember from just ten years ago.*

He *so* wanted to meander through Hyde Park, which was now on his left—to reflect beside the Weeping Beech, to listen to the yammering of whatever it was the protesters at Speakers' Corner were protesting today. But he scooted forward, his head down in earnest . . . until he saw something flickering in front of him as he walked up Park Lane, across from the Dorchester Hotel. He squinted as he tried to ascertain the source of the flashing light. Finally, he determined it was attached to the bus in front of him, was emanating from a digital readout on the back of the conveyance that, until a moment ago, had said "Red Route."

Now, however, it bore a very different message:

DALTON

Then:

10 PM TONIGHT

Followed by:

GREENWICH FOOT TUNNEL

The architect glanced at the pedestrians around him to see if anyone else had spotted the message. But everyone had their heads buried in their phones or were admiring the parkland on their left. When he glanced back at the bus, the readout once again said, "Red Route."

"Seriously?" he muttered softly. "The FOOT TUNNEL? You want to meet THERE of all places?" He knew the long dank tube beneath the Thames to be one of the creepiest places in all of London. On top of that, it wasn't likely they'd be alone at that time of night, and they certainly wouldn't be inconspicuous. He exhaled in frustration as he jogged across Park Lane at Upper Brook Street to get to his appointment with C. J. and Anisa.

He approached Hanover Square from the side that was guarded by a towering statue of William Pitt, otherwise known as William Pitt the Younger. *Had I been in charge,* Lee chuckled to himself, *I would have nicknamed him "Little Pitt."* He didn't know much about the statesman, other than he had served as prime minister and led England in its wars against France and Napoleonism. And that he was *not* the William Pitt who had given the American city of Pittsburgh its name. That honor belonged to Little Pitt's father, William Pitt, First Earl of Chatham.

"Being the son of someone renowned is *such* a pain, isn't it, Dalton?" the statue uttered. Lee studied the face of the statue, which seemed to be looking at some distant point in space. "Don't worry," it continued. "When I was young, everyone thought I was too aloof, too superior, just like you. And just like you, they kept comparing me to my father, kept comparing my accomplishments to his." Lee blinked several times, hoping that might make the voice vanish. Or at least stop talking about *him.*

"But eventually, I won them over. The same way you are winning people over now. I marshaled everyone to a cause and inspired strength in those around me, so together we could vanquish the threat we faced. And in the end, they called me, 'the Atlas of our reeling globe.'"

Lee thought he saw the head of William Pitt twist ever so slightly in his direction.

"You probably feel a little bit like Atlas, don't you, Dalton? Well, you might as well get used to it, because the burden you bear isn't going away any time soon." Again, Lee blinked, but the statue's head now appeared to be at its original angle. The architect took two or three deep breaths and steadied himself.

Oh no. It's happening again, he thought, as he made his way into the park.

When he finally located his colleagues deep in one heavily shrubbed corner of the green space, C. J. was lying on her back, making what resembled snow angels.

"Ah, right, Dalton, there you are," the commander bellowed as she raised herself from the ground and brushed off the leaves and twigs that had collected on her slacks. "I was beginning to worry you might have been nefariously detained somehow." Lee traded nods with Inspector Nassir, whose pained smile resembled the one worn by a teenage girl having to tend to her younger sister.

"Sorry, C. J.," the architect replied. "The weather being so lovely and all, I decided to walk over here, and the traffic slowed me down more than I expected."

"Walk here, did you? All the way from your accommodations? That would be quite a journey, indeed." She cleared her throat some and reached up to pull a clump of stubborn leaves still clinging to the top of her head. "Well, you Americans do love your fitness regimens, don't you?" She smiled. "Don't get me wrong, I'm quite in admiration of it. It's just . . ." She stopped and looked both ways, as if someone might be eavesdropping on their conversation. "To be frank, I am quite a slave to drinking chocolate." At that, she threw her head back, patted her sides and gave Lee a toothy grin.

Lee returned her smile, weakly. But his brow soon furrowed, and he pointed to the ground.

"Um, you were . . . frolicking?" He wiggled his finger back and forth, horizontally.
She squinted, then nodded.

"Oh, right. That. No, not frolicking, really. I was calculating what the radius might have been for Mr. Tinti's topple here after he got shot. I'm quite sure I am about the same height as our victim, so I thought I'd get a sense of exactly where he might have originally been standing, given where his body was found. You know, to make sure, the place where he was shot, and the arc of his fall, all add up." She was looking down at the ground now, a thumb and forefinger pinching the sides of her lower lip together as she considered the scene. "Your associate, that lovely young woman . . ."

"I think you're referring to Bree."

"Right." She continued to pinch her lip in silence for a couple of moments, then looked at Lee. "She's quite attached to that ball of yarn of hers, isn't she?"

Lee issued something between a snort and a chuckle.

"I suppose so," he answered softly. C. J. nodded and smiled.

"A sign of separation anxiety on her part, I gather. *Anyway,* Bree said something this morning that got me to thinking. Her question about whether someone might have placed Mr. Tinti here after murdering him somewhere else did make me consider the possibility our victim might have been shot elsewhere *in the park,* and then moved to this corner in an effort to conceal the body."

Inspector Nassir leaned in. "We wondered whether the killer might have dragged the corpse into the bushes to make sure the body wasn't discovered too quickly, to maximize the window of time they would have had for a getaway," she offered.

Lee studied where C. J. had been on the ground and visually followed the path out into the rest of the park.

"And your conclusion?"

C. J. squinted again, then shook her head. "I do not believe such was the case. It appears *Signore Tinti* was accosted right here and then fell straight back into the shrubbery. The trajectory works out. If you'll look right there, the grass does appear to be somewhat matted, as if someone or something was dropped upon it. We've not discovered any tracks that would have been made by his heels being dragged across the grass or mud in this direction." She jabbed an index finger at several small darker splotches on the ground. "And if I'm not mistaken, those would be indications of dried blood."

Lee nodded as she spoke, turned, looked in the opposite direction, then back at the pair. "So, we believe Mr. Tinti was slain sometime around midnight, is that correct?" he asked.

Inspector Nassir raised one finger. "Actually, I just got a text from the medical examiner saying they've narrowed the time of death to between midnight and half past."

Lee began to nod again. "And the gates were locked. . .?"

"Hours before that," C. J. filled in. Lee shoved his fists into his pockets and scrunched his face in contemplation. Then, without warning, he strode deliberately away from the women and toward the park entrance nearest them. After he had traveled a good distance, C. J. called out, "Are we to wait here, Dalton, for a formal invitation to accompany you?"

Lee swiveled, flapped one hand as a summons, then resumed his stride. He paused to let a young couple breeze through the entrance before he stationed himself immediately next to it. He cupped one of the locks to examine it and shook the gate to gauge its sturdiness. Then stepped back a bit to study the concrete path leading from the entrance before trudging through the gate to inspect the pavement outside.

Nothing. Or nothing out of the ordinary, anyway.

"Let's check the other entrances," he said, scurrying them outside the fence and along the green space's outer perimeter. At the second entrance, Lee noticed several gouges near the bottom of the gate, but the fortification itself seemed as sturdy as the first. "Probably someone using the gate to scrape mud from a metal-toed boot," he surmised. The third gate was adjacent to what appeared to be the vestiges of some years-long construction project, so the space they had to view the gate and surrounding area was much more restricted. Still, nothing seemed amiss there either.

"Would it help us, Mr. Lee, if you told us what we're looking for?" C. J. tossed the question out as they approached the final gate.

"Probably," Lee answered with a broad grin. "The problem, C. J., is I'm not sure what that is."

As the trio neared the fourth gate, a toy poodle on a rainbow-colored leash barked at them ferociously. The older man who was walking the dog offered his deepest apologies, then used his right toe to nudge the dog in the ribs so it would move along.

"Well, *that* little kick was entirely unnecessary," Lee said, frowning. His brow remained furrowed as he scanned the pavement just outside the fourth gate. His attention was drawn to a large dark scuff mark on the curb adjacent to the road. As he bent to peer at it, Inspector Nassir said, "It looks like a shoe print."

Lee ducked his head lower. "Indeed, it does. A partial one anyway."

"Of course, it could belong to anyone," the commander added, but Lee was already studying another, smaller smudge just to the right of the first. Inspector Nassir was already beside him, photographing both marks with her phone.

"I'll see if we can determine what category of shoe made these," she said, "although that's doubtful."

"Yes, I share your pessimism," Lee replied as he headed back into the park through the gate, the pair in tow. Once inside, he veered sharply to the right and scanned the grass alongside the fence. After a few steps, he stopped and bent again. "The grass, it's heavily matted here and . . ." He pointed to another trampled spot a few inches away. "And over there, but *only* in these two places," he said almost to himself. The others bent over his shoulders for a look, and silently nodded.

"What would be the significance of that?" C. J. queried. The architect said nothing for some time, then put his hands on both knees and pushed himself back into a standing position. "I'm not really sure there is any significance to it, C. J. Or that there's no significance." The two women exchanged concerned glances but said nothing.

Lee turned and took several large steps toward the center of the park area, stopped, turned back. Putting his hands on his hips, he looked down and then peered up. His eyes riveted on something above the heads of the commander and her associate. He moved toward them, but as he reached the lower branches of a birch tree, he raised one hand and plucked something dark that was caught among the leaves. The two women moved toward him.

"A piece of fabric?" Inspector Nassir raised her phone to photograph the object.

"Not just any fabric," Lee replied. "It's a high-quality silk, I'd say. From a shirt. Or maybe a suit or a sports coat, even." He held the ragged-shaped fabric at one corner, reviewed it one way then the other. As he did so, Inspector Nassir pulled a small clear bag and a pair of tweezers out of her pocket.

"I guess it's a good thing I brought these items with me after all," she said, prodding the fabric into the bag.

"We should have an analysis from the laboratory by noon tomorrow," the commander intoned.

Lee acknowledged C. J.'s statement, but his attention was back on the gate.

"Anisa, did you say Mayfair is pretty active around midnight?"

Inspector Nassir sealed the bag with her thumbs. "Mayfair is, yes," she replied. "Most of the district has clubs and cafés that stay open late, so people are usually around then." She tilted her forehead to the stolid buildings across the street. "But this is actually one of the quietest quarters within Mayfair. It's mostly banks and business offices along this block. Not much nightlife. Why?"

Lee was studying how the fence enclosed the park.

"I was just thinking . . ." He strode a few steps to their left, to a location just to the right of the statue of William Pitt. "Here, one might be able to get into the park without a lot of difficulty," he called out, as the others ambled toward him. "Getting over the fence wouldn't be simple, but once you're on the other side, you have an unobstructed path to the rest of the park." Lee began to walk toward C. J. and Anisa but stopped short of them. "But look, here," he said, pointing to the fence. "It would be much more difficult to get into the park from here. First, anyone standing in that intersection over there would easily spot someone trying to get in. Then, the interloper faces the challenge of getting beyond that thick row of hedges on the other side of the fence—hedges they wouldn't have to contend with down there."

C. J. wrapped her arms around herself. "So, you're saying you think Mr. Tinti and the murderer for some reason climbed over the fence after hours down there, near where you found the footprints and the piece of silk?"

Lee squinted some, chewed on his upper lip.

"I am sort of sure, but I'm not, like, *absolutely sure*. It's just . . . there's something about this fence, and its height . . ."

Everyone was quiet for a moment. Then C. J. decided to offer a suggestion.

"If it would help, Dalton, we could come back here tonight around midnight to view the vicinity around the time the murder took place." Lee thought about that for a couple of minutes. He swiveled around and smiled.

"That is an excellent suggestion, C. J.," he replied. "Only I can't tonight. I have an engagement later that I . . . can't possibly postpone."

7

Lara was gratified Lee had given her an assignment connected to the case. Not that she wasn't already busy—keeping the architectural firm running could often be more than a full-time job. Especially when they were away from the home office, as they were now.

But the assistant Lara had hired several months back had proved to be exceptionally competent.

Which meant Lara had more time to be bored.

Which meant Lara relished the idea of *an adventure.*

There was another thing, though. Ever since her father had decided to align himself with The Organization, she possessed far more passion for bringing that group to its knees than anyone else in the firm realized. She wanted Lee to understand that. She wanted him to *appreciate* that. By giving her this responsibility, it appeared he finally did.

She tugged at one side of her tweed skirt, crossed her ankles beneath the desk, and tapped at the keyboard on her laptop. She knew she probably looked like a dinosaur to the younger members of the firm, who zipped all over the internet on their tablet computers and phones (Had she actually seen Warren looking up the status of their flight across the Atlantic on his *watch?*)

She didn't care. *Surely,* she told herself, *the proper posture and typing proficiency she'd acquired in secretarial school so long ago still had some merit.*

Carefully, she consulted the legal pad beside her computer, the pad upon which Liam had scrawled the passwords she would need to enter the government's street cam database. She placed her index finger beneath the first string of letters and numbers, and gingerly entered them into a vacant field on her screen.

Her reflection on Liam brought a sly smile to her face. She had certainly had doubts about him when he joined the firm just before they took on the case in Miami. But since then, he had proved to be more beneficial to the firm (and more personable) than she had imagined. In her career, she had learned that young men with his looks and charisma often used those gifts to take unfair advantage of others. She was thankful that he had proven (thus far, anyway) to have a good heart.

She reviewed the pad once again and entered another password. She was thinking, *I have to say, Liam's scientific background and his knowledge of the latest technologies have proved remarkable,* when, sure enough, the small circle spinning in the center of her screen stopped rotating and *she was in.*

Lee had asked her to produce a list of the street cams installed along the perimeter of Hanover Square. But true to her work ethic, she committed to doing one better. She entered enough data to generate a list of all the cameras located within three square blocks of the park. *If we can't catch the killer in the middle of the act,* she thought, *maybe we can catch him coming or going. Or her.*

It was taking a couple of moments for the request to be fulfilled, so she sat back in her chair, lifted her head, and took in the room. The furnishings were dignified but not stuffy. She loved the cream-colored lace curtains that graced the windows looking out on the quiet side street below. If she'd been put in charge of selecting their accommodations, she could not have found a better fit than this lovely residence. A quick glance at the screen told her the request was still being processed.

Lara felt a warm gel envelop her from the shoulders down. Her relationship with Lee had recalibrated to what it had been. The firm could not possibly be more successful, and everyone respected her for her role in that success. Now, Lee was finally asking her to take a more active role in their cases. Everything seemed to be coalescing the way it should.

Then why, she asked herself, *do I still feel a . . . void?* The gel stopped coursing through her body, turned cool and brittle. A light sadness now seeped throughout her. Outside, a shallow bank of clouds slowly muted the sunlight.

Her screen flickered; the list of street cam locations had arrived. She scanned it, scowled slightly. She had hoped for more cameras than the list outlined; it appeared they would be able to review the footage of only three or four within a block or so of the square. And then there was the issue of whether they were in proper working order, which was rarely the case. Carefully, she pressed the control key and the letter "P" on her keyboard, to send the search results to the printer in the corner of Lara's room.

After a few whirrs and clicks, the list appeared in the output tray. She decided to print three more for others on the team. *I know I should probably be emailing this list to everyone, or storing it somewhere on— what do they call it, the cloud?* She sighed and chuckled at the same time. *I think I'll just leave all that to the younger associates.*

Quickly, she logged out of the government database and went to check her email. To her surprise, there were only three new messages. One related to a routine administrative issue her assistant in California had copied her on. Another was a reminder to renew her membership in an international architecture society she belonged to.

The final email was an inquiry from the provincial government of Victoria in Australia. They were interested in The Lee Group submitting a proposal for the design of a new multisport facility in Melbourne. Lara sniffed a bit. *Well, Liam would no doubt love that,* she thought. *But government agencies can be such bears to work with.* She had to acknowledge they had an edge, given the impeccable reputation The Lee Group had earned over the years. *And I am certain,* she thought with a laugh, *that Dalton would love to produce something that would make people forget that monstrosity of an opera house in Sydney.*

She exited her email account and was about to close the browser when her eyes fell on an advertisement at the far right of the screen. It appeared to promote a reading of Tarot cards or one's astrological chart. Neither would normally appeal to Lara, but the photograph of the spokeswoman hadn't just caught her attention; it had, (for some reason) captivated it. She was elegant, probably in her early to mid fifties, and resembled an ambassador, or the CEO of a cosmetics firm. She wore a black turtleneck sweater with a stunning silver necklace capped by a pendant in the shape of the infinity sign. Her short, upswept hair was raven black, her skin a lustrous cream. Lara thought the woman wore a bit too much mascara, but she had to admit that it gave the woman's green-gold eyes an exotic—one might even say hypnotic—quality. She was not really smiling; instead, her expression was more like one worn by someone who has just divined some tantalizing gossip that she *could not possibly wait* to share.

Beneath the woman's photo were the words

How Might YOU Benefit from
Delfina Delgado's Special Gift?

Lara bent closer to the screen and continued to read.

She has advised presidents and prime ministers, has predicted winning lottery numbers and terrifying natural disasters. Learn how to put Delfina Delgado's special gift to work for YOU, at www.delgadospecialgift.com.

The link took Lara to a video that instantly began to play. It was Madame Delgado herself, wearing an ensemble not unlike the one in the advertisement. She was sitting at a desk much like the one Lara was sitting at now, only the wood appeared to be ebony, a perfect complement to Delfina Delgado's hair. Over the woman's right shoulder was a gloppy abstract painting that struggled to evoke a rainy day in some European city. On the wall behind her left shoulder hung a triumvirate of crosses in blue and gold. Resting on the desktop, near her left hand, was a crystal orb on a round, black pedestal. It sat next to a small silver chalice and a notebook bound in burgundy leather.

Delfina Delgado bore the same intense expression as she had in the advertisement, and her elegantly manicured hands rested peacefully in front of her, one on top of the other. It became quickly apparent to Lara that this woman was—or at least considered herself to be—a psychic.

"I have had premonitions ever since I was a child, ever since the age of three," the video began. "I remember playing once in the cornfields on my grandparents' *latifundio* outside Seville. Suddenly, I saw a large ball of fire in the sky. I was in such awe of its power and its fury. Being a child, I thought it was a comet, or maybe even the Second Coming, which I had heard the nuns in my school speak about so often.

"As it turned out, on the very next day, a silo on our farm that had just been filled with fertilizer exploded, killing one of the workers. And it sent a fireball into the sky exactly like the one I had seen the day before. I was shocked, of course. But this is just one example. There are many, so many examples. This was only the beginning."

The woman did not look at the camera during her dialogue. Instead, her eyes flitted just to the left or right of it, as if she were speaking to a small group of people seated in front of her desk. At this point in the video, however, she turned her head like a ventriloquist's dummy and stared directly into the lens, which zoomed in on her face.

"But this is not about me. This gift is not mine alone. We all possess it—it is inside all of us, for it is divinely sent. I have it. *You* have it. We just need to . . . cultivate it. *Nurture* it. The same way we cultivate any other talent, like public speaking, or singing." She paused, licked her lips once, then resumed the thread. "That is precisely what I have devoted my entire life to. To educating myself, to striving to understand my gift, and to using it only for the very best purposes. The highest purposes. And I tell you, doing that has brought me great happiness, unimaginable success." Here, she flashed a smile.

The moment seemed more than a bit staged to Lara. And yet, for some reason, she found herself inexplicably drawn to this woman. She could not recall having had any psychic experiences herself, but she remembered her mother having them now and then. Once as they were on their way to a vacation in the north of Finland, her mother spontaneously instructed her father to take a cutoff from the main road. He had pushed back, saying the alternate route would add too much time to their trip, but her mother had insisted. After they reached their destination, they learned that a tall spruce had fallen across the main road, crushing two cars at almost precisely the moment they would have been traveling through that forest. Then there was the time her mother (without provocation) began to weave a long yarn about a beloved aunt with whom she had picked flowers as a very young child. As she waxed on about the *rantukka* and *sinivuokko* they would pull from the soil, she became quite misty-eyed and somber. That very night, Lara's mother received a call from the aunt's husband informing her the aunt had passed away earlier in the day from a heart attack.

Lara pondered those experiences, returned her attention to Delfina Delgado, who was now displaying for the camera a small item she had plucked from a collection of curios on her desktop.

"I have found in my experience that a talisman such as this can be enormously helpful in helping us cultivate our clairvoyance. Everyone should have a talisman, I believe, should always carry one with them." The camera moved in on the trinket she was holding, a coin-shaped amulet decorated with stars and triangles. "This talisman was given to me by a tribal shaman I consulted many years ago in the American state of New Mexico. I keep it close to me at all times, even when I am cooking, even when I am sleeping, and I have found that ever since he gave it to me, the frequency and accuracy of my premonitions have increased dramatically. My visions have become much more vivid, and I recall them much more easily. It has been a . . . godsend to me."

Lara leaned forward to study the amulet, which seemed to spin on its own power between the woman's fingers. It was mesmerizing. What's more, it triggered an emotional response within her, like the melody of a tune that she had not heard for decades but that reconnected her to some moment of intense delight.

She stole a glance at the clock on her computer screen and started. It was much later in the afternoon than she realized, and she had quite a bit to do to get ready for the following day. She clicked away from the video, sat back in her chair, resting her wrists on her computer as she wondered what it would be like to be able to predict the future. Perhaps even *control* the future through the careful execution of such talents.

With the fingertips of her right hand, she began to rapidly tap the front edge of her laptop. After some time, almost inaudibly she said, "Interesting. Very, very interesting."

8

Roberto stood across the lane from Hanover Square, arms wrapped tight around his torso, in part, because he was shivering (although the temperature was moderate for a September evening in London).

You better not be coming down with the flu, he chastised himself. *You always come down with something right after a long flight. It's all that recirculated air. It pumps germs all over the place.*

He was also hugging himself, in part, because he was feeling vulnerable (although he was far less conscious of that). After the little trick he had tried to pull on The Organization in Miami, they were not allowing him to actually see Isabela any more. He could hardly stand it, but he also knew he had no leverage in the situation. The sense of powerlessness gnawed at him, roiled his stomach.

But two weeks ago, they'd sent an email saying he could exchange a text conversation with her. It wasn't ideal—how did he know the person on the other end would really be Isabela? He felt confident he knew his little sister's linguistic patterns, could spot even a good impostor. But then again, she would soon be—what did they call it these days—a tweener? So, he had to consider the possibility she had grown into someone very different from the Isabela he had helped raise back on the island.

It didn't help that his last image of her was one of her bound, gagged, and looking more frightened than he had ever seen her. More frightened than he had ever seen *anyone.*

Those cabrons! he exclaimed to himself.

When he arrived at the park, it was already closed. But he was glad, because that's how he wanted to survey it, for now. Most of the team was back at the flat, deeply engrossed in their computers, and Dalton was off on one of those mysterious meetings he traipsed off to now and then. He had decided his boss had some sort of fetish he was ashamed of but needed to engage in wherever their work took them. Maybe he was into that plushie scene, which made no sense to Roberto whatsoever. Or maybe he was off seeking heroin or hashish.

Whatever it was, Roberto didn't care. Heaven knows, he was in no place to judge. One day he had a mild crush on his boss, the next he was checking out every other woman under the age of forty who crossed the street near him.

Recently, he'd given himself permission to raise that threshold to forty-five.

He knew for a fact he wouldn't mind having some fun with that agent who had shuttled them in from the airport. *What was her name . . . Alisa? Anisa?* He envisioned her wearing black lace garters and a matching bustier, and wielding in one hand a long leather crop.

That's it, he suddenly decided. *Dalton's into sadomasochism.*

He was strolling along the pavement just outside the park, letting a couple of fingers slap along the pickets of the iron fence to his left. In the street, a red, double-decker bus that claimed to be heading for Oxford Circus hissed alongside him as it stopped for traffic; immediately behind it was a Royal Mail delivery van painted the same shade of red. A few steps back, he had seen the scuff marks that Lee had mentioned back at the flat, but he didn't really see how they could be connected to the murder. He figured some skateboarders had probably left them there.

As he was finishing that thought, his fingers knocked against a picket that shifted slightly beneath his touch. The designer paused, stepped back, and nudged it again with his fingers. It was still attached at the bottom of the fence, but at the top, it moved several centimeters.

He stood on tiptoe to inspect it, pushed it back with his thumb.

Looks like a bad spot-weld job, he thought.

But the additional gap caused by the detachment was barely as wide as a fist, and certainly wasn't large enough to let a leg slide through, much less a complete human being. He stepped back toward the curb, stood on tiptoe again, resumed his normal stance, and shrugged his shoulders.

That was when he spotted the mime.

Roberto vaguely recalled noticing some type of busker entertaining a small crowd at the far end of the lane when he had first arrived at the park. But now, the street entertainer was leaning back against the fence, watching Roberto impassively. *Looks like I'm busted,* he told himself.

He sauntered over to the guy and nodded but got no response. The mime did not wear the typical uniform of his craft. In place of the usual black beret, he wore a gold-colored top hat sporting a large purple flower at the base of the brim. Instead of the usual black-and-white-striped boatman's shirt, his shirt was emerald green with large red buttons. And the requisite black slacks were replaced by orange parachute pants, trimmed in blue.

He *did* evoke the look of others in his craft, however, in that his face was slathered with white clown makeup, which was accented by excessively red lips that arced into a perpetual frown.

"Hey, buddy, do you work this park very often?" Roberto ventured.

At first the mime seemed not to hear him, but after a while, he responded with one long, slow, affirmative nod.

Roberto glanced one way down the lane, then the other.

"You ever see anything strange go on around here?" The street entertainer squinted, indicating he didn't understand the question.

"You ever see anything . . . weird . . . see people in the park late at night? People hanging around when they aren't supposed to?" A smile emerged from the mime and he replied with another slow nod. He hooked one thumb over his shoulder in the direction of the park, created a fist with his right hand and jabbed it into his left forearm.

"Ah, drugs. Right, sure." Roberto looked at the pavement, decided he might as well cut to the chase. "Any chance you were here one night earlier this week? See anybody get in a fight? Hear gunshots, maybe?"

The busker's face stiffened, his eyes took on a suspicious glint. But he didn't respond.

Roberto leaned his head back to look at the night sky. *This isn't going anywhere,* he acknowledged to himself. He dug into his pants pocket to check his phone—it was time for the conversation with Isabela. He nodded bluntly at the entertainer. "Check back with you later." He swiveled away, but immediately felt a leaden clamp on one shoulder. The mime had one palm extended and wore an expression that, on one level, suggested a plea, on another, suggested a threat.

Oh, I get it, he told himself.

Roberto rummaged in his right pocket for a few coins and dropped them into the open palm. The mime glanced at the currency, shrugged his shoulders, and doffed his top hat as Roberto retreated across the street.

Shit, I totally forgot about the currency rate, he told himself as he landed on the opposite curb. *I probably gave him something like twenty dollars.* Just then, his phone buzzed with what appeared to be an incoming text.

He pressed the Message icon. The screen opened not to text but to a video. A tall, reedy male with heavily gelled blond hair, and a wisp-thin mustache curled at both ends, blinked several times. Then, as if given a cue, he jolted erect and began to speak. His voice was clear but altered, the way newscasts shield the identity of an interviewee wishing to remain anonymous.

"Mr. Bermudez. As you know, we have suspended contact between you and your sister for almost a year. We are offering you this one last chance to maintain communication." The speaker leaned in some toward the camera, a move that distorted his face to twice its normal width.

"Let me say that again, Mr. Bermudez," he continued. "ONE. LAST. CHANCE." The speaker's mustache seemed to fold into a snarl under its own power. "No funny business. No efforts to guess where your sister is, no attempts to manipulate the conversation. If you agree to these terms, press the red X that will appear on the screen after this video concludes and you will be connected to your sister via text message." The image froze—five seconds later, the X appeared.

He pressed it. And waited.

The screen went gray. He waited some more. "C'mon!" he whispered. The screen flickered and finally one word appeared.

'Berto?

He breathed heavily. *Si,* he typed back. *¿Cómo está?*

I'm okay. I got to have a Mallorca for breakfast today! Well, it wasn't really a Mallorca, but it was close. Like a big donut with lots of sugar on top. First time!"

He smiled, issued a breath of relief. *It's her,* he thought. *Mallorcas had always been her favorite thing for breakfast.* But his smile soon faded. *But if that's all they've given her to eat."*

'Berto. I want to play a game.

Okay, he typed. **But I . . .**

Remember back on the island, when we used to play 'E-O'? I want to play that.

His mind whirred, trying to recall the game. They'd played lots of games when they were still all together in Puerto Rico.

And then it hit him. And why she wanted to play it. E-O was her abbreviation for Every Other. It was a game he had concocted in which he would say a sentence to her, but the real message he was trying to convey would be carried by every other word in the message he spoke. He had used it as a means of teaching her the alphabet and how to construct sentences. He had forgotten it altogether. Couldn't believe she recalled it.

His temples began to pound. This was dangerous territory they were venturing into. But she seemed hell-bent to blaze the trail.

Okay, I get to go first, her next message said. He waited, but it was as if the screen had frozen. He shook his phone—still nothing. Then it dawned on him that she was probably trying to construct her message properly. It took a lot of concentration to do so, he remembered.

Finally, a few words appeared on the screen.

Can I go see . . .

He smiled. He had always enjoyed playing this game with her. Under these circumstances, he *loved* it.

Go see what? he texted back.

A pause of several seconds. Then . . .

The sand lot, and the girls . . .

He chuckled, shook his head. Wow. *She's really good at this,* he thought. He took a moment to compose his reply.

Which girls?

A long pause this time. Too long, it seemed. He began to worry he had lost her.

Finally . . .

In all grades of school I ran from!

The exclamation mark was a signal she had finished. He'd decipher it soon but wanted to make the most of their remaining connection. And he felt he needed to cover for her, as well.

We'll see. Someday, I will take you back to that sandlot and to all the girls who attended that school you ran away from when you were six—ha ha. He halted, then added, **Anything else u want me 2 tell the family back home? Anything u want me 2 say to Mama Minga and Tio Santos?**

Her answer was quick. **Just that I really miss them and really love them. And that I'm doing just great.**

He rolled his eyes. He knew the first part of her message had been authentic, because it was a phrase she had recited repeatedly over the years. But the last part. That was pure public relations. He knew there was no way in hell she was doing just great.

With deliberation, he began to unravel the message she had delivered during the game. But quickly shot off one more casual message to her. **Really?** he wrote. **That's all you have 2 say for yourself? No silly jokes? No lessons from the books you've been reading?** He was scrolling back to the dialogue of their game, making note of every other letter in her comments.

Can I go see the sand lot

I see sand . . .

. . . And the girls in all grades of

And girls, all of . . .

His heart pounding, he kept decoding.

School I ran from!

I from.

"All of I from?" he blurted out. "What the hell? That can't be right. I must have misread the message somehow."

He flipped back to the last part of the conversation.

. . . All grades of school I ran from!

He already had the beginning of the message. *I see sand and girls all of . . .*

I from. He exhaled in exasperation. "This can't be happening!" he whispered.

And then, he got it. Understood the mix-up. She had broken the rules of the game but had been clever in doing so. Had put two words together to form one. He just hadn't caught it. Until now.

All grades of school I ran from

She hadn't intended the last set of words to be read as, "All of I from."

She'd meant them as, "All of I ran."

I see sand, and girls of . . . Iran.

He was interrupted by her reply to his last question.

Yup, that's all, 'Berto. Didn't have as much 2 share as I thought, I guess.

He was shaking. She had shared far more than those idiots realized. Far more than he ever hoped she might. But he knew he needed to temper himself here. He had to stay calm.

Okay, but you're going to have to come up with something more interesting the next time we chat, he typed back. I'm a busy man, you know, ha ha. He added a smiley face.

She returned one.

Then the screen went black and the phrase "Power to the cause" appeared in a bold white font.

As Roberto charged off in the direction of their flat, he saw the busker eyeing him from beside the fence, his mouth contorted into a fake, frozen smile.

9

"Has anyone seen my ball of yarn?"

Bree was standing in the doorway separating the flat's narrow dining room and the adjacent living room. Her hands were on her hips and her head turned first that way, then this.

Liam, reclining on the back legs of a round-backed wooden chair, scratched at his upper chest, glanced around the room. "What color is it?"

Bree frowned. "Well, I guess if you don't know what color it is, you haven't seen it, now have you?" she said. She let out a huff then swiveled to leave the room just as Roberto was tramping his way into it.

"Hey, you missing a ball of yarn, by any chance?" he asked without looking at her. The designer grabbed an apple from a blue bowl on the dining table, then dropped into the chair across from Liam's. "There's one sticking out from under the back of the armchair in the library," he continued. "Sort of cherry red?"

"The library? How did it get in there? And it's *scarlet,* not cherry . . ." Roberto hurried his bite into the fruit he had purloined, then assumed a mischievous smile.

"Liam was playing hacky sack with it in the living room and kicked it into the library. Then he nudged it under the chair with the toe of his shoe. I think maybe it's how he flirts with women."

"Dude!" Liam flew his right arm toward Roberto the way a fisherman casts a line into the water side-handed. "That's the last time I . . ."

"All right, everyone, gather round." Dalton had marched into the room and was unrolling a large sheet of parchment paper that bore a meticulous rendering drawn in pencil. Lara sidled in behind him, peered over his shoulder when she got closer. They could hear Warren clambering down one of the two staircases leading to the ground floor.

"Parchment paper?" Liam exclaimed. "Wow, aren't *we* the 21st century architectural firm!"

"It was the only version of the schematics I could quickly get my hands on," Lee countered.

"Does anyone want some tea?" Lara asked meekly. "I think I could use some tea." Getting no takers, she padded over to a cabinet and began to hunt for the kettle they had used earlier.

Warren plopped onto the table next to the drawing. "What is that . . . Westminster Abbey?" Lee continued to stare at the outline as he pressed his palms into the table a bit more firmly.

"I'd like to think my senior architect can tell the difference between the drawings for a park and the drawings for a church," he replied.

"Bree, do you want some tea, dear? There appears to be some Clipper Organic White here if you want that."

Lara craned her head in the direction of Bree, whose head first shook back and forth but then slowly slid into an up-and-down motion. Without her yarn, the senior designer seemed adrift, tapping her fingernails on the tabletop with the speed of someone taking a timed typing test.

"All right, let's concentrate, shall we?" Lee asked. "So, this is Hanover Square, where the victim's body was found. Actually, it was found precisely THERE." The architect jabbed a finger at the far upper corner of the drawing, where a grove of trees and shrubs created a large green splotch. "The time of death was sometime just after midnight; however, all the gates to the park were locked several hours earlier."

"Was the corpse naked?" Everyone turned in unison to look at Bree, who was slicing a knife through a small brick of white Stilton cheese.

"Noooo, it wasn't," Lee replied. He waited a few beats for Bree to explain why that was top of mind for her. But she said nothing, so he added, "Does that disappoint you for some reason?"

She swallowed, then patted her lips with a napkin.

"No. I mean, I didn't mean anything . . . raunchy or anything. I just said that because, well, I thought if he WERE clothed, maybe there was something on his jacket—a leaf, or maybe some twigs on his pants— that might tell us where he had been earlier that night. But if he wasn't wearing any clothes, well . . ."

"Then there wouldn't be any of those things." Lee nodded, let out a small smile. "Yes, I see where you were going, Bree. Well, I believe that C. J.'s team has at the very least combed through all of Mr. Tinti's pockets for any personal belongings. But your idea that there might be some foreign substance on his clothes not native to Hanover Square is an intriguing one. Would you mind following up with our friends at Scotland Yard on that?" The senior architect nodded and returned to her cheese.

Warren leaned in.

"So, do we absolutely know the park was locked before midnight? That there was no way he and the assailant could have entered through a gate someone had forgotten to secure?"

Roberto cleared his throat. "I may have something on that," he said. "It's probably not anything significant, but . . ." He went on to describe how he had come upon the loose fence picket during his visit to the square. "I mean, it only creates a small gap," he said. "It's odd, but probably not all that relevant."

Lee chewed the inside of one cheek for a moment. "No. Good work, Roberto," he finally said. "I'll want to have a look at that."

Liam had shoved his head toward the drawing, was sniffing around it like an anteater foraging for grubs. "Are we even sure there was just one assailant?" he asked.

Lee reflected on their questions for a moment. "We're not, Liam," he finally replied. "But even with the loose picket Roberto just brought up, I can't see how one person could have gotten into that park after hours, much less two or more."

He turned to Warren. "And to answer your question, it's not impossible for someone to climb over the fence. In some places, it's not that high. But there were police here and there, patrolling. What would cause Mr. Tinti to want to go through all of that? How could they have entered the park without drawing attention to themselves? You can see here . . ." Lee pointed along the lower rim of the drawing and ran his fingertip along it. "The road is fairly narrow between the park and the buildings across the lane from it. It's that way all the way around, really. And even at midnight, there are a few pedestrians in the area. So . . ."

Lara squeezed behind Lee, a teapot held high in one hand, a cup and saucer dangling from the other. "Don't move," she said softly to her boss, "or your backside will look like the Sahara during one of its harshest droughts." Once she had cleared the architect and began to pour some tea for Bree, she looked over her shoulder at the architect. "Is there any possibility Mr. Tinti was already in the park before it closed? Perhaps he ran into his killer there before the gates got locked and then never left, for some reason. Maybe that person persuaded him to stay in the park after hours, said they needed to discuss some urgent matter with him, convinced him to play an extended game of chess or something like that. Then, after it got dark enough, they . . ."

Lee stretched both arms out and placed them on either side of the drawing. Hung his head and twiddled his fingers on the tabletop. After several minutes, however, he straightened up, tilted his head one way then the other, and sighed. "We have a lot of work to do. And, it's getting late." He looked around the room and suddenly became businesslike.

"Here's what I'm going to ask of you. Lara, I want you to delve into Mr. Tinti's background as best you can. See what sort of online profile he had, if any, who he communicated with, that sort of thing. Roberto, I want you to continue to scope out Hanover Square and the surrounding area, talk with any cops you see patrolling there, find out what the foot traffic was like in the park the day of the murder and, if you can, that evening as well. Bree, you and Warren can accompany C. J. and me on whatever interviews she decides to conduct. Serve as my backup ears, if you will."

"What about me, boss?" Liam had tilted his chair onto its back legs, the fingers of both hands interlocked behind his head.

The architect smiled. "Liam, your assignment is the most critical of all. The Organization didn't kill Mr. Tinti because they didn't like him. He either knew something about their next little plot to upend freedom as we know it and was about to tell someone what that plot was, or he got in the way of it somehow. I need you to do some digging online to find out what The Organization might be planning. Find whatever chatter you can. Identify who or what they've targeted, determine a vulnerable location, identify whatever weapon of destruction—mass or otherwise—they plan to use this time."

The young Aussie looked deep into his boss's eyes and eventually tossed him a coy smile.

"On it," he responded.

Lee returned the smile, nodded once, looked at his watch.

"What is it, Dalton? Do you have somewhere you need to be this hour of the night?" Lara asked the question with one eyebrow arched.

The architect turned and gave his second-in-command a narrow, forced smile.

"As a matter of fact," he replied, "there is."

10

It wasn't a fog that crept over the city during the evening hours. And it certainly wasn't a toxic smog like the one that killed more than four thousand Londoners in 1952.

What had settled low across the cityscape, reducing Lee's visibility to some extent, was a soupy layer of charcoal-gray clouds. To make matters worse, a steady spit from the clouds dripped onto his forehead, a repeated, irritating drip that never became even a mist, much less a shower. The pavement near him was clammy but not really wet; an acrid smell pierced the air.

He patted his brow with a purple-and-brown kerchief that had caught his eye at a bazaar the last time he was in Istanbul, but within seconds, the moisture pricked his forehead again, like acupuncture needles inserted to ease a migraine.

He was standing on the narrow scraggly footpath wedged between the Thames and the back of the entrance to the foot tunnel. Here, the river bowed out and back, but it was so dark, and the flint-colored clouds merged so often with the shale-colored water, that its arc was virtually indistinguishable. But Lee could vaguely make out across the waterway the profile of a smokestack or two—eerie jagged spires that resembled the knobby fingers of some aged crone.

Behind him, the entrance shaft loomed. Designed by civil engineer Sir Alexander Binnie, it featured a circular brick base topped by a green, glazed dome. It and its twin across the river were now more than a century old, providing a stark historic contrast to the ultramodern skyscrapers of Canary Wharf nearby. Not that he could see any of that in this late-night gloom.

Lee really didn't want to enter the foot tunnel. And yet he knew he absolutely had to.

He checked his phone; it was time. The fact the meeting was taking place in the foot tunnel—in *this* dank, creepy, foot tunnel in particular—didn't help. He knew, however, that what was making him squeamish wasn't really the tunnel but the thought of descending the narrow spiral staircase to access it.

He decided not to look down, but to think about his parents instead and grip the railing like there was no tomorrow. *Hell, for all I know, there may be no tomorrow,* he told himself. It helped when he thought about the last conversation he'd had with the person he would soon meet, when he was told his father might be interested in becoming a turncoat . . . *It's a lie,* he thought, *fake news.* And every time he repeated that to himself, he clutched the rail that much tighter, turned his knuckles that much whiter.

With every few steps, the temperature seemed to drop a degree or two. The mugginess slowly gave way to a soggy coolness similar to what he remembered from his playing in his cousins' basement in Colorado.

Eventually (and not without one mild episode of vertigo) his shoe landed on concrete, a contact that reverberated far more than Lee thought it should. That's when he realized he was the only person inside the entire length of the tunnel. Which was strange, given the passageway was used twenty-four-seven by pedestrians and cyclists making their way from one bank of the river to the other.

But at this particular hour, on this particular night, he was its only occupant.

How do they do this? the architect silently asked himself.

He sighed quietly and peered down the long tube in search of some marker, some beacon, that might indicate where his colleague wanted him to go.

Nothing.

The smell of the river seeped through the cast-iron walls—eventually he decided that what he was smelling was a peculiar mix of river and vomit.

He took a few tentative steps toward a faint grating noise in the distance, a metallic sound like that made by an ancient lift struggling to ascend. But the sound was intermittent, not constant. A motor would kick in, the churn of gears and cogs would last about ten seconds, then stop. There'd be silence for a while. Then, the cadence would repeat its ominous cycle. It wasn't long before Lee could precisely predict when "the motor" would kick in and when "the lift" would reach its destination.

Except . . . the lifts that served the tunnel were not currently operating. And although he was walking deliberately toward the sound, it seemed to grow fainter as he approached it.

He paused. Cocked one ear to the side. Listened in vain. Resumed his stroll.

The noise returned, only this time, overlaid upon it was another, more syncopated sound that also registered at a regular interval but was off-beat of the grating. A sound that had been brisk when it began, but now seemed to be winding down.

Footsteps.

"You're standing on the wrong side of the tunnel, Dalton," a voice whispered from behind. "You're in the U.K. now, remember? Keep to the left, please."

He whirled around—it was the person he had come to meet.

"How . . . where . . .?" he stammered. "I mean . . . how did you . . . I didn't hear you come down the stairs."

His friend smiled. "I *didn't* come down the stairs."

Lee waited, but it appeared he was supposed to accept that comment as a satisfactory explanation. He took a couple of steps forward.

"So, why did you kill Antonio Tinti? How did he get in your way? What form of mass hysteria do you have planned this time? Why in London? Why *now*?" It all came tumbling out. There was impatience in his tone, but no anger.

His companion also edged closer, and with the approach, Lee crinkled his nose. So did the other person, who lifted one shoe and turned its sole upward.

"Sorry, Dalton, it appears someone failed to respect the No Animal Fouling sign back there." After some scraping along the concrete floor, Lee's companion stared at the architect for a few seconds then blew out a long whoosh of air.

"You need to understand, Dalton, that *I* did not kill anyone, *they* did. *I* do not have anything planned, *they* do. Don't turn this into an incrimination of *me*. I'm your ally, remember?"

Lee emitted a soft exhale of disgust. "I . . . they . . . it's all the same and you know it." He glanced up at the other, who was using the unsoiled shoe to trace random circles on the pavement. The circles slowed as the other's glare met Lee's.

"And you know it doesn't work that way, Dalton. I don't just reveal what I know because you choose to interrogate me. So why do you persist with that approach?"

Lee appeared chastised. He lowered his head, began to trace his own circles.

"Why isn't there anyone else in the tunnel right now?" he asked.
A smirk appeared on his associate's lips, then vanished.

"Because we have the power to make that so whenever we want to. And, because you and I have confidential business about your father we need to discuss."

Lee scowled. "What is it now?" he muttered. "Oh, let me guess. There's yet another document I need to sign. Some contract that gives you permission to induct him into your little club. Papers that transfer all his assets over to you. That . . ."

"Stop it, Dalton!" The rebuke was tinged with more venom than Dalton expected. "You know we don't need any papers for that. We don't require your signature for anything. Be very clear, my friend, that what's destined to happen isn't predicated on your *approval*."

Lee was breathing heavily through his nostrils now; fists had formed in both pockets of his slacks.

"Then what is it we need to discuss?"

His counterpart took a couple of steps forward, seemed to soften.

"He . . . well, actually, he insisted we pass along some good news to you, as well as a message."

Lee's expression turned from one of exasperation to one of wariness. The acrid smell intensified.

Through a forced smile, the other person said, "The fact is, Dalton, once your father completes his . . . matriculation with us, he and your mother will be released from their confinement. Well, that's probably not the right phrase to use. Let's just say the area they have been restricted to will be expanded. Significantly so. They will have nicer quarters than before, will receive three meals per day instead of just two . . ."

Lee had to quell his impulse to push his confidant into the tunnel's opposite wall.

"I'm trying to assure you that whatever discomforts they've had in the past will be . . . well . . . just that . . . in the *past*. They'll have much more freedom to come and go as they please. They will even be allowed to enjoy some of the programmed entertainment we offer. Of course, we'll continue to monitor them. And, if there are any outbursts, or any acts of insubordination . . ."

Lee gave a sarcastic look. Glanced down the tunnel and then back at his associate.

"I thought your cult was all in favor of people being able to exercise their free will whenever they wanted to."

His counterpart sniffed a couple of times but did not respond to Lee's retort. The architect waited for a reply and when he realized none was coming, followed up with, "You said a minute ago that he also wanted to pass along some sort of message."

"Right. The message." The intermediary pulled in suddenly, seemed reluctant to proceed. "Well, I doubt you're going to find this news anywhere near as uplifting as what I just shared with you."

Lee's eyelids lowered.

"Say it."

A long pause. Then, "To be honest, Dalton, you really should be grateful to us. We knew you'd probably be skeptical about this *volte-face* of his. So we gave him permission to pass along a message to you, actually encouraged him to do so. Something that would convince you his intentions of joining us are sincere. And when we asked him what he wanted to say to you about his decision, his reply was that we should tell you that he's never been so serious about anything in his entire life."

It was as if someone had tethered Lee to a generator and then flipped on the switch.

"What? He said that? Those exact words?"

The expression on his companion's face went from matter-of-fact to commiserative.

"Yes, Dalton. I'm afraid he did."

The architect swiveled away, took several stumbling steps, looked at the tunnel's arched ceiling, and chuckled.

"Unbelievable," was all he could utter as he staggered back to his original position.

For the next few moments, it seemed as if someone had lowered a soundproof chamber over them. Lee shook his head a couple of times but said nothing. He could tell he was being scrutinized.

Finally, the other person coughed, fidgeted some. "It's time for me to go. It's getting quite late. We can't hold up the flow of pedestrian traffic across all of metropolitan London forever." There was a slight scrape and then his associate was darting down the tunnel, one gloved palm raised shoulder-high in a half-hearted farewell.

"Wait!" Even Lee was surprised by the fervor in his voice.

The person reversed course some.

"If you'll recall, this isn't a one-way relationship," Lee intoned. "You don't just summon me and tell me what it is I have to do, or what it is I'm not allowed to do, and then strut off, as if that's that. I'm supposed to get something from you in return. Something that will help me with my case. If you'll recall, we're sort of in this together, remember? *If you'll recall,* I can make your life quite miserable if I want to."

He was winded from the tirade. Took a moment to regain his composure.

"So, it's time you give me something helpful. Time for you to give me something I can really *use.*"

His associate's head hung in a demonstration of repentance. After a while, Lee heard the person inhale sharply.

"All right, Dalton. I'll give you something." One foot extended and made more circles on the concrete. "Often, when someone wants to throw someone off the trail, they'll behave like the magician who doesn't want you to spot the mechanics of his trick."

The speaker thrust one hand out to the left. "They'll create some type of ruckus, perform some sleight of hand, over here . . ." The fingers on the extended hand began to wiggle violently. "To distract everyone from the really significant thing that's taking place over here." The speaker's other hand shot out to the right, slowly tightened, then pivoted to give Lee the bird.

"Don't get so distracted by the left hand, Dalton, that you fail to pay attention to what the right hand is up to," the speaker continued. "For to do so, in this case, could be quite disastrous."

With that, the speaker turned and marched back toward the staircase, as the imaginary lift began yet another ascent.

11

C-O-M-B-U-S-T-I-B-L-E.

Lee was more than pleased with himself. Not only had he completed the acrostic, he had completed it in record time.

In record time *for him*, anyway.

He set the word puzzle book on the coffee table and turned his attention to the weather outside. Gradually, the winds had picked up overnight, but now they were fierce, infusing an otherwise tranquil morning with a turbocharge of fury. He watched as a large delivery box scooted along the pavement then impaled itself against a tall iron fence, and a pedestrian toppled sideways into a parked car. She grabbed the door handle to steady herself against the gale and prevent her body from being blown into traffic.

Global warming, Lee told himself with a shake of his head. *It's making everything more extreme.*

He checked his phone and was glad to see he had an hour before he needed to pad downstairs and hand out some assignments to the team. He appreciated their current excitement about being in London, but felt he needed to direct it toward the dilemma they'd been brought here to solve.

And maybe direct them away from one another for a while.

He reached for the copy of the *Times* that he'd retrieved from outside his door earlier that morning. As much as he had tried, he'd been unsuccessful at adopting online news sources. He enjoyed the feel of newsprint between his fingers; preferred the power that came from turning pages rather than scrolling through them.

Call me antiquated, he said to himself, knowing that many people did.

He scanned the headlines that blared from the front page:

Pound in retreat as realities of Brexit set in

England advances to world soccer quarterfinals

Sheffield couple say 'allo to sextuplets

Sextuplets, Lee exclaimed to himself. *I can't even imagine.*

His eyes flitted across teasers for stories about how a post office had helped a rural town revitalize, and how a legendary talk-show host was now running for Parliament, when they landed on a headline in the bottom right of the page:

Rogue nuclear threat bringing
world leaders to London

In about ten days (the story said) the leaders of the nations that comprised the G7 would assemble in London to consider how to respond to the successful test of a missile sent over the Caspian Sea by the nation of Urkbekistan. Accompanied by their diplomatic attachés, they would discuss instituting economic sanctions, as well as redeploying their nuclear warhead arsenals as a means of heading off an attack by the rogue nation.

Lee chewed the inside of his left cheek as he read the headline once again. Then he counted how many days had elapsed between the discoveries of the murders they'd investigated in New York and Miami, and the onsets of the disasters The Organization had tried to launch in those cities.

Tallied how many days had elapsed since Tinti's body was discovered and how many more would transpire before the world leaders arrived for their meeting.

Read the lede of the story once more.

Jumped when nearby tree branches scraped the window next to where he was sitting.

Felt his muscles twitch and his stomach contract.

12

He noticed the coat before he noticed her.

A massive, blue billow of a coat that she clutched to her breast as if it were a priceless bedspread she was delivering to a friend. Given the stiff winds they were encountering, he could not fathom why she was carrying the coat rather than wearing it. But carrying it she was, as she waddled toward him from the far end of the long, narrow crescent.

It was unusual (but not unheard of) for London to be experiencing a squall like this in September. Rain this time of year was not uncommon, but these winds were both vexing and peculiar. *Likely the remnants of one of those Atlantic hurricanes we sometimes get the last gasp of,* he thought.

With no warning, an intense gust slammed them from one side. He steadied himself by gripping the iron railing to his right; the woman, however, staggered backward and to one side, like Humpty Dumpty set to take a great fall.

His impulse was to dash forward, grab her arm, and guide her along the pavement until she reached the other end of the crescent behind him. But something told him she didn't want his help, wouldn't welcome it at all. So, he chose to show respect to his elder and let her indicate somehow that she wanted his assistance.

After a moment, the winds lessened. She steadied herself, bundled the coat more deeply into her bosom, and trudged toward him again, struggling some to navigate around two sedans that were partially parked on the pavement. *At least she had the good sense not to wear a hat in this weather,* he thought. *Women of her generation can be quite silly about such things.*

They now were only ten to twelve steps away from each other. Shafts of sunlight pierced the clouds, then retreated. He studied her and wondered if he would ever confront the sort of challenges she seemed to be facing at her age.

Hoped he never would.

The wind pummeled them again, but the gust was shorter and less intense than the previous one. Soon enough, they were back on track and just a couple of meters from each other.

As she neared, she glanced up at him. He saw her face soften in anticipation of whatever pleasantries they might exchange. Her abundant lipstick, and her dark gray curls (slightly matted) vaguely reminded him of a favorite aunt on his father's side. *Winifred, was it? Guinevere? Something like that.* He remembered only two encounters with the relative, both when he was very young. But she had quickly endeared herself by taking him to see a freak show at a county fair and by regularly plying him with Double Deckers and Jelly Babies.

They were side by side now. She was still smiling at him, but as they came upon one another, her gaze faded to steel.

"Level Seven!" she hissed as she doddered past him.

He stared straight ahead for a moment, his breath in complete suspense.

"SEVEN?!" he blurted in response.

He knew the protocol, kept moving forward. But he couldn't resist a glance over his shoulder to see if she planned to offer some form of reply.

The woman just trudged on, however, her stooped back lurching from one side to the other.

Once he was well beyond her and rounding the end of the crescent from which she had come, he exhaled heavily and rolled his eyes upward.

Bloody hell! he thought as he quickened his pace. *This is going to be far worse than even I had imagined!*

13

Bree did not find her ball of yarn under the back of the armchair in the library. In fact, it wasn't in the library at all.

It was on top of the armoire in the room Liam and Roberto were staying in. Too far to the back, and too high, for her to claim it without the help of a step stool she spent ten minutes trying to locate.

"You're pigs," she exclaimed, hurling the ball at Liam as they gathered for breakfast. The yarn bounced off his flexed arm and plopped to the floor.

"Aw, truly Bree? Do you really think that? Because, if you do, I'm absolutely devo'ed. I like to think I'm a fairly respectful bloke. I could have been a real pig, you know, and completely unrolled it before I hid it."

Bree fumed.

"And, I could have thrown my knitting needles at you rather than the ball of yarn." She glared at him for several seconds. "Let me rephrase that," she continued. "I could have thrown my knitting needles *into* you. With great pleasure."

Lara breezed into the room, a manila folder in one hand. "Is this a stately residence populated by some of the world's most accomplished architects and designers, or a dorm filled with out-of-control college students?"

"The latter, Lara, you know that." Roberto had sauntered into the room. Warren arrived, only a couple of steps behind. "Those two have a crush on each other but they refuse to admit it," Roberto added, sniffling some. "Just like that freshman couple in the coed dorm who hit it off at the orientation kegger but don't know how to deal with it."

Bree and Liam looked at Roberto, slack jawed.

"He's right, you know," Warren said to them as he dropped into a chair. "Either that, or you two are already messing around and you're just now having your first spat."

The jaws of the pair went even slacker.

"Either way, it's okay, really it is," he added quickly. "Just let us know which it is, so we'll know what we can say and what we can't say."

Bree gurgled half a reply when Lee marched into the room.

"What do we know?" he blurted. "Lara, the street cams. What do we have? And what do we know about Tinti?"

The interrogation broadsided the firm's director of operations, jolting her out of the nanny role she had been in a moment earlier. She flipped open her folders, moved some pieces of paper first this way, then that.

"Well, Dalton, um, the streetcams." She took the paper on the bottom of the stack and moved it to the top and craned her neck forward toward it, like a mother bird feeding a worm to its offspring. "Three were operating that night, it appears. None of them were immediately adjacent to Hanover Square but one is about a block away, and two others are within three blocks of the park. Unfortunately, one of those three was out of commission on the day of the murder and one of the others was only operating from eight in the morning until three in the afternoon, when it went on the fritz." She hesitated, looked at her superior, who gave her no cue. "Of course, the Tube stations nearest Hanover Square might also provide us with video footage," she went on. "But that will only be helpful to us if we know who, specifically, we are looking for. I mean, I really doubt we're going to see anyone on the videos brandishing a pistol in midair."

Roberto snorted, then quickly morphed his response into a hoarse cough. He was feeling a lot better after having bombarded his system the night before with a heavy dose of echinacea, but he wasn't out of the woods just yet.

"And Tinti?" Lee barked. Lara squinted at her boss, wondering why he was suddenly in such a militaristic mood.

Once again, she reshuffled the papers inside her folder. "Mr. Tinti. Our victim. Yes, well from what I've been able to assemble, Anisa had it right. He seemed to lead a fairly humdrum life. Lived in a flat somewhere between Angel and Islington. Apparently, he'd take the Underground into Mayfair every morning, usually arriving at the tailor shop by ten. I was able to do a little research on some websites where people offer their opinions about different businesses in the area and found that . . ." She shuffled her papers again. "That he generally had a good reputation among his clients and with his management. Everyone spoke highly of his work ethic and his friendliness."

Lee waited, raised both eyebrows. "That's it?"

Lara returned his gaze and looked back down at her papers.

"Um, well, yes." She moved things around again. "Except that . . . until recently, he had a girlfriend."

When she looked back at Lee, he appeared preoccupied with a button—or some stain—on his shirt.

"A girlfriend?" he replied absentmindedly.

"Yes, a Betty . . . Naughton. A widow. Owns a clothing boutique in Chalk Farm. He mentioned her quite a bit online for about nine months and seemed quite taken with her. But then, all of a sudden, he stopped posting about her."

Lee continued to swat at his button or stain. "Well, that's interesting," he replied. He made one last flick at whatever he had been focused on and straightened up.

"Thank you, Lara. I'll pass all of that on to C. J. and see what she wants to do with it." He moved his torso slightly to the right. "Bree? What have you learned? Were any interesting foreign objects found on Mr. Tinti the night of his murder?"

The senior architect looked warily at her boss.

"Not . . . really," she answered. "I mean, I contacted everyone involved in moving his body from the park to the morgue. *Everyone.*" She paused and let out a sigh. "He had a few coins in one pants pocket, nothing unusual. Near his breastbone, someone found a piece of cellophane that maybe tumbled out of his shirt pocket when he fell backward to the ground. Probably put it there after eating some candy." She shrugged her shoulders. "Sorry," she said with a slight whine. "I did my best."

Lee nodded. "We're still awaiting the results of the analysis on the piece of fabric we found in the park, and the shoe print as well, but C. J. tells me we'll probably have those by morning." The architect glanced around the room. His eyes landed on Liam, who was busy drumming his fingertips on his knees.

"Mr. Wilding, what do you have to say for yourself?" The Australian didn't say anything for several seconds. Then he straightened up, clasped his fingers on the tabletop in front of him, and became quite businesslike.

"You asked me to see what chatter I could find out there, Dalton, and, well…" He unclasped his fingers and placed both palms face down. "There's a lot of chatter out there, to be honest. Loads. Especially on the message boards and in the chat rooms where *they* like to congregate." Everyone leaned toward Liam; the room suddenly felt as if it had taken on the characteristics of a giant vacuum.

"I haven't gotten a sense of what the chatter means yet," he said meekly. "But I'm seeing lots of comments about some sort of reckoning, some type of retribution about to get underway. In London, specifically."

No one said anything for almost a full minute. Slowly, Lee began to nod. "All right, then. Continue to monitor those sites, Liam," he said in a monotone. "Follow the chatter as best you can, try to trace it, if possible." The architect breathed out heavily, pulled his phone from his pocket to check the time. "I need to let C. J. know about all of this."

***

The commander's outgoing voice mail message said she was busy taking a music lesson but that she would, "return your call in a jiff." And that she did.

"So, your team has come upon some fascinating tidbits has it,

Dalton?" she said, sounding as though she had just finished a hundred-meter dash.

"Well, I'm not sure 'fascinating' is the right word, but 'important,' yes." He paused for but a split second before adding, "Your outgoing message . . . it said you were in *a music lesson?*"

"Yes! My weekly saxophone lesson. I play with a little jazz combo in a club out in Hoxton once or twice a month." She took another deep breath. "It's not that I need the lesson to remember how to play, really. I've been playing ever since I was in secondary. I just like having the additional practice between my gigs. Keeps my lips moist, if you know what I mean."

Lee shut his eyes and tried to envision someone as short as Clara Josephine Digby maneuvering a woodwind as elongated as a saxophone. He kept them closed, and squeezed them even tighter, when she began to rattle off such terms as *scat, 18-karat,* and *balloon lungs.*

When it appeared as though she'd exhausted her musical résumé, Lee filled her in on all that his team had uncovered. When he mentioned the online discussions Liam had come across, she exhaled heavily.

"Yes, well, I must say I'm rather cheesed off they've decided to bring their little shenanigans to our fair city. But it would be false of me to say that I'm surprised. I mean, the moment we discovered that our corpse came with a bona fide version of their calling card, we knew exactly what we were dealing with." She coughed once and then it sounded as if she had turned from the mouthpiece to spit something onto the floor. Soon enough, however, her voice was back.

"Sorry about that," she wheezed. "A hair—or something—started tickling my larynx." The architect shut his eyes again, shook his head, did his best to keep from snickering.

She cleared her throat once more and was suddenly back to her official demeanor. "So, that's all very interesting, yes, very interesting indeed. I will make the phones jangle on my end to ensure we get the video footage from the Tube stations nearest Hanover Park. Be sure to ask your associate—what is her name . . . Laurel?"

"Lara."

"Right. Have Lauren send to me as soon as she can a list of the stations she identified."

Lee decided correcting C. J. was futile at this point. "I will," he replied.

She sighed again, more deeply than before. "I must say, Dalton, I'm inclined to agree with your designer about the fence picket. I can't see how it could factor into Mr. Tinti's murder. So, I'll leave any follow-up regarding that to you and your team, if you don't mind."

"Yes," was all he said. The line went quiet again. Then, he heard a fierce scratching on the other end, a chafing that ended with something metallic hitting a hard surface and Commander Digby cursing softly.

He could only imagine.

Eventually she regained her composure and resumed the conversation.

"Well, between Mr. Tinti's coworkers at the tailor shop and his girlfriend—excuse me, his *former* girlfriend—I'd say we have some people to interview, wouldn't you, Dalton? I'm going to place a call right now to Chalk Farm and I'll get back to you once I have arranged things with Miss Naughton and . . ." She let out one deep grunt followed by a higher-pitched one. ". . . And once I've gotten this saxophone back to my flat without any nicks, scrapes, or dents."

14

Betty Naughton was as iridescent as the façades of the buildings in Chalk Farm that occupied the same block as her shop. The swath of silk she had fashioned into a turban was robin's egg blue; her drop earrings were coral. Her blouse combined those colors and added black for contrast; her genie pants were an intense purple.

Her personality, however, was more cautious than colorful. At least, it was with the investigators. With C. J.'s consent, Lee had invited Bree and Warren to observe the interviews.

"Now, THAT is a skirt!"

C. J. was in a back corner of the shop, holding in her right hand a hanger from which dangled a canary-yellow skirt with a lariat motif stitched in brown. The bottom edge of the skirt was ruffled and, in Dalton's estimation, much too short for the person who was admiring it.

"You know, I have the *perfect* pair of boots to go with this," the commander exclaimed. "I picked them up a few summers ago when I was working on a dude ranch in Wyoming." Lee and his team looked at each other with consternation; it was when he saw the same pinched expression on the face of the shop owner that he knew they were all in agreement that C. J.'s choice of attire was not just ill-advised but nudging her into particularly dangerous territory.

Betty had asked her assistant, Corinne, to bring everyone some tea, but her hospitality halted when the questions turned to her relationship with Antonio Tinti.

"Oh, I don't know, he was a nice-enough guy, I guess," she mumbled as she put a lighter to a cigarette protruding from her mouth. Standing behind a tall counter at the back of the shop, she inhaled deeply and blew out smoke with an equal amount of fervor. As it floated in Lee's direction, his nose twitched. The scent that arrived with the smoke wasn't quite clove, but it wasn't far from it either. She caught her assistant's attention. "Corinne, dear, bring me that ashtray," she said.

The shop girl did as she was told, then skittered to one side of the store to fold a series of cardigans stacked haphazardly on a pedestal table. Lee noted, however, that the assistant seemed to be keeping a wary eye on the interview.

"Exactly how did you and the victim meet, Miss Naughton?" C. J. had returned the skirt to its hanger and was now focused on questioning the business owner, two decisions that caused Lee to emit an audible sigh of relief.

"We met online. On one of those internet dating sites." Betty Naughton blew another plume of smoke. "What a bunch of rot *those things* are. Nothing but losers on there, trust me." She stubbed her cigarette into the ashtray as if to emphasize her disgust, but within moments her fingers were fidgeting for another.

C. J. cocked her head to the left. "So, you viewed Mr. Tinti as a loser, did you?"

The question caught the woman off guard, softened her.

"No, Tony was . . . fine, I suppose. I mean, I'm sure he'd be a great companion for a lot of women out there. It's just that . . . he was . . . well . . ."

C. J. waited for the woman to finish her sentence, but when it became obvious she wasn't going to, the investigator decided to finish it for her.

"A sack of potatoes in bed, is that it?"

Everyone in the shop, including Betty Naughton, stiffened. Bree immediately pretended to look for something in her purse; Warren turned quickly away and moved toward a shelf full of leggings intended for women.

"What? No! Well . . . possibly. I mean NO, that wasn't a factor, really. What I'm trying to say is . . ." She was grasping for another cigarette, along with a way to finish her sentence. In her fluster, she knocked the ashtray from the counter. The shop owner dropped to her knees to clean the mess and her assistant dashed over to assist. Once the chaos had subsided and Corinne had swept the ashes into a dustpan, Betty Naughton put both elbows on the counter and cradled her forehead in both palms.

"Oh . . . I just feel dreadful," she moaned. She lowered her palms to bury her face in them. After a few quick, shallow breaths, she moved her hands to the countertop so she could see C. J. and the others.

"Look, I liked Tony, I really did. He was a sweet guy. But it just wasn't a match. I like to go dancing and drink mai tais, he liked to play board games and drink seltzer with lemon. I enjoy Indian food, Ethiopian food . . . he was a steak and potatoes sort of guy. We'd go out a fair amount, but he really didn't have much money, which wouldn't matter to a lot of women, but . . ."

She looked down at the counter (*In shame?* Lee wondered) then glanced back up at C. J. and the others.

"I was planning to break it off after a couple of months, but then Niccolò—that was his son—died in that terrible accident, and I just couldn't bring myself to go through with it when he was hurting so. And he *really was* a nice guy. We laughed a lot. He'd bring me irises from the florist shop near his flat." She looked away from them for a moment. "He treated me as if I were Queen Elizabeth . . ." She looked at Corinne, who instantly looked down at her stack of sweaters.

"How long did you date?"

The shop owner looked away, thought about the question longer than seemed necessary. "About eight or nine months, I guess. Not quite a year."

"And when did things end?"

"A couple of months ago. He rang me up one night and asked if I wanted to go to one of those little mini-golf courses . . . the ones with the waterfalls and windmills?" She sighed heavily. "I remember thinking to myself I would rather hurl myself off the cliffs of Dover than do that. That's when I knew I just had to end it. So, I told him on the phone I felt we needed to see other people. That *I* needed to see other people."

"How did he take that?"

The shop owner shrugged her shoulders. "Well, he certainly wasn't cheery about it, but he seemed okay." She paused, seemed to be revisiting the conversation. "He *was* surprised, wanted to know what he had done wrong," she added. "I told him 'nothing.' That I just needed to do something different, that's all.

"I mean, how do you tell somebody that, for some sick reason even you don't understand, you can't seem to be satisfied with nice and normal?"

C. J. responded with a nod, studied the woman's face, then jotted a couple of sentences in her notebook. When she was finished, she set her pen down and put one palm on top of the other.

"Mr. Tinti died under some rather . . . unusual circumstances," she said. "Were you aware of anyone entering his life during the time you two dated? Someone who seemed to . . . move in on Mr. Tinti's day-to-day activities in any way? Someone who might have seemed friendly at the time, maybe too friendly? Or too unfriendly?"

The shopkeeper's head was tilted back as she lit another cigarette. At that precise angle, and with the afternoon sunlight filtering through the shop's front windows, Lee thought she resembled a majestic grand dame from the British stage.

"No, I can't say that I do. At least, he didn't mention anybody like that to me. And I don't remember meeting anyone like that while we were together."

A crash startled everyone–Corinne had knocked over a bud vase that had been resting beside the sweaters she was folding.

"Oh, my stars, I'm so very sorry, Ms. Naughton," she uttered as she stooped to collect the shards of porcelain that lay scattered across the shop's wooden floor.

"Well, there certainly seems to be a bad case of the dropsies around here today, doesn't there?" C. J. announced. Betty Naughton had circled around one end of the counter and was now bent beside her assistant, picking up the stray pieces that had not yet been collected.

Lee was certain he heard a brief, almost frantic, exchange of whispers take place between the two women. Soon after, they rose almost simultaneously. Betty took the shattered remnants of the vase from Corinne's hands and strode gingerly toward a rubbish bin in one corner. Corinne, meanwhile, smoothed her jeans, smiled at C. J. and Dalton, and walked meekly toward them.

"There was someone he played bocce with," she began. She glanced at the floor. "He said there was a new member there that he didn't like very much. They'd had a row or two, maybe more." She tilted her head up to look at them directly, but her countenance was grim. "I heard Tony–Mr. Tinti, that is–say he wouldn't be surprised if the guy attacked him, he was such a hothead. So when I heard that Tony had been murdered, I couldn't help but wonder if it might have been that man at the bocce court."

As Betty emerged from the corner, Lee noticed she was peering intently at Corinne, like a stage mother hoping her child was not about to flub her audition.

C. J., who had been scribbling again in her notebook, raised her head and studied the young woman's face.

"Thank you for that information, young lady," she said tenderly. "We certainly want to probe every possible avenue. Did Mr. Tinti tell you anything about this person? Do you remember a name? What he looked like? Why they had these rows?" The commander looked first at Corinne and then at the shop owner.

"I remember Mr. Tinti mentioning he was Eastern European– Serbian, Croatian, something like that," Corinne replied, picking up steam. "And Tony did mention once that the man was very short, and . . ." Her bravado evaporated. "That's really all I know, other than he said the guy kept accusing him of cheating." She looked at Betty who nodded once and smiled.

C. J. went back to her notebook. "And do you happen to recall where it was they played bocce, the name of the club?"

Corinne took an eager step forward. "It isn't a club. It's the bocce court in Hampstead Heath. On the east side, over near the swimming ponds. Apparently, there's a group of men who meet there regularly. He'd go there and play every other week or so."

Lee found it fascinating that although it was Betty who had been Mr. Tinti's girlfriend, it was Corinne who had delivered such a confident narration of Antonio Tinti's activities.

C. J. looked up from her notepad and grinned.

"Well, this has all been quite helpful, ladies, truly it has. And I do say we've consumed far more of your time than we should have, so my apologies for that. Do I assume correctly that if we need to follow up with either of you in the coming days, we can find you both here?" Both women nodded that they could.

"Well, then," C. J. said, rising, "with that we'll bid you, *adieu.*"

As they all headed toward the front door, Bree turned to Corinne. "Here's my business card. Do you have one of yours on you, by chance? I'd love to get your thoughts on . . . some of the looks that will be popular this autumn. What might translate well over on our side of the Atlantic, if you know what I mean."

Corinne flashed an embarrassed grin. "Um, sure, yes, just a moment, let me get you one."

A few minutes later, the group was about to exit the front of the shop when Lee noticed that C. J. was nowhere to be seen. He quickly scanned the premises and discovered, to his dismay, that she had floated back to the canary-yellow skirt in the corner. She was once again holding it up by its hanger and staring at it as if she were in a trance. Finally, her gaze drifted away from the skirt and caught Betty Naughton's eye.

"I hate to bother you, really I do," she said somewhat sheepishly, "but I was wondering if by any chance you offer some sort of layaway plan here."

15

Liam had never liked the term, "the dark web." It lent a sinister personality, he thought, to an online world that merely meant to offer anonymity.

Sure, it was where a lot of people went to score some coke or heroin. Or watch the type of porn you'd never find on the clearnet . . . (Goats? Really?) Or purchase more than a few weapons of mass destruction.

But Liam viewed all those activities as just a part of human nature and thought calling them "dark" was being too judgmental.

He preferred the term, "the *deep* web." Because it implied probing. Skulking . . . below the mainstream surface of things, far beyond (and beneath) the conventional, mundane world that 99 percent of the population is content to live in. Probing . . . really, really, deep, like someone in a diving bell, crawling along the ocean floor in search of sunken treasure. He knew the two terms didn't refer to the same thing, that the sites that make up "the dark web" comprise but a tiny fraction of all the sites one can visit on "the deep web."

Still, for some reason, "deep" appealed to his psyche more than "dark" did. *But, now, Dalton,* he thought with a laugh. *I bet he's more into the dark stuff.*

He clicked on the image of a lightning bolt that was on his

computer screen, the icon for the Thor browser that would send him surreptitiously into the virtual bazaar of the bizarre. Just as the browser's home page and its search bar were appearing, his phone buzzed. A text had arrived.

Got a sec?

It was Bree.

I have a couple of theories about the murder I'd like to get your thoughts on.

He sighed heavily, grabbed his phone with both hands, let his thumbs fly.

Can't. Deep into research. Besides, it's sorta late.

Liam set the phone down, it buzzed angrily back.

A plate of caramel slices just showed up down here. And it's not even ten yet. He could just hear the lilt of temptation in her message, like a melody one of the Sirens would play to lure Odysseus to shore. **I know how much you like caramel slices, Liam . . .**

He grabbed the phone, hastily typed, **Not now,** then tossed the device back onto the desk.

Fuckin' 'ell! he thought. *That woman does know how to taunt me . . .*

It was second nature for him to navigate to those online chat rooms where The Organization was likely to have conversations. Within a couple of moments, he was in one of the rooms he had found most reliable over time, the room where he had recently been reading comments about The Transformation coming to London.

He scanned the screen, looking for any reference to some day of the week, any particular month of the year, *some* specific time frame that could be a clue to when they might be planning their next event. Or, what that event was going to be.

But things looked quiet tonight. There were a lot of the typical rants about the West's imperialistic ways, prayer requests for relatives and friends who were either undergoing a surgery or desperately in need of a transplant, inquiries as to whether someone had a couch they might sleep on when they arrived in Milwaukee or Singapore or Capetown.

He knew, of course, that even in this anonymous netherworld, they wouldn't just blatantly announce their intentions. Whatever information they needed to convey would be carefully sheathed in a seemingly innocent statement, deftly coded so only those the message was intended for could decipher it.

But he was on to their patterns, understood their methodology: short sentences, often out of context (or without any context whatsoever). Sometimes (but not always) containing numbers, or perhaps even anagrams, that provided the critical details one could need to carry out . . . something catastrophic.

He scrolled haphazardly through the conversations. Someone asking where they could find a cheap prosthetic leg. Another person making sure they had not paid too much for a set of crystal goblets. A torrent of epithets toward both the prime minister of England and the American president.

One post filled with numbers caught his eye, but on closer inspection, he decided it was benign:

**Have earned more than US $20,000
this month alone from my website
devoted to clairvoyance. Click here to learn
how you, too, can earn up to $300,000 a year!**

He shook his head. *Now that's a lurk if ever I've seen one,* he thought.

There was a tap at his door. He froze, glanced around, carefully lowered the screen of his laptop, and looked back over one shoulder.

"Who is it?"

He heard a cautious clearing of the throat.

"It's Margarida, Mister Wilding."

The housekeeper. *What in bloody 'ell is she doing at my door at this hour?* He yanked his t-shirt out of his gym shorts so it would dangle in front of him, ran his hands through his hair, headed for the door, and affected his killer smile right before he opened it.

Margarida stood stiff, her lips taut. Her right arm was extended up, about face level, and in her hand was a plate containing a small, haphazardly arranged tower of caramel slices.

"Miss Bree said you were working late and might like these," she announced dutifully. "I will get a glass of warm milk to go with them, if you want."

Liam smiled tepidly, raised his eyebrows.

"Ah, I see. Blackmail it is."

Margarida pulled her head back a couple of inches and assumed an offended look.

"*Cómo?*"

Liam accepted the cookies, looked sheepish in return.

"Aw, I'm sorry, Margarida. Not you . . . Bree. She's wanting me to do something for her. So . . ." He raised the plate to indicate the snack was the blackmail he had been referring to.

"Oh. I see," the housekeeper replied unconvincingly. She began to step backward, stopped suddenly.

"The milk. Do you want?" The look on her face indicated she hoped he'd say no.

"Naw, I'm good Margarida, thanks. Really . . . thanks loads. If you see Bree, tell her I'll ring her up in the morning."

The housekeeper nodded once, then fled for the staircase.

He shook his head and trotted back to his desk, quickly shutting the door behind him and locking it. Setting the plate to the side, he peered at the screen to see if anything incriminating had appeared in his absence. There were a few more posts labeling all North American and Europeans as infidels (he took some comfort that his Aussie and Kiwi brethren weren't targets of their wrath, this week at least). There were more requests for lodging, several more for funds someone hoped to use to start some sort of cyber currency business.

He quickly grew bored. After scanning a few more posts, he reached for one of the caramel slices, gave some thought to watching a little porn.

When one new comment instantly intrigued him:

**This is to confirm that the set of
Titania luggage you requested will arrive
at Heathrow on the flight we confirmed with you
by text earlier this week.**

That was all it said, which was one of the reasons the comment had caught his attention. *Who asks someone to send their luggage to an airport?* he asked himself. *And, they still make that brand of luggage? Because I haven't seen it in, like, the last fifteen years.*

He toyed with *Titania* as an anagram, but could only come up with *I attain*, which was intriguing but led him nowhere. He squinted to see who had posted the comment—someone using the handle IvyMike52—and reminded himself to keep an eye on him (or her) in the future. Then he performed a quick search to see if any other posts had been made under that handle over the previous month or so, but none came up.

Which made the comment all the more suspicious, in his view.

The Aussie drummed his fingers on the desktop, allowed his gaze to drift back to the post about the clairvoyance website and the alleged fortune one could make from such an enterprise.

Maybe that's what I should do, he thought. *Read palms online. Become a virtual psychic. Market myself as Liam the Magnificent or something like that. Maybe that way I'd meet some rich bird who'd set me up for the rest of my life.* He adjusted himself inside his gym shorts. "Look into my crystal balls," he murmured with a chuckle.

As his gaze drifted once again to the advertiser's post, his face took on a glum expression.

I'd sure be making a lot more money than I am at this job, he thought.

16

"*Where* is Liam?!"

Dalton Lee was squinting because of the sunshine streaming in through the dining room sheers. It was a morning light atypical for London; a light that was brilliant, a light more like what one might expect to encounter in California . . . or the south of Spain. As glorious as the view was, however, the winds outside still raged, continuing to wreak havoc on those trying to conduct their daily affairs.

Roberto, his advancing flu having beaten a quick retreat, shrugged off Lee's question about Liam and went back to his phone. Bree shook her head slightly. She was licking caramel off her left thumb with the gusto of a three-year-old licking frosting off the beaters of an electric mixer.

"I dunno where that boy is," she replied. "I tried to connect with him last night, but he seemed to be sinking into some sort of deep dark space."

In the adjacent kitchen, Warren set his coffee cup into the sink with far more force than he intended.

"Sorry about that," he called out. He dried his palms on a dishtowel then returned to the dining room. "Well, he told me he wanted to hunker in and try to find out what The Organization might be up to.

You know how intense he gets when he's on the hunt."

Lee's mouth slunk to one side, and he squinted even more tightly.

"I do appreciate his intensity," he commented. "But not if it's going to interfere with his punctuality."

"Apologies everyone." The cyber expert sauntered into the room, wearing a coral-colored t-shirt, gray shorts and purple flip-flops. If he had combed his hair, it wasn't apparent; and yet, somehow, the tousled locks landed in a way that seemed intentional rather than aimless. He scratched the back of his neck, smiled at everyone, then spotted Bree in the corner.

"Aw, Bree, that was quite the treat you blessed me with last night," he said, beaming. At that, everyone sat up straight. Mortified, Bree raised the morsel of food left in her hand.

"Caramel slices," she announced too boldly. "I sent him a plate of caramel slices. He's . . . a growing boy. Needs his calories."

"And eat them all, I did," Liam responded as he pulled out a chair, turned it backward, and straddled its seat. He then looked back over his other shoulder and grinned wide at his co-worker. "Happy to discuss the case whenever you want to, Bree. I'm around all morning. And this afternoon. Just say when."

The stolid look on her face fizzled and she raised her eyebrows.

"Really? Okay, sure. You tell me. I'm available. All day, really. You decide. Whatever works best for you. Anytime, really. Even a day or so from now."

"Well, it's *so nice* to see everyone getting along so well." Lara had entered the dining room just as Liam and Bree's conversation was at its peak. "But rather than sit around and sing another verse of 'Hallelujah,' how about we all try to advance our agenda a little bit? I think Dalton has some ambitious plans for us all today, isn't that right?"

The architect had repositioned himself around one corner of the table so the sunlight would no longer impede his view.

"Well, yes, there are a couple of interviews we need to accompany C. J. and Anisa on today."

Bree ducked her head.

"C. J.—she's not going to be wearing that fringed yellow skirt to the interviews, is she?"

Lara raised her head a couple of inches and sniffed.

"Excuse me, but something's burning," she announced.

Roberto started and then dropped his phone.

"That would be my toast," he replied, leaping from his chair and darting for the kitchen.

From across the table, Warren looked at his superior with a seriousness the architect had not seen from his employee in some time.

"So exactly what is the plan for today, Dalton?" he asked.

Lee glanced at the doorway to the kitchen in hopes Roberto would soon bound back through it. But the clanging in the distance signaled that the designer might not return for a while, so the architect cleared his throat and leaned forward.

"C. J. wants to interview Mr. Tinti's co-workers at the tailor shop first," he said. "As we all know, a victim's place of work can be the perfect spot for The Organization to embed one of their own. Then . . ."

More clattering from the kitchen made Lee pull up short. Lara frowned toward the architect, shook her head, and leaned back in her chair several inches.

"Do you need us to send a fire brigade in there, Roberto?" she called out.

The designer trudged back into the room with two pieces of heavily buttered and heavily charred toast on a plate that was much too large for them. After he seated himself, Lara stood up, reached across the table, picked up a serving dish, and moved it closer to Roberto.

"I think you may need some marmalade to get those down," she told him.

"AS I WAS SAYING . . ." Lee blared above the din. Once he had everyone focused, he flipped open a notebook in front of him to consult some of his notes. "After we observe the interviews at the tailor shop, we'll see if we've learned anything else about the bocce player Mr. Tinti was having disagreements with and whether we can interview him or not."

Everyone nodded, waited for more.

"Liam, have you come upon anything interesting online?" he continued.

The Australian scratched his chest and gave the question some thought.

"I believe so, Dalton, but I'm not entirely sure." He went on to describe the unusual post he had stumbled upon the night before about luggage arriving at Heathrow. "My plan is to keep monitoring that person and the other chat rooms—unless you'd rather I do something else."

"No, that's fine, Liam, keep at it. That message does seem more than a little suspicious. Only . . ."

Bree decided to enter the discussion. "Only, it seems to me, if the luggage contained something dangerous, like explosives or some sort of toxic chemicals, then they probably wouldn't be sending them to Heathrow. Because anything dangerous like that would be immediately detected by security. Wouldn't it?"

Lee nodded. "It would," he answered.

The room remained quiet in contemplation for a few seconds. Eventually, Lee broke the reverie by nodding toward Lara.

"Ah, my turn, is it?" She reviewed her notes. "Well, let's see. I sent C. J. a list of the street cams we'd like footage from. Rather than make C. J. do it, I took the liberty of contacting London Underground and London Buses and asked them for any feeds they might have, but I haven't heard back from them yet."

Lee was tapping the tines of his fork against his chin.

"Yes. And it might not hurt to check the shared-ride services as well to see if they have any footage," he added. "Given the fact the murder took place around midnight, my assumption is our assailant walked to the park. Then again . . ." Lee increased the velocity of his tapping. "Who knows."

"What do you want *me* to do, Dalton? Do you want me to come along on the interviews?" Roberto had finished his last piece of toast and now was sitting forward in his chair, his hands clasped one inside the other.

A subtle smile formed on the architect's face.

"I'm going to have Bree, Warren, and Lara come along on today's interviews," he said. "I want you to keep monitoring the park, to continue to explore the surroundings, keep watch on whomever you see there. I have this odd feeling we may have missed some important clue there . . .

"And then, of course, there is also the distinct possibility that—as they say—the killer will return to the scene of the crime. If they haven't already."

***

When they assembled in front of the tailor shop, they discovered C. J. was *not* wearing the yellow skirt. In fact, she looked more kempt and professional than they had ever seen her. Her business suit was trim, but amply fit her hefty frame, and her sky-blue blouse looked crisp and pressed. A simple watch adorned with a silver band, and a matching silver necklace, completed her wardrobe.

Most impressive of all, Bree could not find a single missing button on C. J.'s shirt or jacket, nor a frayed hem on any of her attire.

"My heavens, C. J.!" Dalton Lee exulted as they arrived. "Don't you look stunning today?!"

His colleague reddened briefly, then studied herself.

"Yes, well, in this job, one has to wear some *haute couture* at one point or another," she said. "A pant suit commands only so much respect, I've learned."

Anisa was similarly attired but chose to hang back and let C. J. run the show. "Your team, Mr. Lee . . . have you, have all of you, unearthed anything interesting yet?" The younger woman whispered the questions to Lee as they headed toward the shop's front door.

The architect shook his head. "We have a few intriguing leads," he replied. "But nothing concrete. Yet."

"Same here," she countered. "We haven't heard back about that piece of fabric you found snagged on the tree branch, but I do know the analysis of that footprint you also found came back inconclusive. Except that it was likely made by some sort of casual shoe, which doesn't really help us much."

Lee nodded and shrugged his shoulders. "Shall we, then?" he said, extending one arm in the direction of the tailor shop's front door.

As they filed into the tailoring establishment, Lee found himself instantly taken aback and impressed. Even though the shop occupied a prestigious address on Savile Row, he wasn't prepared for the interior they encountered. He had expected some sort of hunting-club ambience, with forest-green walls, tufted leather sofas, and perhaps a fireplace flanked by mounted deer heads. Instead, the shop was urbane and serene, with a dove-gray ceiling, mahogany display shelves that wrapped the entire perimeter of the room, and three oval-shaped free-standing counters the colors of espresso and cream. In a far back corner, a thirty-something salesclerk in a tight brown suit appeared to be showing dress shirts to an older gentleman who wore a small black tam and corduroy jeans.

Spinning around on their right to welcome them was a deeply tanned male with longish black hair combed behind his ears.

"Ah, you must be Commander Digby," the man said as he squeezed out a smile and extended one hand in Bree's direction. C. J. lunged forward and grasped the man's palm before Bree could even blink.

"*I'm* Commander Digby," she said, pumping the gentleman's hand, "and this is my assistant, Inspector Nassir." C. J. then gestured toward the architect and his entourage. "Mr. Lee is here from America and observing the investigation. And these are his colleagues. You would be . . . ?"

"Armando, madam," he replied, nodding. "Armando Cortes, the shop's manager." He extracted a card from his jacket pocket and offered it to her with both hands. "The owners informed me you would be coming sometime today to discuss the circumstances of Antonio's . . . Mr. Tinti's . . . passing."

"Yes, we'd like to ask you a few questions about him, if that's all right," C. J. replied. She swirled her eyes around the room and noted that the older man in the tam was now looking in their direction. "Is there someplace we can go where we can be . . . *un peu plus discret?*"

Armando ducked his head and jutted it forward. "I'm sorry. What?"

"Discreet. Circumspect, if you will. Is there someplace where we can have a conversation that won't be overheard?"

He reared back his head and smiled broadly. "Ah, of course, madam, why didn't you say so? Please, follow me."

Like a *maître d'* leading a party to some VIP room, the manager escorted them toward the back of the shop. "I should probably prepare you," he tossed over one shoulder, "the back of the house is nowhere near as elegant as the front."

As the group moved forward, Lee examined the numerous bolts of luxurious fabrics on display. Positioned upright in the rich mahogany cabinetry that lined the room, the bolts resembled soldiers standing at attention for an important inspection. He spotted an outstanding gabardine on his left, and on his right a worsted wool he would pay two years' salary for. As he perused the variety of fabrics around the room, the architect noted that the older customer in corduroy pants was once again staring at them, a half-smile on his face. Lee dipped his head in the man's direction as a form of acknowledgment; the man returned the nod, but at half the speed. To Lee, the expression on the man's face seemed to say, *We know each other, but you don't realize that, do you?*

The shop manager had been correct. The luxe feel of the store's display area up front gave way in the back to a sterile, warehouse-like space that was bathed in garish fluorescence. Lee found himself squinting again; the others unconsciously wrapped their arms around themselves as if they had just strolled into a supermarket meat locker. The room was cluttered with sewing instruments and the torsos of mannequins, some of which had measuring tapes draped over their shoulders.

"It's very congested back here, I do apologize," Armando said, smiling nonetheless. "But it's the only place we have that can provide us a bit of privacy."

"It will do. Let's get underway." C. J. had suddenly decided to assert her authority. "First of all, Mr. Cortes, can you recall what Mr. Tinti's mood was on the day of the murder? Did he seem out of sorts for any reason? Did he seem at all concerned or anxious?"

The manager studied the floor for a moment; a serious look replaced his smile.

"No. Not at all. I mean, he certainly wasn't *joyful* that day. After his son died, he understandably had become more reserved." His gaze went from the floor to the ceiling. "I do recall that over the last few weeks he had experienced more than one run-in with someone he played bocce with."

C. J. stopped writing, looked up at the manager, and nodded.

"Yes, we know about that gentleman and are trying to locate him. Do you know anything about him? His name? Where he lives?"

Armando now had one elbow resting in the palm of his other hand and his fingertips gently covering his mouth. He remained silent for a few seconds, then shook his head.

"No, I can't say that I do," he replied. "I know he exasperated Tony more than once, but I don't recall any details about him. And I don't remember Tony mentioning anything about him in the days leading up to the . . . the days leading up to his . . . demise." He paused, reflected, shook his head once more. "No, that week, he basically came into the shop, did his work, and left. I would say that week seemed especially unremarkable."

A lanky gentleman in his late fifties tried to squeeze around everyone. His impeccable attire and erect posture gave him the air of an accomplished butler. But his sagging jowls and world-weary attitude implied he was exhausted from serving whatever master employed him.

"Ah, Malcolm! These are the people investigating Tony's . . ." The manager let slide the obvious end to the sentence. Malcolm turned to the group and his jowls sagged even further, as if he had just been informed he was going to have to work unusually late that evening.

"Yes, an unfortunate matter, most definitely," he intoned. He did not respond to C. J.'s effort to shake hands.

"Forgive me, your name is Malcolm . . .?" C. J. was writing in her notebook again.

"Malcolm Hensleigh, madam." As he spelled the name for her, he seemed to grow increasingly tired. When he pronounced the final *h*, he did so in a hoarse whisper. C. J. nodded constantly as he offered the letters; finished her notation with an overemphatic dotting of the *i*.

"Thank you, and your role here is that of . . .?"

"I am the skilled tailor here," he replied. Lee noted the man seemed to add a distinct emphasis to the word "skilled."

"I see," C. J. said, continuing to scribble. "Now, can either of you describe what Mr. Tinti's daily schedule was like? At what hour would he arrive at the shop? When would he take his breaks? When would he leave for home?"

The two employees looked at one another, then away, then back at one another again. Finally, Malcolm Hensleigh cleared his throat.

"Mr. Tinti usually arrived here at ten in the morning, sharp," he said. "If there is one thing I can say in his favor, it's that he was punctual." Dalton Lee cocked his head at the remark, which he thought criticized the deceased more than it complimented him.

"Around one in the afternoon, he would take about a forty-five-minute lunch break," the tailor continued. "Then, depending on his workload, he'd stay until half past four or five in the afternoon. On rare occasions, half past five." He paused, and a smirk appeared on the older man's face. "Not that any of the extra minutes he put in actually showed up in the cuts of the suits he produced."

"All right, Malcolm, that was uncalled for!" Armando narrowed his gaze at the tailor, who appeared nonplussed by the reprimand. Bree, Warren, and Lara discreetly exchanged looks of embarrassment at the overt dissing of a deceased workmate. A little perturbed himself, Lee looked away, only to discover the older man studying him yet again through the doorway separating the two rooms (despite the fact the salesperson talking to the older gentleman was passionately pointing out some intricate detail on the shirt in his hands). The customer's eyes appeared to gleam (*Did one of them have an emerald cast to it,* Lee wondered) and his mouth remained contorted in a shape that fell somewhere between a grin and a grimace.

The architect floated away from the discussion with the tailor and sauntered toward the older gentleman. As he did, the customer uttered a few syllables to the sales clerk, who immediately tucked the shirt under one arm and headed toward the front of the store.

"I'm sorry, but do we know one another?" Lee asked, extending his hand. As their palms met, Lee noted the color of the man's left iris was, indeed, a deep emerald-green. The right eye, however, was most certainly brown.

The other man pumped Lee's hand vigorously.

"Not really," he said quietly. He shook Lee's hand several times more. "But then again, perhaps."

The architect tilted his head to one side. They remained focused on one another, saying nothing for several seconds. Finally, the older man heaved a deep sigh.

"It's really unfortunate, Mr. Lee, that you and your colleagues have chosen to come here," he said softly.

The architect stiffened.

"How do you know who . . . what makes you say that?"

The man held Lee's gaze for some time, not blinking once the entire time. Then, he sniffed quickly and offered one quiet chuckle. "If you'll excuse me, Mr. Lee, I think my ride is here." The emerald eye finally blinked, but in slow motion. "Oh, and I might recommend that you and your friends also book some form of transportation and take it as far from London as it can possibly carry you . . .

"While you still have an opportunity to do so, that is."

Lee stood stunned; the other man whirled around and—all evidence of older age suddenly evaporating from his demeanor—bounded toward the shop's front door. The salesclerk who had been attending the man seemed to have retreated down some side corridor, although Lee could not see any such passageway.

The architect wanted to chase after the older man, or at least warn C. J. that a member of The Organization was in the process of eluding them. But he checked himself. He knew from experience that by now, the man had likely darted down some secluded breezeway, blended into the madding crowd.

As they always do, Lee thought.

He sidled back to the group, his shoulders slumped.

"What's wrong? What was *that* about?" Bree whispered.

He merely shook his head. "Later," he replied.

"And precisely how long have you worked here, Señor Cortes?" C. J. asked.

"Just over three years, madam."

"And *you*, Mr. Hensleigh?"

The tailor made himself taller, lifted his chin a couple of inches.

"I'm proud to say that I've been employed here for twenty-eight consecutive years."

"I see. That's very impressive. You've likely seen a lot of men in their underpants then, haven't you?"

The tailor's jaw dropped. His expression morphed from one of boredom to one of indignation.

"I dare say not, madam!" he exclaimed. "All of our clients use the dressing rooms we provide for them."

C. J. twirled her head around to examine the space they were in. "Oh, right, of course, my error. I suppose I should have known that, given the, uh, locks there on all those stalls, and all." She consulted her notepad again and issued a sly smirk as she did so.

"What else can you tell us about Mr. Tinti?" she offered, her head still down. "Was he prone to taking his lunches in the park? Did he regularly meet anyone here at the shop?"

Anisa took a step forward. "Also, what about the customers he did tailoring work for? Were there any unusual experiences there?"

The two men immediately exchanged glances. Malcolm began to utter something, but Armando raised one palm.

"Generally, everyone is very pleased with our work here. However, several weeks ago there was one customer—Mr. Fakhoury. Omar Fakhoury, I believe. He ordered several suits and—strangely enough— asked specifically that Tony do the tailoring. He said that Tony had performed some tailoring for a friend of his, and that the friend was very pleased with Tony's product." The store manager took a breath. "The gentleman picked up his suits about a month later but came back into the shop the following day. He said the tailoring job was unsatisfactory and he demanded a refund."

"He was *irate*," Malcolm added. "*Screaming.*"

Armando rolled his eyes, retrieved his diplomatic smile. "He was not happy," he agreed quietly.

Anisa nodded. "And who is this Mr. Fakhoury? How long has he been a customer of yours? And do you know why he wanted the victim to work on his suits?" Again, the tailor and the manager looked to one another.

"This was his first purchase from us," Armando replied. "I don't know much about him except that he is from the Middle East . . . Lebanon, if memory serves me correctly. And I have no idea why he wanted Tony to do his tailoring. I do know, however, that he must have an impressive disposable income."

"Why do you say that?" C. J. asked.

"Because he ordered twelve suits from us in the most expensive fabrics we carry. It was our most lucrative order in the fifty-nine years we've been in operation."

Anisa raised one hand a few inches. "And, I'm sorry, but you said he was pretty unhappy with the tailoring Mr. Tinti provided. Did he have a good reason to be?"

Armando glanced at Malcolm, who raised both eyebrows.

"Possibly. But not necessarily. Between us, Tony's tailoring that month probably left a lot to be desired. He was still grieving the death of his son. However, we also noticed that Mr. Fakhoury had put on some weight between the time he had the suits tailored and when he came to pick them up. There was probably more than enough blame to go around, to be honest, but personally, I thought Mr. Fakhoury's reaction was . . . extreme."

"I didn't," Malcolm said.

The room remained quiet for several seconds, then Armando picked up the thread again.

"And, it all worked out in the end, actually. Malcolm agreed to fix the suits and Mr. Fakhoury seemed fine with that." A tinkling sound from up front indicated someone was entering the shop. "I really wish I had more valuable details to share with you. Tony was one of those employees who come in every day, do a good job" (Malcolm loudly cleared his throat as the shop manager uttered this), "and keep to themselves most of the time. He became even more like that after the passing of his son. I do know he liked to take his lunch at one of only a couple of the cafés in the area, when he wasn't bringing in some sandwich in a paper bag, that is. He really was that much the proverbial creature of habit. He had a dating relationship for a while with a woman in Chalk Hill, I do know that. But it didn't seem to last very long, and I'm not sure why it ended. Other than that, I can't think of anyone else he had any repeated interactions with, much less anyone who'd want to . . . harm him."

Malcolm ducked his head a few inches. "Um, may I be excused?" he asked quietly. "I need to attend to one of Mr. Fakhoury's suits. I believe he's coming in to pick it up later this afternoon."

Armando and C. J. nodded simultaneously, and the tailor trudged off, shaking his head as he vanished around a corner. As C. J. reviewed her notes, the shop manager began to tap his right foot.

"Do you have any other questions?" he asked as his eyes darted over C. J.'s shoulder to a customer who had just arrived.

"No, no, you've been quite helpful, Armando. Thank you so very much. I *would* like to get a list of the customers Mr. Tinti had tended to over, say, the past month or two." The shop manager nodded and glanced once again at the customer out front.

"Okay, then," C. J. continued, "if I should happen to think of any further questions, I will ring you at the number on the card you gave me. And . . ." she began to dig into a jacket pocket . . . "should anything significant come to mind, please don't hesitate to phone or text me at this number." She extended a card, one corner of which was folded downward, Lee noted.

He hoped she hadn't recently used the card to floss her teeth.

Armando graciously led them toward the front door but abandoned them the moment their route intersected that of the newly arrived customer. But as Lee was about to exit the doorway, the architect did a one-eighty.

"One quick question, Mr. Cortes," he called out. The shop manager took a few steps forward and smiled broadly at him, but Lee thought the joy seemed forced. "Do you happen to know the name of that customer your salesclerk was attending to in the front room while we were asking questions in the back." The shop manager took on a quizzical look.

"Who? I'm sorry . . ."

"The older gentleman with the black tam and the corduroy slacks. He was being helped by your salesclerk in the brown suit. Do you know who he was, by any chance?"

Lee assumed the specific details he offered would jog the shop manager's memory. Instead, Armando's puzzled expression intensified.

"I'm sorry, Mr. Lee, I'm just not following you," he replied. "I didn't see anyone in a tam enter the shop. And I'm the only person working the sales floor today."

17

As soon as everyone had gathered outside, Lee related to C. J. and Anisa his experience with the older man in the tam. They agreed that even with the resources they could bring to a search, locating him now would be difficult, if not impossible.

"*If* it's even a *him*," C. J. said, dusting some lint off her jacket. "The white hair beneath the cap, the green eye . . . all likely to mislead you, I'm sure. These connivers . . . they are, if anything, masters emeriti of disguise. So it's not beyond the realm of possibility, Dalton, that you were actually having a conversation with a university coed, or a pensioner widow they've recruited from one of our northern suburbs."

Lee sighed. "It's maddening," he blurted.

C. J. patted him on the arm. "It is, indeed, *mon frère,*" she replied. "Quite maddening."

Out of nowhere, the strains of "Ride of the Valkyries" pierced the air. It was C. J.'s phone, alerting her to an incoming call.

"Excuse me just a moment," she said to the others. She yanked the phone out of an inside jacket pocket, swiped its screen to unlock it and placed it to her ear. "Yes, hello? Yes? Oh, Armando! Yes, we're still standing just outside the shop, would you like for us to come back in? No? What's that?" She fell silent, began to nod regularly, then made a low murmuring sound. "Uh-huh. Yes. Oh, I see. Well, yes, that is quite interesting. Yes. Yes, thank you for letting me know that. I do appreciate your passing along that piece of information." She moved the phone a couple of inches from her ear to replace it in her jacket, but quickly returned it. "Oh, and Armando!" she called out. "If any other detail comes to mind that you think might be important, *do not hesitate* to ring me." She nodded a couple of more times before pressing the disconnect key.

The others waited for what seemed an eternity before C. J. finally broke the suspense.

"Well, I wasn't expecting *that*," she began. "I was about to point out that if Malcolm Hensleigh has been working at that shop for twenty-eight consecutive years it was highly unlikely we could put him on our suspect list.

"But. . .? Lee offered.

"As it turns out, something our *skilled* tailor failed to tell us was that he took a one-year sabbatical recently and only returned from it about five months ago."

The rest of the crew took a few moments to digest the news. Finally, Warren broke the silence and articulated what he suspected the others were already thinking.

"I've known lots of terrorists who needed less than a year to train for an assignment," he said.

***

They decided to have some lunch and wait to see if any more information came in before they scheduled their afternoon.

"Let's stroll over to The Breakfast Bar—there's one just a couple of blocks from here," C. J. said. "I know we're having lunch, but they have a chorizo hash I'm quite fond of that they serve all day long, and a full sandwich menu as well." She nudged Lee in the ribs. "I'll bet they can even whip up a blinding grilled cheese for you, my friend."

Lee's jaw went a bit slack. "How did you know I like grilled cheese sandwiches?"

An impish smile took over the commander's face.

"Let's just say your dossier was quite comprehensive," she replied. On their way to the diner, Bree directed their attention to a charming Georgian structure across the street with a To Let sign in the front window.

"That's adorable!" she exclaimed. "I could live there!"

C. J. tossed a droll look over her left shoulder.

"Yes, dear, you could. If you have a thousand pounds a week to spare."

"That's not bad at all," Bree replied. "That's . . . wait, you said one thousand pounds *per week?* That's . . ."

"About four thousand pounds a month," Warren interrupted.

"For a flat that's probably the size of one of your closets back in California," C. J. added.

Bree's enthusiasm wilted just as they arrived at The Breakfast Bar's front entrance.

Once they were inside, Lee began to squint again. Not because of the sunlight (which had faded quite a bit over the course of the morning) but because of the Technicolor interior that welcomed them. One wall was painted aquamarine, another was tangerine, a third leaned toward a deep violet. Each wall had at least two colorful metal signs, reminders of British breakfast brands from days gone by. The floor had a black-and-white checkerboard pattern and the stools at the counter came in either fire-engine red, lemon yellow, or royal blue.

"Wow, I feel like I'm having an LSD flashback," Bree said, her jaw agape. A moment later, she realized everyone was gawking not at the interior but at her. "Or, what *I've been told* one is like," she emphasized.

As luck would have it, a party was leaving the only table large enough to accommodate six people.

"If you'll wait a moment, I'll ready that for you," said a middle-aged woman of South Asian descent whose apron stains bore evidence to a busy morning.

A few minutes later, they descended into their chairs and picked up the menus the server had placed for them. C. J. was the last to get settled, dropping into her seat like someone who had just completed a ten-mile hike.

"I don't like to admit it, but I'm somewhat anxious, Dalton," she said, opening her menu but then closing it immediately. She raised an arm, summoned the woman who had seated them, and asked her to bring a glass of water, no ice.

"What's made you so uneasy, C. J.? I think we're making some headway."

"Oh, I suppose," the commander replied, now fanning herself with the menu. "I know we'll likely ferret out our murderer eventually, especially with all of you on our side." She held the menu steady for a minute, gazed into the distance. "It's just . . . will it be in time to prevent . . .?"

Everyone looked up from their menus in anticipation of her completing the sentence. But no one needed the sentence completed. And they all shared the same sense of dread.

"The luggage! I'll bet it's for body parts!" Bree had set her menu upright on the table top and was peering over it with a look of determination.

"What on earth are you talking about?" C. J. inquired. Lee then told the Scotland Yard detectives about the unusual posting Liam had observed online.

Bree barreled forward. "I just got to thinking, maybe they plan to set off a bomb, or unleash a virulent strain of some sort. But they don't want any evidence left behind as to what caused the catastrophe. Don't want forensics to be able to identify the source. So, maybe their plan is to put the bodies of the deceased, or their body parts anyway, inside the luggage and then . . . um . . . ship all the bags over to . . . uh . . ." Bree's battery rapidly wound down once the impracticality of the scheme became apparent.

"Wait, did the message specify the luggage had anything in it?" Anisa asked. "Or did it say it was empty?" Lee's teammates glanced at each other and shook their heads.

"I don't remember Liam saying the message indicated one way or the other," Warren replied. Anisa nodded.

"So you could be right, Bree, that the luggage being sent here is, in fact, *empty* luggage, so it won't arouse any concern as it goes through security. *But,* instead of putting body parts in them, maybe they plan to pack them with explosives, or something like that, after they've arrived here."

Bree studied Anisa for a minute, then vigorously bobbed her head. "Yeah, exactly," she said. "That was my other thought."

Lara closed her menu and crossed her wrists on top of it.

"Isn't that a lot of trouble for them to go to? If that was their plan, why wouldn't they just buy a set of empty luggage here?"

Anisa was nodding again. "That would be the sensible thing," she replied. "But maybe they think a purchase here would be a lot easier for us to trace. Or possibly, they embedded some sort of tracking devices in the luggage on their end so they could monitor all the bags throughout the trip."

C. J.'s frown turned to a scowl.

"Much to my chagrin, if our fair city has more than its share of anything," she said, "it's people who have expertise at building bombs."

The server came to take their orders. Lara noticed Lee seemed unusually obsessed with the description of the restaurant's grilled cheese sandwich. She watched him as he mouthed the description of the sandwich not once, not twice, but six times. After the sixth run-through, she placed a palm on his forearm.

"This isn't The Savoy, Dalton," she said. "It won't be astounding, but I'm sure it will be fine."

When the server came to Dalton, he hesitated, looked at her, stared back at the menu, then glanced at her once more.

"Your grilled cheese sandwich . . . is it pretty good?" She scanned the menu for a minute, looked at him, gave a big shrug.

"I guess so. Customers seem okay with it. I haven't really eaten it myself."

The architect winced at her non-committal reply. He looked at the menu once again, pointed at it.

"This calls it a 'toastie.' A 'cheese *toastie*.' I don't like it when my grilled cheese sandwich gets too toasted. It's not *too* toasted is it?"

The server did a quick check of the rest of the diner to see if another table needed attention then decided she had to answer him.

"Yes. That's what we call them here. Cheese toasties. I can tell the cook to go light on the toasting, if you want."

"That would be splendid," Lee said. "Oh, and the walnuts . . ."

"You don't want the walnuts?"

"No, I do not."

The server sighed and moved over to Lara, who gave the young woman a beatific smile.

"You can relax, dear. I'll be presenting nowhere near the challenge he just did."

Once the server was heading for the kitchen, they returned to discussing the evidence in front of them.

"The belligerent customer–Mr. Fakhoury–he seems to me like someone we might want to look into further," Anisa said. "We never did get a solid answer, did we, as to why he specified it should be Mr. Tinti who should tailor his clothing?"

The server was back at their table now, bearing beverages and condiments.

"No, we didn't," Lee replied as he spread his napkin across his lap. "And I found that pretty odd. If Mr. Tinti were a superior tailor with an international reputation, I could perhaps understand it. But if we are to believe his colleague, that wasn't the case at all, even if he was working on Savile Row."

"I wonder whether there wasn't more than a little bit of professional jealousy in Mr. Hensleigh's comments," C. J. interjected. "The fact may be that Antonio Tinti was a far better tailor than Mr. Hensleigh cared to admit."

Their server had turned to go back to the kitchen but halted midstep and whirled toward them.

"Did you say 'Antonio'? Mr. Tinti? The tailor who works in the shop over on Savile Row? Did something happen to him?"

"I'm sorry," C. J. answered. "Did you know him?"

She nodded. "Yes. We all did. He came here for lunch all the time. Sometimes he would have breakfast here, too. He was a nice man."

C. J. discreetly checked the name tag at the top of the server's apron, took the woman's hand and squeezed it. "Well, I am so sorry to be the one to deliver the unfortunate news, Mariam, but Mr. Tinti is deceased."

Mariam pressed the palm of her free hand to her lips. "No! When?" She twirled around to a younger server who was walking past her.

"Bridget, did you hear that? Mr. Tinti? That nice older man who worked in the tailor shop? They say he's *dead.*"

The other server's face dropped and she rushed to the table.

"Oh, that's terrible!" she exclaimed. "How did . . . I mean, was it a heart attack?"

A pained expression crossed C. J.'s face. Noticing it, Lara stepped in.

"Unfortunately, someone took Mr. Tinti's life," she replied. "He was murdered."

The two women drew their breath in simultaneously.

"I can't believe it!" Bridget responded. "I knew I hadn't seen him this week, but I thought maybe he was away on holiday, or had the flu or something. He was so sweet—gave me two big tips a couple of weeks ago just for bringing him extra rolls."

Mariam nodded. "Yes, he was a very kind man. Never complained about his order, even if I could tell the cook hadn't gotten it quite right. I felt very sorry for him, losing his son the way he did. And now *this.*" She was standing closest to Bree, and her attention seemed to get diverted by the architect's flowing tresses. "Your hair—you know, it's really lovely," she said. "You should never cut it."

Bree blinked, broke into a small smile, allowed her right hand to float up toward the mane of hair she was quite proud of.

"Why, thank you. And no, I plan to always wear it long. Although it *is* a headache to take care of."

"*Excuse me.*" C. J. was attempting to steer the conversation back to the investigation. "Mariam is it? Bridget? Could we come back in the next day or so and ask you a few more questions about Mr. Tinti? You might have some information that could be of value to us. But only when it's convenient, of course, and when you don't have quite so many customers."

The two women looked at each other and nodded.

"Tomorrow afternoon might be a good time," Mariam offered. "Both of us end our shift at about three."

"So, then," C. J. said, beaming at the pair. "Three it is."

The servers returned to their duties and the diners waited for their food to arrive. While C. J. focused on a text she'd received, Anisa gave the team her suggestions for London landmarks they should try to visit during their stay.

Once C. J.'s texting conversation had come to an end, she placed her elbows on the table and rested her chin in both hands. Her expression went from blissful to thoughtful.

"Dalton, do you ever wonder why those who align themselves with The Organization are so committed to creating havoc and destruction?" she asked.

The architect scoffed once, stopped wiggling his fork back and forth.

"I spend every single day wondering about it, C. J."

After a moment, the commander cocked her head to one side. "Come to any conclusions you care to share with us?'

Lee smiled broadly and narrowed his gaze at her.

"Well, I've decided they're really not all that different from the rest of us. In the fun-house-mirror world they operate in, they probably see themselves as outliers whose rightful place in our society has been denied them by rules and regulations they find oppressive. So when they set out to destroy the core of what makes societies like ours civil, they think of themselves as patriots.

"But we know, of course, that the way they execute their little *Transformation* is just as structured and rule-driven as mainstream society. They claim to worship individual freedom above all else but travel as a pack, professing their allegiance to something beyond any individual—The Cause. They say they honor equality yet designate certain members of their cult as the leaders and others as the grunts tasked with carrying out their dirty work. And, of course, if one of those grunts fails to carry out an assignment properly, that person's freedoms fall by the wayside. They stop being respected as a contributor to the cause and become a traitor, whose extermination is justified because their presence now represents a threat."

He paused to take a breath.

"It's that thing," he added, "where those who have been oppressed, but then gain power, become blind to how they are turning into the next wave of oppressors."

Somewhere a spoon clattered to the floor and everyone at the table jumped. It would take several seconds before everybody and everything had resettled into some semblance of normal.

Their plates arrived. C. J. swooned when the chorizo hash was set in front of her. But Lara needed just one glance at Dalton to determine he was not at all pleased with his sandwich.

"Whatever you do," she whispered, *"don't* make a scene."

After two cautious bites, he returned the soggy bread to its plate and discreetly shoved it to one side.

When they had finished their meals, C. J. instructed Mariam to give her the check.

"C. J., let me take care of my team's share, please." Dalton was leaning across the table in an effort to pluck the bill from the commander's grasp.

"No way, José," she replied with a mischievous smirk. "I do appreciate your gesture of generosity, my good fellow, but you'd be absolutely gobsmacked by what a police commander earns in this country."

As everyone was heading for the door, C. J. placed a hand on Lee's arm and indicated she wanted him to hang back with her for a moment. Once the others were on the pavement beyond, she turned to him and flashed a conspiratorial look at him.

"Dalton, when we were in the shop, did you hear Mr. Hensleigh mention that he expected Mr. Fakhoury to pick up one of his suits this afternoon?"

"I did," Lee responded. He plucked a wrapped peppermint from a basket next to the cashier and proceeded to unwrap it.

"Yes, well, while we were in the middle of the meal, I texted Armando to let me know if Mr. Fakhoury was indeed going to make an appearance. He just got back to me to say an assistant to Mr. Fakhoury called to confirm he'd be in around half past two.

"I'm thinking it might be prudent of us to pop in and have a little *tête-à-tête* with the best-tailored man on earth, don't you?"

18

"Mama! Look at that!"

Thema turned in the direction her three-year-old daughter was pointing. Their journey from Accra had been exhausting, but she felt rejuvenated now that they were finally in the arrivals area of Heathrow's Terminal 3. She found the clamor and crush of all the people in the baggage claim area oddly comforting. It reminded her of the ambience of their village back in Ghana.

"Yes, Abina, that is called a conveyor," she replied. "Our luggage will be on it very soon."

She readjusted the brightly colored duku on her head as her daughter returned to the plushie toy she had brought as a distraction. She was keenly aware that the cantaloupe, lime green, and purple hues of her headdress made her stand out in the baggage area, but she did not care. She was a contemporary woman and was delighted they were relocating to a place as civilized as England. But she refused to abandon her cultural heritage in the process.

Why isn't Kwasi here, she wondered. *Our flight was twenty minutes late in arriving.* Her husband was an excellent provider, she acknowledged, but miserable when it came to managing his time.

"Mama, look at that!"

This time, it was the digital arrival board that captured Abina's fancy as it flickered with new flight updates every few seconds.

"Yes, baby child," she murmured. She attempted to re-interest her daughter in the small stuffed dog. Abina buried her face into the toy's soft back and caressed it as if it were her own child.

Thema peered out the windows in front of them, tried to envision themselves happy and prosperous here. Her husband's new position as a mathematics teacher at a primary school somewhere west of London seemed promising. It certainly provided a salary he could never earn back home. Still, the cultural divide seemed daunting to her. As a girl, she had consumed many of Jane Austen's works, even dared to read D. H. Lawrence's *Lady Chatterley's Lover,* despite the fact her aunt denounced it as something, "spoken by the tongue of the devil."

However, the hubbub around them in no way resembled the orderly, mannered England she had come to love through reading. *Somehow, we will make this work,* she told herself.

"Mama! Mama! Look at *that!*"

Abina had now tossed the plushie toy aside and was trying to squiggle out of her mother's embrace. Thema looked over her right shoulder to see what peculiarity it was this time that her daughter had found so riveting.

When her own eyes landed upon it, however, she quietly exclaimed, "Oh my. Yes. Look at *that!*"

Two very tall and very muscular men were wheeling a long narrow luggage trolley toward them. But the cargo they were transporting was not the typical jumble of backpacks and duffel bags stacked helter-skelter atop one another.

Instead, the items on the trolley were as neatly queued and identical in appearance as a flock of penguins marching toward their breeding ground.

A set of cocoa-brown suitcases, all made with luxurious top-grain leather, each marked with a simple brass nameplate that read "Titania."

Seven leather suitcases, to be exact.

19

Fearing that a swarm of people might make Omar Fakhoury suspicious, Lee sent Warren and Bree back to the residence. "Think about what we want to ask the waitresses when we question them tomorrow," he told them.

Once they were out of sight, the architect ducked his head and assumed a hushed tone with his colleagues from Scotland Yard.

"Are we agreed we need to question Mr. Fakhoury about his disagreement with the deceased *and* explore how the other tailor . . . what's his name?"

"Malcolm," Anisa answered. "Hensleigh."

"Yes, Hensleigh. Do we also want to ferret out just what he was up to during that little sabbatical he failed to tell us about?"

C. J. was staring off at some low point on the horizon. She nodded slowly as Lee spoke.

"Yes, I do believe we are in agreement on that point, Dalton. Total agreement. However . . ."

The roar of a passing motorcycle interrupted her. She grimaced, then waited until the vehicle was at the end of the block before she attempted once again to complete her thought.

"As I was saying, I do believe we need to question Mr. Hensleigh on that matter. *However,* I would like very much to tread carefully on that front. Not show our hand to him too early in the poker game, if you know what I mean."

Lee scrunched his face, indicating he didn't know at all what C. J. meant. Anisa stepped closer, caught Lee's glance, and smiled.

"Here in the U. K., we sometimes use an interrogation technique that's different from the one your investigators in the States use," she said. "Your police in America like to badger suspects, pressure them, try to break them down. Here, we prefer to just let our suspects talk without any sense that we are investigating them, per se. We find that if a suspect thinks the conversation is a casual one, they're a lot more likely to reveal details that will incriminate them . . ." She smiled again at Lee, and he felt a small quiver run up the back of his neck. "Or prove they couldn't possibly have committed the crime."

Lee flashed a grin at the end of her sentence, then let it drop when he realized nothing she had said was even remotely humorous.

"I see," was all he could muster in response. "Fascinating."

They approached the tailor shop cautiously and craned their necks toward the front windows to scope out the interior before they entered. It had a few more customers than before, Lee noted, but they appeared scattered in isolated locations throughout the space, like mannequins abandoned inside a defunct department store.

The moment they entered, Armando caught C. J.'s eye from the back of the shop. He abruptly excused himself from a conversation he was having with a man in a cream-colored suit and took several rapid strides toward them.

"Mr. Fakhoury is in the back," he said, almost breathless when he reached them. "Come with me."

"Yes, well, before you do that." C. J. had Armando's right elbow gently cupped in her right palm. "We were hoping my associate here, Ms. Nassir, could have a word with Mr. Hensleigh, if he is available." Her comment was more of a command than a question.

"Why . . . certainly," the shop manager replied, looking anything but certain. His brow was slightly furrowed, as if someone had just spoken to him in Swahili. "I *think* Malcolm has returned from his break. I'll check just as soon as I've introduced you to Mr. Fakhoury."

When they entered the next room, they encountered the back of a tall, broad-shouldered male sporting dense dark hair and a gray sports jacket accompanied by black slacks. He was speaking passionately to a short, middle-aged woman whose expression registered something between amusement and bewilderment.

Armando made a meek attempt to interrupt the man. "Um, Mr. Fakhoury, if I could . . ." Lee braced for a bellicose eruption.

Instead, Omar Fakhoury offered a broad smile when he swiveled around, and raised both of his thick, yet expertly tweezed, eyebrows in anticipation. The woman he had been haranguing took the interruption as a perfect opportunity to skulk away.

"Mr. Fakhoury, these are the . . . individuals I mentioned earlier. They'd like to have a word with you. Here, why don't you use my office?" Armando took a few steps forward, then dramatically pulled back a tall, drab-gray sheath of fabric, revealing a space that was not much larger than a medium-size dressing room.

"Of course, I am very happy to help," Fakhoury replied. Although the man's tone was genial, Lee thought he saw his grin fade some once the introductions had been made. As they squeezed into the manager's office, Armando caught Anisa's attention and nodded his head to the right, indicating she should follow him.

Fluorescent light flooded the cramped quarters, making everyone look (at the very least) oddly pale and (at the very worst) somewhat ill.

C. J. cleared her throat. "Thank you for taking a few moments to speak with us, Mr., um, Fackery, . . ."

"It's Fa*khoury*," he replied with a tight smile. "Rhymes with 'the jury.'"

"Yes, Fakhoury, thank you. Of course. I'm sorry, I've never been very adept at pronouncing the names of all of you sheiks, Bedouins, and whatnot."

Lee closed his eyes, exhaled, decided it was a good time to examine his shoes. They were in desperate need of a shine, he concluded.

"I am from Lebanon, madam," the customer responded, his smile growing increasingly taut. "Beirut to be precise. It's a city of almost two million people. I was educated here in the United Kingdom and in France, and my business takes me all over the world. I can assure you,

I have never ridden a camel or lived in a tent." His smile suddenly went wide again. Perhaps a bit too wide, Lee thought.

C. J. smiled weakly in return and started to inspect the customer more intently.

"Yes, well, I'm not clear as to whether the shop manager discussed with you why we're here."

"He didn't," Fakhoury replied. "Except to say that you are with the police and that your interest in talking with me has something to do with the tailoring I had performed here? I'm sorry . . . I guess I am very confused." C. J. looked at Lee, who was still in deep introspection over the condition of his footwear.

"I see. Yes. Well, it's our understanding that you had a bit of an altercation a few weeks ago with the gentleman who originally tailored some of your suits." The man's face clouded.

"Ah, yes. I was very unhappy with the quality of the work he performed. It wasn't acceptable work from any tailor, much less one employed here on Savile Row."

"Of course." C. J. extended both arms and placed her palms solidly on the top of the desk behind her. "And I believe there were some harsh words exchanged between you and Mr. Tinti, is that correct?"

The businessman's brow creased. He tilted his head back and looked down the bridge of his nose at his inquisitor.

"Yes, well, I suppose I became somewhat emotional when this . . . worker . . . said I wouldn't recognize a well-tailored suit if it bit me on the ass. I have been wearing the very best suits available for more than fifteen years now, and I fancy myself a bit of a connoisseur of men's fashion. So, of course, I felt that my expertise was being challenged by this little . . ." He stopped and took two deep breaths. When he finished, his mood shifted. "I became upset, but I apologized. Let me rephrase that. I *sent* an apology. By email. After the fact." He tilted his head back another couple of inches. "If I may ask, what is this all about?"

It was C. J., now, who tilted her head back. She took a moment to study Omar Fakhoury from top to bottom. His jacket, slacks, and shoes were definitely expensive, she noted. But his taste in jewelry—a glimmering tie clasp, a gaudy belt buckle—reeked to her of newly minted wealth. *There's oil money here somewhere,* she surmised.

She finally decided she was prepared to break the silence. "Mr. Tinti was found murdered a few nights ago. In Hanover Square." She allowed a dramatic pause to keep the man before her in suspense. "Do understand, Mr. Fakhoury, we're not suggesting in any way that you are responsible for his death. But surely you can understand it is incumbent upon us to talk to anyone who might have had words with our victim in the days leading up to his murder."

Lee noted another shift in Fakhoury's body language. The businessman shoved both hands into the pockets of his slacks, widened his stance. *A pugilist getting ready for a prize fight,* he thought. But Fakhoury tilted his face back to its original position and his face seemed to soften.

"Murdered? That's horrible. I . . ." His look suggested that his mastery of the English language had suddenly left him.

"Again, you're not accused of anything," C. J. added. "That said, can you tell us where you were around midnight on the evening of the sixteenth? A week ago Monday."

"A week ago Monday? I was in Manchester that day," he said quickly.

"And what were you doing there?" Lee watched closely as Fakhoury slowly morphed from someone shocked by the announcement of a murder, to someone increasingly wary of his surroundings. If this was an example of the interrogation technique Anisa had described, it didn't seem to Lee that it was working.

"I drove there for a business meeting, spent the night at a friend's home, then drove back here the next day."

"Was your friend there as well? Did the two of you have dinner together, perhaps?"

"No. He is in a remote part of Indonesia on a work project. He lets me use his flat whenever I am in Manchester. It's more comfortable and convenient than a hotel."

"No doubt," C. J. replied. "No doubt. And . . ." She glanced at her wristwatch. "Around what time did your business meeting conclude?"

Fakhoury looked toward the ceiling. "Around four in the afternoon as best I can recall." C. J. looked to Lee, who was now reviewing the buttons on one of his sleeves.

"So that would have been early enough for you to return to London by, say, eight or nine that evening. But you chose to stay in Manchester?"

"I did." Lee noted the man's responses were becoming more terse. C. J. sighed, turned around, picked up a small stapler on the desk behind her, and tossed it from one hand to the other.

"Finally, Mr. Fakhoury, I'm curious to know what sort of business activities you're engaged in." He studied her, took more time than necessary, Lee thought, to compose his reply. C. J. gripped the stapler in one hand now.

"My business? I have more than one. I am in banking, international finance. I help arrange loans for small to medium-size businesses here and throughout Europe. I also dabble some in import-export."

"I see," C. J. replied. "Import-export. Yes, that can mean a lot of things, can't it? In your case, it would be the import-export of precisely *what?*" Lee took a moment to study his colleague, who seemed more than ever before in her element as a commander.

The financier stiffened, took half a step back.

"I know you said I'm not an official suspect in the murder you are investigating," he said, his head tilting back yet again. "But I think you should direct any other questions you might have to my solicitor."

***

Anisa sidled up behind Malcolm Hensleigh, who was using a measuring tape to calculate the length of a jacket sleeve. Without turning around he muttered, "I know this isn't *your* suit jacket, young lady, so what is it that you need?"

Okay, she thought. *That was odd.*

She took a few more hesitant steps forward. "I'm sorry to bother you," she began. "But, it's . . . my boyfriend. He lives in South Africa, and he's always wanted a Savile Row suit—more than one, to be honest. Anyway, someone recommended your services to him, but when he came here on holiday several months ago, the management told him you weren't available. That you were . . . away?" She paused to gauge his reaction. He seemed unmoved by the comment. "He's coming back to London in December, so I thought I'd see if you were going to be here then. So I could surprise him with the gift of a tailored suit. I wanted to ask you about this when we were in here earlier, but . . ."

The tailor snickered once and repositioned the measuring tape.

"Yes . . . no doubt the *cross-examination* out there got in your way." Slowly, he shifted the upper half of his body so it faced her. When their eyes met, he took on an almost grandfatherly expression.

"Such a lovely young lady," he began. "And yet, you choose to have a boyfriend who lives halfway across the globe." He stopped, narrowed his eyes some. "Now, I find that quite curious."

She swallowed heavily, prayed to Allah that the tailor was not on the verge of unveiling her deceit.

"And how old is this *paramour* of yours?"

"He's thirty-four now. But he'll turn thirty-five between now and December."

"Oh, what joy," the tailor responded. He flipped the jacket over and started measuring it from one shoulder to the other. "I don't suppose you happen to know the length of his inseam?"

Anisa squinted. "No, sorry, I don't."

He breathed in heavily and looked back at her. His benevolent gaze had soured even further. "Doesn't matter, as I wouldn't be able to assist you anyway," he announced. He delivered his decree with the curtness of a professor telling a student she had once again failed a critical exam. "To be honest, I can't fathom how your beau would have become familiar with my work, for we tend to be quite discreet around here as to which tailors undertake which tailoring projects."

His glum look descended into a bitter scowl.

"But, more to the point, I cannot be of help because I fully intend to be gone from this establishment by the time the Yuletide rolls around."

***

Anisa caught up with C. J. and Dalton down the block from the tailor shop. The early shadows of twilight that were beginning to creep across the district added to the trio's defeatist mood.

"Did he explain *why* he expected to be gone by December?" C. J. inquired. Anisa shook her head.

"He was pretty coy with the details he was willing to share with me.

I think he was more than a little suspicious."

"Any chance he shared some information about where he went, or what he did, while he was on his sabbatical?" the architect asked.

She slowly smiled at him, carefully moistened her lips before replying.

"Actually, I did have some luck there. I also told him I was on the hunt for some interesting vacation destinations, and he told me he could highly recommend a village on Cyprus he spent much of last year enjoying."

C. J. and Lee turned toward one another. "Well isn't *that* just the cat's whiskers?" the commander exclaimed, her mouth agape.

"I'm sorry . . . I'm not following," Anisa replied, perplexed.

C. J. patted Lee on one shoulder, then turned back to her associate on the force.

"Do we all think it was by complete coincidence, or calculated design, that Malcolm Hensleigh spent much of last year on an island that's only a thirty-minute flight from the country Omar Fakhoury is from?"

20

The next morning, Dalton Lee stood on the pavement in front of the team's temporary residence, hands on his hips, a grimace on his face.

Before him was the beautiful Maicoletta he had paid a pretty penny to have shipped to him from Southern California. The people who stored the vintage scooter for him had done a magnificent job of ensuring that the chrome body glistened. The cherry-red leather seat was supple and lustrous. Even the headlight was in perfect working order.

There was just one problem. One *really big* problem.

It had a scratch.

Not just any scratch, but a six-inch-long scratch that started just below the little "a" in "letta" and plummeted toward the scooter's floorboard.

Lee looked as if some great shift in the laws of physics had taken place. As if gravity had failed to anchor the scooter to the ground and, instead, had elevated it skyward and tossed it into outer space, or the molecules that made it a solid had rearranged somehow and turned it into a vapor.

"This is entirely unacceptable!" the architect said, rounding the bike and crouching like a wrestling referee peering to see whether a competitor has been pinned to the mat. He was on his phone immediately.

"C. J., this is Dalton. I have a scratch."

"No, Dalton, what you have is an itch," she replied matter-of-factly. "A scratch is the action you take to quell the itch. With your fingers."

"Not me. The bike. My Maicoletta. It's what has a scratch. On one fender."

"I'm sorry. What?"

"I said my bike has a big scratch on one fender."

But C. J. seemed to be talking over him, as if she were now having a second conversation.

"Hold on, Dalton. Something on my end here." Her voice faded a bit as she moved the phone's mouthpiece away a couple of inches, but he could still make out most of what she was saying.

"A toucan? No. No, I *do not* want a toucan. What? No, absolutely not. Because I have no *need* for a toucan, that's why. Right. Exactly. NO TOUCAN."

She was back.

"Sorry about that, Dalton. Someone poking their head into my office without an appointment. Anyway, about your vehicle. I'm very sorry to hear about the scratch. Was it parked outside? Did some of our city's illustrious vandals attack it while it was sitting out in some vulnerable location?"

Lee looked to the heavens. "No, C. J. No. It arrived that way. The damage happened during shipment."

"Oh, I see. Well, I'm not sure there's much our Metropolitan Police can really do to assist then, Dalton. I'd recommend you contact your insurance company as soon as possible. Beyond that, I guess you'll just have to chalk this up as one of those *que sera sera* situations."

As she spoke, Lee was caressing the length of the scratch with the fingertips of his right hand. When he reached the bottom of the mar, only his middle finger was extended.

"I know, C. J.," he replied softly. "I just needed to vent."

"Understood." C. J. suddenly sounded quite decorous. "Now, about our case. A few pieces of information have drifted in." He heard a shuffling of papers, wondered whether C. J. would ever embrace the digital age.

"My team has *finally* performed a thorough sweep of the park and its immediate vicinity," she began. "No gun was found. Neither was Mr. Tinti's phone."

"Which means the killer probably still had the gun with them after leaving the park," Lee concluded. "And possibly the phone, as well."

"Exactly. Now, as for that fabric you so keenly spotted in the tree branches. You were spot-on. It's a top-of-the-line silk. Could be from a shirt, could be from a suit. Could be from someone's bedsheet, for all we know. And, given where you found it, it may have something to do with Mr. Tinti's murder. Or, it may have absolutely nothing to do with it."

"I see. Will your team be checking to see if it matches one of the silk fabrics sold in the tailor shop we visited? That might be beneficial, don't you think?"

"Yes. Absolutely. That's one item on our very long list of things to do."

Lee was inspecting the scratch again, trying to rub it away with his right forefinger. "Don't forget, C. J. I have a lot of team members with me who share an interest in helping."

Several seconds of silence passed before C. J. replied. "I can't begin to convey to you just how much I appreciate that, Dalton. Truly, you have no idea."

He made a mental note to get Warren or Bree on it as quickly as possible.

"Now, Team Scotland Yard *has* found the time to work through the list of Mr. Tinti's clients that the shop manager sent over to us," she added. "They've done quite a bit of cross-checking and apparently found no one on the list using the name of a character in *Wayward Planet,* or some other offbeat, but related, alias. All his customers appear to be on the up-and-up."

"So what do we do now, C. J.?"

"Well, as luck would have it, Dalton," the commander continued, "I've learned Mr. Tinti's fellow bocce enthusiasts are convening this morning for a match over at Hampstead Heath. How about you and some of your entourage meet me there so we can learn a little bit more about that hothead who accused Mr. Tinti of cheating.

Shall we say about half past ten?"

***

The overcast skies weren't helping Lee's mood. But there didn't appear to be any rain on the way, there was that. *How could the movers have been so careless,* he fretted, his head swirling with a mix of anger and despair. *What in the hell did they use to protect the scooter—tissue paper?*

A few steps ahead of them, C. J. was tromping across the parkland like General Patton marching through Luxembourg. Anisa was a few steps behind her, moving more gracefully over the uneven terrain—while Lee, Warren and Bree formed a V shape in the rear, with Lee at the point of the V.

Quietly, Warren asked Bree, "Did C. J. get a haircut? She doesn't look anywhere near as much like Spock from *Star Trek* as she did when we first met her." His co-worker, a voluminous pink tote bag over her right shoulder, elbowed him in the ribs and shot him a conspiratorial smile. Then she cleared her throat.

"I've been wondering, if this bocce guy is the murderer, why didn't he just kill our victim here? In Hampstead Heath. This has way more secluded places to hide a body than that little park in Mayfair."

C. J. stopped midstride like a pointer preparing to indicate to a hunting party the location of the prey. She swerved around slowly and smiled gently at Bree. Her eyes drifted to the tote bag on Bree's arm.

"Breeze, is it?" she asked, taking a step forward. "That purse of yours is . . ."

"It's BREE."

"Yes, of course, BREE. Rhymes with chimpanzee. Anyway, I was about to say, that purse of yours is absolutely . . . Amazonian! Like an *armoire,* it is. What on earth do you have in there, if I may pry?"

The senior architect raised her chin an inch or so, set her jaw tight.

"I brought my knitting," she answered. "I like to knit sometimes while interviews are underway. It helps me stay centered. Forces me to listen." Her tone lightened. "Anyway, to answer your question, I have a couple of works in progress in here, some patterns, some extra yarns."

She paused, smiled tightly at C. J. "And, some very sharp needles."

C. J. scrutinized the young woman in front of her. "Of course, you do," she replied. She continued to study Bree, then cocked her head to one side. "Given its size, I thought perhaps you had the victim's corpse in there, as well, and planned to show it to the bocce players to get their opinions as to exactly how the murder might have taken place, that sort of thing."

For several seconds, no one took a breath. Then, C. J. let out a whoop and slapped her right thigh. "That was a joke, Bree. A jest. A *bon mot*, as the French would say. That rucksack you have there is *astonishing*. Truly it is. And so much more fashionable than this weathered duffel I've been lugging around. I *must* have one, and you're going to help me acquire it. Now as for your comment, you are correct. There are all sorts of copses, thickets, brakes, and boscages here that would be splendid places in which to murder someone and conceal the remains. Absolutely."

She began to stroke her chin between two fingers. "However, I'm thinking the fact Mr. Tinti was found in Hanover Square does not necessarily *exclude* the person we're about to meet as his assailant, does it? And isn't it also very possible that if this antagonist of Mr. Tinti is the murderer, it's more likely he would have arranged the murder far from a place they were both associated with? To deflect suspicion, *n'est-ce pas?*" She stopped, looked once again at Bree's tote. "Does that also come in mauve, by any chance?" she asked.

Bree considered C. J.'s assertion for a moment, decided it had merit. A flash of a smile flew across her lips.

"I suppose you're right, C. J.," she replied quietly.

"Of course, I'm right," C. J. bellowed, offering a toothy grin. "But your questions are helping us frame the case, Breeze . . . truly, they are . . . and you MUST continue to ask them!"

Bree glanced at Warren and Anisa, chuckled a bit and took a couple of large steps to catch up with the commander, who was tromping forward again. C. J. slowed, however, as they approached a hefty man who looked more like the skipper of a boat than a participant in a bocce match.

"Fieldston Tucker, I presume?" C. J. had her right hand extended toward the man, who wore a gold-buttoned blue blazer, white slacks, a captain's hat, and a cravat with a paisley pattern in red and blue. "I recognize you from the description you gave me over the phone."

"Ah, you must be the investigators," he replied, firmly shaking C. J.'s hand. "More than happy to oblige. I'm afraid we're going to have to call off our match anyway. One bloke's got the stomach bug that's going around, another has a sink that's all gummed up."

"I'm sorry to hear that," C. J. replied, "although it does provide us with more time to talk now, doesn't it?" She reached for the edge of his jacket, stroked it some. "Aren't you rather dapper to be fiddling around with wooden balls and sand and such?"

He looked down at her fingers. "My, that's quite a bear paw you have there, isn't it, Miss . . .?"

Stung by his comment, C. J. let go of his jacket like an archer releasing an arrow.

"Digby," she answered with a nod. "And these are my assistants, Ms. Nassir, Mr. Lee, Miss Westerman, and . . . um . . ."

"Warren. Warren Jackson," the architect offered, stepping forward to shake the man's hand.

"Nice to meet you, all of you," he said. "No, I'm afraid I don't play much anymore. I'm what you might call the group's unofficial mascot and referee. A while back, one of the players took me aside and said, 'Field, old chap, your palsy has gotten the best of you. How about you sit out the matches but hold us to the rule book and arbitrate any challenges that arise?'" He paused for a moment and peered past C. J.'s elbow. "Some people might have thought that a cheeky thing to say," he continued, "but I think it was right nice of them, don't you?"

Everyone but C. J. was staring at his hands, which (they realized for the first time) were planted solidly on an elegant wooden cane.

A tender expression danced across the commander's face.

"Most definitely," she replied. Suddenly, she snickered. "Imagine the havoc you would have inflicted on your front lawn if they hadn't said something and you had continued to try to mow it!"

He reacted as if a sour aroma had drifted under his nose. Then he studied the grass for a moment, smiled broadly, and pointed at C. J.

"By Jove, you're right!" he exclaimed, laughing heartily. The look on his face, however, indicated he wasn't quite sure he understood what was so humorous.

"So, Mr. Tucker . . ."

"Please, Miss Digby, call me Field. Everyone else does."

"All right then. And you must call me C. J. Now, what is your line of work, Field?"

"Oh, I'm retired from the Royal Mail. Have been for about five years."

"Worked in one of the offices, did you? Administration? Did everyone refer to it as the . . . *Field* office?" Lee and his team exchanged painful looks with one another.

"No! None of that bureaucratic nonsense for me! I delivered the mail! My streets were up in the northwest, in Stanmore Park."

"I see. And how long have you been coming here to play bocce?"

He turned his head some and scratched his chin.

"I'd say about three years. The wife tolerated about a year or two of me in retirement and then said, 'Out of the house with you, or I'll break your neck.'"

"And how well did you know the victim?"

"Tony? Oh, he was a heck of a bloke. Punch in the gut when I heard what happened to him. I mean, don't get me wrong, he could be a gnat at times. Would take forever to pitch the ball. Would pepper with you with questions about your retirement fund, and what sort of investments you had, and how much you withdrew each year, those sorts of things. But he was all right, although not the sort of bloke you'd go have a pint with after a match, really. Cordial, but kept to himself mostly. Especially after his son died."

C. J. nodded, ran her tongue along her lower gums.

"We heard he had some battles with one of the players here."

The former postal carrier took on a downcast look.

"Oh, right. Our resident firebrand, Karlo. Quite the donkey, that one. I haven't the foggiest why he picked on Tony the way he did. Or why Tony reacted to Karlo the way *he* did. It was odd, really. Quite odd. Tony was usually this mild-mannered, milquetoast sort of fellow, you know what I mean? But then Karlo would accuse Tony of moving his ball when no one was paying attention, or some other infraction most of us didn't even realize there was a rule against, and suddenly, go-along-to-get-along Tony would blow up like one of those cyclones out in the Irish Sea."

C. J. cleared her throat. "So, this Mr. Karlo . . ."

"No, no. Karlo is his first name. As for his last name, don't ask me to pronounce it. It's one of those funny Eastern European names. With lots of k's and lots of c's. And all those little punctuation marks."

"Got it. So, this Karlo. Do you think he could have . . .?"

"Killed Tony? Heavens, no." The retired postman stopped, thrust both hands into his pockets. "I mean, Karlo did yell at Tony a lot. Got right in his face several times. But *murder* Tony? In cold blood? Karlo's never gotten physically violent with anyone as far as I know, and I really can't see him getting violent, and oh, lookee here. If it isn't Mister Congeniality himself."

They all turned and saw a short wiry man with curly dark hair and thick eyebrows trudging toward them. His face was scrunched into a scowl, which Lee suspected was the standard-issue expression of someone who, for some inexplicable reason, was perpetually unhappy.

"Field," the young man grunted as he trudged past Lee and his team. As he passed, he scanned everyone as if he expected any one of them to jump him at a moment's notice.

"Sorry, chap, but it looks like there's not going to be a match today. Too many of our brethren have had to bow out for one reason or another." Karlo put his hands on his hips, raised his eyebrows, blew a long breath out. Although he was dressed all in white, he gave off a grimy appearance, as if he had just changed the spark plugs on a car.

"Too bad," he grunted.

The bocce referee glanced sheepishly at C. J. and her entourage, then back at the young man. "Before you go, Karlo, these people might like to have a word with you. Metropolitan Police. They're here about Tony. His . . . death . . . you know."

Lee waited for the man to launch into some sort of bombast. Instead, he just squinted at them. "Yes. His death. I feel very bad for the family."

"Did you know any of them?" C. J. asked.

Karlo looked at the ground, rubbed his chin as if he were trying to remove some of the grime he oozed. Lee determined the scowl was, in fact, fixed permanently to the young man's face. "No, I didn't."

C. J. chose to press on. "You didn't really get along with Mr. Tinti, did you?"

Lee expected the young man to erupt. Instead, he laughed.

"No. We get along okay. I mean, he didn't like it when I point out what a cheater he was. And a liar. Which he was. All the time. But, no, it was . . . you know . . . how I play the game. Part of the competition. 'Messing with somebody's mind,' as you say here." His manner was amiable, but the scowl had returned to his face.

"I have to ask, Mr . . .?"

"Kovačević."

C. J. turned to Field, who raised his eyebrows as if to say, "I told you so."

"Ah, yes, well, I do need to ask where you were around midnight on the night Mr. Tinti was slain."

Karlo's body seemed to coil inward, like a jaguar retreating from a swarm of anacondas.

"Why? You think I kill him? Why would I kill him? You just think I kill him because I come from Croatia, don't you? Well, I no murder anybody. I think I want a lawyer!" With each sentence, his voice grew sharper.

"Now, Mr., um, Karlo. There is no need for you to get into such a roil. We're not accusing you of anything. We're just gathering data. We thought it possible you were near the scene of the crime when it occurred, maybe overheard something, that sort of thing."

That seemed to calm him, but the scowl deepened.

"I didn't see anything. Or hear anything. At that time, I would have been in my flat, asleep. I go to bed at half past eleven every night. I work hard. It's too bad for him. But I know nothing about it."

C. J. sighed, looked at Karlo's feet. His shoes seemed cleaner than the rest of his attire.

"What sort of work do you perform, if I may ask?"

His chin tilted up.

"I work in a shipping warehouse in the afternoon. At night, I do some janitor work. In two department stores on Oxford Street. The nicer stores. This is my day off. I'm a good worker. Always on time."

"I'm sure you are. Do you share your flat with anyone? Is there someone who can . . . verify you were sleeping there that night?"

Karlo breathed in through his nostrils, seemed to be restraining himself.

"I don't like where this is going," he said, his teeth now clenched. "I leave now."

As he strode off in the direction he had come from, C. J. called out, "Karlo, would you know anyone who might have wanted to do Mr. Tinti any harm?"

The young man halted then pivoted sharply toward them.

"Oh, I would have loved to harm him, believe me," he yelled back. "But I say the truth when I tell you I'm not the one who got the pleasure of killing that bastard!"

21

They had one more task that day—to interview the two employees at the restaurant they had visited the day before. Lee was restless, and Bree and Warren were eager to explore whether the swatch of silk Lee had found in Hanover Square might be connected to the tailor shop where the victim had worked.

Lee turned to C. J. "So, what was your impression of . . ." He gave her a coy smile. "Mr. Mxyzptlk?"

Bree decided to answer instead. "Well, if you want to know the truth, I think he's the one who did it," she replied sharply. "One minute he's saying he was just messing with the victim's mind, then two minutes later, he's telling us he regrets he didn't have the pleasure of killing him. Cannot trust that one, no sirree, not one bit. In fact, I can't believe we just let him stroll away from us."

C. J. glanced at Lee and smiled weakly.

"Well, dear, we didn't really have any grounds for detaining him now, did we?" She slowed her pace, breathed a long sigh. She seemed deflated. Or weary. Possibly both. "However, once again, you raise a valid point, Bree." The senior architect smiled to hear her name pronounced correctly for a change. "Although I didn't get a sense our friend from Croatia was murderous, I must say he did come off as duplicitous. The good news is, I've already texted headquarters and instructed them to put a watch on him. Depending on where he lives, and how well his home is monitored by cameras, we may be able to determine if his alibi of being asleep on the night of the murder holds up or not."

"I'm putting my money on the answer being 'Not,'" Warren said.

When they entered the restaurant, Lee hung back to take a handful of the peppermints from the bowl near the front door. He decided it might be best to secure some of the wrapped candies in the event the bowl got depleted before the group was ready to leave.

Mariam was sitting in a booth near the back, chewing the nails on her right hand. The place had about eight customers, all of whom were seated near the front door. Bridget was tending to them, but she caught C. J.'s eye and indicated with a quick nod she'd join them as soon as she could.

Mariam brightened as they approached.

"I was hoping you'd come. I was afraid you might have forgotten."

They settled themselves into her booth and the one behind it. Bree, sitting across from Mariam, reached into her tote and began to work on a knitting project she had in process.

"Oh, you do knitting!" Mariam exclaimed, her smile growing. "I *love* to knit. When I can find the time, that is. My nana back in Lahore taught me. We used to have so many beautiful yarns to work with in Pakistan. But not so much anymore."

"I can just imagine," Bree said as she worked a ball of purple wool that exited her bag at the slightest tug. "Really gorgeous, I'm sure."

Mariam eyed Bree's accessories with envy. "Perhaps we could knit together sometime!" she suggested. "I just received a set of ebony needles I would love to show you."

Bree was flattered. "I am!" she replied. "Let me know how to contact you and I'll give you a call . . ." She looked over at Lee, who nodded. "If I'm able to get some time away from the investigation."

Mariam clouded a bit, placed one palm on the back of the other. "But of course," she said quietly.

"I'm sorry," C. J. said. "I don't believe I caught your last name when we were here yesterday."

"It's Talpur. It's my family name. I was married for a short time, but I went back to my family name a few years ago."

Bridget swooped by, out of breath. She set a cell phone on the table, directly in front of Mariam.

"You left it on the tray station again," she said to her co-worker. Then, turning to the rest of the group, asked, "Anyone here need anything? Coffee? A soda? Sorry, I promise I'll come sit in a jiff. Two more people just sat down in my station. I was supposed to be off by now, but we're one short today." Everyone indicated they were fine, but she seemed determined. "Aw, I remember you," she said grinning at Lee. "You're the one who's got a thing for cheese toasties. One cheese toastie coming right up." Lee raised a finger and uttered a quick guttural sound to try to stop her progress, but she was gone long before he could form a syllable.

The group turned its attention back to Mariam.

"So, Miss Talpur," C. J. began, "can you tell us how often Mr. Tinti . . . the tailor . . . frequented this place?" She leaned back against the seat, wrapped her arms around her torso.

"Oh, he would come here a lot. At least three or four times a week. Sometimes five, even. Would always sit in the same booth, if it was open. That one, up there." She pointed toward the booth at the front of the restaurant that was in line with theirs. Lee found it interesting that anyone sitting on the side of the booth that backed up to the front of the restaurant would be out of the sight of anyone walking in through the front door.

"Did he ever speak of being afraid? Of there being someone who wanted to hurt him?"

Mariam thought about that, slowly began to nod. "Maybe, yes. Often, he would come in here just after he played that game with the little bowling balls. What is it?"

"Bocce?" Anisa offered.

"Yes. That's it. It is Italian, I think? Anyway, there was someone he played that game with who treated him very badly. He talked about it a lot." The team members exchanged looks.

"Did you ever get the sense Mr. Tinti was . . . fearful of this person?"

The server thought about that for a few seconds, slowly began to nod again.

"Yes. I think maybe so," she replied, as if she were in a trance. "He never really talked a lot when he was here. He told me he was diabetic, so he always ordered eggs and toast, or maybe a cutlet with tomatoes on the side if he thought he needed to lose some weight." She broke her trance to look directly at them and laughed. "He never really needed to lose any weight," she added. "For a forty-eight-year-old man, he was still in excellent shape."

But her smile vanished, and soon she was staring off into space again. "However, I notice recently he would jump a little bit, and look over at the door whenever someone come in. Anyone. And a couple of times, he would put money on the table and leave before he had finished eating. Without telling us."

Anisa leaned forward. "Did you ever ask him *why* he did that?"

Again, Mariam nodded methodically.

"Yes. One time, I caught up to him as he was heading out the door and asked him if something was wrong with his food. He said, 'No. There is never anything wrong with the food, Mariam. But since my son died, everything's gone wrong with my life. I'm afraid I will have no one. I'm afraid for my life.'

"Then he turned and tore off down the street. Like somebody was chasing him."

Anisa was about to ask Mariam why Tinti might have feared for his life when Bridget came crashing into the conversation again. This time, she plopped herself down next to C. J.

"I am *so* sorry, it's been absolutely mad here today. But Juliet's finally arrived, so I can take a few to chat." They scooted down the booth to accommodate her.

C. J. smiled at the young woman. "Thank you for taking time to speak with us Miss . . .?"

"Griffiths," the waitress responded. "With an 's' at the end."

"I see. Griffiths. We do so appreciate your speaking with us, Miss Griffiths. Let's begin, shall we, with how often you waited on Mr. Tinti."

She blew out some air. "Not very often, really. Mariam was usually the one to take care of him. I'd wait on him once a week. Maybe twice."

"And did he talk to you much about what was going on in his life?"

She smiled wistfully. "Not a lot. I mean, he was definitely a funny bloke. Not 'ha-ha' funny, but quirky funny. In an endearing sort of way, you know? I think we bonded some because I ran track in university and he told me he'd qualified for the Olympic track team something like, thirty years ago? We both like action-adventure movies. I grew up in Southport, and he said he spent a summer there back in the day. Then he was nice enough that time to lend me some money when me mum got behind on her taxes, so . . ." She halted, looked at the tabletop for a second. "I know what you're probably thinking. It wasn't like *that* at all. We never went anywhere together or anything like that. We weren't a couple. He was just this lonely guy who turned into a friend of sorts. That's all. We did have buckets of laughs when I first started to wait on him. But that stopped when his son died." There was a ding.

"Ah, there's your toastie," she said, winking at Lee. "Back in a sec."

"Really, miss, you don't ha . . ." But Lee gave up, for she was already out of sight.

They turned back to Mariam, who was chewing her nails again. She stopped when she noticed everyone staring at her.

"Are there any other details you can think of, Mariam, that might lead us to whoever murdered Mr. Tinti?" Bree asked. "Did he ever tell you he thought someone was following him? Did he ever mention receiving a threatening phone call, or email?" She glanced at Lee, who nodded his consent at her inserting herself into the interview. After all, he had instructed her and Warren to come up with questions they might ask the servers.

The waitress shook her head, but Lee thought he detected a glint of insight deep within her eyes.

The sandwich arrived. To the casual observer, it looked perfectly fine. But Warren knew they were in trouble after Lee's first bite. The architect's nose went one direction while his lower lip went the other. His breathing grew shallower, and Warren was pretty sure Lee's right leg was bouncing as if it were trying to prime a pump of some sort.

"Excuse me," Lee barked, tossing his napkin to one side and scooting off one end of the booth. Within seconds, he was marching toward the doors to the kitchen.

"Uh-oh," Bree said.

When Lee found the cook, he offered the dark-haired man a forced smile.

"Hello. Would you mind my giving you a little instruction on how to craft a grilled cheese sandwich one can actually . . . swallow?"

"Sorry?" the cook replied.

The architect waved off the answer with his right hand as his eyes darted around the small, cluttered kitchen.

"First, the white bread you're using is fine," Lee announced as he dragged two thick slices from a package sitting on the counter. He tossed the slices into a nearby pan. "However, you should only brown each slice for about two minutes. You're browning them way too long."

The cook leaned in and looked over Lee's shoulder. "Only two minutes?"

"Yes, if that," the architect replied. "And you need to use more butter. *Unsalted* butter. And for heaven's sakes, *American cheese*. Not cheddar and *definitely not* the provolone you're using."

Lee nudged the bread slices around the inside of the pan with a spatula as the cook nodded and watched intently.

Five minutes later, Lee returned to the booth carrying a plate that bore a new sandwich accented by two sweet pickle rounds. The cook was next to him, one arm draped over the architect's shoulders. Warren noticed that a small pat of butter clung to the architect's tie.

"This guy really knows his stuff!" the cook bellowed, an index finger pointed at Lee. "I can't believe all the things he taught me in just five minutes!"

It took a while for Lee to get seated and for the cook to recount the many nuances associated with making a cheese toastie that Lee had imparted to him, and for C. J. to regain control of the investigation.

Which she eventually did.

"If there's *anything* else you can think of, Mariam, please contact me here." She handed the waitress a business card, which she quickly secured in the purse beside her.

"Like Bridget said, when Tony started coming here, he'd talk some. He'd go on about his work at the tailor shop and disco dancing," she said. "But he became a different person after they killed his son."

Lee had been mid-bite when Mariam spoke the line that would

alter the trajectory of their investigation. He stopped chewing, set the sandwich onto the plate, and looked over at C. J.

"I'm sorry," the commander said quickly. "You said, 'when they killed his son.' You must have meant, 'when his son died.' It was our understanding that his fatality came about as the result of an automobile accident."

Mariam smirked a little then gave C. J. a penetrating look.

"Yes, I know that's what the official report said," she replied. "But Mr. Tinti told me just a couple of weeks ago he suspected his son's death was *anything but* an accident."

22

Lara posed before the mirror, head tilted up, her left hand gently stroking the necklace that had arrived that afternoon. The talisman that dangled from it seemed a little smaller, and a little lighter, than Delfina Delgado's website had described it.

But its glimmer captivated her. For reasons she could not pinpoint, it truly seemed to have given her a greater sense of confidence. Or perhaps it had just evaporated most of her concerns.

In either case, she somehow felt calmer and more assertive.

She searched for the small card that had accompanied the necklace. Its instructions were typeset in a blunt, modern font, but it seemed to her that the psychic had signed the message personally. *Then again, given what they can do with technology these days . . .* she reminded herself.

The instructions were on her desk, under the box the necklace had arrived in. Carefully, she unfolded the card and read:

This necklace includes the talisman, crafted by
Acoma Indians in the American state
of New Mexico, that you saw me discuss
on my video. I hope it brings you the serenity

**and clarity mine has given me. As soon as you
put it on, close your eyes, place your right palm
on the talisman and focus on the first image
that comes to mind. Attach a wish to that
visual image. If you wish passionately enough,
within 24 hours, your wish will come true.**

The message continued:

**As a result of your US $300 purchase, Larra,
you have received a complimentary membership
in Ms. Delgado's Inner Circle. This entitles you
to receive our special newsletter, as well as
discounts on other items that can remove any static
that is hindering your clairvoyance and boost
your ability to generate tranquility. Once your purchases
reach the US $1,500 level, you will qualify for
an exclusive reading by Ms. Delgado herself.
You can also secure such a reading by sending
the full amount to us by way of credit card or PayBuddy.**

It didn't really bother Lara that the psychic had misspelled her name. *How often did I see my name spelled that way while I was growing up,* she asked herself as she turned back toward the mirror. *Besides, I may have made a mistake. I probably entered it that way into the order form and didn't catch it.*

She looked at the card again, dreamed of what it might be like to receive a personalized reading from Delfina Delgado. *Who knows,* she told herself, *maybe she would impart some information that would help us solve the case.*

Instantly, she chided herself for believing such folly. Then her mind drifted back to the other items she had perused on the website, items that might bring her purchase total to fifteen hundred dollars. There was that lovely, silver table clock that she had admired. *What was its price? Five hundred dollars?* There were earrings and a brooch and scarves she had liked, but those were all smaller-ticket items that, together, wouldn't get her to the magic number she needed for a personal reading.

Oh, I'm being ridiculous, she thought. *I should just send her the full amount in one payment. I can afford it.*

She examined herself in the mirror again. The necklace looked resplendent against the black cotton sweater she had on. *Time to put it to the test,* she told herself. She placed her right palm atop the silver charm and allowed both eyes to close gently. Took a breath . . . and waited.

What first came into her mind's eye was an image of her motherland. A tranquil meadow filled with lilies of the valley. And a small grove of silver birches beyond. She sighed. *Well, I was hoping for the identity of whoever murdered Antonio Tinti,* she thought. *I guess I'll have to run with this, however.*

She squeezed her eyes tighter, found herself suppressing an urge to cry.

"I wish to connect with my *kotimaa* again," she whispered. "Let me once more connect with my beloved Finland."

***

Liam was pacing his room and his heart was galloping. He had never experienced anything like this before in all his years of probing the dark web.

Shit! These mongrels really mean business.

He stomped toward the small dresser on his left, balled up one fist, and hurled it toward a stack of jeans that had just exited the dryer. Three pairs tumbled onto the floor; those remaining looked like they had been sideswiped by a tornado. He placed both palms over his nose and mouth and took several slow breaths. Waited for his heartbeat to return to something close to normal. Strode back over to his laptop on the desk.

The message was still there:

How do you make an Aussie boy cry?
Grind his tennis-pro sister into pebbles of sand
and then sell them to the people
who maintain the courts at Wimbledon.

Better stop monitoring our conversations, you drongo, or you'll be weeping something more than just crocodile tears, mate.

Below the message was a symbol of sorts, a crude skeleton face engulfed in flames.

He kicked at the laptop but only grazed one side of it.

How? he asked himself. *How did they find out it was me? How is it they always seem to find out, always seem to elude detection?*

He urged himself to calm down and reminded himself of the many times The Organization had faltered and let their guard down.

Had been completely foiled.

And yet . . .

He repositioned the computer, sat down in front of it, and closed the browser. A surfing magazine nearby caught his eye. He flipped through the pages and spotted a board he liked a lot. Royal blue, with yellow racing stripes from nose to tail. He knew he couldn't afford it, sniffed once, then tossed the magazine onto a nearby chair.

He had to admit that the mention of his sister had been a sucker punch to his rib cage.

His mind drifted back to a neighborhood tennis court near their home in Queensland. Caryn was in her tennis whites. (*No way she'd be caught in those silly pastel or neon outfits worn now by some of the players,* he recalled, chuckling.) She was bending over him, readjusting his grip on the racket so his backhand would have more force. She was probably nineteen, maybe twenty. He was ten. Her dark blonde hair was pulled back and held perfectly in place by a white visor that cast a shadow on her face but did nothing to diminish her impeccably white smile. Tiny silver orbs for earrings. Soft pink lipstick. The hint of a floral bouquet, wafting from her hair.

Her look at him was earnest. The dutiful instructor. But suddenly their eyes met, and he was taken to some sophisticated space of knowing, to some intersection of bonding and familiarity that made him feel more mature, and more connected, than ever before.

"You'll get this, Liam, you will," she said, smiling. "Right now, you're young and sort of slim, so I'm okay with you using a two-handed grip for your backhand. For now."

He nodded. "Yeah, me too," he replied.

She comprehended him. He comprehended her.

"But pretty soon, when you start to get some muscle, I want you to wean yourself from the two-handed grip and move to a one-handed grip, okay?"

He nodded again. "Okay."

"You'll know when you're ready to make the switch," she said. "You'll feel it in your . . . soul." That surprised him some. "Soul" wasn't the sort of word Caryn used much.

He smiled at her. She knew. And he knew.

"Now, I'm going to have to depend on you to make that shift on your own," she continued. "You've got to realize, I won't always be around to look out for you when it comes to things like this."

The fury surged in him once again. But he used the breathing techniques he'd learned from a yogi he'd met in Thailand a few years back to quell the rage, return himself to calm.

He reclined in the chair and studied the ceiling for several seconds. He thought about checking in with Lara but decided he needed to keep working. On something. Anything. Because the last thing he wanted was for Dalton to think he was some sort of bludger.

He reopened the Thor browser on his computer and logged back into the dark web. But this time, he signed on to a network that would shield his computer's IP address and into an account he hadn't used in over a year. He decided he'd search for the names of some of the people that Dalton, C. J., and the others had recently interviewed.

Just to see what might come up.

It didn't take much rummaging in his knapsack to find the piece of paper with a list of names Lara had given to him earlier in the day. *God, her penmanship is awesome,* he thought as he scanned the list.

He chose to search for the women first. *Maybe I'll get lucky and find out one of them runs an international prostitution ring,* he told himself. Although he knew it was unlikely anyone on the list, much less the women, would use their real names for a questionable transaction on the dark web.

But you never know, he thought.

He typed "Betty Naughton," the name of the victim's ex-girlfriend. *As far as I'm concerned,* he told himself, *when it comes to murder suspects, ex-girlfriends move to the front of the line.* He hit "Search," but quickly got a message: "No Results." So, he went back to the list. The next name was that of the young assistant in the ex-girlfriend's clothing shop. "Corinne . . . Haim? Helm?" He peered closer, decided it was Holm. Typed it. Again, nothing.

Pretty quickly, he determined that the females on the list were either upstanding girls or experts at disguising their depravity online. *Probably the latter,* he thought, scratching his head. He turned his attention to the names of the men. *Well, from what they've told me, that tailor the victim worked with is a total wuss,* he thought. *Little use checking on him.* He ran an index finger down the list, stopped at "Omar Fakhoury."

Now, he sounds questionable, he told himself.

He tapped the name into the search field . . . incorrectly. Tried again . . . got it wrong again. *F-A-K-H, damn, those people spell their names weird,* he said to himself as he punched the keyboard.

Sat back in his chair when a few results came up.

Slowly, he scrolled through them all. There were a couple of posts Fakhoury had made on a message board devoted to the sale of bitcoins—but he was advocating against them as investments. He also had a couple of message board comments criticizing the current regime running Lebanon. But they seemed more reasonable than radical. Fakhoury did seem to have corresponded with an arms dealer at some point, but as best as Liam could tell, the inquiry was more about the history of the guns than how to purchase or import them.

He flipped through several more random comments on myriad bulletin boards and websites but stopped when he hit a search result showing more than twenty messages between Fakhoury and someone with the handle Taylor54W39. He opened the first message, the content of which made him shift forward in his chair:

Ready to receive the shipment.
Eager to distribute over the next several weeks.

He rapidly clicked on the other messages in the string. All referenced either "acquiring the items for release," or "needing to find less overt ways to ship the items," or "excited to have found a new supplier eager to work with us so long as they can do so discreetly." One message in particular, however, galvanized Liam's attention:

**We must be certain the upcoming transfer
does not raise the suspicion of customs officials.
Time is of the essence.**

He had no way of figuring out what it was they planned to transfer, but maybe he could identify the person who was planning to receive the items, whatever they were. He swept Taylor54W39 into the browser's search engine, prompted it to look for that moniker elsewhere on the dark web. But the search tool returned only the stream of correspondence he had just reviewed. *Nothing else out there?* he thought. *On the entire dark web? That's bizarre.*

So, he opened a regular browser to search the clearnet. Typed in the same string of characters and numerals, hit "Search." Several results appeared, but Liam frowned since most of them seemed bogus replies unconnected to the individual he was searching for.

Then one result in the middle of the list jumped out at him. It linked to a comment someone had made on a local blog post in support of England exiting the European Union. He tapped on the link and quickly scanned the blog for the comment.

And there it was. Taylor54W39.

And at the end of the comment, a name. Liam squinted at it, looked over at the list of names nearby.

There was a match, but he wanted to be certain of it. On a hunch, he did a quick background check of the person in question.

He was right. The individual had incorporated (as many people do) a lot of personal information into their handle. And the more he studied that handle, the more the identity seemed lock-solid:

54, the person's birth year. W39, the most common size of a man's waist. Taylor, a homonym of the person's profession.

I guess the old bloke isn't quite the wuss I thought he was, Liam said as he turned to the list and drew a large red circle around the name of the victim's former co-worker, Malcolm Hensleigh.

***

It was to be a working dinner. Fortunately, Margarida had prepared a sumptuous beef bourguignon as a reward for their hard work.

"If any of you are now this vegan thing I hear about," she said, "I'm afraid you're out of luck." Even if someone at the table had been vegan (and Lee had been known to experiment now and then with the dietary regimen) the bouquet wafting from the kitchen would have converted them in an instant.

"I know you haven't had much time to do so," Lee said to Warren, "but have you and Bree had any luck identifying the source of that silk I found in Hanover Square?"

"As a matter of fact, we have," Bree replied as she put her knitting aside. The room fell quiet in anticipation. She nodded at Warren to provide the details.

"Not only is that particular grade of silk one that's used in the tailor shop where Antonio Tinti worked," he said, "it's from the shirt he was wearing the night he was killed." Warren stopped to gauge the reaction of everyone around the table.

"But . . . wasn't it, like, snared in a tree branch?" Roberto asked.

Bree nodded. "Pretty strange, huh? Apparently, it came from the side of one of Mr. Tinti's cuffs. Because it was small, and he fell backward into the shrubbery after he was shot, they didn't notice it when they moved his body. Or if they did, they didn't record it. Probably assumed it had torn loose during his fall and was among all the leaves, or in the shrubs somewhere."

"Excuse me," Margarida suddenly bellowed, reaching over Lee's shoulder to set a bowl of beef, and broth, and onions in front of him. "I hope everyone notice that I fill your bowls in the kitchen and bring them to you rather than put everything in the center of the table and make you do it yourselves." They murmured their appreciation in unison and began to position their napkins to minimize any splatter.

"How would part of Mr. Tinti's cuff end up in a tree clear across the park from where his body was found?" Lara asked as Margarida was setting the bowl in front of Lee. Lara smiled and nodded once at Margarida as the cook made her way back for another bowl. "I mean, it makes me wonder if Bree might have been right in the first place. That perhaps his body was moved to the bushes after he was killed elsewhere."

Once all the other dishes had arrived, everyone picked up their cutlery to dive into the feast.

"Well, I'm not convinced of *that*," Lee said between chews. "But it is puzzling, isn't it?"

"You know, the body could have been planted there, to throw us off," Roberto offered. Lee was pleasantly surprised to see his designer focused more on the details of the case than the apps on his phone.

"Maybe," Lee answered, cutting into a carrot. "But it's hard for me to see the assailant taking the time to do that. Their attacks tend to be tactical, not theatrical." He turned to his second-in-command.

"Did you find out anything interesting about our victim?"

Lara took a deep swallow, patted her lips with her napkin, and ducked her head.

"Not a great deal, I'm sorry to say. Mr. Tinti was not much of one for taking selfies or posting cute kitty-cat videos." She reached for the glass of burgundy that Margarida had poured for her and took a sip. "There is his online dating profile, but he hadn't updated it for almost a year. And that only provided basic data about him. Nothing new or particularly insightful there, I'm afraid. And neither London Underground, London Buses, nor the more popular shared-ride services, have been much help either. They're terribly short-staffed right now, or so they say. And without a detailed description of who we're looking for, they're reluctant to release any of their surveillance feeds. Passenger privacy and all that."

Lee nodded, tapped the tabletop impatiently. Lara went back to her meal.

"I have something," Liam said quietly.

"Let us guess," Roberto said with a wink. "The victim was actually one of the biggest purveyors of assault rifles on the dark web."

"No, I haven't made *that* connection yet," the Australian said matter-of-factly. He went on to share his discovery of the string of communiqués between Omar Fakhoury and Malcolm Hensleigh.

"Wow," Bree mumbled through a mouth full of vegetables.

"That *is* powerful stuff, Liam. Great work," Lee added. "I'll alert C. J. to that as soon as we're finished here. Still, did I understand you to say the correspondence isn't clear as to what it was Mr. Fakhoury planned to ship to Mr. Hensleigh? And, that we don't have any evidence that their messages are connected somehow with the messages you saw about luggage coming into Heathrow?"

Liam nodded. "That's right, Dalton. But, if I can somehow connect both sets of messages to either Fakhoury or the tailor, or to the same account at least, that would be . . ."

"Incriminating," Roberto interjected.

Lara turned to her co-worker.

"I'm happy to help you with that, Liam. I'm not sure there is much more background research I can do on Mr. Tinti, at this point."

"I'd welcome that," he replied.

Lee turned to the firm's chief designer. "And you, Roberto?" he said, raising his eyebrows. The Puerto Rican glanced at his phone, then back at his superior.

"I've been a little preoccupied, Dalton, sorry," he answered. "But I have all of tomorrow set aside to scoping out the square again. Promise."

The architect nodded. "I understand," he said softly.

At the opposite end of the table, Lara elevated her spoon and took a long, final sip of the broth at the bottom of her bowl. Her eyes were closed so she could savor the tantalizing mix of flavors Margarida had created as part of their entrée.

When she opened them . . . her right hand went weak and the spoon it was holding tumbled into the bowl.

"Lara! Are you all right?!" Bree barked, putting one hand on the woman's back.

But Lara couldn't respond. Her gaze was transfixed on the pattern etched in the bottom of the bowl, a pattern that, throughout the meal, had been completely hidden by the beef, the broth, the vegetables, and her spoon.

A pattern consisting of a tranquil meadow filled with lilies of the valley.

And a small grove of silver birches beyond.

23

"What in the hell is *wrong* with you? What part of 'do nothing whatsoever to call attention to yourself' *do you not seem to grasp?*"

The slap landed slightly askew, hitting the person's cheek with the bluntness of a baton.

"I . . . I didn't *call attention . . .*"

This time, it was the back of the hand, smacking the opposite cheek cleanly, violently. The victim tried to scoot the chair a couple of inches to one side, but the floor was too slick to allow his shoes any traction.

"Let me make this one point very, very clear," the attacker sneered as he plopped a Malteser into his mouth. He used his tongue to nudge it around the inside of his mouth before swallowing it almost whole. "You are *not* going to bollix this Transformation the way some of our less-talented associates have bollixed others. Did I not stress to you during our little trip on the Underground that we expected you to keep as low a profile as possible? That you were to go about your business until we were ready to cut you loose? Yes, you completed your assignment, and for that we are very appreciative. But to be viewed as a successful patriot in *our* book, you have to possess more than just a steady aim. We also expect you to have an abundance of guile. An impeccable sense of timing. The ability to suddenly exhibit the qualities of a chameleon and creep along the wallpaper completely undetected.

"Do you *understand?*"

The person in the chair nodded, slightly at first, then more vigorously when the assaulter raised his left hand as if to strike again.

"This Mr. Lee is no idiot," he hissed. "An idiot *savant*, perhaps, but a *savant*, nonetheless. One miscue, one errant word from you, and trust me, he will put two and three together and somehow suss out precisely why the number seven is so important to us. Am I making myself quite clear to you *now?*"

Another slap. This one was softer, but it landed directly at the center of a previous blow. His prey let out a muffled yelp, struggled once again to push the chair away from the barrage.

The assailant dipped a hand into the candy sack, extracted another Malteser, and sucked on it in silence as he studied his sitting target for two or three minutes. Just beyond the open transom windows, the wail of an ambulance reached a crescendo in the night, then waned. There were voices on the pavement below, urgent. Soon enough, they diminished as well.

Finally, with great deliberation, he began to nod his head, crouched in close.

"You know, you're probably not aware we have had quite a bit of success dealing with rogue agents. In Madagascar, for example. One of our comrades there made complete hash of what had been, up to that point, the perfect execution of the perfect plot." He stared off into a far corner of the warehouse and scowled as if he had spotted a rat. "Do you have even the slightest idea what happened to that agent after we caught up with him?"

The response was a rapid head shake 'no.'

The batterer sneered again as he stood back and pulled himself tall. He combed the fingers of one hand through his hair then staggered back a few paces, almost stumbling in the process. He righted himself, then trudged over to a long table made of petrified wood, the only item in the entire vast space (save for a few extension cords that resembled sleeping snakes on a smooth riverbed). Scattered across the table were a variety of beakers and canisters—some amber, some green, others brown—many of which appeared to have words or phrases scribbled on their surfaces with a black felt marker. He selected one, picked it up, squinted at the wording, then set it down. Picked up another—a rectangular, copper-colored tin that resembled a petrol can. "Ah, there you are," he said with a low cackle. He seemed almost drunk now, what with the swagger and slurring he displayed as he returned to his captive.

He bent low again, blinked rapidly several times, then reared back and began to uncap the can.

"Well, here's what I was told," he said, peering at the cap he was manipulating. "They claim the mist alone seared the lungs of that agent fairly quickly, causing severe respiratory distress within five minutes." The cap came free. He flicked it to the concrete floor and watched it roll off into the darkness before he moved closer to the chair. An intense, vinegar-like aroma floated from the can.

"But it was the *solution,* of course, that caused the truly horrific damage, corroding the intestines the way flesh-eating bacteria devour skin."

The captive gripped the chair and shut both eyes tight as the speaker tipped the can enough to allow a trickle of fluid to cascade onto the knuckles of his hostage's taut right hand. Savoring his complete control, the dominator glared from above, heavy lidded. A small smirk formed slowly on his lips.

"But that's what you should expect to happen, isn't it?" he added, "when you're plunged into a vat of muriatic acid."

24

The next day was cool, overcast.

Lara's reaction at dinner the night before had piqued Lee's curiosity. She had told them she was perfectly fine, that she had suddenly recalled something important she needed to do.

He wasn't entirely convinced, however.

His phone buzzed just after breakfast, and even he was surprised at just how knee-jerk his reaction was to the sound. The clandestine meetings he was called to now and again had him on edge. He knew he was obliged to attend them. There was even a time when he had looked forward to them. But no more.

The message was not from his confidant, however. It was from C. J.

I think we should take a stroll this morning . . . discuss things.

He agreed. All the loose strings and duplicitous characters had his head woozy. And, he wasn't sure any of them were responsible for the murder of Antonio Tinti.

But he had a feeling one of them probably was.

He decided to skip that morning's copy of the *Times*. The relentless headlines about the wars and famines across the globe were beginning to depress him. Even more depressing were the advertisements encouraging people to preorder items "to ensure delivery in time for

Christmas."

For God's sakes, it's not even October, he thought.

The architect took a final sip of coffee and headed for the shower.

***

C. J. told him she wanted to stroll through Mayfair, to soak up the neighborhood Antonio Tinti had worked in . . . and died in.

"I know the district can be pretentious beyond repair," she told him. "But it just has this *je ne sais quoi* that for some reason is calling me today. Humor me, Dalton. Maybe something in the neighborhood will give us a spark of insight into the murder."

The forecast called for light showers, so both had umbrellas when they met up in front of Burlington House, home of the Royal Academy of the Arts. Hers was teal, his smoke gray with a very small Buffalo Trace bourbon label imprinted on opposite sides.

"It was a promotional item they sent along with the case I ordered," he confessed.

Lee let C. J. know he did not necessarily share her disdain for the area. To him, it was the more affluent parts of many mid-size North American cities that were doing the "pretending," communities filled with homes that evoked pretend castles and streets named for European cities and regions no one within five miles of those streets had visited in their lifetimes. Mayfair, in contrast, was the real thing. Superaffluent to be sure, but he found the neighborhood aristocratic, not affected. Subdued, not showy.

"Take this place," he said, pointing up at Burlington House. "An exquisite example of Palladian architecture, really. Originally, there was a rather fuddy-duddy home on the site that was built around 1665, I think. But fifty years later, when Lord Burlington asked the architect he had hired to give the house a Palladian flair, that became one of the most important moments in the history of English architecture."

"Really?" C. J. said, sniffing. "It still looks rather fusty to me."

Lee chuckled. "Well, *you* may not like it, C. J., but this was the first and most important of all those buildings across the United Kingdom with pediments, porticos, and the proportions like those found in classical Greek and Roman temples. Even Monticello, Thomas Jefferson's plantation in Virginia, owes a debt of gratitude to this building."

C. J. registered that she was, perhaps, a few degrees more impressed with the building than she had been a few minutes earlier.

"See those Venetian windows in the end bays?" Lee asked, pointing toward the main block of the structure. "Those were the first Venetian windows to appear in England. And can you believe that the British government almost demolished this gorgeous and historic structure so it could build a modern campus for the University of London? Fortunately, enough people were so outraged by the plan, it was scrapped. That's when the Royal Academy moved in and a new architect, Sidney Smirke, added that third story to the main block."

They sauntered on along the north side of Piccadilly and soon approached the Green Park Tube station. The Ritz Hotel was on their left, and that reminded Lee he really should bring the team there in the days ahead for one of its legendary tea services. A light mist began to descend, but neither Lee nor C. J. thought it intense enough to require the protection of their umbrellas.

C. J. sniffed once and cleared her throat.

"I'm curious . . . what's your sense of things, Dalton?" She was squinting at the pavement as they strolled, like a kindergartner inspecting a new pair of saddle oxfords.

"By things, I assume you mean the murder?"

Her reaction was more of a wince than a smile.

"Sorry, yes. I get so consumed in these goings-on, I forget you have other things to occupy your time. Your architecture practice. Your team. The gash on your motorcycle."

"It isn't a *gash*, C. J. It's just a scratch. It will buff out, I'm sure. And it's a motor *scooter*, not a motorcycle. A *vintage* motor scooter at that. It took me *forever* to find it, and then another forever to summon up the courage to buy it."

She smiled weakly at him as they continued down Piccadilly. After several steps, Lee stopped abruptly.

"I'm sorry, C. J., I never did answer your question, did I?" he said. "But I'm afraid I'm going to answer your question with another question. What is *your* sense of things? What's *your* take on the cast of characters we've interviewed so far? I have my theories. But you know this place, and these people, far better than I do."

They resumed their walk. She clamped her umbrella between her armpit and breast, swung both arms out in front of her, and interlocked the fingers of one hand into the fingers of the other.

"Well, we know the murderer is lurking somewhere nearby," she replied, "because we know The Organization always worries that if they extract them too soon after the murder, it will redirect our attention onto that individual. That said, no one we've met thus far has really impressed me as someone possessing the *chutzpah* to shoot someone at point-blank range. Even that young firebrand we met at the bocce court—what's his name?"

"Karlo," Lee answered.

"Yes, Karlo. He strikes me as being a lot like most of the Chihuahuas I have come across. All yip, but not much nip, if you know what I mean."

Lee suppressed an urge to burst out laughing.

"So," she continued, "I can't say I am thoroughly convinced we've actually met the murderer face-to-face. *Yet*, that is."

Lee nodded as they walked, tilted his head again.

"What do you make of the communications we found between Omar Fakhoury and Malcolm Hensleigh?"

She exhaled. "Yes, well, that *is* one of the more intriguing angles of our investigation, isn't it?" she replied. "That and Mr. Tinti's contention that his son's death may not have been the accident it appeared to be."

"I was hoping you would mention that," Lee countered. "That's an avenue we probably need to explore as quickly as possible, wouldn't you say?"

"I . . . would," C. J. replied slowly, drawing the two words out in such a way that Lee wasn't entirely sure that she did. She then let out a heavier sigh of exasperation, which caused him to squeeze his brow. "Sorry, Dalton," she said in response to his concern. "I guess I am just at a point where the last thing I need right now is yet another avenue to pursue. An avenue that could turn out to be only one more cul-de-sac."

Lee decided to steer them away from the clamor of Piccadilly and into the heart of Mayfair. They made a right turn at Bolton Street and another quick right at Curzon, which had them soon sauntering alongside Berkeley Square Gardens.

"Maybe the soul of Tinti's son is in there," he said, pointing toward the skinny, four-story townhouse with the number "50" cleanly displayed above its front door. "Shall I knock and see if he has any information he'd be willing to share with us?"

C. J. grinned broadly, put both palms to her face. Although the four-story townhouse now contained a book and antiquities seller, it was legendary as one of London's most haunted structures. One version of the tale insisted that the attic bore the ghost of a young woman who committed suicide by hurling herself out a top-floor window. Other versions identified the specter as belonging to either a small girl killed there by a punitive servant, or an older recluse who'd been rejected by his fiancée.

"Oh, Dalton, you know one cannot be a serious investigator and believe in such nonsense," C. J. said as they moved on.

"True," Lee confessed. "But it's an important reminder to us, isn't it, that people often weave detailed stories about what they've seen and heard that have no basis in fact and actually reveal just how easily swayed those people really are."

The commander nodded along with him, looking deep into his eyes to determine just who among the many people they had spoken to over the past few days he might be referring to.

"I'm beginning to wonder if Tinti's son was more involved in his father's murder than we thought," he continued. "Not directly, of course, but . . . indirectly. Are we sure there was no calling card from The Organization on the son's body?"

C. J. shook her head. "I saw nothing in the files about a page from *Wayward Colony* being found on his body. But then again, our team isn't likely to win a Nobel Prize for meticulousness. I'll have some of my associates do some more digging into that. It's quite possible they overlooked it."

Lee looked straight ahead and wondered if it was by coincidence or divine providence that they were approaching Grosvenor Chapel, one of the city's more charming places of worship. "Do you think our Good

Father is telling us he'd like us to turn our minds away from murder and vengeful spirits?" he asked, leaning in toward C. J. She flushed some.

"Oh, that has always been one of my favorite chapels here," she replied. "If you've never been inside, you should make the effort someday. You absolutely must feast your eyes on the vault above. The composition of the Holy Ghost descending into glory in the form of a dove is truly breathtaking."

Lee nodded. "I'm sure. Wasn't this the chapel that became a harbor of comfort for so many American troops during World War II?"

"It was. In fact, it's the ongoing popularity of the chapel among Americans that has sustained it to this day." She halted and looked over at him. "Sort of like our relationship, I'd say."

Lee smiled, then noticed the commander's energy appeared to be flagging.

"Do you need to sit, C. J.? Do you want to rest for a few minutes?" he asked.

She waved him off. "No, it's just my knee. I'm beginning to get the twinges, I'm afraid. However, the doctor says surgery is probably another couple of years off, at least. So not to worry. Nothing I can't soldier through."

That made him decide to steer them toward the hotels along Park Lane. If C. J. was underestimating her discomfort, the hotels could be a convenient place for them to dash into if they needed a quick respite. *And any one of them could supply us with an excellent spot of tea . . . or bottle of champagne,* he thought.

The first hotel they encountered was 45 Park Lane, London's contemporary nod to the Art Deco hotels in Miami Beach. Somehow, the hotel's architects had managed to take a 1960s-era office building and give it all the verve and curves of a place one might expect to spot Cary Grant or Merle Oberon. He loved how the profile of the building approached the intersection like a steamship churning its way down the Mississippi River. However, he wasn't all that keen on buildings from one decade pretending to be from another, and the fact the hotel had once housed a club in which the waitresses scampered around in bunny suits only soured the renovation for him that much more.

He *was* in love, however, with the next hotel just one block up. The Dorchester, which opened in 1931, was genuine Deco and true to the era in its period furnishings and ambience. He knew the hotel had hosted luminaries as diverse as writers Somerset Maugham and Ernest Hemingway, entertainer Danny Kaye, jazz singer Alberta Hunter, General Dwight D. Eisenhower, and director Alfred Hitchcock. That said, he also knew the British viewed its exterior as very American and quite unremarkable.

He had to acknowledge that architect William Curtis Green's expansive use of reinforced concrete had given the hotel a bunker-like personality. But it was that fortitude that gave the hotel the reputation it earned during World War II as one of the safest and quietest buildings to take shelter in during the Blitz. Meanwhile, he found the hotel's interiors to be quite sumptuous, especially the Oliver Messel Suite, named after the designer who in the 1950s remarkably transformed the space to look exactly like a Georgian country home.

C. J., however, looked at the hotel as if it were caked in mud and exuding a horrific stench.

"If you ask my opinion, it's *very* Elizabeth Taylor," she uttered in a tone that made it clear the actress was NOT one of C. J.'s favorite celebrities.

"Well, she was born here, you know, and that *Welsh* companion of hers, Richard Burton, did stay in The Dorchester quite often back in the sixties," Lee offered.

The commander was not impressed. "Still a hussy, as far as I'm concerned," she replied, a dour look on her face. He studied his colleague as they meandered up Park Lane. Her comment had made him wonder whether she might have been a spurned bride at some point. Finally, he summoned up his courage to ask.

"Excuse me, C. J., it's really none of my business, but . . . is there . . . anyone special . . . in your life?"

He knew he was being cheeky, asking someone so British something so very personal. But the commander looked at him not with disdain, but with glee, and slapped him mightily on the arm closest to her.

"Oh, Dalton. How charmingly silly of you. There is no need for you to fret about my romantic life. I am doing *very well* in that department,

I can assure you of *that!*"

He arched his eyebrows, waited for more. Instead, she turned away, picked up her pace, and began to admire the buildings they were strolling past.

They were now going back in time, architecturally. Looming ahead was another of Lee's favorite structures, the Grosvenor House Hotel, built in the 1920s on the grounds of the former residence of the Dukes of Westminster. It was the first hotel in London to offer guests a separate bathroom and entrance lobby for each bedroom, as well as running iced water in every bathroom. When it first opened, it also served as the headquarters of the International Sportsmen's Club, so its facilities included Turkish baths, a swimming pool, squash courts, and a gymnasium.

"Did you know the Great Room in there was built as an ice rink?" he asked his colleague. He hoped that by shifting their conversation to the world of architectural trivia, he might move them on from the *faux pas* he'd committed by asking about her personal life.

"I must say I did not," she answered with what Lee thought to be legitimate interest.

"It *was*," he said, deciding to run with the thread. "It used to host skating demonstrations by Sonja Henie and Cecilia Colledge. And Queen Elizabeth took her skating lessons there as a child. In 1935, they turned the space into the banquet hall it is now, but most of the rink's machinery still exists beneath the ballroom floor."

"I had no idea," the commander replied.

The hotel's aura of class and decorum was quickly dented, however, when they happened upon a chorus of angry voices just beyond the front door. Lee could see that several of the protesters carried placards, but he couldn't quite make them out.

"What's their beef?" he asked C. J.

"My guess would be the G7 summit," she said. "As a security measure, we've floated publicly that this is where the meeting is taking place when in fact, it's taking place at The Connaught." She tried with little success to discern the comments on the crowd's signs and the substance of their rhythmic chants. Finally, she shook her head. "But then, for all we know, they could be yelling about all the drilling in the

North Sea, or the coral poaching that our Chinese friends insist on undertaking. I must say, I never cease to be amazed at the panorama of trivialities out there that some of the most comfortable people on the planet seem to get upset about."

Lee glanced over at his colleague. "The summit. Have you considered that could be the target . . .?"

"I have, Dalton," she interrupted. "It's not for public consumption, mind you, but we're substantially increasing the security planned throughout the city. More guards, more cameras. That sort of things."

"Good," Lee said in a chipper tone. However, the commander seemed less than confident. "What's wrong?" he inquired. She looked over at the protesters, sighed softly.

"It just seems it's near impossible to make a place truly impenetrable these days," she replied. She looked back at the architect. "Especially, a place that's impenetrable by *them*."

Lee gave her a smile of condolence, but his grin rapidly faded when he noticed that one of the protesters seemed to be glaring at him. The young man with a full beard and gloriously colored tattoos down both arms had a piercing stare. After a moment, he slowly turned his sign around. Its crudely written message read

Butt out, Dalton Lee, OR ELSE

The architect's heart skipped not one, but several, beats.

"Did you see that, C. J.?" he asked, tapping her heavily on one shoulder.

"See what, Dalton?" Her attention had been shanghaied by a flock of geese that were rising from behind a thicket in Hyde Park across the street.

"The protester. Over there. The one with . . ."

But the young man with the tattoos seemed to have vanished.

Or, had he really been there in the first place, the architect asked himself.

He was certain he had been. Then again, maybe he wasn't so certain.

When he and C. J. finally rounded the far corner of the hotel, they veered right, and Lee had to step quickly to avoid a small triangular barrier the city had erected to keep pedestrians from stepping into a hole in the pavement. "I'm not sure which obstacle is worse," Lee said with a huff. "The hole . . . or that cautionary barrier."

"The hole," C. J. shot back almost immediately. "Trust me."

Almost immediately, they were upon the London Chancery Building, the former home of the US Embassy. It was another structure that exuded an aura of force and austerity . . . and another structure Lee admired as a grand representative of an important architectural era.

Eero Saarinen, a comrade of Lara's father, had designed the building in the 1950s, and the phalanx of squares and rectangles on the structure's façade helped reinforce that fact. It was the first embassy in London built for that purpose, but it was also a brutal, modern interloper dropped into a neighborhood rich with elegant Georgian landmarks. That, and the enormous golden eagle centered above the top floor, had made it more than a little controversial when it opened in 1960.

"Not many people realize it was inspired by the Doge's Palace in Venice," Lee whispered. He adored the unapologetic symmetry of the building, both outside and in, a sense of orchestrated order and calm found in so many American libraries, schoolhouses, and government buildings of the time. But Lee was nowhere near as fond of the new embassy in Nine Elms, a gaudy, towering cube that in his opinion called far too much attention to itself. He was at least comforted to know that even though the building in front of them was slated to become a hotel, the developers were required to maintain Saarinen's original design in their renovation.

They pressed on, heading back east toward the heart of Mayfair. C. J. interrupted the silence with a question that baffled Lee.

"And what about you?" she asked.

He shifted nervously. "Me? What about me?"

A soft smirk appeared on C. J.'s face.

"You asked about me. Now I'm asking about you. Is there someone? You're . . . how old, now, Dalton?"

Lee felt as if both of his legs had gone leaden. He dipped his head first to the left, and then to the right, as if to stretch his neck, even though his neck wasn't really tight. He peered ahead in hopes they were coming upon another architectural landmark that he could talk about. None appeared on the horizon, however.

"Well . . . I'm forty . . . ish," he replied. "And there are, well, lots of people, really."

"Lots of people you'd like to settle down with?"

"Well, of course not. I mean . . . lots of close friends. And associates."

"Associates," C. J. replied nodding. "I see." She took a few more steps before adding. "By 'associate,' are you referring to someone like . . . Lara?"

That's when Lee tripped on a crack in the pavement, a move that sent him hurtling forward like someone making a running, horizontal dive at a swimming pool. His right fingertips, and C. J.'s quick grasp on the back vent of his jacket, prevented him from tumbling face down onto the pavement. Still, he needed a couple of moments to stabilize himself before responding.

"Lara is . . . a dear friend," he said, with much more gravity than the sentence required. He readjusted his jacket and checked to ensure he had not wrenched something. "We look upon one another with great . . . esteem."

C. J. kept a game face. "Ah. Esteem, is it? But of course," she replied.

"And if I were you," the architect continued, "I'd be very careful, for I could bring up that little display of intimacy I saw you exchanging the other day with our friend at the bocce court."

That seemed to end the discussion. Which was fine with him, for he felt more comfortable discussing matters of architecture than matters of the heart. And there were so many other buildings here in Mayfair he'd love to experience, and show to C. J.

Buildings such as The Connaught Hotel, where the G7 meeting would occur. He found it to be an Edwardian masterpiece, with a suite that had housed French president Charles de Gaulle as he helped plan the D-Day landings, and a lobby boasting a staircase so admired by the American designer Ralph Lauren that he had a replica of it installed in his boutique in Manhattan.

Or, One Mayfair Church, which was no longer a place of worship, but was still an outstanding example of the Greek Revival Style favored by John Peter Gandy during the 1820s. And, thanks to Sir Arthur Blomfield's additions to the church in the 1870s, a place whose façade and elegant porch were still considered among the finest in the city.

He even yearned to become reacquainted with the Hotel Beaumont and Antony Gormley's sculpture, ROOM. He was fascinated by the artist's peculiar vision of designing a structure that served as a sleeping quarters inside the hotel, *and* a sculpture that projected from the hotel in the form of a giant, crouching cuboid figure patterned after the artist's physique.

But it was nearing noon, and the gentle mist they had occasionally experienced throughout the morning had now evolved into a steady, dreary drizzle. So, he guided them over to Brook Street, where Mayfair's Georgian architecture was on grand display. They stopped in front of the adjacent terraces numbered 23 and 25.

"Quite the musical legacy here," he said to his colleague.

"Really?"

He nodded toward Number 23, an oatmeal-colored building whose ground floor housed a clothing boutique accented by a door painted fire-engine red.

"That's where Jimi Hendrix lived for a time," he said, glancing up to the windows. He then pointed to the structure on the right, which was constructed of brown bricks offset by reddish-brick lintels above each window. A leather-goods retailer occupied its first floor.

"And the classical composer George Handel lived up there somewhere. Shortly after it was built, I would imagine. Both buildings look pretty much the way they would have looked when they were constructed in the 1720s."

Their umbrellas were up now, and the rain was beginning to pelt them. The nearby pedestrians were scrambling for cover; Lee and C. J. huddled underneath the closest overhang they could find, a slate-blue awning attached to a building that housed a knitwear shop.

"You do know Hanover Square is just a couple of blocks in that direction," C. J. reminded him, pointing vaguely toward the east. "Did you want to go take a *look-see* after the rain has let up?"

He shook his head, gripped his umbrella more firmly.

"I do need to go back there," he began, "but I want to make my return at night. As close to the time of the murder as I can. And I want Warren to come with me. I need him to help me explore a theory that I have."

He turned toward C. J., expecting her to have a look of intrigue or anticipation on her face. What he was met with, however, was a look of deep concern.

"C. J.?"

She stared out at the torrential rain.

"It's just . . . their scheme. If they are planning to launch their Transformation during the G7 summit, I fear the consequences could very well be . . ."

Methodically, he followed her stare out at the pouring rain and gripped his umbrella even more tightly.

"I know what you're going to say," he told her. "And I agree. The consequences could be more catastrophic than we ever imagined."

25

Of course, it was raining. And, of course, Roberto had failed to bring an umbrella.

In his eagerness to prepare for another conversation with Isabela, he hadn't checked to see what the weather might be. Maybe it was a good thing that they were going to converse by text, not video.

Either way though, raindrops splattering on his screen wasn't going to make the exchange any easier.

The showers had dispersed whatever crowd might normally have been at Hanover Square in the middle of the day. Only a handful of pedestrians were gliding across the outer corners of the square, intent, it seemed, on observing some important appointment. No one was lounging inside the park, and no one was sauntering along the pavement that formed its perimeter.

The graphic designer checked his phone--his messaging date with Isabela wasn't to begin for fifteen minutes. He gave some thought to hanging out beneath the awning that covered a café patio across the street, but he didn't want to irk the proprietor by making him think he was some sort of vagrant. So he strolled alongside the fence that lined the park and scanned the landscape for some clue that might be valuable.

Although, by now, anything worthwhile is probably long gone, he said to himself.

When he came around the next corner, he saw the mime slumped against the ironwork he had been reclining against when Roberto first met him. The clown's hands were deep in the pockets of his baggy trousers and his head was bowed. Roberto couldn't tell if the guy was deep in contemplation or consumed with depression. Or asleep.

Roberto decided to be bold in his approach. To get the entertainer's attention, he cleared his throat and scuffed one shoe against the pavement as he neared. The mime turned his head, but otherwise didn't acknowledge Roberto's advance.

"So, I'm thinking maybe you know more about what's been going on in this park than you're letting on, *amigo,*" Roberto said, lifting his chin a notch. He was now standing only an arm's length from the busker, who eyed him with fatigue.

"I'm thinking maybe you were involved somehow in what took place here a few nights ago. What do you think?"

The mime did not immediately answer, but instead, rolled his eyes skyward, closed them, and slowly shook his head. He remained in that position for several seconds. Finally, he exhaled heavily.

"Give it a rest, guvnor," he muttered. "Can't you show a little sympathy to a bloke who's trying to eke out a living but can't get a break from the weather?" The entertainer's face was still tilted up, his lids were still shut. But eventually, he lowered his head, opened his eyes, and turned in Roberto's direction.

"Let me guess . . . Mexican? Brazilian? No, I'm putting my wager on Colombian. Your machismo act is *very* impressive, guvnor, really it is. But it does get tiresome rather quickly, you know?"

Roberto flinched. "I'm Puerto Rican and proud of it," he replied, thrusting his face forward a couple of inches. Then he had a glimpse of enlightenment and realized even *that* response had reinforced the busker's stereotype of his lineage. "So, you *can* speak," he added quietly.

The clown shut his eyes and shrugged his shoulders.

"When I want to. And only to whomever I want to."

Thunder resonated softly in the distance, but to Roberto, it seemed the rain was easing up.

The mime inspected his shoes for a time, then sighed and turned to Roberto with a bored expression.

"Exactly what, or who, are you trying to find here, old chap? Has your teenage daughter taken up with some pimp? Has your heroin dealer suddenly gone quiet? Did someone steal your priceless watch and you think they're trying to sell it on the street? Or did some little tart you met here give you the old heave-ho and you're hoping to run into her again like some lovesick puppy?"

Roberto studied the busker's face closely.

"None of that," he answered. "I'm following up on . . . a murder. Over there, across the park. It happened about a week ago. You notice anything?"

The mime swiveled in the direction Roberto was pointing, paused for a moment, then swiveled back. His expression of disinterest was no different than it had been when he turned away. He shrugged his shoulders again.

"Sorry, guvnor, but I wouldn't know anything about that. My shift here ends around eighteen hours, except in the summer when I might hang around until twenty or even twenty-one." He extended both arms and used his palms to whisk away the droplets of rain that had accumulated on his brightly colored trousers.

Roberto glanced at his phone; it was almost time for his conversation.

"Antonio Tinti. Does that name mean anything to you?"

The designer thought he saw a tic cross the entertainer's face the moment he uttered the tailor's name. But the clown pursed his lips in an exaggerated frown and shook his head.

"He's a tailor. Over on Savile Row," Roberto continued. "Short, balding but not entirely bald. Someone shot him in the park. At point blank range."

The mime shrugged his shoulders again, extended both palms upward, shook his head once more. He had returned to his silent routine.

This time, the thunder sounded closer, insisted more that everyone respect its presence.

Roberto scoffed in frustration, turned, and trudged across the street so he could initiate contact with Isabela. When he glanced over his shoulder, the busker was wearing a steely expression.

Like a hawk considering its intended prey.

Roberto pressed the phone number they'd sent him to start his dialogue with Isabela. For a change, Roberto didn't bump up against any technical difficulties or delays in making the connection. His little sister even seemed to be in a cheerful mood.

Maybe they're finally loosening the rope a little bit, he said to himself.

He was eager to pick up the game where they'd left off so he could extract some more details about her location. But she began the conversation with what he thought was an odd deflect.

'Berto, what are the ingredients for making *arroz con gandules?*

He double-checked to make sure she hadn't already started playing the game. Once he verified she hadn't, he scratched his head.

Rice and pigeon peas? he typed back. He had to think. **Onion. Some *sofrito?* Um, tomato sauce. Maybe olives and capers.** He waited a few seconds before he started typing again.

Why? Are you planning to do some cooking soon? ☺

Her response took some time to arrive.

No, silly. It was one of my favorite foods when I was a kid. I really miss it, and I couldn't remember what it was made of. Just curious.

"When I was a kid." That shattered his heart into shards. She was only eight the last time he saw her. Now she was on the threshold of becoming a young woman, and unable to remember the ingredients of her favorite dish.

Let's talk about something else, he typed. **You go first . . .**

***

To the random observer, their talk was an entirely innocent one—about how proficient she had become at jumping rope, about the emergence of a mole on the back of her leg, about the fact she had experienced her first period, and about her yearning to play once more at the beach near their old home in Puerto Rico.

To anyone adept at the game known as Every Other, however, their conversation was a cleverly executed transfer of code.

Back at the residence, Roberto sat alone at the dining table, his cell phone in one hand, a pencil in the other. He would glance at the screen, then scribble on a crisp white notepad to his right. Then back at the screen, then another scribble.

He felt like a cryptographer, although he knew what they had undertaken was rudimentary compared to what those who work in intelligence units deal with.

Thank God these terrorists aren't geniuses, he thought to himself.

When he jotted down the final letter of Isabela's surreptitious message, he sat back in his chair and blew out a long, slow breath. A smile crept across his face as he read all the information she'd passed on to him.

Heard the guards talking.

Moving us to a jail. A famous one.

Named for somebody? Evan? In the northwest!

He knew exactly where they were taking her. The Evin Prison in Tehran. Colloquially known as Evin University because of all the Iranian intellectuals imprisoned there over the years. *So that means the government of Iran is cooperating with The Organization,* he thought, his blood pressure rising.

Still, he now knew exactly where in this big wide world they were going to be imprisoning his dearest Isabela. He needed only one last piece of critical data to rescue her from years of confinement, to bring this madness to its final end.

When, exactly, would she be arriving there?

26

"So, this is nice."

Bree removed the needles, yarn, and stitch markers from her tote and set them on the coffee table in front of her. Her praise of Mariam's apartment had merely been an effort to be polite; in truth, the place was perhaps one half-step above a dump. The furniture, though dated and mismatched, showed little wear. But newspapers cluttered the floor. The lamplight behind the sofa Mariam reclined upon was dingy, and the lamp's aluminum shade had not been dusted in weeks. A vaguely rancid aroma seeped from the kitchen. And, a cat Bree was sure had ringworm kept eyeing her menacingly from one corner of the room.

"Thank you. You're very kind. Would you like some wine?" Mariam was rising from the couch before she had finished her question.

"YES!" Bree pulled herself in once she realized her response had come off more enthusiastic than she had intended. Within moments, she wondered if she should have asked for tea, rather than accept alcohol from someone she hardly knew.

Over the clatter in the kitchen, she heard Mariam ask, "White or red?"

"Um, either is fine. Whatever you have the most of." She sank into her chair again, afraid now that her comment had made her sound like quite the lush. The cat began a low hiss at her and slunk to a spot behind a bookcase.

"I'm so glad you called me at the restaurant," Mariam said as she returned with filled glasses for the two of them. Bree's eyes grew huge when Mariam set down in front of her what looked more like a fishbowl full of red wine than a glassful.

"Oh my, that's . . ."

"A Pakistani wine," Mariam interrupted. "Homemade by the Kalash tribe near the border with Afghanistan. My cousin came to visit a couple of months ago and brought some with him. Drink. I think you will like it." Bree's right palm flew to her breast as she began a series of short coughs.

"I'm so sorry. It must be the night air . . . or something," she suggested. She lifted the goblet and tilted it tentatively toward her lips. Took as slight a sip as she could. Contemplated how best to conceal her disgust once she managed a swallow.

And was pleasantly surprised with its taste. It had more of a mineral bite than she would choose but other than that, it wasn't just tolerable, it was a wine she thought she could actually enjoy.

"What are you knitting?" Mariam asked, suddenly full of motion. She cleared a collection of trinkets off the top of the table between them, readjusted the pillow to her left, took a gulp of wine, moved her needles (from one side of the table and then back again) as well as a rosewood yarn bowl Bree assumed was from Pakistan.

"Um . . . a shawl," Bree replied, watching Mariam's agitation with increasing alarm. "To wear. At night."

Her host stopped rearranging things and peered at Bree suspiciously.

"I thought you were from Texas, or one of those warmer American states. Why do you need a shawl?"

Bree took a larger sip from the wine, jerked her head down to one side as the alcohol traversed her throat.

"It's Arizona, actually" she answered, smiling tightly. "And, I'm from *northern* Arizona. Near the mountains, not the desert. It gets very cool there in the evenings. Same thing in Southern California, which is where I live now . . .

"So I imagine you must really be distraught over Mr. Tinti's murder."

Mariam returned the forced grin, continued to look at Bree with a measure of disbelief.

"Distraught? No, not really. I mean, yes, of course, it's sad when someone dies. But no, I wouldn't say I am distraught."

As she began to knit, Bree peered at her companion across the table. Mariam's accessories were all exquisitely crafted. But she noticed the server seemed clumsy and uncertain as she worked her needles.

"Oh, really? I just thought that since you had such a regular relationship . . ."

"There was no relationship!" Mariam looked as if she were scolding a child. "He was just a customer. And not much of one at that!"

Bree's brow furrowed further. "I thought . . ."

"That we were close friends? That we were—how do you Americans say it?—BFFs? No. Not at all. He come to the restaurant, and I serve him. Sometimes, he wants to talk, and I listen." She paused to look at some point beyond Bree's right shoulder. "Well, sometimes I listen. But mostly, I pretend I am listening. He never say anything interesting, so why would I listen? Why would anyone listen? All he ever talked about was his disco music. And how much he missed his ex-wife. Then he would leave. Maybe he would put an extra pound or two with the check. But not very often. Definitely not often enough."

She stopped again but looked directly at Bree this time.

"Your hair . . . you must use some special conditioner on it? Is it an American brand? Japanese?"

Bree paused. "I . . . have no idea, really." Mariam returned to a slumped position as Bree shifted uncomfortably in her chair. She decided to change the topic, if only temporarily.

"What do you like to knit, Mariam?" The question came to her, in part, because she had been squinting to identify what was unfolding between Mariam's needles, but couldn't make out the item no matter how hard she tried.

The server frowned slightly, bobbed her head one way, then the other. "It depends on the season," she replied. "I've never tried a blanket or anything like that, but in the winter, I have made a couple of dishcloths. And I've knitted a lot of arm covers."

Bree instinctively glanced at the arms of the sofa Mariam was sitting on and was mortified to see her companion followed her gaze. The woman's look turned steely. "For my relatives in Pakistan," she said. "Not for me."

Bree smiled weakly. "I'd love to see them some time," she lied. "I'm sure they're lovely."

The comment seemed to brighten Mariam. She flashed her first smile of the evening. "Yes, I think so. I like to mix some interesting colors together. Maybe I will knit some for you. How long do you think you will be here? With your work."

Bree retreated some. She knew not to reveal too much information about their investigation. "It's hard to say. We think we're making some progress, but . . ."

"Let me tell you this." Mariam was frowning again, and she had thrust her head forward as if she were sharing a secret with a big sister. "I think the tailor and his son were doing something illegal. Dealing drugs, or something like that. I think that is why they killed him. Maybe why they killed both of them. I think maybe Tony didn't pay someone the money he owed them, or he was going to snitch on someone, and they didn't want him to do that. So . . ." She stuck out her right hand and imitated a gun going off.

Something Mariam had said caused Bree to stop knitting for a moment and reflect on an avenue she wanted to share with Lee and the others when she returned to the residence that night.

"Why do you think Tony and his son were involved in something illegal?" She resumed her knitting, began to watch the server's hands more intently. They seemed to be going in opposite directions, fighting each other first to loop the yarn and then to unravel what she had just finished looping.

For a few moments, the waitress just peered at her knitting, her lips taut, nodding her head repeatedly as if someone invisible were rocking her. But before she could reply, someone rapped gently on the door. Bree wondered how her companion would react, given her unusual state. She waited warily to see if Mariam's eyes would bulge or her frown deepen even more.

Instead, her mouth contorted into a small, conspiratorial smile. "Excuse me, will you please?" She rose from the sofa like a geisha who'd been summoned by her patron. Although her pleasantry had been in the form of a question, Mariam didn't wait for Bree to answer. And Bree noticed Mariam didn't really walk to the door so much as float toward it.

The architect sat still, pretending to knit, straining to hear any syllable she could.

But it was all in vain. Mariam opened the door just a crack and spoke in a tone hardly above a whisper. Bree could tell the visitor was male from the resonance of his timbre, but he joined Mariam in keeping the conversation as discreet as possible. She also could tell that the two of them were speaking English, for she heard the word "later," and then, "arriving." That, and a short laugh, which either could have uttered. But that was all she could deduce.

The door shut, and Mariam returned to her sofa with a gait far more heavy-footed than the one she'd used before.

"More wine?" she asked, her brow more wrinkled, and her expression more dour, than when Bree had last seen her.

"NO THANKS!" The architect bit her lower lip at her third unfortunate slip of emotion. But Mariam seemed not to mind. Her thoughts appeared to be elsewhere altogether. Suddenly, she started. "Oh, that's so beautiful!" She reached toward Bree's hands and clutched the free end of the shawl the architect was creating. "Really, that's just lovely, Bree. You *must* teach me how to make something like this. I am so uncoordinated when it comes to knitting complex things like those lace patterns. Will you teach me?"

Bree had no desire whatsoever to spend more time with the sad, erratic woman. But she also felt deep inside that Mariam knew some secret, possessed some clue, that could lead them to Tinti's killer.

And then, as if Bree had spoken her thoughts out loud, Mariam delivered precisely that.

"Ah!" she blurted. "I forgot. You asked me why I thought Tony and his son might be involved in something illegal." Mariam padded into a small side room, where Bree could hear the waitress rummaging through papers of some sort. A drawer opened, and there was more rummaging. Another drawer opened, and Bree heard what sounded like the lid of a metal box being opened.

Seemingly out of nowhere, the cat bounded into her lap. Bree froze, but then worried the feline might sense her discomfort and use it as motivation to attack. Instead, the animal sat quietly, examining her the way some passerby might study a Chippendale desk displayed prominently in a store window. She recognized it to be a Bengal cat, which she knew can look feral but is domestic. She considered petting the animal but decided against it, worried the cat's hair might cling to her yarn.

The animal began to nuzzle her thigh. But when Mariam strode back into the room, it stiffened, turned toward its owner, arched its back, and let out a threatening hiss before darting off the chair toward its favorite bookcase.

Bree looked questioningly toward Mariam, whose expression registered an emotion that straddled fear and confusion. Very softly the waitress cleared her throat.

"I didn't want to speak of this to your friends," she said, her eyes wide. "To be truthful, I didn't think it was very important. But maybe." Her palms were interlocked in front of her, as if they concealed a delicate feather or flower. "Once after Tony left and I was clearing his table, I found this."

She tilted one palm outward to reveal a piece of notebook paper folded into a tiny neat square. Bree looked first at it, and then at Mariam, who nodded at her.

"Take it. Open it."

The architect did as she was instructed and methodically unfolded the slightly yellowed notepaper. She could tell there were only a couple of words on it, words written with a ball-point pen. But she couldn't make them out, as they were upside down.

So she inverted the piece of paper, took a deep breath in.

"HELP ME" the note said, its final "e" trailing off into an indistinct blur.

PLEASE

If you would, please post a review of this book on any of these websites or your own book blog:

amazon   BARNES&NOBLE   **BookBub**   goodreads

iBooks   ®Rakuten kobo   Smashwords

The more reviews a book gets (regardless of the star rating) the more people who buy the book.

So thank you for getting the word out (either for or against) this mystery thriller.

If you know author Jeffrey Eaton, please **do not** mention that in your review, for it is likely to lead to your review being pulled. Other than that, however, have at it.

And **thank you!**

Note: You only need to have an account with Amazon, iBooks, etc. to post a review there. You do not have to have purchased the book there to post your review.

murderbecomes.com

CORNET

27

They could walk there. Easily. He knew that but wanted to take the Maicoletta nonetheless.

"The crisp night air will do us some good," Lee said to Warren. "Besides, it's dark. No one will notice the scratch."

Warren chuckled as he hiked a leg over the back of the seat. "No one can see the scratch in *the daytime*, Dalton. It's barely noticeable. Even with, like, a magnifying glass, you can hardly see it."

Lee thought that was an exaggeration but decided not to press the issue. He wanted to stay on good terms with his resident cat burglar, for he was really going to need Warren's expertise tonight.

Lee inserted the earbuds connected to his phone and fiddled with the controls to start some music for the ride. As he did so, Warren tapped the architect on the back, then tugged gently on the earbuds.

"Let me guess," Warren said, flashing a big smile. "Puccini?"

"No," Lee replied.

"Mozart?"

Warren's superior shook his head, began to smile.

"Sondheim? Adele? The Academy of St. Martin in the Fields?"

Lee's headshake took on a much wider span, as if he was trying to dry his hair in the wind.

"The Pointer Sisters," he called out over his shoulder. "The extended release version of 'Jump for My Love.'"

Warren threw his head back and guffawed. "Whoa. The eighties. You do realize I was still wearing onesies when that came out."

Lee rolled his eyes and put on his helmet. "Thanks for making me feel like Methuselah," he said as he revved up the scooter. "And for the record, I was only three or four myself."

Warren punched his boss in the back.

"Okay, maybe six or seven," Lee confessed.

As they zoomed off, the head of The Lee Group reminded himself that he needed to be careful. The pavement was slippery thanks to the day's intermittent showers, and even now, they found themselves underneath a gentle mist. Fortunately, it was almost midnight, so there were not many vehicles on the road.

He decided to take a circuitous route—first down to Wellington Arch and the Australian and New Zealand war memorials and then back across Mayfair to Hanover Square. For one thing, doing so would put them at the park more to the moment when Tinti had been shot. And Lee, for some reason, had an inexplicable, almost adolescent desire to ride circles around the arch and the equestrian statue of the Duke of Wellington.

The air felt sleek against them as they zoomed along Park Lane. For some time, they said nothing to one another as they admired the muted moonlight while keeping watch for the errant car or lorry that might potentially sideswipe them.

When the Pointer Sisters' song came to an end, Lee yanked out his earbuds and tucked them into the light gray cardigan he was wearing. He decided it might be a good time to broach a subject with Warren that he knew his senior architect might be a little uncomfortable with.

"I've been wondering, have you heard anything from Hannah recently?" Lee yelled over his left shoulder.

Warren seemed somehow to shrink, and scoot closer to his boss, at the same time.

"Not really," came the reply. A pause. "But I didn't expect to. We pretty much decided we should both probably just move on."

Another longer pause. Warren shifted on the seat, first forward, then back.

Uh-oh, I did make him uncomfortable, Lee fretted. But Warren was suddenly talkative again.

"I've been meaning to apologize to you about that, Dalton," he shouted. "For what happened in Miami. I probably wasn't as engrossed in that investigation as I should have been. I wasn't very . . . professional, I'm afraid."

"No need to apologize, Warren," Lee yelled. "You helped us clear one of the key suspects, remember? And, as for Hannah, well, you were just being . . . human."

He felt the body behind him soften—and embrace his upper torso more tightly—at the same time.

"Agent Weiss is a wonderful person," Warren continued. "An *awesome* person. I admire her enormously. I *miss her* enormously. I . . ." He decided to shift the mood. "I have no doubt she is impressing the hell out of her co-workers in Los Angeles right now."

He scooted closer to Lee again and moved his face closer to his boss's ear.

"And we need to bring my wife home, Dalton. Soon. I really need her." He paused, then added, "The other day, Natalia told me she can't remember her mommy's face anymore."

Lee's heart crumpled.

"We will, Warren, I swear. I am doing everything in my power to bring back your wife, Roberto's little sister, Bree's friend . . ."

"And your mother and father. I know. We all know you are doing everything you can, Dalton. We never think that you are not. But at the same time, you shouldn't believe you're going to be able to save everybody. It can't all be on your shoulders. It's *not* just on *your* shoulders. Know that."

At that moment, a black cab traveling alongside them went "thunk" into and then out of a small pothole, spraying them with the rainwater it had collected. Lee immediately throttled down so they wouldn't skid and adroitly kept the scooter under control.

"Well, so much for that shower I took this evening," he muttered to his companion.

They entered the circle and moved to the left, navigating their way around the Machine Gun Corps Memorial, also known as The Boy David. Lee had always found the statue to be both odd . . . and oddly alluring. Made of Mazzona marble, the central column of the memorial supported a nude version of Goliath's slayer, David. However, David's pose (one hand on one hip, the other on Goliath's sword) somehow came off as both macho and Vegas showgirl. Making the memorial even more peculiar were the Vickers machine guns that flanked David on a plinth below.

"It's sort of one-part Rambo, one-part Rihanna," Warren called out to his boss. Lee nodded quickly.

"I know," he shouted back. "Isn't it amazing?!"

They proceeded clockwise around the circle, taking their time to study The Boy David and the Australian War Memorial, a landform comprising green-gray Australian granite that rose from the pavement like the contours of the Australian landscape. Lee felt one of Warren's arms unfold from around his waist. He seemed to be fiddling with something on his body.

Lee called out, "What are you doing back there?"

"I was trying to find out what all that wording is on the memorial," Warren replied. "This says it lists the names of all the towns that sent Australian men and women into service in the first and second world wars. It says there are more than twenty-three thousand towns listed."

Lee slowed the scooter to a crawl so he wouldn't have to yell.

"What do you mean by 'this'? How did you suddenly find that information?"

Warren clapped a hand on one of Lee's shoulders.

"The memorial's website. I called it up on my watch, Dalton. Easy peasy."

Lee emitted a low whistle and shook his head. "I need to catch up," was all he could say. As the architect sped the scooter back up, his younger associate said, "Shouldn't we be heading over to the park?" Gradually, they re-entered the traffic flow.

"We will," Lee replied loudly. "I just want to go around the Boy of David one more time."

They approached the statue from the rear. Warren, a little embarrassed by the statue's nudity, looked in every other direction.

However, Lee slowed the scooter again, kept studying the artwork intently.

Aren't you going to say something to me, he thought. *Don't you have some clue about the killer? Isn't there something about The Organization's intentions that you need to share with me? Or some criticism of my behavior? Or maybe some important life lesson you feel the need to impart?*

He waited for a response, but The Boy David only smirked in return.

It was Warren's voice that startled the architect out of his reverie. "Why are we going so slowly?" he called out. "You look like you're waiting for something to happen."

Lee took one last furtive glimpse at the statue before they headed east onto Piccadilly. Once he had maneuvered them onto Regent Street, he slowed again and looked over his left shoulder.

"Warren, do things ever . . . talk to you?"

His senior architect hesitated. "I'm not sure what you mean. The forms of certain buildings, and some songs, really speak to me."

"No, by 'talk to,' I don't mean 'inspire.' I mean . . . 'converse.' 'Interact with.' Do things . . . do inanimate objects . . . ever converse with you?"

Warren thought for a moment. It struck him that, more than once, Dalton had seemed to be already speaking to someone when Warren had entered a room . . . with no one in it but Dalton. He recalled the same thing happening when they were strolling through a park or across someone's lawn, or in a department store. Only it never happened when he was right beside Dalton. It seemed to take place only when Warren was a short distance from him.

He started to say something, but then remembered Dalton's question had been about *him.* "No, I can't say that they do, Dalton. Or, if they have, I must not have found whatever they said very interesting."

Warren had hoped to bring a little levity to their conversation. But he could tell from his boss's body language that his response had only caused Lee to slump in disappointment.

***

187

When they got to Hanover Square, no one was in the vicinity.

Absolutely no one.

Not in the park (which, it being midnight, was closed). But, also not in any of the lanes that helped formed the square. No matter which direction they looked, they saw not a single person . . . save for one twenty-something, accessorized with hoodie, earbuds, and skateboard, who caromed off one corner of the park before picking up his board and disappearing into the night.

"Well, we can't assume the area was this desolate the night of the murder," Lee told Warren. "But if it was, it would sure explain why no one saw or heard anything."

They acknowledged it *was* early in the work-week. And, that it was just after midnight. Also, that it had been raining for much of the day. Still, the architects found it odd the square was so completely void of humanity.

"Feels like a scene in some zombie apocalypse movie," Warren countered.

Lee edged the Maicoletta onto the pavement and propped it against the fence. Within seconds, he had the vehicle securely locked and tethered.

"Let's take a walk," he whispered to his accomplice.

Roberto had provided Lee with the precise location of where he should be able to find the loose picket in the fence. But the architect was having a difficult time identifying it.

"Maybe it was on the opposite side of the park," Warren offered.

Lee, his hands on his hips, shook his head. "No, he clearly said it was almost directly opposite where the motorcycles park." Only three bikes were in that spot behind them at present, but the pavement clearly indicated it was the location Roberto had referred to.

"Not the bicycle racks? Because there's scads of them all the way around the park."

Lee had started ambling back toward the locked gate. He shook his head once more.

"No, he definitely said 'motorcycles.'"

The architect then whirled around and headed back toward Warren. Only this time he pressed each iron rod in the fence, as if he were late for a meeting and trying to summon an elevator.

Nothing gave way.

"Someone's fixed it," Lee concluded. "I'll circle back with Roberto, but I am certain this is the semicircle of the fence Roberto told us about. If that's the case, it may be the fastest this city—or someone else—has ever repaired a park fence."

Warren decided to make his own test and got the same results. "So, what now?" he asked.

The architect dug into his shirt pocket and retrieved his phone. Turning on the flashlight app, he directed the light as best he could over the shrubs and into the park.

"What are you looking for, Dalton?

Lee moved the device to the right, then the left, then froze it in place.

"That. I was looking for that footprint. There." It was the print and the matted grass just beyond the shrubs that he had spotted a couple of days earlier. They were diminished, but still discernible. He broke out in a smile and turned to his employee.

"And this is where you come in, Warren," he said. "You're taller than I am. So I want you to scale the fence and see whether . . ."

"My other foot would reach the print if I hopped all the way over?"

The architect broadened his smile and nodded. "I would have asked Roberto to do it but . . . well . . ."

This time it was Warren who nodded. "I get it. Say no more. He's probably a little hefty for that assignment." In order to gain some upper-body flexibility, he removed the light windbreaker he was wearing. And before Lee could blink, his employee was crouching on the highest horizontal rail that ran the length of the fence.

"How do you do that without toppling over and impaling yourself on the finials?" Lee whispered.

Warren looked down at his boss and winked. "We learn that in our first semester of cat burglar school," he whispered back.

With that, Warren turned and stood tall on the fence, balancing himself like an aerialist about to traverse a tightrope. He lifted his right leg straight ahead of him and then set it back down when he began to wobble. Composed himself, then did the same with his left leg. From below, Lee marveled at his associate's equilibrium . . . and nerves of steel.

With no warning, Warren then leapt backward off the fence and onto the pavement. Once he brushed himself off, he stood erect and turned toward Lee.

"Nope. Doesn't work. There is no way someone could have reached that spot just from climbing the fence and taking a hop. The footprint is too far beyond the shrubs, even for me."

Lee gave his employee a sober look. "Which means whoever made that print either made it after they were inside the park . . ."

"Or they somehow were catapulted into the park from back over there," Warren added, pointing to the other side of the lane.

Lee took a deep breath, frowned. "That's . . . not the outcome I was hoping for." He thrust his fists into his pockets and turned his attention toward the pavement. That's when he saw the remnants of the scuff marks near the curb that he had noticed on his previous visit.

The architect swiveled around, looked back at the fence, then at the scuff marks. Calculated the width of the lane behind him and Warren, and the width of the pavement beyond that.

"Yes. A catapult," he finally said, a slight twinkle in his eyes. "You know, Warren, you may have actually hit on something there."

28

The day did not begin well.

First came Bree's recounting of what Mariam had shown her. The note deeply unsettled Lee, for although he knew that all the murders they investigated had victims, it disheartened him to come face-to-face with their misery, their sense of helplessness, their belief there might have been someone out there who could rescue them from their fate.

But did not.

Then there was the report C. J. delivered to him over the phone.

"I've circled back with everyone who attended to the automobile accident that killed Niccolò Tinti," she said. Her statement was followed by a loud honking noise, a blare that sounded as if she were clearing out all her sinuses. Nonplussed, she barreled on with her commentary. "No page of *Wayward Colony* was found on the son's body, Dalton. Nor anything similar to that. Everyone is quite sure of it. It seems he darted across a street, outside of the crosswalk, just as a car came around the corner. His death was instant, the coroner says. The driver even stopped to render aid. No charges were filed."

Lee released a long breath. "So that means that unless The Organization has suddenly gotten very sloppy with its practices, his death truly was an accident. And, that we're at . . .""

"Another dead end. Yes, I know. *Quel dommage.*"

Lee wasn't clear whether his peevishness stemmed from the case now seeming once again to be at a standstill or from C. J. now seeming perfectly capable of finishing his sentences. He decided to switch gears.

"Oh, I meant to ask you . . . our friend Karlo . . . has any surveillance footage turned up that supports or refutes his claim he was at home asleep when Tinti was killed?"

"Ah, yes. Karlo," was immediately followed by another honk even deeper than the first.

"I'm concerned about you, C. J." the architect said. "You sound . . ."

"I'm fine, Dalton, fine. It's just the infernal barometric pressure. We must have another high approaching us from Spain, or the Hebrides, or some such locale. Whenever the pressure starts to rise, all my cavities start to feel like a family of porcupines have taken up residence inside them. It's annoying to no end, I'm sure, and I ask that you pay no mind to the cacophony I'm creating. It comes, it goes."

He waited for her to answer his question about the surveillance tapes. When she didn't, he gave her a nudge.

"Oh, of course, the footage, yes. Well there was some, and it does seem to corroborate Karlo's alibi. It does show him entering his building about the time he said he did. And it doesn't show him leaving that same way.

"However . . ."

Lee braced for another honk. But it never materialized.

"However, what?"

"However, there are always back windows and fire escapes and other sorts of mechanisms that enable one to escape detection of security cameras depending on their location, aren't there?"

Lee was beginning to wonder whether C. J. was truly on their side.

"I suppose," he replied, more glum than before. He began to caress the long, wooden drawer pull attached to the desk he was seated at, stroked his fingertip along its entire length, from left to right. The fact was, he was also still nursing the jab to the solar plexus he had suffered the previous afternoon when he received the estimate from a nearby body shop for removing the scratch from his Maicoletta. He started to caress the drawer pull again, this time moving from right to left.

That suddenly reminded him of something. "Do you have a measuring tape, C. J.?"

"A what?"

"You know, a measuring tape. One of those little gadgets that has a flexible ruler that pulls out and then snaps back when you're done with it."

"Oh, we call that a tape measure, Dalton. Yes, I'm sure we have one around here somewhere. But why do you need one?"

Now he was rapidly brushing his fingertip back and forth along the top of the drawer pull. He decided to play coy.

"Obviously, C. J., because there's something I want to measure," he replied, his lips now arced in a definitive smile.

***

He was *that close* to pressing the final digit of the telephone number.

But he exited the call instead. Started the string of numbers again. Got halfway through, then gave up.

He sighed, started to pace the room. *You're a forty-year-old man, Dalton. Stop being so ridiculous.* He punched two digits, then jabbed the home key. Swiveled to his right and glanced out at the branches of the London plane tree that stood just beyond his window, its leaves hinting at the earliest turn of autumn . . . which made him only more melancholy and more exasperated with his emotional stasis.

But she's so lovely, he reminded himself.

He raised his index finger one more time to dial her number, to see if she'd have a drink with him in some chic secluded bar, or even some raucous rowdy tavern.

But pressed an entirely different phone number altogether.

"Um, yes, I was referred to you by . . . an associate," he uttered when a voice picked up on the other end of the line. "I was wondering if I might be able to meet someone there, to explore a few things?"

The voice launched into a series of questions about his insurance situation, how pressing his need was to see someone.

"Just what is it you need to explore?" the voice concluded. Lee's breathing went shallow and rapid; to steady himself, he grasped one arm of the club chair next to him. *Maybe it would be better to delay this until after I return to the States,* he thought. For a moment he seriously considered hanging up and upswallowing into the nearest rubbish bin.

"Well . . . it's possible I may be . . ."

"It's all right. We're here to help. No matter what it is you are grappling with." The voice that had seemed curt and perfunctory a moment earlier suddenly seemed caring. Almost maternal.

"I guess, it's possible that . . . I am hearing . . . voices," he replied. The moment the word "voices" left his lips, he felt a lightness and coolness permeate his body, a deep serenity embrace his soul.

***

He was about to leave the residence through the front door and head up the block to the gym where they had workout privileges, when he heard steps behind him. It was Lara.

"Dalton, we think we've found the gun," she called out.

"We, as in you and Liam? Or we, as in you and Warren?"

His second-in-command ducked her head.

"Well, no. I meant someone on C. J. and Anisa's team. All of us, together, I meant."

Lee allowed a tiny grin to emerge.

"It's a Glock G19?"

"Yes."

"And they found it . . . oh, I'm sorry . . . *we* found it where?"

At first, he thought her crabbed expression was meant to admonish him for his little jab. But once she answered him, he knew it was a genuine look of gravity about the situation.

"It was at the bottom of a dumpster," she intoned. "No more than a quarter-mile from the bocce court at Hampstead Heath."

Lee raised both eyebrows, squinted, and nodded slowly. "Well, that's certainly interesting, isn't it?"

Lara returned his nod but said nothing more.

"I don't suppose we were lucky enough to be handed any prints from the gun," he asked.

"No. Either the murderer used gloves or did an outstanding job of removing the prints before tossing the gun aside. And the silencer that was attached to it, as well."

Lee continued nodding, adjusted the towel that was draped around his neck. "I would agree." He thought some more, raised his chin. "Then how do we know for sure it is *the* gun?"

A cool look returned to Lara's face. "Are you making fun of me?"

Lee frowned with concern. "No, why?"

"You said 'we' again. I thought maybe you were taunting me."

The architect looked abashed and stepped forward. "My mistake, Lara. No, I really meant 'we' that time. Even though *they* were the ones who found the gun."

Lara's sternness intensified.

"You know what I mean," Lee said.

She sighed. "Ballistics confirmed a match. That's all I know."

Lee nodded again and let out his own sigh of exasperation.

"Well, I was really hoping to get a workout in. Even if for half an hour." He uttered that more as a question than an explanation as he looked at his closest associate.

Lara smiled at him. "Run along, Dalton. Lift your weights. We'll take care of things until you get back."

The architect raised an eyebrow. Lara instantly replaced her tone of encouragement with one of pronouncement.

"What I meant, Dalton, was, *I* will take care of things until you get back."

***

He didn't need to lift weights. What he needed was a spin class. No . . . what he actually needed was the heavy-duty distraction a spin class provides.

So he could process the numerous threads that were folding into, and unraveling from, the investigation.

And so he could summon up the courage to ask Anisa out on a . . . He couldn't quite bring himself to call it a date. It was more like . . . a private social engagement, perhaps? Yes, he liked the sound of that.

Given their work situation, any get-together they had would need to be in private. And, of course, what they would be doing would be social in nature. When he reached the word "engagement," however, he pulled up. *No. That sounds too much like a commitment,* he thought, shaking his head.

As he mounted a cycle positioned in one far corner of the gym, he ran through the alternatives. *Encounter? No, that sounds like we're just going to bump into one another.* He pressed the START button on the console and set the speed of the bike to his liking. *Session. What about session?* He thought the word had potential, until he remembered a session is also what one has with a therapist. He edged up the speed of the cycle. Lots of other words traipsed across his brain, but he instantly rejected them.

Finally, he hit on the perfect choice. *Appointment! Yes, that's perfect—it's a social appointment. Like the appointments I have with clients. Where we sit, and we talk, and sometimes we have a drink while we're sitting and . . . talking about things.* A smile of satisfaction came upon his face as he nudged up the speed even more.

Yes, I can certainly ask her to join me on a private social appointment, he assured himself. *How could she possibly reject an offer like that?*

The wording settled, he turned his attention to the case. He was disappointed to learn that no one had found a calling card from The Organization on the body of Antonio Tinti's son. It appeared the automobile accident had been just that. And yet, Bree had raised an intriguing question when she recounted to him her experience with Mariam the evening before.

"And then she said, 'Maybe Tony was going to snitch on someone, and they weren't going to let him get away with that.'" Mariam's thoughts about Tinti's murder had gotten Lee to thinking. *Maybe Tinti and his son weren't involved in some illegal activity, but what if Tinti's son knew somehow what The Organization was up to? And then shared that with his father?*

Lee's pace was starting to surpass that of the pedals. He punched the up-arrow on the speed control even higher.

And, what if The Organization somehow found out Tinti knew about their plans and . . . Lee's legs and the cycle's wheels were now spinning so fast, the three people who were exercising nearby turned to look at him.

"And so THAT'S why they murdered him!" he cried out. An older woman on an elliptical trainer behind him instantly stopped pedaling and took her towel and water bottle to the opposite end of the row.

He lowered the speed to a level he could manage. For now, his idea was mostly conjecture. But his instincts told him he should encourage his team and C. J. to look for evidence that would corroborate it.

Just then, the video screen on the cycle's console began to flicker. The cricket match it was broadcasting first went black-and-white, then to static. After a few seconds, the static disappeared, leaving a black, imageless screen in front of him.

Their satellite dish must have gone down, he said to himself.
But as soon as he completed that thought, a series of words in a crisp white font appeared.

TIME TO MEET AGAIN, DALTON
I HAVE MORE INFORMATION TO SHARE
ABOUT YOUR FATHER
AMUSEMENT PARK AT KILBURN GRANGE
TOMORROW NIGHT, 11 PM

Lee checked discreetly over one shoulder, but everyone else in the gym seemed engrossed in their workouts and oblivious to what had just occurred.

When Lee looked back, the message was gone, and the cricket match was underway again.

England was beating Sri Lanka by five wickets, with four balls remaining.

29

The gun—discovered at the bottom of an olive-green dumpster two blocks from Hampstead Heath's popular bocce court—was indeed, *the gun.*

A Glock G19. But not just any Glock G19. A dove-gray Glock G19 sporting a handle that had been retrofitted with a cover made of matching dove-gray leather.

"Does that tell us anything? That the killer was a dove hunter, perhaps? Or maybe a female who wanted her hand more protected from the kickback?"

C. J. and Anisa had set up the conference call with Dalton the moment he had returned from the gym. As he waited for them to respond, he took a quick, discreet swig of the banana and blueberry smoothie he'd persuaded Margarida to make for him as a post-workout meal. But as he lowered the glass, he thought he heard Anisa chuckling on the line.

"No, Dalton. It probably means the killer just wanted it to be a really fashionable kill." It *was* Anisa who had been chuckling, and she ended her response with another, shorter laugh. The architect felt his cheeks warm.

C. J. decided she needed to chime in.

"As we could have expected, all serial numbers and other forms of identification have been removed. No prints, either." She paused. "They train their assassins well."

Lee took another swig of the smoothie and swished it around his mouth before swallowing. A hasty effort at oral hygiene.

"I'm somewhat surprised the dumpster hadn't been emptied," he offered. "I mean, it's been almost a week now since Tinti was murdered. Are we *certain* this is the murder weapon, and not just a similar Glock someone tossed into the bin a few days ago?"

"I wondered about that too, Dalton." Anisa's tone now sounded warmer. "But there was a sanitation worker's strike here that ended either the day you and your team arrived, or maybe the day after. Apparently, it's taking them a while to catch up. Which, as it turns out, was to our benefit."

Lee came up with one other possible lead.

"Where in the dumpster did they find it? I mean, was it in a certain corner? Was it dead-center?" He winced after that unintended pun but decided to plunge ahead. "I'm wondering if we can determine the direction from which the murderer tossed the gun. Whether they were walking north, or headed west?"

"It was in the northeast corner of the bin, I do know that," C. J. answered. "But Dalton, experience tells me it's impossible to extract anything from that. If it were tossed with any meaningful velocity, it likely caromed off one of the walls."

"So . . . the gun is of no help then?" Lee set his smoothie down on the table next to his bed and strolled over to the window. The sky was sepia colored, even though it was only approaching noon. *Does London get dust storms,* he wondered.

"Not necessarily," Anisa replied. "We're checking our underground channels to see if anyone here has sold a gun like it in the past few weeks. It's doubtful, but not outside the realm of possibility. Remember, this isn't America. The black market for these types of weapons is a lot smaller here than it is where you're from, Dalton. Who knows, maybe we'll get lucky and stumble on a transaction."

"Well, it's been absolutely jolly talking to the both of you," C. J. interrupted, "but I must vamoose. I'm already late for a meeting at

Number 10 about the G7 summit. You two carry on, and I'll check back with you in the afternoon. *Sayonara*."

There was a click. He and Anisa were now alone on the line.

"Would you be interested in meeting me for a private social appointment?" he blurted, his eyes squeezed tight as he delivered the line he had practiced repeatedly. There was no reply for several seconds. Lee thought he was going to die.

Finally, she responded. "You mean . . . a date?"

Now, Lee *was certain* he was going to die. "Well, I think of it more as . . . um . . ."

"I'd love to, Dalton. Why don't we meet for cocktails at Club Canton? Say about eight?"

He was impressed. Club Canton was all carved wood and gold leaf—tony to say the least. But it wasn't her suggestion of an opulent location that impressed him. It was her suggestion of a place that was the intersection of the two things he cherished most—elegance and Chinese culture. Somehow, she had already found a way to push his buttons . . . which made him anxious.

"Oh . . . okay," he said just as his phone began to tumble from his hand. He miraculously caught it midfall by thrusting his free hand across his torso to grasp it, the way a right fielder might snare a smacked line drive.

"Great. See you then." She clicked off before he could respond. Lee stood beside his bed for a couple of moments, staring at his phone. Eventually, he shook his head a couple of times. Sighed some.

"So," he whispered to the room. "That just happened."

***

"Sounds like your night with the waitress was festy."

Liam was sitting sideways in one of the dining room chairs, his feet propped upon the chair next to him. He was wearing a navy-blue t-shirt and frayed jeans and his laptop was near his right elbow. He had offered the comment to Bree, who was seated across the table, but his attention was riveted to the screen in front of him.

She was knitting again, her ball of yarn decidedly smaller than it had been a couple of days earlier. A sly smile came across her lips. "You wouldn't have believed it, Liam. I mean, it wasn't *horrid*, it was just . . . icky. She's very odd. The place was a mess. And then there was that cat."

Liam aimlessly tapped a few keys. "What do you make of the note the tailor left?"

Bree quickly dipped her head to one side as she contemplated the question. But then she turned toward him and took on a questioning expression.

"Are we flirting with one another?"

"What?! No! I'm not, are you?"

Bree paused. "No, of course not. It's just, you know, what they were saying about us a couple of days ago. That you and I were . . . having an affair. Or trying to. I'm not, at all. But I just wanted to be sure we were on the same page with that."

Liam continued to stare at his computer screen. He had either had been deaf to her comment . . . or was ignoring it.

After a while she asked, "What are you reading?"

He let out a deep, sad sigh.

"It's one of those stupid online ads. For some psychic. I'm trying to figure out what it is about these ads that make otherwise rational people hand over their life savings to someone they don't even know. I read somewhere that some of these scumbags can pull in up to a million a year off elderly people. I don't get why they're allowed to get away with it." He took in a large breath, glanced in her direction, but not at her. "You didn't answer my question. What do you make of the note?"

"I dunno," she replied, her fingers working more feverishly. "Dalton doesn't think Tinti had the *cajones* to get himself mixed up in something nefarious." The speed of her hands was such her needles began occasionally to clack. "But I'm not entirely convinced he's right. It's the meek and timid ones you always have to keep your eyes on."

"Don't you think that note was sorta weird?" Liam still wasn't looking at her. The discreet movement of his lips told her he was reading something on the screen.

"What do you mean? It said HELP ME. Two simple words. What's weird about that?"

He glanced up and over the screen to her.

"I didn't mean the wording of the note was weird, just that . . ." He went back to the computer and typed a few characters. "I meant, isn't it a weird note for him to have written if he were truly involved in something illegal? What sort of person who has voluntarily chosen to deal drugs, or run guns, or traffic thirteen-year-olds, or whatever, suddenly asks a waitress to help him? What's *she* going to do? How is *she* going to help? If he really wanted help to get out of some illegal activity or blackmail situation, he'd just go to the police, wouldn't he?"

Bree looked sideways at her associate. Liam didn't usually display such an interest in the deduction part of an investigation. She was pretty impressed with his first attempt to do so.

"I guess . . . I mean, that makes sense to me," she quietly replied. She moved her needles some more, then stopped. "Unless, maybe, he was so deep into the activity he was afraid he'd be sent to prison if the police found out?"

Liam shook his head.

"Naw. He'd get immunity if it was something really big and he could hand over the power brokers. Besides, where would he have found the time and the opportunity to be involved in something so complex? He worked all day in a clothing shop. People knew where he always ate breakfast, where he ate lunch. From what you've told me, they could even tell you which booth he always sat in. It's not like he was some sort of lorry driver who could go missing for a few hours whenever he wanted to."

He fell silent for a moment and went back to reading words on the screen. Then he shook his head twice, as if trying to rouse himself out of a trance.

"Naw, the more I think about it, I don't think he was asking Mariam for help at all. I think he knew something, had possession of something, and was afraid of what might happen to him because of it. He wasn't asking Mariam for help, he was asking the universe for help. Because he felt trapped. Like some rabbit surrounded by foxes."

Bree continued to knit and watch Liam out of the corner of her eye. She was amazed by how he was able to effectively scan the constantly changing information displayed on multiple browser windows simultaneously. And keep a conversation going with her (sort of) as well. His head darted left, then right, then left again; now and then he'd lean forward and tap a few keys on his computer. She became accustomed to his rhythm; relaxed into it some.

And then, it all changed.

"Whoa, what's this?" the Aussie suddenly barked. He thrust his head forward, moved his lips rapidly, then shoved his upper body against the back of his chair, placed both hands on top of his head and let out a long exhale. "Fuck me dead," he uttered.

"What?" Bree replied, dropping her knitting to one side and dashing over to peer over Liam's shoulders. Silently, she read the sentences on the screen he'd been reviewing, putting her right hand on his right shoulder as she did so.

"Wait, what's that a reply to? Scroll up," she commanded. Liam did as she instructed, and she read the beginning of the chat message he had come across. Put her left hand on his left shoulder and pressed both her palms down to steady herself. Let out a deep exhale as well.

"Oh my God," she whispered into Liam's left ear. "If that doesn't confirm Tinti's son was somehow involved with The Organization, I don't know what does."

30

"So, tell me again. *Why* are we buying groceries?"

He wasn't pushing the trolley down the aisle so much as thrusting it forward with the sole of his right jackboot. Despite her age, and the arthritis in her hip, she was doing a fairly good job of keeping up with him, lagging only a step or two behind.

"Well, we're buying groceries because . . ." She paused as she strained to reach a higher shelf filled with baking-related items. "Fetch me one of those bags of sugar, would ya' luv?" she asked, her breath labored from the stretch. "That one. The seventy-five-gram size." He complied, placing the sugar into the trolley for her, and then used his boot to shove the conveyance forward once again.

"As I was saying, we're *buying groceries,* because I am out of chocolate and pizza toppings and dog biscuits for Molly," she responded. "Also, I want to make a pie." She waddled a little faster to catch up with her companion; once she did, she lowered her voice to a register just above a whisper.

"We're *in a grocery store,* however, because I figured you were far less likely to erupt in an outburst here like the one you had when we passed each other on the crescent the other day. I can't believe you uttered which level the attack had been elevated to!"

Although she wasn't carrying a coat the way she had that day, she appeared to him to be just as rotund. Maybe more so.

"Sugar?" he said. "Chocolate? Pizza toppings? *That* doesn't sound like a very nutritious diet, Charlotte."

She ambled forward, flashed a sarcastic smile that she knew he wouldn't see given he was now three full lengths ahead of her.

"Nigel, when you get to be my age, you'll view proper nutrition as a worthwhile but quaint relic of the past, like shining one's shoes every Sunday evening or taking all of one's woolens to the cleaners in early September."

He pushed the trolley, which edged forward a few inches then suddenly veered to the right and smashed into a display of mayonnaise. He grabbed hold of its handle, repositioned it for a straight maneuver down the aisle, then nudged it once again with his foot.

"Oh, and I didn't . . ." He was wagging his head from one side to the other. "I didn't erupt in an 'outburst.' I was merely taken aback, that's all. I mean, aren't you more than a bit surprised at the level . . ."

He could feel the admonishing frown piercing him from behind and chose to soften his voice in obedient response.

"Aren't you surprised with, you know, the *severity* of what we're expected to do?"

They rounded the end of the aisle and started up the next.

"Oh, now, would you look at that! Molly's favorite biscuits are on sale!" she announced with glee. "Now *that's* going to be light on me pocketbook, it is." She set the biscuits in the back of the trolley, then placed one palm on the young man's back.

"Let me explain something to you, Nigel. When you've been working to bring about The Transformation for as long as I have, you're not surprised by anything. Or you shouldn't be, that is. You need to understand, luv, I watched limbs jettison from torsos when we bombed that bank in Johannesburg. Saw children stagger blood stained and bruised from beneath that shopping mall we caused to collapse in New Delhi. It's gut-wrenching at the time, certainly. It can even make you wonder at night if you're still a human being. But, when you're truly committed to helping people throughout the world know the unimaginable joy of conquering the elitists who control them, it's simply something you prepare yourself for. It's what you come to expect.

"It's what you choose to become hardened to."

She moved her head to one side, squinted at him a bit. "You *are* committed to The Transformation, aren't you, Nigel? You're not just participating in it as a lark, I hope. I do so want to believe that you are fully, wholeheartedly committed."

He nodded, slowly at first, then with much greater enthusiasm. "Of course, I am, Charlotte. You know that. I *want* you to know that. I want you to be *completely confident* that I am totally committed to the cause."

Her head was still tilted to one side, but her expression shifted from concern to satisfaction. "Wonderful," she replied. "Now *that's* the sort of vigor I like to see in our associates."

She glanced around them, coughed once. "It's probably time we get around to discussing how things stand . . ."

But a young father with two kids in tow was now approaching them from the other direction. She turned toward the shelf nearest her and pretended to inspect the nutritional details on a jar of peanut butter. Once the family had finally passed, Nigel raised his eyebrows in her direction; she indicated it was all right to proceed.

"Did I hear that the shipment we've been expecting successfully arrived at Heathrow?" he asked. As they turned into the next aisle, she nodded. She stopped to consider a large bag of marshmallows, decided against it.

"And the people we hired to manage that shipment for us. They performed as we needed them to?"

Again, she nodded as she tossed a tin of cocoa powder into the trolley.

"They sent the correct number of briefcases? And those briefcases look identical to . . . those they are going to replace?"

She crouched low to read the price of several cans of condensed milk sitting in a box on the floor. In response to his question, she looked up at him, smiled broadly, and nodded once again without saying anything. Groaning some as she stood erect, she placed several cans of the milk into the trolley.

"Well, good then," he replied. "You know, Charlotte, I conducted a significant amount of research to identify just the right accomplices for that job. Finding just the right items for this assignment and getting them shipped from one hemisphere to another without raising anyone's suspicions were no easy tasks, believe me. I'm pleased to hear it all went as . . . perfectly . . . as it did."

She glanced over at him and shook her head slightly as she began to stroll down the aisle toward the dairy section.

"So I guess that means everything is set to unroll in a few days? And that you are happy with my oversight of this part of the assignment?"

It wasn't clear whether she let out a sigh of exasperation or a grunt of discomfort. Probably both. But when she looked back at him, her expression was one of a proud relative, even though they'd known one another for only a few months.

"Yes, quite happy," she answered.

She slid her purse off her shoulder and carefully unlocked the clasp. She then plunged her left hand in and rummaged around until she landed on what she was looking for. Finally, she raised that hand out of the purse as deliberately as she had lowered it.

"You've performed exceedingly well over the past couple of weeks, Nigel. I am very pleased with the outcomes. I'd say you deserve a little reward, don't you?"

He looked down at her outstretched palm and was delighted to find it held a Double Decker candy, ready for the taking.

31

Their delve into the background of Niccolò Tinti was swift and comprehensive. And it revealed that the twenty-two-year old was as unremarkable as his father, if not more so: Average student who dropped out of university after his first year of study. Two minor run-ins with the law, one for possession of marijuana, the other for vagrancy while he was staying with a friend in Liverpool.

"His father was a Savile Row tailor. Why would he resort to begging in public?" Lee asked C. J. He heard a low whooshing sound on the other end of the phone, like air conditioning vents operating on high. The sound would ebb, then ascend, then ebb again, then ascend again. "And, are you . . . vacuuming your office?"

The whoosh went away, then returned.

"Yes," she replied bluntly. "We had a bit of a mishap here in my office. The cleaning crew won't be here for several hours so I'm taking care of it." He waited for her to elaborate but soon realized that wasn't going to happen.

"Mishap?" he probed.

"Yes. A mishap. Or, as the Germans would say, *ein unfall*. With . . . some chocolate."

Lee burst into a silent smile. "No doubt some *drinking* chocolate."

The whooshing intensified for a couple of moments, then ceased altogether. He heard some low grunting on the other end and what sounded like the canister of the vacuum slamming into something metal. In time, C. J. returned to the conversation.

"No doubt," she said softly.

The architect decided to abandon his question about the vagrancy charge. "What about the friend in Liverpool? Any link between him and The Organization?"

"It was a her. And no. She's a part-time bank teller, part-time actress. As best we've been able to tell, their friendship centered more around a passion for cannabis than a passion for terrorism."

Lee nodded as C. J. spoke. "Well, I think we've come across something here on our end, C. J. Liam was doing some online research and came across a message Tinti's son sent across one of the channels The Organization likes to use. To be more precise, Tinti's son answered a job listing."

"A job listing? What type of job?"

"A courier job. Someone was looking for a courier to retrieve a set of identical luggage. At Heathrow."

C. J. was silent for some time. "I see. Just one message?"

"Yes. I'm guessing he accepted the job and they then took their correspondence underground. And I should be clear that Liam hasn't *definitively* traced that listing to The Organization, but . . ."

"But it's probably only a matter of time before he does." C. J. went quiet again, then perked up. "I must say, Dalton, that Liam of yours is quite the Sherlock Holmes. Or given his nationality, maybe I should say, quite the Crocodile Dundee? I'm very impressed with the contributions he's made to this investigation so far. I think he'd make a splendid fit with the rest of us here at Scotland Yard."

Lee didn't say anything for several seconds. But when he did, his response was good-natured but stern.

"Don't you dare, C. J." he muttered softly. "Don't you even dare."

***

When he spotted her in the banquette, his knees buckled. Fortunately,

209

there was a small railing nearby for Lee to clutch onto as he descended the small staircase leading into Club Canton's private dining lounge. She wore her hair down and it sprawled luxuriously across her tanned shoulders. Her emerald green dress was form fitting, but not revealing. She had obviously spent a great deal of time on her eye makeup for he noticed her eyes in a way he never had before. Intensely dark lashes framed gray-green irises that hypnotized him (even though she was looking not at him but at her phone, which was resting on the tabletop). Her lip color was soft and subdued.

Thank heavens I didn't choose the rep tie, he told himself.

As best he could tell, she had reserved the private dining lounge for just the two of them. A dining lounge that served *twelve people.* Reserved, for *just the two of them.*

"Hello," he said, barely loud enough for her to hear. Anisa glanced up, beamed, and slid her phone to the far side of the table.

"Hello, Mr. Lee. Glad you could make it. Why don't you sit here at the end of the table? The appropriate seat for the boss, wouldn't you say?"

He did as he was told, sliding into the fuchsia-hued club chair with a rounded back. Quickly, he clasped the hand of hers closest to him and glanced around absent-mindedly.

"Wow. This place is packed. I hope the service doesn't suffer."

She chuckled but immediately removed her hand and lowered her head as a waiter approached to take their drink orders. "I'd like a Mother of Pearl," she said with confidence. "With the most top-shelf tequila you have in stock."

Lee looked over at her, arched both eyebrows. "Tequila? Really? And it's accompanied by . . ." He checked the menu in front of him. "Blood orange shrub and pomegranate molasses. Well. Okay then."

The waiter nodded, cocked his head in Lee's direction. "And you, sir?"

Lee scanned the cocktail offerings, didn't find what he was seeking but decided it wouldn't hurt to ask.

"I don't see Buffalo Trace bourbon on here . . . do you carry it?"

The waiter frowned, shook his head. "I'm sorry, sir, I'm afraid we don't."

The architect looked pleadingly at the waiter. "You sure?"

The waiter's expression went from sympathetic to peeved.

"*Quite* sure."

Lee blew a little air through his lips, perused the menu further. Eventually he chose to veer toward the conservative end of the spectrum.

"All right then, a Bombay Star for me. Easy on the frankincense bitters, please."

The waiter departed and Anisa leaned forward.

"That's a terrific tie, by the way."

Lee beamed on the inside, played coy on the outside. "Oh, this old thing? I found it in a vintage shop in Milan," he replied. "I almost didn't wear it tonight. I thought it might be a little . . ." He stopped to study the lavishness around them. "A little staid for the occasion."

"The Great Dalton Lee? Staid? *Never!*" she said with a deep laugh.

He wanted to study her, like a portrait in the Louvre. He reached down and fiddled with a trouser cuff instead. *Well, this seems to be going well,* he said to himself.

They invested some time toward getting to know one another. She shared how she grew up the smartest kid in her town back in Jordan, and how she cobbled together a host of scholarships to first attend Cambridge, then the University of California at Berkeley.

"Did you know I also went to Cambridge?" Lee said with a wink.

"You're a Cantab, too? Get out!" She smiled, shook her head in amazement. "Such a marvelous experience I had there. Have you been back recently? Are you going to go visit while you're here?"

He reflected on the question. "You know, it *would* be great to see old Cam again."

She slapped at his forearm. "Oh, you must Dalton! You won't believe how much it's changed. And, how much it hasn't." He resolved to find the time for a quick visit.

She went on to relate how she had planned to become an archaeologist, but that law enforcement had stolen her away from excavation sites. "I have this intense need to see justice prevail," she said. "The reward you get from bringing in a criminal is immensely more satisfying than the one you get from unearthing a mastodon tusk, believe me."

Later, when he became the focus of their conversation, he downplayed his ascent to the position of the world's preeminent architect but did share insights into some of his favorite projects. "There's just something about taking the angles and arcs and planes we're all used to seeing and rearranging them in a way that's fresh and unexpected," he told her. "I suppose that's another way of imposing justice onto a dangerous, disorderly world."

"Well, it's the way *you* do it," she whispered. "And, you do it very well."

He swallowed hard, had to admit he was enthralled with everything about her. She was bright but not haughty. Gorgeous but down-to-earth. And at this very moment, smiling at him with a look of . . . was it longing? he hoped.

She sat back and assumed a more serious mood. "So, we now believe Mr. Tinti's son may have been involved in The Organization, is that right?"

Lee took a sip of water, nodded as he swallowed it.

"Yes. We don't have a lock-solid connection yet, but it makes sense. We do know the younger Tinti agreed to transport several suitcases being sent to Heathrow, which means he likely was involved in whatever scheme The Organization has planned here. And likely confided as much to his father before he was killed. There's no evidence The Organization orchestrated the son's accident, so it appears that was an unfortunate coincidence.

"Somehow, The Organization learned that Niccolò Tinti had told his father about the plot. Maybe because he wanted to back out, or maybe because he hoped to recruit his father to join the cause."

Anisa winced. "Are we certain the latter didn't happen? Maybe that's why they killed the father? Maybe Tinti *did* get involved and then double-crossed them later."

The waiter came to take their orders, then swiftly departed. Lee contemplated Anisa's premise and as he did, the strains of a jazz combo beginning a set floated into the room from the floor above them.

"Well, I guess that's not out of the realm of possibility," he acknowledged. "I can't *prove* that isn't what happened. But . . ."

"But what?" She was leaning forward again and the bouquet coming from her was intoxicating Lee more than the cocktail he had ordered. A cocktail that Lee had deemed a liberal pour, to say the least.

"But, terrorist and double-crosser doesn't fit Tinti's profile, does it? Remember, Tinti was boring. His whereabouts were predictable. And Liam said it best, I think. When would he have found the time? The poor sap didn't have a wealth of spare time to begin with it seems, much less enough spare time to commit to a complicated operation like those The Organization carries out."

Anisa took an extended sip of her Mother of Pearl. Lee sensed the tequila was beginning to relax her inhibitions.

"You know what frustrates me the most about this, Dalton? Even if everything you say proves true, our knowing *why* Tinti got killed doesn't seem like much of an achievement. We still don't know *who* murdered him, and we don't know what it is The Organization's planning to do here. And we have to figure out the former, if we're going to stop the latter."

A surge of passion swelled up in Lee. It was as if someone had suddenly upended the table from below, and he felt an obligation to straighten it and rescue her from the upheaval at the same time. He had nothing but the best of intentions, but he felt compulsions to protect her, encourage her . . . and pounce upon her.

That's when the exotic dancer arrived.

Dressed all in gold, the young woman with the dark brown tresses didn't dance into the room so much as slither into it, undulating her hips and bosoms and shoulders in such a way that Lee was reminded of the online description he had read of a toy that had been popular in the 1950s:

**A Slinky can perform a number of tricks,
including traveling down a flight of steps
end-over-end as it stretches and re-forms itself
with the aid of gravity and its own momentum,
or appearing to levitate for a period of time . . .**

Well, she was definitely levitating right now, immediately beside the world's most prominent architect. Within a couple of inches of him, to be exact. Her moisturized fingers swept across his cheek and chin, her thighs intertwined with his. She would turn that way, before violently swiveling one hundred and eighty degrees, this way. Lee felt as if he were being entertained by a cyclone drenched in emollients and colognes.

And the next thing he knew, he was dancing alongside her. He hadn't volunteered, of course. The dancer had pulled him from his chair and spun him around, with one arm of hers wrapped around his waist. He wasn't quite sure what sort of step they were doing—to Lee it felt like a samba mashed up with a fox trot. With a little bit of The Twist (or was it The Watusi?) thrown in. This involuntary display both aroused and embarrassed the architect, but when he got the chance to look over at Anisa, her chin was propped in both of her palms and she wore a look of bemusement on her face.

The *pas de deux* ended as abruptly as it had begun, leaving Lee in a whirl of bewilderment.

Anisa clapped her hands lightly. "Bravo. Encore," she said softly.

Lee shook his head back and forth, as if to dislodge an attic full of cobwebs. "No encore, please. That should never have happened. And I'm not entirely sure *how* it happened. I'm so sorry, Anisa. That was disrespectful of me."

She slapped at him again. "Oh, Dalton, don't be silly, it was fun. No need to apologize. You looked giddy with delight. No one should take that away from you."

He straightened his tie, brushed his finger down the bridge of his nose. Picked up his napkin and took a quick spoonful of the king crab sweetcorn soup he had ordered.

She gently placed a palm on the back of his free hand. "I'm glad we did this. I was hoping we could spend some quiet time together."

"Yes," was all he said.

She carved into one of the wasabi prawns on her plate, took a delicate bite, and chewed in silence. He flashed a quick smile at her, which she returned before consuming another bit of prawn. Neither said a word for several moments.

He felt very warm. He wasn't sure if it was from the soup, the dancing, or . . .

As they dined, the ambience in the club shifted slightly. The jazz trio above them, which had been playing smoky ballads, had at some point veered into pop classics more suitable for a hotel lobby bar. Lee wasn't fond of the style of music, but he did like the tune they were playing at the moment, a 1970s Top Ten hit by a group called The Doobie Brothers. As he finished his soup, he realized he was silently humming the chorus, something about what a fool believes, and how no wise man possesses the power to use his reason to dismiss what he wants to be.

Or, something like that.

"So, I was thinking, Anisa, that maybe . . ."

"Yes?"

"That perhaps we might, um . . ." He hesitated, looked down at his empty soup bowl. "There's this cottage in the Lake District I've had my eye on. For some time really. I've gotten to know the owner quite well, have let him know I want to buy it from him whenever he's ready to sell. Anyway, I can rent the cottage pretty much any weekend, and so I thought, maybe . . ."

He glanced up . . . and froze. When he had looked away from her to take a spoonful of soup, she was beaming with contentment. When he looked back at her, however, her expression had changed to befuddlement. And then, embarrassment.

"Oh, Dalton, I . . . didn't realize. You had . . . you have . . . romantic feelings? Oh, my gosh . . ."

He felt warm again. Much, much warmer than before. "Well . . . I . . ."

"I'm *so* sorry, Dalton. I had no idea. I feel just awful. I mean, I have a steady boyfriend. Well, sort of. These days, he's spending most of his time in South Africa, managing a couple of the diamond mines down there. We see each other every month or so. Maybe it's every six weeks. Anyway, we're quite serious, and . . ."

"I see. Really, it's fine . . ."

"I mean, it's an absolute privilege and all, that you, of all people . . ."

"Not to worry, Anisa, really. It's nothing for you to be ashamed of. Wait. That's not what I meant. What I meant was . . ."

A waiter approached to take away their plates. They dropped the conversation and rearranged their napkins and utensils until the server had removed himself from the vicinity.

Anisa chose to resume the dialogue. "Look, Dalton. I need to say something. I am flattered beyond the moon, I truly am. You're incredibly charming, and so cute and all, and . . ."

"Cute? You think I'm *cute?*"

She leaned forward and took hold of his forearm. "Cute is a good thing, Dalton. Got it?" One side of his mouth crinkled some. She'd melted his indignance.

"I may not be in a position to have a romance with you, but, funny enough, I wanted to come here tonight because I do have a proposition, of sorts, I'd like to make."

He arched an eyebrow. "A proposition?"

She leaned in even closer, and it took every fiber in his being to lower his heart rate and focus his vision.

"Earlier this week I got a message from my family. Over time, they've scattered around the world, but the largest bloc is still in Jordan. There's this cousin. Growing up, we were like brother and sister, we did *everything* together, even attended some of the same university classes. I got my degree in archaeology and he became a photojournalist.

"Anyway, last week he went missing. He was working on some investigative piece he was being pretty discreet about, except to say it had something to do with the psychology of terrorism. He had been working on it for over a year and I'm guessing he had stuck his nose into a lot of places he probably shouldn't have. Anyway, this week, my family told me that . . . they . . ."

Lee felt as if his internal organs were on an elevator that was plummeting to the bottom of its shaft.

"They received a body part?"

She nodded, tears welling up in her eyes.

"Which . . . ?"

"He was a *photo*journalist, so . . ."

The elevator inside him plummeted to the basement.

"One of his *eyes?*"

She nodded again, more rapidly. Her palm began to clutch his forearm with intensity. "Dalton, I actually do want a relationship with you, but a professional one. Here's my proposition—I want to join your team. I *need* to join your team.

"As quickly as I possibly can."

32

Lee thought it disturbing enough this rendezvous had to take place on the verge of midnight. It didn't help that it was also taking place immediately after his evening with Anisa, and everything that experience had delivered.

But seriously, Lee thought as he neared the unlocked gate he'd been told to enter, *whose bright idea was it to put an amusement park for children on a site with the name Kilburn? Kill. Burn. I mean, whoever's responsible for the marketing of this place ought to be . . .*

A breeze had kicked up, and from somewhere nearby it carried a sharp industrial smell, like sewer gas. *Well, that could certainly explain the "burn" part,* he thought.

And, the sky seemed off to him. There was no forecast for bad weather, but the late-night clouds had a green-gray cast. Even the glow of the moon behind them appeared hesitant, erratic, as if it were a bulb connected to a rheostat that someone was nudging first one way, then the other. Then there was the wind, which blew gently most of the time but would occasionally surge unexpectedly in a way that caused Lee's lapels to flap.

Undeterred, however, he prodded himself on to his appointment.

When the word "appointment" came to mind, he began to reflect on

Anisa and the "private social appointment" of theirs he had left forty-five minutes ago. He wasn't sure what to make of it, how to respond to her request. On one hand, he was eager to bring her onto the team immediately. Now that The Organization had kidnapped someone close to her, she certainly fulfilled the primary requirement for being a part of his team. And her background in archaeology would certainly make it easier for her to pass as a member of his architectural firm.

And yet, hadn't he just threatened C. J. when she hinted she might like to poach Liam and install the young Aussie on *her* team? His threat was in jest, but still . . .

The more he thought about it, the more certain he became that Anisa's connection to the investigation should remain indirect for now. Perhaps, when the timing felt right, he could engage C. J. into a conversation about Anisa's future.

It took him more than a couple of moments to find the metal gate he had been instructed to enter. But as he approached it, the gate swung open several inches, creaking softly as it did.

Must have been a breeze, he assured himself (even though no breeze had been blowing when the gate opened). He inspected the gate closely as he crept through the narrow gap its opening had provided. It looked like every standard-issue metal gate he had ever seen. When he shut it behind him, however, he thought he detected a click that made the closing seem more secure than normal. He took a couple of steps backward, pushed the gate with three fingers.

It wouldn't budge. Tried again. Same result.

But he didn't panic. With both hands, he could easily vault the gate if he needed to, and really, why would he even need to? *This is a carnival site,* he reminded himself. *And I know very well the person I'm meeting. I shouldn't have any need to flee this place, even at this hour.*

Out of curiosity, he nudged the gate once more, only with substantially more force.

Locked tight.

He turned toward the center of the grange and squinted to identify the forms ahead. The amusement rides looked not like instruments of entertainment but like monsters from some sci-fi flick. Supporting towers, in the dark, became menacing giants; the rides themselves resembled remnants of some alien invasion.

I find nothing about this place even remotely amusing, Lee declared to himself.

He trudged on but had no idea where he was heading. He could barely see the end of his nose, so he was unclear how he was supposed to spot the person who had summoned him. He suddenly tensed when a critter skittered across the top of his shoe. *Probably a rat,* he told himself.

It was two rats, one twice the size of the other.

And then came a screech. On his right, very close. At first, he thought it was the call from an owl. Instead, it came from one of the rides, one of the tamer attractions that locked fairgoers into several sleigh-like compartments and then hurtled them in a circle as the floor rose and fell beneath them. The floor of the contraption was moving ever so slightly, causing metal to scream on metal. And yet, there was no wind coming across the grange to propel the ride forward.

"Quit toying with me," Dalton called out. "I know it's you."

The only response was the continued shriek of steel. But now it was coming at a lower pitch and lasting much longer than before. Over time, it became barely audible, then ceased.

That's when the wind resumed, with enough force to almost topple the architect. Somewhere nearby, he heard a scuffing of shoes, then, "I'm on your left, Dalton, not your right."

Lee steadied himself in the sudden gale and squinted over his left shoulder, ducking his head forward. "How was I supposed to find you when you're wearing nothing but black?" he said to the indistinct form.

"You weren't supposed to find me," came the reply. "I was supposed to find you."

Lee didn't know how to respond to that—decided not to. He shoved his head forward again and widened his eyes to take in more of his counterpart.

"That outfit . . . it makes you look like a bat." He heard a scoff.

"Likely not the first time someone has thought that."

Lee edged closer and, as he did, the other person floated nearer to close the gap. "I hate to tell you this—well, no, I don't really *hate* to tell you this because you really need to know—these rendezvous of ours are starting to grate on my nerves," he said.

"I know. And I completely understand, Dalton. I'd even go so far as to say I sympathize. That's why I've decided to be a bit more forthcoming with you during this little chat of ours."

"Forthcoming?"

"Yes. As to what's in store. Of course, I'm not going to divulge the type of data that would let you and your colleagues thwart our plans. But I *can* give you some pertinent details that should make your trek out here worthwhile."

Lee waited. Sensing the architect was not as enthused by the announcement as one might expect, the speaker decided to elaborate.

"The Transformation is set to begin sooner rather than later, Dalton. Within the week, actually. There's really nothing you can do about it; we've plotted each step with expert precision. I really do like you, so I urge you to remember what I said when we met in the Greenwich Tunnel. Properly considered, expertly analyzed, our conversation there could provide your team with a critical insight . . . some meaningful clue.

"But it's also important you realize it would be pure folly to try to stop our campaign. We're more sophisticated than we were in Miami, and far more strategic than we were in Manhattan. And, we're confident the masses are—how should I word it—more inclined to our point of view? Look at the Brexit vote not long ago, the recent elections in your country and in Germany. Citizens everywhere have grown intolerant of the status quo. They no longer buy the argument that constitutions and bills of rights and covenants and regulations are in their best interest. They know they can manage things far better on their own if someone will just grant them the freedom to do so."

"And you actually believe you and your group of misguided misfits are the ones to do that?"

"That's a bit harsh, don't you think?" The form went silent for several seconds before adding, "Yes, we believe not only that we are the group who can do that, but also the group who *should* do that. To lead the masses to a place of enlightenment that will help them feel as though they are self-directed individuals, not slaves to the ruling class. Encourage them to throw off the shackles that come with common law and inhale the unadulterated euphoria that comes with shaping the quality of one's own existence.

"We're going to carry those imprisoned souls to the river, Dalton, and allow them to drink the water of unfettered freedom. Sooner than you might have imagined."

The wind had abated again. Which was unfortunate, for never had Lee so wished for a gust to blow someone to the opposite end of the universe as he did at this moment. He was seething but was able to restrain his fury before he uttered his response.

"Let me be perfectly clear about one thing," he began. "There is not going to be any Transformation. If I have to travel to the end of the earth and spend every single cent I've saved over the course of my entire career, I will prevent you and your deranged followers from destroying everything freedom-loving people hold dear.

"Mark my words. You *will not* prevail."

The other person shifted from one foot to the other, then back again. Lee had the distinct impression his tirade had landed like a balled-up fist to the solar plexus, although in the dark, he couldn't detect an expression that would supply evidence of that. But he felt like he was on a roll, so he decided to press on.

"Why do you call me to these lectures? What purpose do they serve you? Because I've begun to seriously question what benefit I get out of them. They seem to bring me more taunting than assistance; more shadows than clarity. Really, why do you bother?"

Several moments of silence elapsed. Eventually, Lee heard a sharp intake of breath.

"You know very well *the why,* Dalton. Or, maybe I should say, *the who.* I need to be sure you continue to protect . . . the one I love dearly. You promised you would do that and so far, you've kept your word.

"I'm not about to abandon my colleagues. I cannot risk expulsion by those who've shown me the exquisite tomorrow that beckons from afar. But I *can* turn you in the right direction, dissuade you from some incorrect assumption. Offer a reasonable time frame, suggest a plausible locale, all as a gesture of my gratitude. That's why I keep calling you. Take it or leave it."

The wind returned. Only this time it was a soothing flow, as if they were on a schooner traversing some alpine lake. But then, Lee noticed on the near horizon a phenomenon he had read about, but never observed. Jagged, reddish-orange tentacles, located just above a wall of storm clouds, that flickered as they traveled toward the sky.

"What in the hell . . .?" he muttered.

His companion glanced casually over one shoulder and nodded. "Ah, red sprites. Electrical sparks packed with nitrogen gas just above an active thunderstorm."

"Yes, I know what they are," Lee replied, his mouth still agape. "But one rarely sees them from the ground. Usually, one needs a telescope to see them. And rarely are they so enormous. And so . . . vivid."

The other person smirked at the architect. "Thank you, Dalton. I appreciate the compliment." At that, the flare flickered two or three times, then vanished.

Lee looked at his companion, then back at the now-dark sky, then back at his companion. He sighed, shook his head in frustration.

"So do you have any other fascinating information to share with me?" he asked. An update on the condition of my parents, perhaps? Has the chafing from the manacles you locked them in all these years gone away? Do you still have them blindfolded, or have you somehow found it within your hearts to restore their sense of sight to them?" Even in the darkness, Lee could sense the penetrating look of disdain being sent his way.

"Really, Dalton, that was unnecessary." Several seconds of silence passed. Then, "For what it's worth, your mother is doing quite well. She's made a friend or two since we relocated your parents to their new . . . surroundings. She did take a bit of a tumble a few days ago. Tripped on the corner of a carpet, or something like that. No broken bones, fortunately, although she did come away with a mild contusion to the skull, I'm told."

"You bastards, I will . . ." Lee saw a sallow palm jut up in front of him.

"No. Truly, Dalton. She took a spill. Apparently, her equilibrium hasn't quite stabilized since we . . . released her. I'm told she will be fine over time and that the sensation in her inner ears should normalize in a couple of days."

"And my father? Has he completed his—what did you call it— matriculation?"

"Not quite. He has a couple more milestones to achieve before we consider him an initiate. But that shouldn't take long. Another month or so at most, I'd say."

"And you still persist with this folly that he's committed to joining all of you?"

"Yes. As I told you before, he said to tell you he's never been so serious about anything in his entire life. If you insist on some type of confirmation, I'm sure we have a recording of his interrogation . . . I mean, his interview . . . somewhere."

The dark form shuffled some. "Now, I'm sorry, but I must go. Things are unfolding quite rapidly. Truly, Dalton, it's important you understand we are, at most, a few days away from launch time."

And with that, Lee found himself alone in the grange's vast expanse. He heard another metallic creak behind him. This time, however, it did not startle him, did not even make him wince.

But when he turned to look in the direction of the noise, two images caught his attention. A red sprite bursting brighter than any before it, and the man in the moon sporting a look of despair.

33

It was the most glorious weather Lee had ever encountered in London. The most glorious weather he had encountered in all the time he'd spent in *all of England,* for that matter.

The sky wasn't just blue, it was a glorious, cerulean blue, with clouds so white, so fluffy, so evenly spaced apart, their perfection was laughable. A serious autumn front had swept through the city overnight, lowering the temperature by fifteen degrees. Absent, however, was the dampness one might associate with a chilly autumn day in London town.

Most certainly gone was the smell of sulfur, as well as the bursts from red sprites high in the sky.

To make the day even more delightful, Lee's Maicoletta was now scratch-free.

"Well, thank God for *that*," C. J. said when he informed her over the phone of the scooter's return to service. "I didn't think we were *ever* going to hear the end of your misery over that laceration."

"C. J., it wasn't a . . . oh, never mind." The architect took a quick nibble out of the apricot, blueberry, and ginger scone that Margarida had fetched for him from a nearby bakery. "So, what's on our agenda for today?"

"Well, I think it's time we confront Mr. Hensleigh about those mysterious messages he was sharing online with Mr. Fakhoury. Those messages about shipments that they didn't want our dear friends in customs to notice."

"Good. Yes, I was thinking the same thing. I know Liam's still trying to connect those messages to whoever sent those communiqués about baggage arriving at Heathrow. Maybe Mr. Hensleigh will inadvertently connect the dots for us there."

"You know, Dalton, I am wondering whether Liam might have better luck working in our department and using some of the technology we have here at Scotland Yard. What we use is quite state of the art, I'm told."

"Not happening, C. J."

Things went quiet for a moment. Lee was pretty sure he then heard the commander mutter something under her breath.

"Well, we'll need to tread carefully," she finally said. "If Misters Fakhoury and Hensleigh *are* affiliated with our friends in that cuckoo cult, we don't want to tip them off that we are suspicious of that. Of course, I'd also like to speak with Mr. Fakhoury, but his office told me he is, conveniently enough, in Egypt on business."

"What did you just call them?"

"Who?"

"The Organization. Its members, I mean."

A gentle titter came across the line. "Oh, that?" She sighed again. "Dalton, that's probably the *nicest* name I've called them since I learned they had regrouped. Now, grab a muffler, or a sturdy jacket, and meet me at the tailor shop in an hour. And for heaven's sakes, don't wreck that *michelada* of yours on the way over. I'm not sure I could bear any more whining from you about it."

Lee's eyes were closed; he had his right thumb and index finger pressed tight against the bridge of his nose. "It's called a *Maicoletta*, C. J. A *michelada* is a cocktail made with Mexican beer." He drew in a breath, forced a smile. "It doesn't matter. I'll see you in an hour."

"*Ciao,*" she replied.

***

Armando, the shop manager, met them just inside the front door. "I'm sorry. I got your text, but I didn't have a chance to reply. We've been unusually busy this morning. Unfortunately, Malcolm isn't in today. In fact, he won't be in for the rest of the week. He's on holiday."

"Where . . . on holiday?" C. J. asked. Her head was cocked to the left, and that caused the costume tiara she was wearing to slide a couple of inches toward her ear.

"Egypt, I think it was. Yes, Egypt. I remember him saying he had a desire to see the great pyramids."

C. J. turned to Lee, which caused the tiara to slide even further. Deftly, she repositioned the headwear with a quick nudge of the fingers on her right hand. "I see. Well, when do you expect him to return?"

The manager looked down, rubbed side of his nose with one finger.

"He'll be back Monday, as I recall. Yes, he was only taking a few days off. Now, if you'll excuse me, I must return to my client in the back. I was out yesterday myself, so I'm trying to play catch-up. I hope you understand. Please feel free to linger."

The pair nodded but said nothing.

"So, isn't *that* just the most stunning of coincidences?" C. J. groused. "Egypt. To see the pyramids. And not returning until Monday. Splendid. Just *splendid*."

Lee was quiet, in rumination. Eventually, he said, "It is peculiar. At the same time . . ."

"At the same time what?"

"At the same time, I wonder whether Mr. Fakhoury and Mr. Hensleigh being out of the country at the same time means we can mark them off the list of suspects in Mr. Tinti's murder."

"How do you mean?"

Lee began to rock on his heels. "You know how The Organization operates, C. J. You know how much their operatives like to be in the vicinity when 'The Transformation' begins. Why would Fakhoury and this tailor both hightail it to the Middle East, and be gone for several days, if the group is about to launch whatever little scheme they have in mind this time? Wouldn't they want to be around to . . . enjoy the party?"

"You have a point there, Dalton. You most definitely do. Unless, of course, their scheme necessitates the transport of someone, or something, from the Middle East. And we probably shouldn't put it past The Organization to change up their routine now and again, should we?"

The bell on the shop's front door tinkled, signaling the entrance of another customer. In this case, the customer was Omar Fakhoury.

"Oh, you again," he said curtly, scanning the pair as if they were vagabonds asking for a handout.

C. J. turned to Lee and gave him a look. "Well, isn't this just a box of animal crackers," she whispered. She turned back to the businessman and, to Lee's surprise, took an aggressive stance with him. "Care to tell us what *you're* doing here?"

Fakhoury came across first shocked, then cowed, by C. J.'s question. "What am I doing here? I'm here to pick up a couple pairs of slacks I had tailored. Why do you ask? Have I done something wrong?"

Lee was tempted to reply, 'I don't know. Have you?' but held back. This was C. J.'s interview, not his. Instead, he decided to step outside, so Fakhoury wouldn't feel so outnumbered. He hoped it would motivate the businessman to open up to her.

"No. It's just that, this morning . . ." C. J. pulled back, observing the very warning she had given Lee on the phone. "We were of the understanding . . ." she turned to motion toward Lee only to discover he was no longer there. "I mean, *I* was of the understanding that you were traveling. Your, um, office informed me of that."

"I'm on my way to the airport right now," he replied. His tone was brusque again and he turned away from the inspector and craned his neck toward the back of the shop. "That's why I'm here. I need those slacks for my business meetings tomorrow."

"In Egypt?"

Fakhoury turned back to the inspector and narrowed his gaze at her. "Egypt? No! I'm going to France, not Egypt. Marseilles, to be exact."

"And you expect to be there through the rest of the week?" C. J. had become a cur that refused to relinquish its bone.

"No. It's only a day trip. Well, I may need to be there for a couple of days, but no more than that."

That stopped the inspector in her tracks. But for only a moment.

"Before you depart, Mr. Fakhoury, there are a couple of questions I need to ask you."

"I really don't have the time for this," he said, peering toward the back of the store again. "I need my slacks."

"I understand, but I need to inquire about some online messages we've stumbled upon. I was just wondering if the name Taylor54W39 is one you recognize?"

By the way he responded, one would have thought she had asked him if he had ever embezzled a million dollars or if he would take his clothes off in front of her. His head swung in her direction and the muscles throughout his body constricted. His expression was one of incomprehension, but his complexion was turning a bright crimson.

He was about to reply when the shop manager wheeled around a corner with a couple of zippered bags over one shoulder.

"Here you are, Mr. Fakhoury. Please accept my apologies. I saw you come in via our security cameras and was in the back trying to retrieve your tailoring, but had some difficulty locating it. We're short-staffed today because Mr. Hensleigh is on holiday, so I'm running around like the proverbial headless chicken. Again, my apologies. I know you're in a hurry, but do you want to try those on to ensure they fit?"

The businessman stared at the shop manager for several seconds before responding. "You say he's on holiday? Mr. Hensleigh, that is."

"Yes, he's out of the country for a few days."

"I see." Fakhoury seemed to be working through something in his mind. "No, Armando, thank you, but I don't have the time to try these on. I'm on my way to Heathrow. I'm sure they'll be fine. I appreciate your rushing them for me."

With that, he swiveled around and strode out the shop's front door.

The shop manager studied C. J. intently. "I see you're still here," was all he said.

She tilted her head again . . . and the tiara slid toward her ear again. "Yes. You said it was all right if we lingered. I'm sorry if I misunderstood you."

The manager's look shifted from dubious to solicitous. "But, of course, Ms. Digby. Stay as long as you like." He began to fade away but continued to look at her as he backpedaled toward one of the service alcoves. "And if you find something you'd like to purchase and have us tailor for you, please do summon me."

When he was gone, C. J. issued a smirk. She recognized his last comment as a thinly veiled attempt at sarcasm, given the shop offered and tailored *men's* clothing only.

The bell tinkled again as Lee re-entered the shop.

"Well, that must have gone well," he said. "I don't see any blood or life-threatening injuries anywhere."

"To be honest, it was shambolic," C. J. replied. She straightened her tiara and smoothed her outfit. "Apparently, we caught Mr. Fakhoury just as he was leaving on his business trip. Claimed he's going to France for a day or so, not Egypt. More important to us, however, he didn't react well when I asked if he was familiar with the handle that Liam saw on that message string we came here to talk to him about. Taylor54W39. He was up and out and gone the minute I brought that up."

"Couldn't you have arrested him? Or detained him, at least?"

C. J. frowned. "On what charge? Running late for a flight at Heathrow? If I could do that, I'd be arresting a third of the world's population, every single day of the year."

"Point taken. But, why would his office lie to someone from Scotland Yard about where he was going?"

"Precisely."

And if Fakhoury is headed to France, then why is Malcolm Hensleigh in Egypt?"

"*Precisely,*" C. J. repeated.

The architect was stroking his chin, suddenly stopped. "Wait. Did you say he told you he only expected to be gone for a day or so?"

"Yes. He said his business is in Marseilles, so he expects it to be a short trip."

Lee's eyes grew large. Large enough to pique C. J.'s concern.

"What?" she said. "What is it, Dalton?"

The architect took a deep breath in. "If he's only going to be gone for a day, then he definitely doesn't believe in the art of packing light."

"What do you mean?"

Lee set his lips firmly together before answering her.

"Well, when his assistant went to put Fakhoury's tailoring in the back seat of the limo, I was on the pavement nearby. He had to move a couple of items from the back seat to the trunk to make room for the tailoring and . . . well . . . that trunk wasn't empty, it was filled with luggage.

"A perfectly matched set of six or seven suitcases, I would say."

34

That night, the world's most accomplished architect grappled with a disturbing dream. At one point during the nightmare, he felt as if he were submerged in a pool of ice and incapable of inhaling any oxygen. Moments later, his temples were pounding from what felt like a sudden onrush of clear, unadulterated air.

When he awoke, his fists were clenched, and the sheets were drenched.

This doesn't bode well for the day, Lee thought as he attempted to avoid the residue of perspiration around him. He was right. On the nightstand, his phone was trembling from a cascade of texts sent to him by C. J.

Given this unexpected development, the last one read, **it's best you come to my office as quickly as you can.**

Lee sank into the sheets, giving up on his efforts to keep his fingers and toes away from the sweat. His mind drifted back to the dream that had caused him such distress.

He was riding in a gilded carriage drawn by a stately white steed. His attire comprised a top hat and tails; his countenance was august, yet gay. He was admiring the scenery on display through the window: a meadow flanked by two majestic oaks, bisected by a clear, babbling brook. His hands rested comfortably on his upper thighs, the fingers of one intertwined with those of the other.

Suddenly, the carriage dipped into what felt like a deep, wide rut, and when it emerged on the other side, the sky had gone black. The oaks no longer bore any leaves and the water in the brook was no longer babbling but, instead, was bubbling, like water in a witch's cauldron. Lee leaned forward to ask the driver what had happened.

However, when the person at the reins turned to answer, the architect took a sharp breath in. It was Antonio Tinti, or, to be more precise, a somewhat skeletal version of the recently murdered tailor. The victim's eye sockets were sunk into his cranial cavity, his cheeks were emaciated and wan. To the left of his nose was a bloody bullet hole.

Most concerning to Lee, a tear was trickling down the driver's right cheek.

"I didn't deserve it," he murmured to his passenger as the carriage continued to lurch forward. "Why me? Why did this have to happen to *me?*" The carriage bounced violently for a few seconds, then careened to the right. Frantically, the driver yanked on the reins, the horse whinnied maniacally, and then the conveyance returned to its original track.

Lee looked out the window to avoid Tinti's glare. A crimson starburst was lighting up the night sky—the vestige of a red sprite three times the size of those he'd seen from the amusement park.

"It was my son who was involved with them, not me," Tinti droned on, the tear now frozen midcheek. His voice had taken on a hollow, metallic timbre, as if he were speaking through the amplifier used by those who've had a laryngectomy. "I didn't *want* to be involved. I didn't *ask* to be involved. I just wanted to go to work every day, do my job well every day, and come home every night to my flat and a pint of Guinness.

"Why me?" he asked again, the tear beginning to descend again. "Why *me?*"

The horse was slowing now. The driver made a half-hearted effort to spur the animal into action, but eventually abandoned the effort as pointless.

When he turned back to speak to Lee one last time, all the flesh had disappeared from his face.

"What . . . they intend . . . to do is . . . horrible, unimaginable," he intoned, the pace of his speech now mirroring the horse's gait. "The bloodshed . . . will be . . . staggering. How . . . we will recover I can't . . . possibly . . . imagine. The worst part is, I knew . . . but didn't tell anyone . . . in time. You must stop them. Please, STOP THEM. If you don't stop them, you'll be as responsible as I am for the horror that ensues.

"Don't let there be . . . any more innocent victims. Please. Losing my son was bad enough. Losing my life was . . . *agony*."

That was when Lee had awakened. That was when the texts had started to arrive.

The architect chose not to shave before heading to police headquarters. He wasn't confident he could maneuver a blade with precision.

***

When Lee showed up at C. J.'s office, he was taken aback by her greeting. "You don't seem to be your usual self, Dalton," she said as she swept through several sheets of paper on her desktop. "You look like you've seen a ghost."

He thought about describing his dream to her, then decided to discuss the situation at hand. "So, what's your interpretation of the phone call, C. J.?"

She leaned forward, crossed her arms on the desk, set her fingers on her forearms, and drummed them as she contemplated how to reply to Lee's question.

"I think it's genuine," she said softly. "He seemed legitimate. He offered details. Was the exact opposite of the pugnacious brute we met at the bocce court."

Lee slowly breathed in, then out, noticing that the room's usual medicinal smell had vanished, even if the sickly plants on the window sill had not.

"I was referring to the call you got from Fieldston Tucker. Your texts said you had gotten calls from Mr. Tucker *and* Karlo. You seemed a little smitten with the postman when we were at Hampstead Heath. So, I thought, maybe he was going to ask you . . ."

C. J. scoffed and waved him off. "I *was not smitten*. I am not smitten now. I was merely . . ." A slight smile creased her face. "Ingratiating myself, that's all. Building a rapport. Cultivating a relationship. All in the best interest of the investigation, of course."

Lee returned her smile. "Of course."

The commander raised her left hand to scratch the back of her head. "And *his* call was merely to tell us that he had discovered a few of Tinti's personal effects in his guest bedroom a couple of nights back. Some sneakers, a track suit, and a few toiletries. He said Tinti had asked to stay at his place for a couple nights when the water lines serving his flat got ruptured by the utility crews. He was asking what he should do with them, that's all."

She rearranged the papers on her desk once more. Stopped and stared at a particular page.

"As for Karlo, our Croatian friend was not particularly belligerent, but he *was* agitated when he called in. Insisted for the umpteenth time he had nothing to do with Tinti's death, and then told his story. Said that he had overheard Field . . ." She glanced up at Dalton, who did not flinch. "That he overheard *Mr. Tucker* talking near the bocce court to someone on his phone. According to Karlo, Mr. Tucker was relating all the details of Tinti's death to someone but didn't seem to express much remorse over the situation. He was just relating the facts and saying yes over and over again, as if that was the answer to a series of questions he was being asked by the person on the other line."

"No clue as to who *Mr. Tucker* was talking to?"

C. J. arched one eyebrow at Lee, then refocused her attention on the page in front of her. As she read, her lips moved silently for a couple of seconds. Eventually, she shook her head.

"No. No clue at all. However, Karlo did say the conversation went on for quite some time."

"How long?"

"Ten minutes. That's what makes me think his story is genuine. Karlo was very precise with the specifics. Someone concocting a story out of thin air isn't usually so meticulous when it come to the details."

Lee considered that for a few moments. "I'm wondering . . . in his conversation with Karlo, did Tucker reveal anything about Tinti's murder that only we know? Because, of course, that would tell me he was more connected to the incident than we thought."

She shook her head again. "Alas, from everything I've read, he did not. He did seem to have an encyclopedic knowledge of the murder. Like I said, the call apparently lasted at ten minutes." She blew out some air. "But everything he said on the phone call was public knowledge. Nothing we've held close to our chests."

"Where was Karlo when this phone conversation was taking place? Was Tucker aware Karlo was eavesdropping on him?"

C. J. cleared her throat. "I wouldn't say Karlo was eavesdropping, per se. He *overheard* the conversation. He was . . ." She looked back at the paper in front of her then up at Lee. "In a stall. Our retired postal carrier stepped into the facilities to take the call, didn't realize Karlo was in the process of . . . using the facility."

"Aha." Lee began to rock on his heels and toes. "So, Karlo can't really say *for certain* it was Tucker. He didn't actually see him with his own eyes."

C. J. consulted the report again. "Actually, he did. He emerged from the stall as the conversation was ending. Says Field was more taken aback to see him than was customary, then quickly ended the call."

"Signing off with . . ."

"Ivy Mike. Yes, I called you *tout de suite* when I came upon *that* juicy little detail."

Lee didn't say anything for a while. Then, he ventured forth. "I really have a difficult time envisioning your . . ." Now it was his turn to check himself. "I really can't see Fieldston Tucker executing a terrorist attack on his dear homeland. Or murdering someone. I mean, he seems so . . . patriotic. And daft. And then there is the palsy to consider."

From the look on C. J. face, he was about to receive a serious tongue-lashing. He hadn't bought her claim that she hadn't been flirting with the retired postal carrier. So he would have understood if she had taken his comment as an affront to (dare he say it?) her romantic interest. But her tense demeanor relaxed into a boisterous laugh and an exaggerated roll of the eyes.

"Oh, I *most certainly* can see him as a member of The Organization, Dalton," she replied. "Just think about it. He was a *postal carrier*. For goodness sakes, who knows more about everyone, and everything going on in everyone's personal life, than a postal carrier? What a perfect way to embed yourself into a place and absorb the comings and goings of the people you plan to annihilate. As well as the people you know are plotting to thwart you."

She sighed and shuffled the papers yet again. "Now, whether or not he is *our* murderer is another question entirely. *Perhaps* it is sheer coincidence that he ended that phone call with the very moniker your adorable associate, Liam, noticed in the messages about luggage being shipped to Heathrow."

On her desk, her phone began to trumpet the "Ride of the Valkyries."

"However, I'm not sure I've shared this with you, Dalton, but I am a firm believer that there is *no such thing* as a coincidence." The commander ducked her head as she moved her phone to her ear. "*Pronto?*"

As she entered the conversation, Lee allowed his attention to drift to all the nooks and crannies of C. J.'s office. In a way, he was disappointed. The room's decor seemed pretty pedestrian given the commander's eclectic interests and eccentric personality. He felt certain that somewhere in the room, a saxophone (or maybe even a toucan) should be on obvious display. *And where does she store that tiara she was wearing the other day,* he wondered.

He also made a mental note to ask when he might watch her perform at one of the local jazz clubs. Given the increasingly short window they had to work with, he figured he needed to do that sooner rather than later.

His reverie was interrupted by a shrill cry from C. J.

"WHAT? When?" Her mouth was open, and she was doodling ferociously on the back of one of the papers on her desk. "What were the circumstances? Do we know?" She didn't say anything for several seconds but continued to scribble as if she were capturing the details for a scene in a play before they had entirely escaped her.

"I see. All right. Thank you. Yes, I'll be sure someone follows up on this immediately. Good day."

Lee leaned forward, anchored both arms on the edge of her desk. "What on earth was *that* about?"

Rather than reply, she began to slowly massage her temples with her fingertips, like a fortune teller trying to summon a view of the future. "Do you remember Betty Naughton?" she finally said, her voice a quiet monotone. "Tinti's girlfriend? The one with the shop?"

Lee nodded, even though C. J. wasn't looking at him—her eyes pressed tight. "Well, Bree just left a message with my assistant. It appears Miss Naughton was found murdered in her apartment earlier today."

35

A part of what Lee considered to be just a theory suddenly proved to be reality. By triangulating some activity in this chat room using this avatar, with an email sent from that email address using that oft-repeated phrase, Liam was able to connect one simple message from Antonio Tinti's son to someone associated with The Organization.

"I'm in," said the message written by Niccolò Tinti.

"Power to the cause," came the encrypted, untraceable reply.

Dalton Lee reviewed one last time the evidence Liam had just texted to him, then leaned across the desk and showed it to C. J.

"Well, I'd say that's seals that," she announced, returning the phone to the architect. She drummed her fingers on her desk, studied Lee closely. "The questions before us now are, did Tinti's son tell his father at some point what he was up to? And if that's the case, did The Organization learn that and then silence Tinti before he shared what he knew with the authorities? With us, I mean."

They both said nothing for some time, contemplating the possibilities.

"What about the gun, C. J.? Any details surface yet about its purchase?"

She shook her head. "Unfortunately, no. Anisa is quite the expert when it comes to unearthing such intelligence. It's perhaps the greatest strength she brings to our team."

The commander wasn't looking at Lee when she made the comment, but he had the distinct impression the comment was more about him than it was about Anisa. Especially given the way she had drawn out the words "our team."

C. J. picked up a pen and began to tap it on her desktop. "Tinti senior must have known about the plot and accidentally revealed what he knew to the wrong person."

Lee nodded. "Yes, but who? His ex-girlfriend? Malcolm Hensleigh? One of the waitresses? One of his mates at the bocce court?" He hesitated before adding, "For someone who just wanted to be left alone to blend into the wallpaper, it sure seems like he had a lot of confidantes he could turn to."

C. J. continued to tap her pen and nod in agreement. Suddenly, the pen went still.

"The bocce court. That reminds me. We need to have a little conversation with Field . . . ston Tucker to sort out exactly what was going on with that phone call Karlo overheard."

"What about Betty? Her murder, I mean."

C. J. was already nodding and leaning across her desk to pick up her phone.

"Yes, that's of significant concern as well. I'll ask Anisa to go collect the details about that and then we'll meet with her after we have our little *tête-à-tête* with Mr. Tucker."

Lee chuckled to himself and thought, *Well, at least she's getting better when it comes to faking emotional distance from the old guy.*

***

Fieldston Tucker was happy to meet them at police headquarters. More than that. He walked into C. J.'s office with a bouquet of posies in one hand.

Oh no, Lee thought.

"It came to me that it is quite likely no one ever thinks to brighten the office of a policewoman," he said, extending the bouquet toward the commander. Lee noted that the postal carrier's other hand was trembling significantly as he made the exchange.

"What a lovely gesture, Field, truly it is," C. J. said, smiling broadly. But when she caught Lee eyeing her closely, she adjusted her demeanor to one more dispassionate. "Did your wife help pick these out, Mr. Tucker?"

The postal carrier seemed flustered by the question, but then brightened.

"As a matter of fact, she did! To be honest, I make a fist of it whenever it comes to picking flowers. Once, while I was at university, I sent a spray of lilies to a lovely young lady I was dating. Wrote on the card I thought them to be the perfect symbol of how I felt about our relationship. Turned out her family owned a couple of funeral parlors. Needless to say, *that* didn't go over very well."

Everyone, including Fieldston Tucker, smiled painfully. C. J. scanned the room for a place to put the posies. She finally yanked an assortment of pens and pencils out of a medium-size cup on her desk and stuck them into that.

"Won't those need water?" Tucker asked, pointing toward the flowers with his quavering hand.

"Eventually," she replied. The commander cleared her throat twice, encouraged him to take the chair on the other side of her desk. Lee stood against the opposite wall, his arms folded. He couldn't possibly imagine this feeble gentleman being the one who had riddled Antonio Tinti's body with a hail of bullets. At the same time, Lee's familiarity with The Organization had taught him he shouldn't discount the guy's involvement, either.

"I asked you here, Mr. Tucker . . ."

"Please, C. J., call me Field."

C. J. looked toward Lee, who nodded back. "Yes. Right. Um, I asked you here, Field, to inquire about a phone call you took the other day at the bocce court. In the . . . facilities there."

The postal carrier squinted some. "The one from my doctor about my urinalysis?"

C. J. looked again at Lee. His eyes had fluttered closed and he was chuckling softly as he moved his head left and right.

"No, I don't believe that is the one I'm referring to," she continued. "This was a call . . ." She struggled to think of a conspicuous detail that would help jog his memory. "You went on at length with someone about the murder of Antonio Tinti."

He seemed dazed some, fiddled with the bottom hem of his windbreaker.

"I don't remember that. I don't remember that at all," he replied.

She decided she had no other course of action but to surge full steam ahead. "You went on at length about Mr. Tinti's murder and then you ended the phone call by saying, 'Ivy Mike.'"

Tucker stared at his interrogator.

"Ivy Mike? Right! Ivy Mike! That means I was taking to Raibert MacDonald. My pen pal in Scotland. I say, 'pen pal,' because that's what we were back in grammar school. These days, we communicate by telephone, of course."

C. J. waited for more. It didn't come.

"Of course," she echoed. "We were wondering, Field, about the nature of that call. And why you happened to use that particular sign-off."

"What? Ivy Mike? Oh, I've always used it with him. Raibert and I became pen pals because we worked on a school paper about it."

"About what?" C. J.'s tone betrayed more than a tinge of impatience, Lee thought.

"About Ivy Mike. The States' first test of a full-scale thermonuclear device. Took place on one of those tiny atolls out in the Pacific Ocean. Elugelab Island, I think, although I'm probably mispronouncing it. He and I were already pen pals, and by coincidence, we were given the same assignment in fifth grade—to write about the dawn of the nuclear era. We decided to write about how the Americans developed the explosive in 1952 as part of Operation Ivy."

The mention of the year riveted Lee's attention. *1952. That could possibly explain the 52 in the handle, IvyMike52,* he thought. The architect began to feel increasingly uneasy as he began to envision some connection between the messages Liam had seen in the online chat room, the moniker IvyMike52, the references to suitcases . . . and, now, nuclear devices.

"Jeezus," he whispered under his breath.

C. J. looked briefly at Lee but ignored his comment.

"I sign off all our calls with Ivy Mike, and he always signs off with Dick Garwin."

C. J. looked expectantly at the postal carrier. "Who is . . .?" she prompted.

"Oh, the guy who designed Ivy Mike, obviously."

The commander nodded slowly in return, then replied, "Obviously." She then sat back in her chair and studied the older man across the desk from her. She glanced once at Lee, then returned her focus to the postal carrier.

"So, Field, can you tell us why you were talking to this Mister . . . MacDonald, was it?"

"Yes. And it still is MacDonald."

"Yes. Certainly." She sighed softly before she followed up with her question. "Why were you were talking to this MacDonald chap about Antonio Tinti's murder?"

Again, the postal carrier seemed at sea for a couple of moments.

"Well . . . Raibert lives near Aberdeen now, and there was a notice about the murder that appeared in the newspaper there. It mentioned that Tony played a lot of bocce, and Raibert knew I played it, so he called me to see if I might know him. 'Know him?' I said. 'Hell, I've been naked with the guy!'"

That made Lee duck his head forward a few inches.

"I beg your pardon?" C. J. replied.

Now it was Fieldston Tucker's turn to be exasperated.

"In the showers, C. J., in the showers. Back when I was still playing, we competed in a lot of out-of-town tournaments at clubs that would let us use their showers after we'd finished our matches." His expression veered from disappointment to disgust. He waved his steady hand in the air as if he were swatting away a fly. "I'm not into that sort of thing, if that's what you're thinking. Strictly a man's-man here, no need to worry on that front."

Lee discreetly put a fist up to his mouth and laughed into it.

"I'm sure you are," was all C. J. could muster.

The postal carrier glanced at his watch, a gigantic timepiece on his left wrist with numbers large enough Lee could see them from where he was standing. "Is there any other information you need? I do want to help as much as possible." He paused. "However, I have an appointment with my urologist in about forty-five minutes. Should I call them and postpone?"

C. J. looked to Lee, who shrugged his shoulders. "No, Field, I think that's all we need from you right now," she said. "Except perhaps the phone number of your friend Raibert. We might like to follow up with him on a couple of questions about your phone conversation. Merely protocol on our part."

"Protocol. Right." The retiree pulled his phone from an interior pocket of his windbreaker and used one thumb to skim through the directory. "Here it is. Raibert MacDonald. "See, I told you it was still MacDonald!"

He contorted the phone so C. J. could scribble down the phone number.

"Brilliant!" she announced as she completed the last digit. "Thank you ever so, Mr. Tucker. I mean, Field. We'll be in touch if we need anything further. Oh, and thank you also for the flowers. They add a nice dash of color to the office, don't you think?"

The postal carrier rose to shake her hand and then make his way to the door. He was most of the way into the vestibule when he re-opened the door some. "Don't forget to give those posies some water," he said, pointing toward C. J.'s desk. She smiled but said nothing.

As Tucker was closing the door, he turned and gave Lee a jovial wink. But the architect noticed the twinkle in the man's eyes went dull, and his smile fell completely, before the door had fully shut.

It was a couple of moments later when he also realized the postal carrier had confidently shut the office door with the hand that had once been trembling. And that the cane he had relied upon at Hampstead Heath was nowhere to be seen.

***

Lee decided to walk back to the residence rather than take a cab or the Tube. The air was cool, and sunlight was filtering softly through the late afternoon clouds. His thoughts returned to Fieldston Tucker's testimony, of sorts, and his use of Ivy Mike as a handle.

The architect had done some quick research on his phone, and everything the postal carrier had said to C. J. corroborated with sources online. Operation Ivy was the eighth in a series of nuclear tests carried out by the United States in the 1950s. "Mike" was the name of the first of two detonations carried out under the Ivy banner. The detonation had taken place on Elugelab Island in the Pacific. And Richard Garwin was, indeed, the person who had designed the device, which offered five hundred times the yield of the bomb that the United States had dropped on Nagasaki.

Lee was trying not to be paranoid. But he couldn't help but fret about the recent arrival into London of seven suitcases sent by someone calling himself IvyMike52.

He was ambling along Birdcage Walk now, approaching Buckingham Palace. Silver metal barriers that stood chock-a-block alongside the curb demanded pedestrians observe a sense of order one hardly ever saw in Los Angeles or New York.

In the distance, the neoclassical masterpiece that has served for almost two centuries as the London residence for the British monarchy seemed especially grand today, with the sun bathing its columns and pediments in a gentle, golden gleam.

He wondered how many people knew that the architect of Buckingham House, the precursor to today's palace, almost shoved the Duke of Buckingham off the roof of the building in the early 1700s when the duke failed to pay the architect the commission he'd been promised. Or, that a menagerie comprising everything from crocodiles, elephants, camels, and zebras had, at some point, called the grounds of Buckingham Palace home.

Or that, when Queen Elizabeth (the Queen Mother) and her husband (King George VI) were investigating the lower levels of the castle one day in the early twentieth century, they came across a stranger who had been living in the building for many months, if not years.

At least four architects could claim they contributed to the grandeur that now attracted millions of tourists to London each year, and Lee thought each one of them deserved a prize for how they had helped transform a simple townhome into an architectural treasure.

He was just across the street from the palace now. On his immediate right, a young mother stood on the pavement, holding the hand of her five-year-old daughter. The moppet wore a fuchsia-colored jacket, and white-and-fuchsia tights. In her free hand, she held a large Mylar balloon, both sides of which were filled with the face of a lion.

A large crowd was in front of him, waiting to cross the street, so Lee stood patiently beside the mother and child until the signal changed.

"The palace truly is extraordinary," said the lion on the balloon. "But Anisa was right. You really need to get away to Cambridge as soon as you get the chance, Dalton. Bask in your glory days at university. Because your schedule is going to get very hectic, very soon. And you're going to want a lot of pleasant memories stored up to counter what's likely to happen.

"You don't think I'm . . . *lion* . . . to you now, do you?"

Lee squeezed his eyes tight, tried to resist the lure of the voice.

"There's no reason for you to pretend you can't hear me, Dalton," the lion continued. "We both know you can. Are you . . . *feline* . . . a little uncomfortable with this conversation?"

Lee opened both eyes and discreetly looked first at the mother, then at the four-year-old, and then at the people assembled around him. No one seemed to have heard the lion's monologue. Given the crowd pressed close to him on all sides, he knew better than to reply to the balloon. So, he spoke his reply internally instead.

First of all, your puns are deplorable. Secondly, you're not really speaking to me. I know that now.

He peeked timidly at the balloon. The lion only stared back at him.

And then its lips began to move.

"Then why did you respond to me just now? Of course, I am speaking to you, Dalton. And, no, you don't have to vocalize your thoughts for me to hear them. So there. That ought to give you some . . . *paws*." Dalton thought he saw the eyes of the lion shift first to the left and then to the right, but he wasn't certain of that, and didn't really want to know if he had.

"Now do as I say, friend. Head up to Cambridge for a day or two.

It's essential you do that. Before The Transformation enters its ... *mane* phase."

At that moment, the traffic light changed and the crowd in front of him began to make its way across the intersection. The mother, daughter, and balloon drifted off in the same direction.

But Dalton Lee remained where he had been standing for the last several minutes, his hands in his pockets, dread pulsing through his veins.

36

"Yes, Lara, of course I understand why you'd choose to purchase one of my ten-minute readings before committing to one of my VIP packages. I understand perfectly. However, I feel it important to let you know that the discounts associated with the packages you inquired about *will expire* at the end of this week. So, I urge you to consider moving forward with the purchase of a VIP package as soon as you possibly can. You'll have the freedom then to ask me about anything that may be troubling you, or about a romantic involvement, or about some illness or debt you'd like to see go away. And I'll be able to offer insights and recommendations that are much more in-depth than what I can possibly do in just ten minutes. I'm sure you understand, yes?

"And did I mention that with the purchase of one of my VIP packages, you'll receive, free of charge, a four-ounce bottle of my new fragrance, Prophecy?"

The operations manager of The Lee Group wasn't surprised or disappointed that Delfina Delgado had pronounced her name as if it were spelled "Laura," with an "o" sound at the end of the first syllable, rather than "Lara," with a more open "a" at the end of that syllable.

However, she *was* taken aback some by Delfina Delgado's appearance. In the video Lara had watched, the psychic had an immaculate coiffure, impeccable makeup, and a creamy complexion. She could have been mistaken for a model of fur coats, or perhaps, a movie star along the lines of Catherine Zeta-Jones.

On this video phone call, however, she looked more like someone who would be staffing the counter at one's neighborhood cleaners. Her hair was swept up, but errant strands of it jutted out at odd angles from the top of her head. Her eyes were mesmerizing, in part because her mascara was slightly smeared in several places. Her cheeks were flabby, not taut, and her teeth were dull, not white.

But, I didn't hire her to look pretty, Lara reminded herself. *I hired her to give me . . . counsel.*

"Laura, there are several ways we could proceed with this reading," the psychic began. Delfina Delgado wasn't looking so much into the camera now, but at several eight-by-ten sheets of paper that were fanned out in a wide semicircle on her desk. She tried to glance at them furtively, but each time she looked up from her desktop, she needed a moment to connect with the camera.

Surely those aren't cue cards, Lara wondered.

"If you'd like, you can ask me a series of questions, and I can consult with the oracles to give you an answer to each one," the clairvoyant intoned. "But, remember, we only have ten minutes."

Lara admitted to herself she was relieved Delfina Delgado was neither sitting in front of a crystal ball nor wearing a gypsy ensemble. Her psychic looked more disheveled than Lara had expected, but at least she wasn't coming across as a sad stereotype.

Not yet, anyway.

"Or, I could just absorb the elements of your aura and deliver a forecast based on the vibrations I'm picking up. Whichever you decide."

Lara gave the options some careful thought. On one hand, she was intrigued with the idea of the psychic reading her aura from across the universe and providing her thoughts without any prompt whatsoever. On the other hand, there was a crucial question she was eager to get some direction on.

She flashed back to the day before when she'd been sorting through a series of emails the firm had received. She'd been delighted to learn that The Lee Group had made the short list of designers under consideration for the new national library being commissioned by Myanmar, and that the research assistant candidate who had stood out during the interview process a few weeks back had accepted the firm's offer of employment. However, she felt a malaise drift over her the more she waded through what (for the first time) seemed to be little more than a tedious stack of trivial missives.

Until she came upon that email that had been addressed to her and her alone. An email informing her that Aalto University was searching for someone to lead a new program devoted exclusively to sustainability in architecture and urban design. And that the president of the university (a college classmate of hers from thirty-five years ago) viewed her as *the perfect candidate* to assume that role (although he assumed she was content with her position with The Lee Group).

But adding that, if she were *not* perfectly content . . .

"Surprise me," Lara said into the camera on her computer. "Tell me what it is that you see, and what it is that you feel."

A spark of delight shone in Delfina Delgado's eyes upon hearing Lara's decision, a spark that imbued them a verve Lara had not seen in them since the session began.

"Well, all right then," the clairvoyant whispered, licking her lips gently.

The fact Lara was giving her free rein to offer a prediction without any data to work with seemed to embolden the psychic. Rapidly, she brought the sheets of paper into a stack and, after straightening them, set them to one side. She placed her right palm flat on the desktop and her left palm flat upon that. She tilted her chin upward slightly, breathed in once through her nostrils, and closed her eyes. Her muscles relaxed, and her soul seemed to float to some corner of the galaxy offering perfect repose. Moments passed. Eventually, Delfina Delgado seemed so placid, so transcendent, Lara began to wonder if the woman had fallen asleep.

But then she finally said, "Lara, I want you to close your eyes along with me and begin to take several shallow, but invigorating, breaths," she finally said. Lee's second-in-command did not fail to notice that, this time, the psychic had pronounced her name correctly.

She did as the medium instructed.

"Now, I want you to think of someone you care about very much, Lara. Someone you have only positive feelings for and who you trust completely. Unfailingly. Who would that be, Lara? Who is that person?"

"My mother," Lara responded immediately.

For a moment, the clairvoyant said nothing. Lara couldn't resist opening one eye a few centimeters to ensure Delfina Delgado was staying true to the script and had not ducked out for a smoke. The woman was still there and appeared to be even more in a trance than before.

"Excellent. Now, I want you to envision a roller window shade anchored to the top of your forehead. And your mother has hold of the bottom of that shade and she is going to very, very slowly lower the shade over first your face, then your shoulders, then your torso, then your hips, your thighs, your lower legs, and, finally, your feet."

Lara scrunched her face at that information. On one hand because the scenario seemed so silly . . . and on another because her mother had always been averse to window shades, preferring instead to leave the windows of their home free from heavy cover.

"When you feel an overwhelming majority of the stress leave your body—it could be when your mother lowers the shade past your shoulders, or it may not be until it has passed your knees—whenever it is, I need you to let me know. Do you understand me, Lara?"

She nodded, said "Yes," very softly.

"All right, then, the shade is lowering. It's lowering. It's lowering further . . ."

Lara's cynicism was on full throttle. However, she reminded herself she had plunked down twenty-five-hundred dollars for this reading, so she should perhaps make at least a half-hearted effort to be cooperative. And much to her surprise, about the time the shade dropped just below her bosom, an incredible lightness suffused her body.

"I believe I'm there," she said, a gauzy softness to her voice. "Thank you."

"Ah, but it was you who made it happen, Lara," the psychic replied quickly.

A moment later, Lara heard a bell tinkle, fought the temptation to open her eyes again to catch Delfina Delgado in the act. Lara's composure was so calm, however, she dared not disturb it.

"Now, this is the most important segment of your reading, Lara. A very critical segment. I need you to concentrate on whatever issue you want guidance on. I need you to visualize it, clearly, but at the same time, not think *too* hard on it. Otherwise, you could cast too much of a bias onto it. It's a fine line I'm asking you to walk, a delicate balance between capturing the image clearly in your mind and clutching it too tightly to your soul. Do you think you can do that, Lara?"

Lara began to nod fervently. "I do," she answered.

The bell rang again. "Then, I will wait to receive the image you send me, and soon after, I will give you my perspective on your situation."

Lara pressed her spine against the back of the chair, set both feet flat on the carpet, and allowed her mind's eye to wander. She tried not to force an image to appear. She would wait for whatever impression seemed apt and then gently toss it over the internet to the psychic, like a dove released into a dark, starlit sky.

But it wasn't that easy. Lara's mental clarity was bumping up against a persistent jet stream of concerns and fears and second guesses that made it tough for an image to crystallize. She first saw her father, shaking his head, exhibiting his typical stance of disappointment in her. Then she saw Dalton, boyish and forlorn, flipping through the folders on her desk in California. That scenario eventually melted into another taking place in a lounge filled with professors angrily waving sheaths of paper in her face.

"This . . . may take some time, Delfina," she finally said.

"That's all right, it often does," came the reply. "However, I must let you know there are only about three minutes left in this session. If you'd like to extend your reading by another ten minutes, I'd be happy to add the charge to whichever credit card we have on file for you. Would you like me to do that?"

Lara bit her lower lip for a couple of seconds. "No, I believe we're fine." She took a deep breath, and that seemed to blow away the negative imagery she'd bumped up against. Suddenly, she had a clear view of the email itself. No actions, emotions, or people invaded her thoughts; all she saw (quite vividly) was the line of the email that read "Of course, I think there is no one out there better qualified for this position than you, Lara."

She heard a noise on the other side of the computer screen; it was something between a gasp and a squawk. She didn't know if she was breaking protocol by opening her eyes, but she didn't really care if she was.

Delfina Delgado looked as if someone had inserted an electrical rod into her backbone. Her eyelashes were fluttering, and her mouth drooped open a bit. The clairvoyant's arms were stretched out taut, but it was the backs of her hands, not her palms, that rested upon the desktop.

"I see now, yes, I see *quite clearly* what it is you are seeking," the woman said. Her mouth had closed, but her lips were quivering, as if she were delivering her reading from inside a freezer. "You are not the only one who needs this guidance. It will impact the lives of many, many others as well. Many, *many* others."

Lara's face inched closer to the screen. The psychic was giving a virtuoso performance.

"I am now seeing a solution . . . *the* solution you came to me for, Lara. It is hazy but becoming more vivid." At the word "vivid," the woman's voice increased both in volume and intensity.

"You are torn as to the direction you should take. As to which of your many options you should pursue."

Delfina Delgado now appeared to be levitating from her chair. Her arms were still rigid, but she now was extending them to the heavens. "I see the answer, Lara. I see the answer you must heed. It is coming in just one short word, one short, simple word.

"And that word is . . . *wait.*"

With that, the screen went dark. It flickered several times, then presented Lara with the following message:

**To authorize another ten-minute reading with
THE GREAT DELFINA DELGADO, please CLICK HERE**

37

Bree had learned of Betty's murder from Corinne, her shop assistant. The minute the young woman had been notified of her employer's death, she contacted Bree using the phone number on the business card Bree had given to her at the shop.

"Are you all right, Corinne?" Bree asked. "This must come as quite a shock."

"I guess," was all the shop girl said in reply.

Bree wasn't sure if the young woman was responding to her question as to whether she was all right, or to her statement that the murder must have come as a shock. "I'll check on you later," Bree told the young woman.

"Maybe," Corinne replied.

Betty's body had been found in her flat in West Hampstead. The apartment "appeared" to have been ransacked, but the investigators had some suspicion the melee might have been staged. That said, all her jewelry, both costume and fine, was missing. Also gone was a small portrait, painted by one of Argentina's most renowned contemporary artists, that (as she once confided to Corinne) had been appraised at more than three thousand pounds.

There was no evidence of a break-in. Betty must have known the person who killed her. Just as Antonio Tinti must have known the person who had murdered him.

The shopkeeper was discovered on the floor of her bedroom, and all indications were that she had been smothered with a pillow. She was wearing silk pajamas; she had not been the victim of a sexual assault. A small stuffed giraffe occupied its usual position on the bed, across from the pillow Betty slept on (although it had been knocked onto one side).

Most importantly, no page from the original edition of *Wayward Planet* was found on her body.

"This *can't* be a coincidence, Dalton," Anisa said. The architect, who was in his room at the townhouse, moved the phone from one ear to the other so he could pick up the television remote with his dominant hand.

"Well, it *can* be, Anisa," he answered. "But I agree that it looks pretty unusual. Either it's a high-odds poker hand we've been dealt or . . . all the people in Antonio Tinti's life need to be looking over their shoulders."

The morning news was streaming a live feed from Heathrow. Representatives of the president of the United States, the chancellor of Germany, and the prime ministers of Canada and Japan were shown exiting one of the airport's main terminals with their attachés in tow. After a few vague waves toward the cameras, the leaders and their entourages all climbed into stolid black SUVs and sped off.

Lee felt his stomach do a flip-flop. His chest seemed to be contracting, as well.

"They don't *have* to leave their calling card on the corpse of everyone they murder, you know," Anisa said. "Maybe they've decided to move on from that clichéd ritual. Maybe their egos are such they no longer need to flaunt in front of us what they've done."

Lee let that sink in as he chewed on the inside of one of his cheeks, studied the scene unfolding on the television screen, and tilted his head back to look at the ceiling.

"Maybe," he eventually replied.

***

Corinne had agreed to meet Bree at a coffeehouse only a few blocks from the flat in Swiss Cottage that she shared with two friends. She looked drawn, fearful, and—thanks to a bulky wool jumper topped by a boa-constrictor-like infinity scarf—overdressed for the weather, which was relatively mild.

The young woman took a tiny sip of the macchiato she had ordered and set the cup on the small table in front of them.

"I knew this was going to happen," she announced.

"What? How? How did you know?" Bree responded. "Why do you say that?"

Corinne gave a weak smile and shook her head.

"I just knew." She breathed in heavily through her nostrils and glanced over her left shoulder, then her right, like a second-rate actress in a classic melodrama.

"He could walk in here at any time, you know," she whispered. "And that probably wouldn't be to our advantage." She took another sip of the macchiato, turned, and stared at some distant spot near the front door.

Bree wondered whether Betty's death had caused the waifish young woman to lose her marbles. Started to believe she'd not had many to begin with. "He *who?*" she probed, refusing to follow Corinne's gaze across the room.

The young woman turned back to Bree and sighed heavily. Before the architect's eyes, she transformed from a clandestine confidante into a clinical narrator of facts and statistics.

"She'd started dating someone new recently. About a month and a half ago, I think. I knew it couldn't be good when she said he was an acquaintance of Tony's. I mean, like *that* ever goes well." She was now slurping her beverage more than sipping it. She spent a couple of moments daubing her lips with her napkin before proceeding.

"The new guy . . . he had anger issues. She told me that, as they were getting into a cab on their second date, she spotted a guy who's the boyfriend of one of our biggest customers and waved at him. Well, the date got so mad, he grabbed her by the forearm and yanked her into the cab. Gave her a bruise the size of a kiwi fruit, she said. Told her she

256

should never ever do that in front of him again."

"What's the guy's name?"

The shop assistant turned toward the front door again, her mouth descending into a twisted frown.

"I don't remember," she said robotically. "I mean, I don't think she ever told me."

Bree reclined against the back of her seat and viewed Corinne with more than a dollop of skepticism. When the young woman had arrived at the coffeehouse, she'd seemed agitated, even paranoid. Just like that, however, she had relaxed into a more composed, sensible observer of what had taken place.

Then, without warning, she'd turned edgy again.

Bree ran through the abridged encyclopedia she had stored in her brain to determine which pharmaceutical Corinne might be on. None came quickly to mind. So, she decided to continue the conversation and try not to let Corinne figure out it was actually more of an interrogation.

"Well . . . did she tell you what he looked like? What he did for a living?"

Corinne just stared back at her and slowly shook her head at each question. Over time, her lips curled into something between a sneer and a smile, as if she were amused that Bree would even ask such foolish questions.

The meeting was over before Bree intended for it to be. "I've got to run," Corinne breathed out. Suddenly, she was in a dither. "I need to pick up some groceries. And open the shop."

"The shop? It's still open? What will happen to it, now that Betty has . . .?"

Corinne looked up, as if she were searching the ceiling for the answer. "Oh, I assume she left it to me, I mean, *surely* she did." She lifted her backpack and began to place the straps over her shoulders. "Really, thanks very much for reaching out to me, Bree. It was so kind and, yes, we shall miss Betty ever so."

With that, Corinne darted out the front door. It didn't take but a second for Bree to realize she had just been stuck with the check.

***

In the corner farthest from the library's main circulation desk, Roberto sat at a table poring over a large world atlas, engrossed in a detailed map of the city of Tehran. He was developing a plan to rescue Isabela, and like most people who are trying to look inconspicuous, he was doing a dreadful job of it. Every few seconds, he'd look up from the tome, scour the room, go back to the book, then glance up quickly once again in case he'd missed a pair of prying eyes. Every few minutes he would feign a cough and use it as an opportunity to check out the people in the cubicles beside him.

He was concerned the librarian in the green-plaid skirt had made note of which book he had extracted from the shelves and might now be cross-referencing its contents against some database of hers to see why it might be of interest to an international terrorist (which, he had to admit, he sort of looked like today).

Uncombed hair. Beard stubble. Olive-green army jacket with more pockets than a zoo full of kangaroos. More than one bruised fingernail (the culprit being a drawer in his room that was stubborn to close). He'd paid a lot of money for his leather boots (which came to a point just below his knees), but they were in desperate need of some polishing and buffing.

And then, of course, he was also reviewing the streets and alleyways of the largest city in all of Iran, which just happened to also be one of the world's most renowned havens for anti-West terrorists.

So he wasn't all that surprised (but was startled, nonetheless) when the green-skirted librarian was suddenly standing beside him.

"I couldn't help but notice your interest in The City of 72 Nations," she said quietly. Her hair color, her complexion, and the lilt in her voice told him she either was Irish or had a lot of Irish blood in her system. In her hands, she held out a few pamphlets, fanned out for his easy review.

"These additional maps might be helpful to you. They're much more detailed." She flashed a quick smile of embarrassment. "We keep them in a special collection, so if you don't mind, please return them when you've finished with them."

He looked directly at her face, forced a smile. "I will. Definitely. Thanks." He had the feeling she might be interested in him, but as soon as the maps were in his hands, she turned away and strode back to her desk without a single glance over her shoulder.

Even if she had been coming on to him, he didn't have the time right now to be focused on a romantic dalliance or a sexual conquest, he told himself. His next text conversation with Isabela would be in a couple of days, and he wanted to know everything about the prison they were taking her to, and how he might wrest her from it.

A strategy was coming together, and the maps the librarian had just given him were supporting his plan. One map highlighted the proximity of the Tehran International Exhibition Centre to the Evin Prison and the network of expressways that connected the two. He wondered what exhibitions were on the centre's calendar in the coming weeks, and if any of them might have a booth that would naturally be staffed by someone representing Puerto Rico. That would put him within only a few hundred meters of Isabela. All that remained was for him to select some date on the calendar *after* the date Isabela would be placed in confinement inside Evin, and *around* the time a major expo was taking place at the centre.

Right now, he didn't know either. But he planned to ferret out both as soon as possible.

***

It had taken C. J.'s team more time than they'd hoped to track down Raibert MacDonald. But when they finally did locate him, he was tucking five-pound notes into the G-strings worn by two different strippers in a club just outside Glasgow.

"Ow, you're not going to come along and spoil me fun *now*, are ya'?" he told the detectives who hustled him out the bar's front door. "It's taken me a good two months to get both of those lassies interested in me. Here I have me planned a ménage à trois, and you two polis come along and spoil it all for me."

"I don't think they were interested in you, mannie, so much as they were interested in your fivers," said one of the detectives.

The good news was, he was far more sleepy and slap-happy than inebriated. And the truth be told, he had been ready to depart the club anyway.

And he corroborated every single detail Fieldston Tucker had provided them about the phone call overheard by Karlo Kovačević.

"Ivy Mike? You best believe that wee barra is Ivy Mike," he told the detectives. "And, aye, fur definite, the person you are speaking to at present is Dick Garwin."

He went on to regale the detectives with a story about how he and Tucker had once picked up a couple of prostitutes in the south of Spain, only to discover once they all returned to their hotel room that the women were, in fact, transvestites.

"We forgot to check for the Adam's apples," he told them, nodding vigorously.

C. J. rolled her eyes as she finished relating that escapade to Lee.

"Truly, Dalton, I often wonder out of which laundry basket you men get your brains."

The architect smiled then feigned offense. "Ouch. We're not all like that," he replied.

The commander had moved from behind her desk to a tall metal file cabinet against the opposite wall. The top drawer was so high off the ground, she could barely see into it after opening it.

"That's true, Dalton. Quite true. My apologies." Standing on tiptoe, she plucked two manila folders from the drawer, slammed it shut, and swiveled toward him.

He was surprised to see a sober expression on her face.

"That said, if you think I'm not aware of your efforts to pilfer Anisa from my team, then you are just as foolish as the rest of them."

He shivered briefly. He hadn't expected that. It wasn't that he thought of C. J. as dense. He just thought he was better at keeping a secret than he apparently was. But the commander's expression went from stoic to comical.

"And so you know, I've decided it's perfectly all right," she added, flashing a resigned grin in his direction. "I learned about her . . . family situation . . . a day or so ago. I completely agree she would benefit from being more directly connected to the effort to bring down The

Organization and . . ." She turned away from him suddenly, sauntered back to her chair. "You could certainly benefit from the passion she brings to the job."

Even though he was looking at the back of the commander's head, her loneliness suddenly seemed palpable to him. "You know, C. J., I've decided to take a quick trip up to Cambridge tomorrow," he said. "I'll only be gone for a day. After I get back, I'd love to come see you perform. With your saxophone."

She was beaming when she turned back toward him.

"*That* would be a delight, Dalton," she said as she plopped herself into her chair. "An absolute delight. Let me know when, and I'll try to have them seat you at a VIP table."

Her phone buzzed, and as it did, she let out an irritated grunt.

"Never a moment of peace around here," she said, glancing at the screen. Her eyes widened some as she took in the message sent to her.

"Well, I guess that settles that," she said as she placed her phone back on the desk. "Our friends in the laboratory have been stunningly efficient today, poking around at some specks of DNA we discovered on the nightstand next to where Betty Naughton's body was found."

"And . . .?"

C. J. swatted at a fly that suddenly did a zigzag in front of her face. The pest flew off but soon returned, causing the commander to go into a routine with her hands that resembled a conductor whipping an orchestra into a frenzy. When the insect had finally retreated to a corner of the office, she looked over at the world's most renowned architect and sent him a weary smile.

"It seems the DNA matches that of a teenage hoodlum who's been terrorizing that neighborhood for the past several months. We've learned she hired him at some point to do some heavy lifting around the shop, which would explain why she let him into her flat.

"It appears her murder has nothing to do with The Organization or Antonio Tinti," she added. "Case . . ."

The fly returned, buzzing past her left ear before making a belly flop landing on the desktop in front of her. Without a second of hesitation, she slammed her right palm on top of it.

"Closed," she announced, emphatically. She picked up a sheet of paper and used it to scrape the insect's remains into the rubbish bin beside her desk.

"However," she said, "when one case closes . . ."

Lee leaned forward in anticipation.

"Fakhoury. Either he's extended indefinitely his one-day trip to Marseilles, or he's acquired the super power of invisibility. He never arrived in France. Cancelled his reservation at the last minute and hasn't been seen since. His office claims they know nothing about his disappearance. He has gone on the lam, as we say, and has eluded us for now."

Lee rolled his eyes. "So, Fakhoury *and* Hensleigh. Out of the country. And *incommunicado*. At the same time."

C. J. looked toward the ceiling. "Yes. *Incommunicado*. I like that word. I need to use it more often."

Ten minutes later, Lee texted to the rest of the team what he had just learned from C. J. about Ivy Mike, Dick Garwin, the demise of Betty Naughton, and the disappearance of Omar Fakhoury.

Bree was relieved to learn that Betty's murder had not been at the hands of The Organization. She immediately called Corinne to pass along the news.

But when she rang up the young woman, she got an automated message telling her the number was no longer in service.

A quick call to the shop in Chalk Farm yielded the same result.

38

Bree really didn't want to be here. But for the good of the investigation, she felt she had to be.

As she climbed the stairs leading to the front door of Mariam's apartment building, she repositioned her tote bag to the other shoulder and took several short, shallow breaths. *Who knows what condition the place will be in,* she told herself as she climbed the last step. *Who knows what it's going to smell like?*

She prepared to press the buzzer but, just then, the front door flew open.

"Whoops, sorry about that, I didn't see you standing there."

It was Bridget, a motorcycle jacket thrown over her waitress uniform, a wad of chewing gum in her mouth.

"Hi Bridget. I doubt you remember my name—it's Bree. Mariam and I have a knitting date tonight."

"Right, she mentioned something about that just now. I swear, that woman left her phone at the diner *once again.* So I offered to run it by here before I headed home."

Bree nodded, smiled, and waited.

Bridget lowered her head a couple of inches and shifted into an exaggerated whisper. "Have you learned any more about who . . . you know . . . about who killed Tony?"

Bree started to shake her head but curtailed herself from following that instinct. "We're making progress," she replied, nodding repeatedly. "We're pretty sure we know *why* he was killed. And we have several leads as to who might have been the killer, so . . ."

Bridget's face beamed. "Oh, that's smashing! His family—what's left of them anyway—deserves some sort of closure I think." Her face clouded suddenly. "We all do a little bit, I guess."

Bree smiled but said nothing more. She was eager to get the evening over with.

Bridget nodded once. "Well, I'll be off. Got an early shift tomorrow." The waitress started to trot down the stairs but pulled up before she reached the pavement. Quickly she pivoted back toward Bree, who was now pressing the buzzer. "By the way, I'm rather glad you and Mariam have become friends. As best I can tell, she could really use one."

Bree started to reply but chose instead to wave Bridget along and go back to summoning her host.

She was beyond stunned when she entered Mariam's flat. The floors were vacuumed; the tables and chairs were free of clutter. There was no rancid smell to offend her; instead, a hint of sandalwood filled the air. Mariam, although not glamorous, had pulled her hair up into a neat bun and had donned pressed black slacks and a long-sleeve sweater that bore not the slightest trace of cat hair.

And then there was the cat. The mangy, mean, possibly feral cat that seemed possessed by a whole host of demons. It was now entwined around Bree's ankles, purring as if the senior architect had just walked in with the largest container of catnip on record.

"Well . . . isn't this . . . something?" Bree uttered, a small smile blossoming as she glanced around. She went to set her tote on the floor beside the chair she'd sat in last time, but before she could, Mariam dove below the bag to place a small dish towel between it and the carpet. As she did, the cat let out a sharp yeow and charged across the carpet toward some dark corner.

"I'd hate for that lovely bag of yours to get dust all over it," the waitress said meekly.

Bree cleared her throat and looked around the room. She couldn't be certain, but it seemed that many of the knickknacks were different from those that had been on display the time before. "Oh! I almost forgot!" Bree announced. "I brought some wine. For us to share."

Marian's brow crinkled as she read the label on the bottle Bree had pulled from her tote. "This is from California," she said, a trace of awe in her voice. "So, it must be very good wine. That's very nice of you, Bree, but you didn't need to. I still have several bottles of the Kalashi wine in my pantry. Maybe we should save this . . . for a special occasion?"

"Um, let's have some of this," Bree replied instantly. She dropped her head a couple of inches, aware that she had probably, once again, insulted Mariam out of reflex. Although she had enjoyed the Pakistani wine, this evening she was in the mood for something more . . . cultivated.

As it turned out, Mariam didn't seem offended at all.

"Okay," she answered with a shrug of her shoulders. She padded off toward the kitchen to fill some glasses.

Bree sat back in the chair and considered how best to tilt the conversation when Mariam returned. How she might get the waitress to open up even more about Antonio Tinti and what, if anything, she knew about Tinti's son.

That was about the time she spotted it, pressed close against the opposite arm of the sofa: a medium-size shipping box with a brightly colored mailing label on top. Someone had clumsily wrapped the box with several rows of strapping tape, and multiple postage marks in one upper corner made the package look as if it bore a tattoo sleeve.

Bree's mind drifted back to her previous time in the flat. To a visitor, speaking softly.

"Arriving. Later," he had said. And then Mariam wearing a sullen expression, returning to the sofa.

Her parents had raised her never to pry, but this detective work had taught her otherwise. *If I could just get a peek at the mailing label,* she told herself, rising carefully from the chair.

A short clatter arose in the kitchen. Bree halted, hovered a few inches off the cushion. Waited.

That's when the cat emerged from behind a bookcase, trotted across the room and leapt into Bree's tote. "What? Cat . . . no!" she whispered.

It was too late. The cat was now comfortably curled up and hidden inside her knitting kit. As footsteps moved toward the room, Bree leapt over to the box and read the label as quickly as she could. Instantly, she retreated to the chair and dropped onto the cushion just as Mariam returned with two wine glasses on a simple silver tray.

Bree hadn't been able to make out most of the writing on the label— whoever had mailed the box to Mariam had terrible penmanship, she decided. However, among the inky postmarks at the top of the box was one word that jumped out at her: Cairo.

"I really like this wine, Bree." Mariam carefully set their glasses on the table between them. "Sorry, but I just had to take a couple of sips of it in the kitchen. I love its aroma, and even though it's dry, it has a little hint at the end of . . . nutmeg, is it?" Bree nodded, quickly took a first sip, and allowed the wine to swim in her mouth for several seconds before swallowing it slowly.

"Is it from the county Napa?"

Bree shook her head. "No, Mendocino. A little farther north. But you definitely know your wines, Mariam." She saw an opening, decided to take it. "Did you and . . . Mr. Tinti talk about wines much?"

Mariam frowned. "I'd rather not talk about him, if it's all right with you," she said softly. She pulled at one cuff as she sat on the sofa and leaned forward to retrieve her knitting needles from her bag.

"Oh, I'm sorry. Sure," Bree responded. Inside, however, she sunk. She didn't really want to waste an hour knitting with this woman if it wasn't going to provide some payoff to the investigation. "If you don't mind my asking, why not?" she added.

Out of nowhere, Mariam became clearheaded and detached.

"Well, despite what I said before, his death does sadden me. I am prone to depression and do what I can to avoid situations and conversations that might aggravate it."

She went back to unpacking her knitting project. "I guess I just feel I need to move on from that situation. Tony's murder was very unfortunate, and we have been shocked and upset by it. But I must trust that the police will do their job and find whoever did it. I really have no other choice, do I?"

"No, I suppose not," Bree replied, a wary tone in her voice.

"But, more than anything else, Bree, I'd just like to spend some time getting to know you better." She hesitated, nodded once, then continued. "I haven't mentioned it, but there's something about you—I'm not sure what it is, really—but something that reminds me of a person from my past."

Bree felt flattered and flustered at the same time. *Is she . . . coming on to me,* she wondered silently.

"When I was still in Pakistan, this woman came to our village—she was an American woman, by the way—who had a tremendous impact on me and the other young women in my town. She really affected my outlook on life. Back then, I was trying to help a friend organize a school for the girls in our village. I wasn't allowed to go to school at their age, but I read all the time, about anything and everything I possibly could, especially places outside of Pakistan."

Bree noticed a glimmer of a smile appear on Mariam's face as she related her story. The senior architect thought it ironic, and sad, that after all her curiosity about the bigger world, Mariam seemed to find her happiness not in the cosmopolitan Western city she was now living in, but in the provincial, Third World home she'd left long ago.

"This American, she had so many fascinating ideas about how women should make their way in the world. Revolutionary ideas, for my culture. And not only that, but how governments—even the men in a society—so often suppress our freedoms." Mariam uttered a short laugh. "Really, at first, I didn't know how to respond to her. In some ways, the ideas she presented were—you know—blasphemy to our culture. And yet, I was mesmerized by them. By her. Everything she said, I knew to be utterly and completely true. And, there was something about how she spoke about the glorious talents we women have inside us, and how institutions and traditions so often keep us from developing those talents and using them to benefit a greater good . . . it just stirred up so much in me."

Bree was nodding, transported. To a rally, many years ago in Palo Alto. It was the first time she had heard Carole speak about international human rights and how so many countries were refusing to respect even the most fundamental entitlements of their citizens, particularly the country's ethnic or sexual or religious minority. She'd never given much thought to such issues; in fact, she was at the rally only because she'd nabbed a freelance gig from a women's magazine to photograph the female speakers. A women's magazine she'd neither heard of, nor read.

And just as Mariam had found her core beliefs altered by her colleague, so too had Bree found herself enlightened and emboldened by what Carole had said at that rally. She'd sought out Carole backstage and asked if they could have tea together so she could learn more. And found herself shocked when the activist said yes. They spent almost two hours at that tiny tea café on University Avenue, discussing the evolution of feminism and human trafficking, and sexism in the workplace, and medical and reproductive rights, among numerous other topics. Carole, of course, had done most of the talking, while Bree had done most of the listening. And thinking.

After all was said and done, Bree had become a completely different person.

"And," Mariam continued, "when all was said and done, I had become a completely different person. I am certain the direction of my life was permanently altered by this woman. We became quite close friends for the couple of months she was in Pakistan. We took long walks together, discussed the evolving roles of women in the world, and she even helped me develop some materials for the school that tried to instill those ideas in my students in a way that wouldn't alarm the authorities."

With that, she erupted in a laugh that faded as quickly as it had appeared. She was trying to work her needles again, but her effort was lackluster.

"I stayed in touch with Carole for a few months after she left Pakistan, but then one day, she just seemed to disappear."

Bree stopped knitting. She set her needles on her lap, resting them across one another. Soon, however, they were clacking against each other. "I'm sorry, did you say her name was *Carole?*"

Mariam just focused on her knitting.

"Yes. Carole. Whitworth, I think it was. Or maybe Wadsworth. I don't remember where in America she was from. But I do remember she always wore this beautiful silver pin. I think it was in the shape of a porpoise?"

Bree could not breathe. It was *her* Carole. *Their* Carole, apparently. And it was a dolphin pin, not a porpoise pin. A dolphin pin Bree had spent many days seeking a replacement for when Carole had lost hers during a trip to Zimbabwe.

What in the hell are the odds that . . .? She stopped, totally unable to finish her thought.

She tried to knit, but it seemed her knuckles would clench, or twitch in the direction opposite the one her hands needed to go. She was befuddled and angry; it was too much for her to absorb, much less process. This woman, a waitress from Pakistan, knew the murder victim but didn't want to talk about him. Had a package in her flat that had been sent to her from Egypt. Owned a cat that was now balled up inside her knitting tote. And if that weren't enough, had just revealed she also had been acquainted with the most influential person in Bree's life. For maybe the first time, she had no idea what to do. Should she tell Mariam that Carole had influenced her as well, and had offered her counsel during the most difficult period of her life? Did she dare inform Mariam that Carole was now in solitary confinement somewhere, held prisoner by The Organization in some grotto, warehouse, jail cell, or abandoned fuel tank? That they had severed Carole's upper lip from her face and mailed it to her son as proof they were holding her captive and as cruel revenge for her "incendiary" talk?

Or, does Mariam already know all that?

Perplexed, and somewhat paralyzed by it all, Bree chose . . . to just keep knitting. To let it be. To see how it all played out. To act as if the extraordinary was merely ordinary.

Mariam was humming now and exhibiting a newfound dexterity with her needles. The two of them had consumed two-thirds the bottle of wine. Somewhere beyond the windows one could hear a lilting tune that sounded as if it was being produced by a melodica or pump organ. Bree could not find a clock anywhere in the room, but she swore she could hear one ticking.

It seemed as though everything in the world was right again, and that the aura of eccentricity Mariam always brought to an evening had chosen to leave the building.

Bree glanced over at her knitting companion. "What . . . what *is* that you're making, Mariam?"

An eerie grin took over the waitress's face. "It's a quick little project," she said carefully. "When it's finished, I'll put a rock in the bottom of it and give it a polyester fill.

"It's called a *blood-drop* paperweight."

A couple of minutes later, Bree was scurrying down the front steps of Mariam's building.

"You sure you don't want to take the rest of the wine with you?" the waitress called out from the doorway.

"NO, REALLY, I'm good. You enjoy it, Mariam, my compliments. It was such fun, but I completely forgot I have to meet the others at an earlier hour than usual tomorrow. I can't wait to see the finished version of your . . ."

She couldn't bear to bring herself to finish the sentence. A few steps later, she also realized she couldn't bear to lug her heavier-than-usual tote much farther.

Oh no, she thought. *Mariam's cat.*

As if summoned by telepathy, the Bengal cat poked its head out the top of the tote and scrambled its way out of the bag. The feline took several steps forward, then stopped briefly and looked back at Bree, before resuming its retreat into the darkness.

Bree knew better, but she would have sworn that when the cat had glanced over its shoulder, it had given her a long, sly wink.

39

"Still haven't connected the message about the luggage to either the tailor or the Lebanese businessman, have we?" Lara was trying not to sound disappointed. She appreciated Liam's contributions to the team, she really did. Still, her tone carried more exasperation than she had intended.

"No. Sorry, Lara," Liam replied.

The firm's second-in-command looked away from her computer screen . . . and her heart melted. There he stood, his hands shoved deep into the pockets of his navy- blue corduroys, his head tilted downward in shame. She recalibrated a bit, stood up from the desk and took a couple of steps toward him.

"I understand," she said in the most conciliatory tone she could muster. "I haven't had any luck either. I've tried every decryption software I can think of, checked and double-checked every IP address on the planet. I tried to identify precisely where those suitcases were manufactured to see if I could locate any communication from the factory to anyone else out there on the internet, but . . ." She shrugged her shoulders and shook her head.

"I know," he replied. "I've even looked for seven individual purchases of the same suitcase from seven different locations in a relatively short amount of time. No dice. It's like they magically appeared out of nowhere."

"And much to my surprise, someone I worked with several years ago at the National Bureau of Investigation in Finland wasn't able to turn up anything. And he is probably the very best cyber-investigator on the planet."

Liam glanced up, his hangdog expression hanging even more than before.

"No offense, Liam," Lara quickly added. "I should have said . . . *was* the best cyber-investigator. I am sure that now you are far more than capable than he is."

He stared at her quietly for a few seconds before cracking a scintilla of a smile. "So I've been told," he responded softly.

He moved toward her . . . and she whirled around and stepped quickly back to her desk.

"What now, then? Do you think you're out of tricks?" she asked, her back to him. "Or do you want to keep trying?" Her tone had returned to that of the efficient administrator.

The silence lasted even longer than the one before.

"No, I think I want to keep trying," he finally replied.

***

Lara sent Liam a brief smile as she shut the door behind him. For a moment, she hung by the door, her palms pressed against it. How flattering it would be if he were truly interested in her. But she was mature enough to know he was probably interested only in seeing whether he could get her interested in him.

She had to applaud him for making a woman in her early fifties feel attractive. A lot of men his age wouldn't bother doing even that. Still, she knew better than to seriously fall for his flirtatiousness. Besides, they had more important things to focus on at present. They had made no headway in identifying Tinti's killer. And whatever The Organization planned to do to launch their vision for their Transformation in London couldn't be more than a few days away.

Maybe even within the next day or so.

She set herself back onto the seat cushion and waited a moment to be certain no one was lurking outside her room. Satisfied there was no one in the hallway, she enlarged the browser screen she'd minimized while Liam was there.

It was the page outlining the numerous VIP packages Delfina Delgado was offering that month. This woman had answered both her wish to reconnect with Finland *and* her question as to how she should respond to the job offer from Aalto University. And she had answered both clearly and promptly. She had no reservations now about Delfina's legitimacy. She was more than willing to send the woman any sum to direct her toward the positive influences she needed in her life and steer her away from those that would only do her harm.

Maybe Delfina can even help me better understand why my father defected to The Organization, she thought. *Or ease the grief I've had since my mother passed on.*

She shook her head suddenly, reprimanding herself.

Oh, for goodness' sake, she reminded herself. *She's a psychic, not a psychotherapist.*

She scrolled down and vacillated between the different options. Contemplated the peace of mind a VIP Elite package might provide her and wondered whether the VIP Basic package might suffice.

More than once, her cursor hovered over the check box for each. Finally, she clicked the white square next to the words VIP Elite and hit the button that said NEXT.

That took her to a page that asked her to select the checking, credit, or online pay account she wanted her payment to be drawn from. She hadn't realized—but was thrilled to learn—there were so many different means by which she could execute this fifty-thousand-dollar investment in her future . . .

***

He knew Lara probably thought he was just toying with her. That he was just some insincere lothario who viewed a dalliance with her as more of an ego-building conquest than a genuine expression of affection.

Liam double-clicked on the icons of a couple of chat rooms on the dark web to see if there were any interesting conversations underway. There were more people than usual using the rooms today, but nothing they were talking about looked consequential, much less, apocalyptic. He was being cautious, using the rogue network and online account that likely shielded him from the prying eyes of The Organization. Or so he hoped.

His thoughts returned to Lara. He knew she probably found him "adorable," but flighty. Charming in a raffish way, but too callow to take seriously. Maybe she was right. But the attention he was paying her came from a genuine place. He wasn't clear why, but he felt a need to look out for her (even though she was probably the strongest and most capable woman he had ever met).

Strength can be a deceptive façade, he told himself. He then let out a hearty laugh. *Dude, that may be the deepest thought you've ever had.*

He kept scanning the chat rooms he had been monitoring, then opened another browser window to peek in on yet another set of conversations. His eyes flitted across the screen like a laser pointer, seeking out terms like *luggage, baggage, Titania,* and *suitcase,* as well as such words and phrases as *initiative, revolution, transformation,* and, the winner-winner-chicken-dinner of them all, *Power to the cause.*

Confidentially, Lee had suggested to Liam that he also keep an eye out for any word or phrase that could be a coded euphemism for *bomb.*

His mind meandered back to Lara. But not so much to *Lara* (to be honest, he found her intimidating as much as he found her alluring) as to the reasons why he might be preoccupied with her. Mommy issues? He played with that for a few moments but discarded it quickly. His mum was tanned and athletic whereas Lara was powdered and cerebral. His mother was gregarious, whereas Lara was reserved; undemanding, while Lara was meticulous.

He jolted forward when he spotted the word *explosive* in the middle of some chatter. But it turned out to be an underground journalist making a reference to an expose on a British politician, an expose brimming with details that would likely have "explosive ramifications" on the coming elections.

He relaxed and went back to considering why he was having the feelings he was having. After a couple of more minutes, he shrugged his shoulders, deciding it didn't really matter. He felt some tug to protect an older woman, and that was likely all it was. No need to get all analytical about it; they were co-workers (technically, she was his boss), so nothing should, or would, come of it.

Then he decided to try hacking into the IP addresses used by some former members of The Organization who either had been captured over the past couple of years or had chosen on their own to "come back to the clear side" (what they called the process of undergoing intense deprogramming). He knew that sometimes those addresses—or very similar ones, anyway—got resurrected by new recruits to "the club."

But before he could get a search underway, an icon on his screen began to pulse. It was connected to someone within The Lee Group. He hadn't told anyone, but Lee had asked Liam to surreptitiously install tracking devices on everyone's computers as a security precaution. Not because the head of the firm didn't trust his employees, but because he wanted to protect them should they wander somewhere on the internet where they could get into some danger, or accidentally reveal too much about their side of the investigation.

He leaned forward to see which team member was connected to that icon and what might have triggered the alarm. As he studied his screen, he placed his right elbow on the desktop and dropped his chin into his upturned palm.

Why in bloody hell, he asked himself, *is Lara transferring that large a sum out of the firm's primary checking account?*

40

Lee thought about taking the Maicoletta up to Cambridge. But showers overnight had left many of the roads slick, and it wasn't clear yet when the showers were going to end. On top of that, he didn't want to have to repeatedly hunt for places to park the scooter in a university town flush with cyclists.

So, he opted for the train instead. And was glad he did. No sooner had he settled himself into his first-class seat when a text came in from Anisa.

May have found Tinti's phone
In a wall safe at back of closet
Working with manufacturer to get it unlocked
Will update you when we know more

Had Lee been on his scooter, he would have made an immediate U-turn and returned to London. But they were already ten minutes out of Kings Cross, and the trip took only an hour, so . . .

The architect did view the discovery of Tinti's phone to be an incredible stroke of good fortune. But he also thought it strange the tailor hadn't taken the device to Hanover Square the night he was murdered.

Did he not want anyone finding out who he was meeting that night? he wondered. Then another more sinister option presented itself. *Or did the killer pluck the phone from Tinti's corpse and somehow plant it later in the wall safe?*

The train was about eight minutes late when it pulled into Cambridge Station. To his surprise, the busiest rail station in the east of England seemed unusually serene. But he reminded himself it was midmorning on a weekday, so he shouldn't be *that* surprised.

Since he didn't plan to be gone more than a day (if that), he hadn't brought a suitcase. So within moments, he was exiting the station's long, classical façade, which had been executed by Sancton Wood, the designer of many of England's nineteenth-century railway destinations. He was relieved to see a phalanx of bicycles for hire just outside the exit, which made his decision to leave the Maicoletta behind all the more sensible. Using an app on his phone to unlock one of the bikes, he soon was off on the two-wheeler, heading for the campus that had made him the architect, the man, and (in some ways) the detective, he was today.

On one level, he wished his visit had not been so impromptu. Otherwise, he would have headed straight to Scroope Terrace, and the department of architecture, to have a grand reunion with any professors he'd had who still taught there, as well as the classrooms in which he had learned his craft. Given his current stature in the field, the administration, no doubt, would more than welcome him. But it was early October, so classes were likely in session this morning. And, he didn't want to cause a ruckus. His purpose here was not to stroke his ego but to reconnect with the place that had kindled his passion for architecture.

As well as his passion to do whatever it took to destroy The Organization.

He chose to take Regent Street into the heart of Cambridge and was soon alongside his first stop, the magnificent King's College Chapel, constructed in the late fifteenth and early sixteenth centuries. A grand vision of King Henry VI, the chapel was modeled on a cathedral choir by master mason Reginald Ely. However, its construction got delayed, first by the Wars of the Roses, then by the imprisonment and murder of Henry VI in the Tower of London, and finally by the death of his successor, Edward IV. Thirty-seven years after the foundation stone had been laid, only the foundation and walls made of white magnesian limestone had been finished.

Fortunately, Richard III (and later Henry VII and Henry VIII) made the chapel one of their priorities. By 1515, the main structure was completed and upon Henry VIII's death in 1547, it was widely recognized as one of the world's finest examples of Late Medieval architecture in Europe.

Lee thought it miraculous that the chapel had survived both the English Civil War and the Second World War (although he thought it likely the removal of the chapel's stained glass before the Blitz began was mostly responsible for that miracle). *Thank heavens they did that,* he thought, *for as spectacular as the exterior is, the interior is truly off the hook.*

Although he was a devotee of contemporary forms, Lee could not help but swoon over the chapel's exquisite fan vaulting, decorated with carefully carved bosses featuring coats of arms, wild beasts, and a host of Tudor symbols. Carved equally well, Lee thought, was the screen that divided the antechapel from the choir and bore the initials of Anne Boleyn and the screen's donor, King Henry VIII. And how could one possibly look askance, he thought, at the magnificent painting by Peter Paul Rubens, *The Adoration of the Magi,* placed just above the chapel's high altar.

Knowing that this outstanding example of medieval architecture was only a few hundred meters away was inspiration enough for me to push my learning here that much more, Lee told himself.

From there, Lee maneuvered the bicycle up Kings' Parade to The Senate House, another neoclassical gem. Built in 1722 by the renowned architect James Gibbs, the building for many years had served as the university's parliament building of sorts, hosting meetings conducted by the school's Council of the Senate. These days, however, it mainly hosted the school's graduation ceremonies, and Lee thought fondly on the times he'd watched the son or daughter of some friend or colleague receive a diploma in The Senate House.

He loved how the temple and basilica that comprised The Senate House formed not a square, circle, or rectangle, but a parallelogram. And, of course, the roof of the structure remained dear to the hearts of many Cambridge alumni as the place where on a summer evening in 1958, several students hoisted a beat-up Austin Seven van for everyone to see. By morning, however, the vehicle had vanished, whisked off by either an efficient administration or other students who had become envious of the clever prank.

As Lee made his way toward Trinity College's Great Court, the sky began to brighten. *Perfect timing,* Lee thought, *for if there ever were a space and a collection of buildings that were enhanced by shafts of sunlight, it is Great Court.*

Believed to be Europe's largest enclosed court, Great Court was completed in the early 1600s by Thomas Nevile, an English clergyman and academic. The idea for the court came about when Nevile saw a need to bring some sort of coherence to the buildings and public spaces across the university's campus. He rearranged existing buildings to create the court, bestowing upon Cambridge an architectural masterpiece.

Lee took careful note of the Porters' Lodge and the Great Gate, which features a renowned statue of university founder, King Henry VIII. He chuckled upon recalling the story that in the nineteenth century, students once skulked their way up the gate in the dark of night and replaced the scepter in Henry VIII's hands with a far less regal table leg.

He also took note that the famous clock embedded in the King's Gate (the entrance to the oldest section of Trinity College) continued to chime every fifteen minutes and to note the hour not once, but twice. He knew that was because the clock was installed in the seventeenth century at the request of Master of Trinity, Richard Bentley, who insisted the clock strike once each hour for the college of his mastership, for Trinity, and once more for his alma mater, St John's College, Cambridge.

But Lee's favorite aspect of the Great Court was its chapel, begun by Queen Mary I in 1554 to honor her father. Lee was particularly impressed with the antechapel's statues (honoring such famous Trinity men as Isaac Newton) as well as the Metzler organ that was located within a restored seventeenth-century case built by one of England's most important organ builders, Father Smith.

Most people, however, knew the Great Court best for its renowned run, featured in the award-winning film, *Chariots of Fire*. For centuries, intrepid athletes have made it their objective to run the court's 431-meter perimeter in the forty-three seconds it takes the clock to strike twelve. Lee was impressed that, over time, only two runners had officially succeeded. During his second year at Cambridge, when he was at his fittest, Lee had toyed with the idea of making a go of it. But the idea fell by the wayside when three days before his attempt, he tripped running up the stairs to the commissary, twisting his ankle in the process.

I coulda been a contender, Lee joked to himself as he pedaled the bike away from the area.

On the way to his next stop, it dawned on the architect that the Great Court Run was an excellent analogy for his life these days. He felt he was always trying to outsprint The Organization, to get to them before the clock struck twelve—before they implemented whatever nefarious plot they had in store. He also frequently worried he would trip and twist an ankle (or suffer some other extraordinary act of clumsiness) before he could prevent their plan from moving forward. Lee knew he was growing weary of having to play, *Beat the Clock*.

It didn't help that it was while he was at Cambridge that he spotted the precise time on a clock pictured in the background of a photo discovered during a federal raid in California. The time on that clock had been the critical clue that had helped him solve the assassination of California congresswoman Elizabeth Hirshhorn twenty years ago and bring The Organization to its knees.

Or so everyone had thought . . .

His irritable mood shifted as he approached the two courts that made up the Cripps Building at St. John's College, which no one would mistake for a neoclassical masterpiece. Built in the 1960s to relieve a shortage of student housing, and designed by the renowned architects Philip Powell and Hidalgo Moya, the courts were indeed masterful, but in a more contemporary sort of way.

Lee thought it ingenious how the architects, Powell and Moya, had made a series of horizontal blocks appear less dense. Their addition of cloisters allowed passersby to see through the Cripps Building to the River Cam and The Backs beyond. They also gave an airiness to the project by making the windows highly vertical and by layering onto the faces of the buildings not one but two varieties of Portland stone.

Lee didn't want to travel beyond Northampton Street, so he turned the bike around and headed down Bridge and then Sidney Street, into the heart of the city. A soft breeze had kicked up and for a few moments, he felt like he was twenty-two again, preparing for examinations and fretting whether the designs in his portfolio were sophisticated enough for him to land a position with some esteemed architectural firm.

Had he only known . . .

Moments later, he pulled up beside the chapel of Emmanuel College, more affectionately known as "Emma." Anyone with any expertise in British architecture would instantly recognize this as one of the early works of Sir Christopher Wren, one of England's greatest architects. And here was yet another clock, nestled in the center of the pediment at the top of the chapel. Lee could not believe it when he learned that anybody can now download a track, produced by the BBC Sound Effects Centre, of the clock striking every hour, on the hour.

Lee was aware the chapel's original plain windows had been replaced in 1884 with exquisite, stained-glass versions as part of the commemoration of the college's tercentenary. The figures in the windows ran the gamut from Saint Augustine of Hippo and Saint Anselm, to two of the college masters, Laurence Chaderton and John Harvard, the educator who went on to found Harvard College in America. And Lee was pleased that despite its classical look, the chapel had chosen to assume a progressive place in history when in 2006 it became the first chapel within the Church of England to bless same-sex civil partnerships (albeit only those involving members and alumni of Emmanuel College).

It was as Lee was about to remount his bike that the young man appeared. The architect was standing beside his bicycle admiring the chapel when someone who appeared to be a fresher crossed in front of him, right to left. The youth was wearing black jeans and a gray hoodie, and as he passed, he was staring at the grass near the architect's feet. Lee thought the student looked familiar but couldn't place from where.

"Sir? Sir! Your shoelaces are both untied. Be sure you don't trip over them."

Lee glanced at his shoes, and sure enough, both of his laces looked like wild clumps of overcooked pasta. And then it struck him. He'd had this very same experience once before. Only it had been in Miami on the campus of Florida International University with the exact same young man. Only there, the student had been wearing a t-shirt and shorts, not a hoodie and jeans. But he had uttered the very same concern to Lee and then instructed the architect how to tie his laces so they wouldn't come undone.

"You!" Lee barked. "I remember you! Florida, remember? You helped me with my shoelaces there, too. What are you doing here, in Cambridge of all places? Sorry, I guess I haven't been following your instructions as diligently as I should have."

The young man's face went blank, and his expression went from helpful to fearful. He offered a half-hearted smile, shook his head once, and started to trot away.

Twenty yards out, several faculty members ambled across the green, blocking Lee's ability to see the student. When they had cleared Lee's line of view, however, the young man was nowhere to be found. Lee squinted, then looked at both his shoes. The lace on the left shoe was still hanging loose, but the right lace was tied tight. He chewed the inside of one cheek for a moment.

This has to stop, he lectured himself. *This just isn't right.*

He decided (for the time being, anyway) that the best thing for him to do was to pedal on.

He navigated his way past Downing College, renowned for having one of the first major buildings of the Greek Revival period in England (Lee lamented however, that architect William Wilkins's plan for a grand campus, similar to Thomas Jefferson's vision for the University of Virginia, never came to be.) He then ambled past yet another neoclassical stunner, the recently renovated Fitzwilliam Museum, finished in 1848. He thought about going into the lower galleries to view once again the ancient sarcophagi from Egypt and the funerary couch from Rome, and to ascend to the upper galleries to enjoy the impressive collection of watercolors by J. M. W. Turner.

The architect checked his phone again. It was nearing midday and he was determined to be back in London before six. The train he wanted to take back to the city left just before three, so he had a little more time for sightseeing, but not enough time to explore the museum, he decided.

Where should I go next, he asked himself. He was enjoying his unusual role as tourist but also knew it was, for him, a form of procrastination. A general outline of the murder of Antonio Tinti was brewing in his mind, but he felt he needed more time to let the elements all come together. It would be epic if Tinti's phone contained the final bits of data he needed to determine who had enticed the tailor to Hanover Square to murder him.

I feel like there's this gigantic geometry problem I'm supposed to solve, but I'm not allowed to have a compass, ruler, protractor, or computer to help solve it, he thought. *And, there's this huge hourglass beside me, and the sand in it is rushing into the lower chamber more quickly than I can even grasp what the problem is.*

He didn't have an answer for the geometry problem but thinking about geometry helped him land on where he wanted to head next. The Mathematical Bridge over the River Cam was among his favorite works in town—on many afternoons he had focused on this engineering marvel as he lounged alongside one of the river's tranquil banks.

It was an urban myth that Sir Isaac Newton had designed the quirky bridge without any nuts or bolts, and that those items had been added by students who had dissembled the bridge but were stumped when they tried to reassemble it. In fact, the original version of the wooden footbridge was designed by William Etheridge and built by James Essex in 1749. Lee believed it had been rebuilt on two occasions (in 1866 and in 1905) and that the latest version retained most of the design of the original. Although the Mathematical Bridge appears to be an arch, it is constructed entirely of straight timbers from an unusually sophisticated engineering design.

Lee stood next to his bike, holding tight to the handlebars as he beheld the span for the first time in more than a decade. It was on his last visit here that he realized it was the optical illusion of the arc that had likely influenced his belief that things are not always what they seem to the naked eye.

His next-to-last stop was a bit out of the way, across the river. But his love for contemporary design demanded he look in on the History Faculty Library, to see how well its unusual lines and angles were holding up. Lee recalled that the building had opened in 1968: its design by James Frazier Stirling had actually been an entry in an architectural competition. The building he now was gazing upon was almost identical to that winning design, except for its having been reoriented a full ninety degrees so it would fit on the site specified for it.

Lee decided the design of the brick-and-glass building had held up over time, even if it did exude a 1960s personality. From the side he was on, it resembled a polyhedron, topped by a short, wedding-cake-style pyramid of glass, which in turn, was shielded from the elements by two tall wings of glass and brick that flared out on either side. It was far more intricate and interlocking than that, however, with glass walls that in places stair-stepped away from the street, and ramps and towers that gave the library the appearance of something a very creative five-year-old had assembled from a set of building blocks.

It was the library's interior, however, that Lee was most smitten with. A vast reading room that could accommodate three hundred people featured carrels positioned in semicircular arcs that nested one inside the other. An atrium above was flanked by at least three floors of offices featuring windows partially shielded by white panels. Natural light streamed through the glass windows at the top of the atrium onto the readers below, eliminating whatever stuffy stereotype one might have of a history library.

Often, Lee had come there to read, to think, to dream. Once, a young woman in the carrel next to him had captured his fascination. She had auburn hair, wore a cable-knit sweater, and dark slacks. The more he stared at her, the more he thought she might just be "the one." Sadly, the more he stared at her, the more uncomfortable she became, to the point of discreetly picking up her materials and moving to a carrel on the opposite side of the room.

Lee noticed it was time for him to scoot over to what would be his last, but most meaningful, stop. The residence hall within Old Court was where he had spent two glorious years as an undergraduate (and fellow) while attending Queens' College. Constructed from 1448-1451, the court was the epitome of medieval styling, with Gothic windows coming to a point, square turrets at each corner, and a rectangular gatehouse featuring octagonal towers at each of its corners. He had read that Queens' was the first college in the world to adopt such a look, and the style spread far and wide, eventually inspiring Blair Tower at Princeton University in the United States.

The architect laid his bike on the ground and stood with his hands on his hips, peering up at the building that had served as his home for many months. He tried to picture a young student slumped in one of the rooms' frumpy armchairs, reading Voltaire or poring over a history of Tudor castles the way he had. He hoped that student had the same insatiable curiosity about the greater world that he had back in the day and prayed that student was never thrust into an international maelstrom like the one he stepped into when he solved (in that very room) the assassination of Congresswoman Hirshhorn.

His thoughts floated to the day he first settled into Old Court, his mother and father trailing behind him like courtesans tending to their royal highness. His mother fretted whether the accommodations were large enough for him; his father questioned the integrity of the building's foundation. Their fussing and fidgeting had irritated him at that time; of course, now he'd now pay a hefty ransom to receive so much attention from them.

That was the day his father had played a practical joke on him. They had moved in all his belongings, taken a tour of every nook and cranny of Queens' College, and arranged (and rearranged) every item in his room. The sun was lowering in the horizon; it was time for his parents to leave. His mother kept forestalling their departure, so finally his father stepped up to the task by extending his right hand and wishing his son a productive term ahead.

"Dalton, we know you will make us proud," his father had said, "and that you understand this is the beginning of your life apart from us. Your independence is upon you and I want you to know we plan to rent out your room back in San Diego, since you'll really have no need for it in the future."

It was true that Lee had been eager to establish his own rhythms and routine. But he hadn't expected his parents to cut the cord so abruptly. Not yet. Not now.

"You're . . . renting out my room?" he replied. "Already? You're kidding, right?"

His father gave a look far more grave than any Lee had seen him wear. Then the older Lee raised one hand and placed it solidly on Lee's right shoulder.

"Son," he said, a steeliness in his voice, "I've never been so serious about anything in my entire life."

Lee was crestfallen, and more than a little peeved his father would ruin what was supposed to be such a joyous day for him. However, being the obedient child, he nodded sharply once in reply, before allowing his head to droop in sadness.

His mother offered a brief but firm hug, then the pair scurried out the door. A bit shell-shocked, Lee stood in the center of the room, reviewing his possessions and reassessing his feeling about the word "freedom."

He was starting to place his books into one of the nearby shelving units when the door squeaked, and his father padded back into the flat. His expression was mostly neutral but seemed softer than when he had departed. He ambled toward his son, put his right hand into the younger Lee's left palm and embraced the college student around his upper back. He then ducked in toward Lee's right ear and squeezed his son tight.

"Two things," he whispered quickly. "One, your father will *never* allow himself to show his true emotions in front of your mother. Got that?"

A quick smile broke out across Lee's face and he nodded. Then, his father pressed even closer to his son's ear.

"And, two. If you ever hear me say I've never been so serious about anything in my entire life, know what I mean is the very opposite of that."

41

While Dalton Lee was relaxing on the train that would return him to Kings Cross station, seven people in seven completely different sections of London received the same message simultaneously on their phones:

Christmas has arrived early, luvs!
Come enjoy a slice of pie and help open
the seven presents we've received
from our friends overseas.
3 in the afternoon.
Thursday, October 4.
Room 1101, Ivy Palace Hotel.
No need to RSVP,
for attendance at this gathering is. . .
MANDATORY

***

Autumn blasted its way into London just as Dalton Lee was wending his way from the train station to the team's residence. There had been hints of it in the days before: a cool snap here, leaves tumbling gently to

287

the ground over there, brief but heavy showers now and then.

This weather phenomenon, however, was different. Its personality went beyond forceful; it was *foreboding*. It unleashed violent and sustained gusts that made tree branches dangle like broken arms and colonies of leaves swirl first around one's ankles, then one's knees, and eventually, one's waist. The rain, though intermittent, was torrential. Umbrellas did not just invert, they snapped in two, jettisoning their canopies into the air like projectile missiles aimed at some distant target.

By the time Dalton Lee slammed shut the front door to the townhouse, he was gasping for breath and clutching his chest.

"My God! The weather out there is *appalling!"* he announced as Margarida came to relieve him of his coat. The bones of the residence creaked, and the windows whistled and sighed around him, as he stagger-stepped his way from the entryway into the dining room beyond. Every so often, it sounded as if someone were splashing a mammoth pail of water against every window. Then, everything would turn eerily serene.

"This used to be my favorite season," Lee confessed. "But *this . . . this is . . .* insane!"

Margarida padded off to pour the architect a cup of his favorite jie tea. Bree was sitting at the dining table, but it was almost impossible to see her for all the knitting accessories she had stacked up in front of her.

"Dalton, someone from C. J's team called. They believe they found . . ."

The architect raised his left palm as he slumped into a chair at the opposite end of the table. "Tinti's phone. Yes, I know. Anisa texted me about that while I was on my way to Cambridge."

At the mention of Anisa, Bree glanced at her boss and slowed her knitting.

"Is everything all right, Dalton? Did you enjoy seeing Cambridge again?"

Lee nodded but didn't reply.

She resumed the velocity she'd been displaying with her needles before Lee had entered the room, raising her chin a few inches as she did so.

"Oh, and I spent some more time with that waitress, Mariam."

Lee looked up, waited for more detail.

"Sorry, but she didn't reveal anything valuable about Tinti. In fact, she seemed to me to be avoiding any talk about him at all. Almost every time I brought him up, she changed the subject. Or tried to." One of the balls of yarn rolled off the tabletop and in the direction of the wall behind her. She twisted her torso and extended one arm toward the errant yarn. "For . . . someone who seemed . . . so concerned about Mr. Tinti . . . when we first met her," Bree said, straining to reach the ball with her fingertips, "she certainly seems to have done . . . an about-face." Deftly, she slid one palm beneath the orb, tossed it about two inches in the air to secure it in her hand, swiveled back around, and leaned forward to place the ball closer to the center of the table for safekeeping.

Lee nodded to Margarida as she brought him his tea. "From what I've observed," he said, "her moods are mercurial."

The room fell quiet after that. Lee slurped his tea, contemplated whether to ring up C. J. or text her to learn more about the discovery of Tinti's phone. Bree continued her knitting, but over time, her speed lessened as she periodically glanced at the man who was trying to rescue so many people the team cared about. Her lower lip twitched some; eventually, she set her needles on the table and crossed her wrists in front of her.

"You hear voices, sometimes, don't you, Dalton?"

The architect was in midslurp when Bree asked the question; his cup hung in midair as he wondered how to respond. He never expected anyone to say something like this, so he didn't have a prepared response to deliver.

All he knew was that a wave of anxiety started washing over him.

"Why do you say that, Bree?"

She ran her tongue across her lips, trying to choose her words carefully.

"I've heard you. Actually, I've *seen* you. Sometimes. I've seen you have a conversation with . . ."

The architect waited. Raised his eyebrows. "With . . .?"

Bree looked down at her crafting accessories for a moment, then directly into his eyes. "With *something*. Not *someone*. Some*thing*."

Lee nodded then took a gulp of tea and winced from how hot it was. He picked up the napkin by his left wrist and patted his lips.

"And, that's not normal, is it, Bree?"

She reacted as if he had hurled an insult her way, then focused on a spot somewhere beyond his right shoulder.

"I don't think it's something I want to . . . put a judgment on, Dalton," she stammered. "I mean, at some point, we all hear voices, really. Well, maybe we hear them, or maybe it's more that we *feel* them. Inside of us. I just think that maybe, the voices you're hearing are trying to tell you something important. Something that will help you see or understand some aspect of the murders we investigate, some aspect about them the rest of us don't see or understand." She'd stopped looking over Lee's shoulder and was now studying the tabletop and massaging her fingers. "And that, maybe, those voices the rest of us hear inside of us, you hear . . . from something *outside* of you, like a room, a park, maybe, even, an art gallery." She paused, then seemed suddenly emboldened by some newfound clarity. "I think when you hear a voice, Dalton, it's trying to guide you, send you in the direction you're supposed to go. In the direction we're all supposed to go . . . *with* you."

Lee sat impassive, thought for some time about what Bree had said, then very deliberately set his cup on the saucer in front of him.

"But it's still not normal, is it?" he repeated.

The optimistic expression on Bree's face clouded. As the seconds passed, the corners of her mouth methodically arced downward.

"No," she finally replied, shaking her head gently. "No, Dalton, it's not."

***

When C. J. answered her phone, Lee heard a forceful spray of water in the background.

Surely, she isn't taking this call in the shower, he told himself.

In short order, the spraying ceased. "Ah, Dalton, how are things?

Yes, I'm working late, which is problematic because I have a gig out in Hoxton later tonight. How was your visit to the old alma mater?"

The very moment she finished her questions, the gush of water resumed.

"For heaven's sakes, C. J., what are you . . . oh, never mind," he said. "Um, the trip. It was fine. But Anisa texted me that we've . . . that, um, your team that is . . . found Tinti's phone? In a wall safe?"

The spraying sound intensified for a moment, then stopped altogether.

"Yes. Curious, isn't it?" she answered. "The safe was at the very back of his closet and hidden from view by several hangers full of coats and jackets."

The spraying began again, only this time in short bursts, followed by one long spray. Lee then detected the commander moving the phone away from her mouth. "Graham, would you please set this on the radiator out there to dry?" she asked. "Yes, over there, thank you." Lee heard some shuffling before C. J.'s voice came back full into the receiver.

"I wondered if he perhaps owned two phones. And that the one we found in the safe was a backup. But we checked with his carrier, and they showed only one phone on his account. And there's no evidence of him having an account with another carrier. So it does seem rather odd that he didn't take his phone to Hanover Square, especially if he intended to meet someone there. But maybe he just forgot it. Heaven knows, I forget mine more than I care to admit."

Lee murmured his agreement then decided to venture the idea that had come to him earlier. "Is it possible, C. J., that the killer took Tinti's phone and put it in the wall safe?"

There was quiet on the other end of the phone for but a moment. "Not likely," she responded. "We've had agents stationed outside Tinti's flat since the murder. I know those two agents quite well. If someone was able to get past that duo and enter the building, then heaven help us all."

Lee decided to try another tack. "What about the call logs? Any luck yet accessing them?"

C. J. let out a long sigh. "You know, Dalton, I have enormous respect for your technology companies there in America, I really do." The chair screeched for several seconds before she continued the thread. "But they can be quite difficult at times like this. I appreciate their concerns about personal privacy, and all, but for goodness sakes, we're talking about a murder victim here."

A metallic clank told Lee the commander had just tossed something into the trash can beneath her desk. "But we are persevering in our negotiations with the manufacturer. We hope to hear something positive from them soon."

"There's not much time, C. J." Even the architect was stunned at the urgency in his voice.

"I know, Dalton," she responded just as curtly. "Trust me, I've made them quite aware of that."

***

Liam slumped in his desk chair, with only the computer screen lighting the room.

He wanted to be as inconspicuous as possible and deflect anyone knocking on his door, in part because he had a hunch tonight was the night The Organization would transmit some sort of important instructions to one of its agents in London, and he wanted to be alert if, or when, that happened. And, in part, because all he was wearing was a thick, red hoodie and black bikini underwear. It wasn't that he was trying to make some sort of fashion statement; he'd just been negligent with his laundry, and what he had on was all he had clean.

He clicked away from the video of a married couple in their seventies surfing off the coast of Western Australia and checked the progress of the hack he had underway. "68 %," it read. He shoved himself back in the chair, placed his hands on his thighs, and reflected on his own grandmum, who had worn out more than one surfboard in her time. Lovely woman she was, always smelled of lavender or some such fragrance. Liked to muss his hair with one hand and swat him on the bottom with the other whenever he got rowdy, which was often. She usually had a smooth, dark tan, and although not prone to competitive sports, she would be the first to jump into the cockpit of an ocean kayak to explore a reef or secluded sea cave someone had told her about.

At this point, he sighed and closed his eyes tight. What must have it been like for her at the bank in Perth, holding tight to her purse, as the vice president told her all the money was gone from her account and could not be recovered. Just because she had trusted a young woman who'd rung her up out of the clear blue one day and said she was the niece of a close friend who had recently passed away. Said she'd won the top prize in Lotterywest but couldn't claim the money because she didn't have the 10 percent deposit they required her to put forward while they verified her credentials. Asked if Liam's grandmother could send that amount to her for just twenty-four hours, insisted she'd repay her just as soon as the state released the prize money.

Only there was no prize money and there was no repayment.

His grandmother had to move in with his parents shortly after that. Sixteen months later, she was dead from skin cancer.

He checked the monitor. "83 %," it now read.

He hadn't told anyone, but ever since, he'd been on the prowl for scams targeting senior citizens. Especially those that relied on emotionally manipulative online hoaxes to whisk away—just like that—hundreds of thousands of dollars, or pounds, or pesos, or yen. In the flutter of an eyelash with no possible way of tracing their destination.

"95 %," the monitor said.

He'd studied every hacking technique one could employ against financial transactions. Had learned how to spot fraudulent perpetrators, identify their location, tap into their bank accounts, and a whole lot more. Had purchased every software program he could find that would aid and abet such defensive hacking (as he liked to call it). Had studied how the shysters operated, the names they operated under, where they operated, and how to pin them to the mat.

And now, all his research, and all his investment in data, and processes, and software, and systems, was about to pay for itself. In spades.

The meter monitoring the progress of his action online began to glow red.

"100 %," it read. "Transfer of funds halted."

Liam beamed, scratched his balls, and thrust one fist into the air in jubilation. *Take that, Delfina Delgado,* he exulted.

In response, his computer emitted a ping; the young Australian cocked his head to the side. One of the underground chat boards he had been monitoring had sent an alert.

An emergency alert.

He clicked over to his dark web browser and saw that one of his many underground email addresses had received a message that, based on its origin and its syntax, had a high probability of coming from someone affiliated with The Organization.

But when Liam went to read it, his brow furrowed. It was more of a pictogram than a message. The first image looked like a filter full of coffee, or maybe a teabag. Next came a symbol resembling a subtraction sign, followed by the word "our" repeated numerous times. *Lots* of times. The message ended with what looked like an image of the Seven Dwarfs. Only in place of each dwarf's face was the image of some nation's flag. He recognized the American flag as well as the Union Jack. The Australian flag was not among them.

He tilted his head one way, closed one eye, and studied the pictogram closely. Put his elbows on the desk, cradled his chin in his hands, thrust his face closer to the screen and looked at the images yet another way. Ran through the names of different teas, from pekoe, to Earl Gray, to pu'erh, to oolong. Wondered if perhaps the subtraction sign was instead meant to represent a fraction, or maybe even a hyphen. Added up how many times the word "our" appeared. It came to more than seventy.

He was stumped.

And then in a flash, he got it.

The first picture *was* of a teabag, but it was more about the tea than the bag itself. The horizontal symbol *was* a subtraction sign, after all. The number of times "our" had been repeated made perfect sense to him now. And the seven flag-draped dwarfs represented the countries attending the G7 summit.

Liam punched his boss's name in his phone's contact list and was relieved when the architect picked up immediately. "Dalton, it's Liam," he said breathlessly. "They've sent an instruction to their troops. It definitely looks like they're targeting the world leaders who are coming to the summit."

"What exactly does the message say?"

Liam peered at his computer screen once again, took in one long, deep breath. "I could be wrong, but I'm pretty sure it's saying, 'T-minus seventy-two hours.'"

42

As he descended the steps leading to the subterranean jazz club known as The Bell Jar, Dalton Lee contorted his face. He'd fully expected to hear a clamor bursting from one of London's most popular jazz spots. But there was no clamor, no raucous laughter, no shrieks or screams of an audience being hurtled into ecstasy by the sudden uptick of a combo's tempo.

Most concerning, there was no sound of a saxophone—tenor or alto.

The architect pulled out his phone to make sure he had the right time, date, and location. Satisfied that he did, he stood at the bottom of the steps and . . . scratched the back of his neck.

That's when the door to the club swung open and two behemoths in dark, ill-fitting suits stepped out. Noticing Lee, they crossed their arms and widened their stances. "Are you Mr. Lee?" asked the one on the left. The architect reacted the way he usually did when someone asked him that question. He hesitated.

"Maybe . . ." he replied, taking a couple of discreet steps back.

"Dalton Lee, the architect?" asked the one on the right. The no-neck smiled slightly, as if he were a fanboy, or possibly someone interested in entering the field of architecture (although given his appearance, that seemed highly unlikely). Convinced the men meant no harm and were merely bouncers for the club, Lee nodded.

The friendlier one stepped back so his colleague could open the door. "We thought so. You match the description Miss Digby gave us," he said. "She's looking forward to seeing you. Have a good time."

Lee flashed a quick grin at the hulks, ducked his head, strode through the doorway, and braced himself for whatever he was about to encounter. And what he encountered was the instant realization that getting a seat at the VIP table was not going to be a problem tonight.

As best he could tell, there were four people in the audience. On the opposite side of the room sat a grizzled thirty-something in a cream-colored fedora and dark-rimmed glasses who seemed mesmerized and depressed by some message he'd just received on his phone. At the back of the dimly lit space in a different corner was a grossly overweight male with stringy black hair. He had two fingers pressed to his lips, as if he were smoking an invisible cigarette. Near the center of the room sat an embarrassingly amorous couple (although, given the generation or so that separated the silver-haired male from his giggly squeeze, Lee guessed they weren't so much a couple as a convenient arrangement of some sort).

On the stage to his left, someone wearing dark trousers, and a white dress shirt with the sleeves rolled up, stood on tiptoe to adjust the amber lights that dangled from above. On Lee's right, a beefy young male with skinny, spiky sideburns maneuvered a white rag in ever-widening circles in hopes of getting the top of the bar as clean as possible. Although the employee looked out across the room, he kept his glance vague and impersonal, as if he were calculating how to make a rapid exit.

Lee edged toward the bar and nodded once at the person behind it, who nodded back but continued to clean. The architect's nostrils twitched at the smell of leftover lager in a glass nearby.

"I thought there was live music here tonight," Lee offered. The bartender glanced at the large silver watch on his left wrist, then thrust that hand deep into one pocket.

"There will be, soon enough. What can I get you? Can I interest the American in one of our homeland's more esteemed whiskies? A

Cardhu eighteen-year, perhaps, or maybe a Mortlach Single Malt?"

Lee was not as well-versed on whiskies as he was bourbons, but he didn't want to come off like some blinkered tourist. So he chose to rely on a tactic that had rescued him from many similar situations.

"Whatever you recommend," he said with a smile.

"Take a seat. I'll have someone bring it to you," the bartender responded, turning away from his customer.

Lee reviewed his options and chose a table two rows behind—and a little to the right of—the May-December romance. But the table wobbled due to the unevenness of the floor and spotting nothing nearby he could use to steady it, Lee switched to the table on the left. The Brazilian blowout on the floozy in front of him was now hindering his view of the stage some, but Lee was in no mood to move again, much less interfere with a couple who now resembled Siamese twins.

No sooner had the bartender set Lee's whisky on the table when the combo, including C. J., took their positions on the stage. Lee felt badly for her that no other patrons had entered the club, found it even odder that it was the bartender (not some waitress) who had brought him his drink.

A fiftyish male wearing a pin-stripe suit and too much pomade leaned into the microphone and gave the audience an artificial smile.

"Good evening, lassies and gents," he said, in the voice of someone who'd enjoyed far too many full-strength Lambert & Butlers in his day. "I'm Nigel Rounds, and we are Nigel Rounds and the Old Fashioneds."

With that, the combo burst into a breezy version of "Begin the Beguine." Positioned directly behind both the bass player and Nigel Rounds, C. J. looked (and sounded) like an afterthought. Lee leaned first one way, then the other, with the hopes of seeing her better, but she seemed to keep turning opposite whichever direction he went. And the few notes that did erupt from her saxophone sounded more like bleats from a wounded sheep.

When the number ended, the sparse audience applauded more enthusiastically then Lee expected . . . or felt was justified.

From there, the Old Fashioneds went on to offer up-tempo versions of "I Get a Kick Out of You," "Blame it on the Bossa Nova," "Careless Whisper," "Rollin' in the Deep," and—the number that amused Lee the most—the Rolling Stones' "Honky Tonk Woman." Lee noted two interesting things as the set progressed. With each song, C. J.'s contributions became more pronounced. And when Lee scanned the audience at the end of each number, it seemed everyone else in the room was scanning the audience as well.

The lights lowered a bit more, and the bandleader stepped forward toward the mic, mopping his brow with a large brown kerchief.

"Before we take a rest, we'd like to offer our personal homage to the late, magnificent, John Coltrane, who was born on this very day in 1926. Coltrane was, of course, the greatest jazz saxophonist. Not just in our lifetime, but in all the lifetimes that have ever been lived."

Rounds stepped back from the microphone to mop his brow again, then leaned back toward it. His gaze was intense, but at the same time wistful. "Trane was a master of both mainstream and avant-garde jazz, and he belongs to that special breed of artists whose works become more admired, and more influential, with each passing year after their death. We lost him way too soon, to heroin addiction and liver cancer. Here to pay tribute to—as I like to call him, 'my personal friend, J. C.'— is our own pretty remarkable saxophonist—my personal friend, C. J."

With that, Nigel Rounds extended his left arm, bowed deeply from the waist, and trotted back from the mic as C. J. trundled toward it. She grinned goofily for a second and, spotting Lee at his table, sent him a quick wave.

"Well, let's get one thing straight right now," she said as she struggled to lower the microphone to her level. "No one is ever going to mistake me for John Coltrane." Lee laughed heartily to give her encouragement, but he was the only one in the audience who did so. She nodded once at Lee, then continued. "I want to tell you, that as a young girl growing up in Wakefield, I'd sit on my bed and listen well into the night— well, sometimes well into the *morning,* actually—to Trane's albums. *Soul Train. Lush Life. Giant Steps.* Maybe it's because my parents used to have battle royals almost every night, and I found a friend in the visceral wails Trane would produce from his sax. Maybe it's because I was a dreamy teenager in dumpy Wakefield, and I found my hope for escape from that place in the free-form runs he would improvise. I'm not really sure why I was always so drawn to John Coltrane's music, but all I know is, he will probably end up being my only true soul mate."

Lee, taking a sip of his whiskey, found that comment both telling . . . and sad.

C. J.'s expression, however, switched from reflective to buoyant. "Now, without further ado, here is my valiant attempt to evoke John Coltrane's unforgettable masterpiece, 'Moment's Notice.'"

With that, C. J. grasped the woodwind like some long-lost lover and blew the house to smithereens. Her runs mimicked gazelles darting across Saharan plateaus; her high notes were as clear as Alpine streams. When she improvised, (which she did quite often) she took Coltrane down alleyways even he might have avoided. Her torso twisted this way and that, while her head shook in the opposite direction, flinging droplets of sweat across the small stage.

At one point, it appeared her energy might be waning. But she took one enormous breath and barreled full speed ahead, increasing both the velocity and volume of the runs she produced. When the trumpets or piano took over, she seemed not to relax but to coil into herself and tap her foot as if priming a stubborn pump. Then she'd enter the number again like a full-blown tornado, gyrating with a force that made the walls tremble.

She was not one with the music. She was its dominatrix.

When it was over—exquisitely spectacularly over—everyone sat quietly eyes wide, jaws slack. Even the couple in front of Lee had ceased their public lovemaking, thunderstruck by what they'd just experienced. The architect placed his right palm against his lips and gently shook his head from side to side, then lowered the hand and began to applaud. The other patrons joined him in the clapping, then stood in unison to emphasize their respect.

Onstage, C. J. grinned goofily once more, squinted to see beyond the footlights. She was nodding like a bobblehead and, noticing Lee with a bemused smile on his face, thrust one finger toward him and bellowed, "DALTON!"

***

It took C. J. a minute to reposition the saxophone so it wasn't poking

Lee in the ribs. Satisfied the instrument was at last secure, she fell sidelong into the seat beside him and exhaled several hours' worth of anxiety.

He looked her up and down, let out a little laugh. "So, *you*. Clara Josephine Digby. You're a commander at Scotland Yard and you just did . . . *that*." He set one wrist upon the other and placed them both upon his lap. "I definitely wasn't expecting . . . *that*."

She chuckled briefly, waved off his adulation. "Now, don't get all dotty on me, Dalton," she replied. "Anyone who's spent more than a couple of hours with *Saxophone for DumDums* could probably accomplish the same thing."

Lee pulled his head back. "Be careful, C. J. Don't forget what someone once said about false modesty—that it's the meanest species of pride out there."

The policewoman across from him smirked and tilted her head. "I prefer what I heard somebody on YouTube call it. 'Arrogance's more beautiful sister,' or some such thing."

They both laughed for some time. Lee relaxed his posture and extended his arm across the back of C. J.'s chair. "No, really, C. J. that was *epic*. And, your testimony about why you admire Coltrane as much as you do, and how much his music meant to you while you were growing up? That *really* moved me. I had musical crushes, too, only mine were for Puccini and Pat Benatar."

The bartender approached and took her order for "a perfect Rob Roy, please." Lee drummed his fingers on the tablecloth as he looked around the club and noticed C. J. seemed to be surveying the room as well.

"Would you like another, sir?" the bartender asked.

"Thanks, but no," Lee replied.

Once the bartender had slunk away, C. J.'s demeanor shifted from playful to businesslike. She glanced behind them, then ducked her head. "There's been an interesting development. Remember the friend Niccolò Tinti sometimes stayed with in Liverpool? The young lady who does everything part-time?"

Lee nodded.

"When I spoke with her on the phone a few days ago, I stressed at the end of our chat that if she thought of anything else that might be useful to us, to please contact me. Well she did, this afternoon."

"What did she have to offer?"

"Well . . . she told me she had suddenly remembered Niccolò showing up at her flat a couple of months ago in somewhat of an agitated state. She said he wasn't irate, but was pacing, tossing cups and saucers into the sink, that sort of thing. Anyway, when she pressed him about what was wrong, he told her he'd left in his car some documents related to a new job he had hired on to. A job with some operation whose ethics were less than admirable, he told her. And that his father had come across those documents when he borrowed the son's car to go to the store. And, that when his father returned he 'went to spare over it' (as she put it) yelling until Niccolò Tinti thought his father was going to burst a blood vessel."

"Okay."

"Well, Little Miss Part-Time goes on to say she didn't think to bring it up earlier because Niccolò told her he was more upset about his father rummaging around in his car than anything else. And that, really, it was no big deal, because he had decided TO LEAVE THE ORGANIZATION anyway. After that, she said, he calmed down, so she forgot all about it."

"Leave The Organization," Lee intoned. "She thought he meant some organization in general, but . . ."

"We know otherwise."

Suddenly, Lee wanted another drink, but the bartender was nowhere in sight. "Well, I'd say that closes the loop on the motive for killing Antonio Tinti, wouldn't you?"

C. J. nodded, took a serious swig of her Rob Roy. "Oh, Dalton, so much is happening right now, I probably shouldn't have come here tonight, but I couldn't bear not to."

Lee nodded in commiseration, looked around the room once more. "I'm just sorry there weren't more people here to witness that unbelievable performance of yours," he said. "It must be the weather. It's beastly out there."

The commander sat back in her chair and exhaled again.

"Well, I'm not sorry," she replied. "I'm bloody thankful these are the only people here."

"What? Why?" he countered.

The commander interlocked her fingers, leaned forward on her elbows and ducked her head in Lee's direction. "I wasn't going to tell you, but I suppose I should. I received a death threat from The Organization this morning," she said as quietly as possible. "A pop-up message on my tablet computer at home, of all things."

"What kind of death threat are we talking about, C. J.?"

She gave him a weak smirk. "Oh, you know, their typical foolishness. I think the words 'decapitation' and 'dismemberment' were both in there somewhere." Her smirk faded, and she began to tip her head toward the others in the room.

"I wager you thought all these people here were jazz enthusiasts." He nodded in return. "In fact," she continued, "they're security detail, every last one of them. Here to make certain yours truly makes it through the night without someone sending a forty-five-caliber bullet through her bangs."

Lee turned and examined the others, who appeared to have returned to the poses they'd held when he first entered the club. He pointed at the couple sitting at the table two rows up. "Even them?"

C. J. nodded. "Oh yes, especially them. They're among the best in the business. Martin there worked for MI6 for more than twenty-five years, probably has eight or nine assassinations on his résumé. And is, by the way, gayer than Sydney during Pride Weekend. Felicia, on the other hand, is a mother of three from St. George's Hill who's an expert in using the projectile weapons associated with the martial arts form known as ninjutsu."

Lee shook his head, looked to C. J. for some comfort.

"Perhaps this will make you feel better," she said, tilting her head backward. "That Humpty Dumpty behind us who looks high on PCP? If I remember correctly, he's a loaner from your Central Intelligence Agency." She paused, made meaningful eye contact with Lee. "Much obliged to you Yanks for that, I am."

Lee reached out and clutched one of the commander's arms. "I'll protect you, C. J., I swear it," he said. "I'll do whatever it takes to shield you from harm."

She became the one wearing a smile of bemusement.

"Thank you, Dalton, thank you ever so much for that. I do truly thank you," she replied, squeezing his hand, which, in response, gripped her arm more tightly. "I have not the slightest doubt I am safer under your watch." She let go of his hand and turned slightly away from him.

"But these serpents are extraordinarily lethal, and we know when they set their minds on destruction, there's very little we can do to stop them. And whatever destruction they have in mind, my friend, it's coming any moment now."

43

"I do have to say, Dalton, I'm a little surprised by this. On several fronts." Bree took another sip of tea, her pinkie extended from the cup the way many of the flagpoles jut from the side of the embassies throughout London.

Directly across from her, C. J., in a too-tight floral print, winced at her.

"My dear, given the nature of what we're about to discuss, might I suggest you speak more sotto voce?"

Bree replaced her teacup on the saucer before her, gave the commander across from her a cool, blank stare. "I probably would, C. J.," she replied, "if I knew what that meant."

Sensing the need to serve as a mediator, Lee shifted his body forward in his chair and cleared his throat ceremoniously. "Fill us in, Bree. What is it about our being here that astonishes you so?"

She flashed a quick, taut smile in C. J.'s direction, refolded her napkin for the umpteenth time, then returned her attention to her boss.

"Well, for one thing, I never dreamed I'd actually be experiencing afternoon tea at the Ritz in London," she offered. "I mean, I'm a girl from rural Arizona and yet, somehow, here I am, sitting in a courtyard full of palm trees and surrounded by one of London's most iconic structures." Everyone, except C. J. chuckled at the observation. "Second of all, I never dreamed that hot tea could be so . . . satisfying."

Lee looked bemused and, noting his mirth, C. J. allowed her lips to part in a half-hearted smile, as well.

At this point, Bree ducked her head and softened her voice to an inaudible whisper. "And just as C. J. said, I'm surprised we're discussing the case in such a public venue. I mean, by this time tomorrow, all hell may be breaking loose and we're . . . here?"

Lee nodded, recrossed his legs, scratched the back of his head and sat back in his chair.

"Well, we are architects, after all. So what more appropriate location might there be for us to discreetly discuss our work than a building that's been heralded as an architectural masterpiece from the day it was completed? No one is going to think us out of place, are they?"

In between chews of teacake, Warren said, "If you ask me, I think Roberto looks pretty out of place in a jacket and tie." Roberto elevated his chin a couple of inches.

"No one asked you," he responded.

"Okay, everybody, we'll get to the serious business at hand in a few moments," Lee said, hoping to regain control of the room. "For now, can we spend a couple of minutes basking in the glory of this magnificent edifice?" He scanned his colleagues before offering a definitive nod of the head. "Okay, then, who can tell me when this hotel was completed?"

Liam lazily turned one palm up from the armrest of his chair. "1905," he said. "Or maybe it was 1906?"

Lee nodded again. "Finished in October of 1905 and opened in May of 1906. Good. Now, who can tell me about the architects?"

Warren swallowed heavily, then raised his left hand. "Charles Mewès and Arthur J. Davis," he said confidently. "Both had been educated at the École des Beaux-Arts in Paris, which explains the traditional French classicism throughout the building. Mewès had already designed the Hotel Ritz in Paris, and he and Davis collaborated on the Grand Petit Palais that was part of the Paris Exhibition of 1900."

"Excellent, Warren!" Lee gushed. "You've definitely been doing your homework." The younger architect wiggled his head back and forth and gave the group a self-satisfied smile.

"Thank you, milord," he replied in an affected British accent. He then looked across at Roberto. "Sorry to bother, ol' chap, but might I have a bit more clotted cream?"

C. J. rolled her eyes and shifted uncomfortably in her seat. Lee, sitting beside her, turned his head in her direction. "Are you all right?" he asked with great earnestness. "Do you need to use the facilities?" The commander froze, assumed a stern look, and shook her head no. From across the table separating them, Bree tried valiantly, but unsuccessfully, to stifle a laugh.

"And, finally, who can share some of the other interesting facts about this structure?" Lee said. More than one hand shot up.

"Bree, why don't you start?" their boss said.

"Um, well, although the hotel is a London landmark, it contains no elements of British architecture," she began. "The arcade along Piccadilly borrows heavily from the arcades in the Place Vendome in Paris as well as the Rue de Rivoli there. And the mansard roofs on the Green Park façade, as well as all the tall windows and wall panels, also evoke earlier projects in Paris. The shape of the site is irregular, a fact the architects cleverly hid through the installation of a series of curving walls. The ground floor consists of some pretty luxurious granite from Norway, and the floors above are made from Portland stone."

"I like the lions," Roberto interjected. Everyone looked at him quizzically, waited for him to elaborate. "The green lions outside," he said, pointing vaguely upward. "Didn't you see them? They put these large, green, copper lions at each corner of the pavilion roofs. It's cool, because that's the hotel's emblem." Everyone smiled but said nothing. "Graphic designer geek stuff," he added, offering a bigger smile in return.

"What else?" Lee nudged the group. He glanced around, nodded at Warren.

"The interior is Louis XVI, through and through," he said. "The suite of rooms on the ground floor is recognized worldwide as an example of the world's best hotel architecture. The Long Gallery, running from the Arlington Street entrance to the hotel's restaurant, showcases carpets from Savonnerie, Europe's most prestigious manufacturer of knotted-pile rugs. Over in the southwest corner is this strange staircase that's triangular, but no one really knows why. However, everyone knows that the curving main staircase was constructed specifically so women could enter the ground floor with a grand flourish, emphasizing their large and expensive gowns as they did so."

Lee turned again toward his colleague from the police department. "I could see you doing that, C. J.," he said to her. "Perhaps in that fringed country-western skirt you fancied in the shop owned by Tinti's ex-girlfriend?"

Everyone held their breath. But C. J.'s dour look exploded into uproarious laughter, which she quickly pulled in when others in the room made it clear her zeal was not appreciated. "You're right, Dalton, you're absolutely right," she replied as she nudged him in the ribs with one elbow. "Quite the Marie Antoinette I would be."

Bree edged toward Roberto and shifted her voice into as low a register as she could.

"More like Calamity Jane, if you ask me," she whispered.

When she had finished her comment, she noticed Lee running his right index finger up and down the bridge of his nose, a signal to everyone it was time to put all joking aside. To address the important matters at hand. To lower one's voice and pull oneself *in*.

"So," he said, almost inaudibly. "Where do we stand with Tinti's phone, C. J.?" She frowned and shifted her weight in the chair, as she tugged at her dress.

"I'm afraid we've made no more than a millimeter of progress," she whispered. She emitted an exasperated sigh. "You're from California, Dalton. Don't you know anyone in—oh, what do you call that place, Silicone Valley?—who could help move things along for us?"

Roberto started to titter, but a piercing look from his boss quashed that immediately.

"I believe it's Sili*con* Valley, C. J.," he replied. "And, as it turns out, I do know one or two influential people there. I'll place some calls just as soon as we've finished."

He looked toward Lara. She was staring at the carpet, doing everything she could to avoid eye contact with him.

"Have you and Liam found any connection between the messages Liam intercepted about luggage coming into Heathrow, and either Omar Fakhoury or Malcolm Hensleigh? Anything at all?"

She looked away from the architect. Shook her head casually.

"No, we've not. I think Liam has had . . . other priorities, recently." The architect reeled back a few inches in his chair, sent a puzzled look toward the young Australian.

"Actually, Dalton, I've been working like a jacky trying to connect the two. No luck."

Dalton waited, expecting some explanation of Lara's comment. Noticing Lee's anticipation, Liam sat up in his chair. "I know Lara's been quite conscientious on this as well, but . . ." He glanced over at his superior, but she was studying the carpet again and offered no response. Liam slunk back into his chair and began to play with the fabric of his slacks.

"Okay, then," Lee replied as quietly as he could. "I'm assuming we've also had no luck locating either Mr. Fakhoury or Mr. Hensleigh?"

For the first time, Anisa spoke up.

"Actually, I do have some promising news there. On a lark, I followed up with the tailor shop earlier today, and the manager told me Mr. Hensleigh has just returned from Egypt and is expected to return to work in the next couple of days."

A smile crossed Dalton Lee's lips. "Awesome. It appears this little tea party of ours has generated at least *a wee bit* of positive news." He swiveled toward C. J. "I assume you'll be making an appointment to interview him as soon as possible?"

She nodded once. "Most definitely," she responded.

A young, fair, blonde woman vaguely of Eastern European descent arrived to remove some of their cups and plates. Lee tilted up his head a couple of inches and issued a forced smile (but said nothing) as she went about her duties. No one else uttered a word, as well. They all knew it was unlikely the woman was there to eavesdrop on their conversation, and they also knew it was not at all beyond the realm of possibility. The business they needed to discuss would have to wait until she had cleared all the service items and asked them if they wanted anything else. And had left their seating area and moved to another room, which she did. Eventually.

Once the young woman was completely out of sight, Lee leaned forward, and he (and everyone else in attendance) relaxed. But the architect's expression was stern; he held one finger up in front of him.

"All right," he began. "I want everyone to pay close attention and absorb every word I have to say. From the sound of the message Liam intercepted, The Organization is now less than seventy-two hours away from launching their initiative here. And, given that the national flags superimposed over the faces of the dwarfs in that message just happen to match the nations represented at the G7 summit here this week, it appears that is their target.

"But, it could be something else altogether. Maybe they're planning to use those suitcases to create chaos in the Underground. Or at multiple tourist attractions throughout the city." He paused, looked around him. "Or even within this magnificent specimen of neoclassical design." Each person froze and then turned to look warily around. When the moment passed, Lee rapidly tucked his tie into his dress shirt and bent forward to take one last quick gulp of tea.

"We can stop them, but only if we identify exactly what their initiative is. Or identify who murdered Antonio Tinti, and then coerce the killer to reveal the details of their initiative to us."

"Do you even have a guess at this point who murdered Tinti, Dalton, because to be honest, I am at a complete loss." Bree, physically, was the epitome of composure, with her spine taut and her chin resolute. But the look on her face betrayed a deep well of fear.

Everyone waited for Lee to reply, and it felt as if he took an entire minute to scan the face of each person in attendance before he finally answered the question he knew anyone of them wanted to ask. "I have a theory," he replied in a hushed tone. "It's still blurry, but I plan to do everything I can to bring it into focus as quickly as possible."

He blew out some air, carefully folded his hands on his lap.

"I may not know for sure who the murderer is," he continued, "but I do know this, everyone. We can't get distracted now by any frivolous pastimes we may have been indulging in these past few days." He took another opportunity to look directly at each colleague; when his eyes reached Lara's, she averted them to the left.

"We must stay alert, we must be cautious," he went on. "We must be prepared for the worst-case scenario to evolve into something even more horrendous. For if our experiences in Manhattan and Miami taught us anything, the safety of millions of people—and possibly the freedoms we've cherished our entire lives—depend on it."

44

Lee's nightmare that evening was one-part surrealist painting, one-part Japanese sci-fi flick. The only detail he could clearly recall was his being bound by leather straps to a long flat board that tilted up at one end. Ten masks with menacing expressions floated just in front of him, like icons on a computer screen. The masks kept shifting positions, and as they did, one or the other would dive-bomb toward him, then retreat just as quickly. All the while, a tense, screeching sound blared in the background.

Each mask came with a sound effect, as well. One would hiss as it moved within an inch of his face, another would issue a blood-curdling scream. A third had the roar of a Siberian tiger while a fourth mimicked a buzz saw's squeal. Over time, the features of the masks began to morph, until each resembled someone he knew: his father, Lara, Mariam the waitress, and Malcolm the tailor. The collection then began to spin like reels in a slot machine, delivering a different, but familiar, face with each rotation. First Roberto, then Karlo, then Betty and Corinne. Next Warren, and Anisa, Omar and Margarida.

The spinning of the masks accelerated, until there was a blinding crash followed by seven loud explosions.

Lee awoke, his chest heaving, the sheets flooded with sweat. He squinted to see the clock beside the bed and was relieved that it was barely after six. He, C. J. and a few of the others had an appointment at ten, which had been prompted by a text sent by the manager of the tailor shop, alerting them that Malcolm Hensleigh was expected 'back on the job' that morning.

He closed his eyes, started to drift away. But just a few seconds later was roused yet again by the sound effect he had just heard in his dream . . .

BANG! BANG! BANG! BANG! BANG! BANG! BANG!

***

"Are you sure it's wise for so many of us to be here, C. J.?"

They were standing at one end of Savile Row, a block away from the tailor shop. Dalton, Bree, Warren, Anisa and even Lara stood in a warm early-morning sun, a sun that made the weather unusually balmy for a morning in very late September. Beside them, a flower box abundant with cushion mums and asters decorated a storefront; above them, a Union Flag flapped with pride.

C. J. was matter-of-fact in her reply.

"Yes, I'm sure. As they say, strength in numbers."

Lee led the team down the street. But as they neared the front of the tailor shop, he moved to one side to allow C. J. to take the lead. Warren, who was at the rear of the queue, had not fully made his way into the shop when the manager came skittering up to them from one of the back rooms.

"Why, Mr. Cortes," C. J. said, a weak smile on her lips. "One would think you had eyes in the back of your head."

He gave a short laugh, but the merriment on his face quickly vanished. "I wanted to catch you as quickly as possible, to alert you," he said in a hush. "Mr. Hensleigh is here, but he's not in a very good mood."

C. J. cocked her head to one side. "Not in a good mood, you say? What a terrible thing it must be to return from a respite among the pyramids only to come back . . . irritable." Her expression made it appear as if she had asked the manager a question, but her tone had been quite declaratory. "If you would, Armando, please inform Mr. Hensleigh we need to see him . . . as quickly as possible."

Her abruptness removed whatever sliver of civility the manager had remaining. He frowned to the point of scowling, whirled in the opposite direction, and led the group toward the back of the shop.

They found Malcolm Hensleigh slightly bent over a large cabinet, sewing a button onto a dark wool jacket. He neither turned around nor straightened up when they entered, but instead kept guiding the needle and thread painstakingly through the fabric.

"I've been expecting you," he said softly.

They waited for him to say more, but nothing more came.

C. J. cleared her throat. "Because. . .?"

He sniffed and continued sewing.

"Because I knew one of you would eventually come to appreciate the excellence of my work and ask me to tailor something for you, of course." Even Armando joined the others in sharing looks of amusement with one another.

C. J. stepped forward and moved to the other side of the cabinet, where the tailor was more likely to see her. He did not look up, however. He just continued to work on the button.

"We didn't come here to have you tailor something for us, Mr. Hensleigh," she said. "We came here to ask you what you were doing in Egypt. And what kind of relationship you have with Mr. Fakhoury." At that, he stopped sewing and raised his head a tad. But he gazed straight ahead at the opposite wall, not at C. J. or any of the others.

"Oh, I see," he said, almost imperceptibly. "You've finally found out about that, have you?"

C. J. swiveled to look at Dalton, who reflexively moved in her direction. But she shooed him back with a slight wave of her hand. "Yes, we have," she answered, her countenance grim. "Do you care to explain yourself?"

No one else in the room moved. No one else in the room breathed.

The tailor dropped the threaded needle and placed both palms on the unfinished jacket. He pressed his upper body higher and allowed his elbows to bow outward, taking a deep breath through his nostrils as he did. His exhale was labored, incremental, tinged with great sadness.

"It began a few months ago," he said. "He came into the shop to have several suits refitted. We were in rotation at that time and Tony was the next one up, so he took on the assignment and—as I expected he would—bungled the job. Omar is quite fussy about what he wants, and that was a period when Tony was unusually distracted. Issues with his son, and his lady friend, I believe. He was not at all 'on his game' as one might say."

He swiveled so that his lanky body partially faced the group and he, for the first time, looked directly at them, although it seemed that Anisa was the one he focused on the most.

"I approached Omar on the sly and offered to repair the damage Tony had inflicted on his clothing."

"Did Mr. Tinti know about this?" Lee interrupted. The tailor glanced at Lee as if the architect had just arrived in a puff of smoke.

"Armando knew," he said, gesturing toward the manager. "But, no, I chose to keep Tony in the dark about what I had done. I may not have been one of Tony's greatest admirers, but we tailors do retain some semblance of loyalty to one another." He raised his head a few inches, as if someone had just sent him a message via telepathy. "At least, some of us do, anyway."

C. J. studied the tall man beside her, squinted some. "Go on," she said.

He sniffed a couple of times, turned his body fully toward his audience, and leaned back against the cabinet, bracing himself with both palms. "After I altered Omar's apparel, he approached me and offered a reward of sorts. A . . . token of his appreciation, if you will."

"A set of matching luggage?" This time, it was Anisa who chose to interrupt. The tailor frowned at her as if she'd emitted a belch.

"Good heavens, no, young lady, what on earth would cause you to say something so ridiculous as that?" he replied with disdain. Slowly, he shifted his gaze back to C. J., offering her a meek smile. "That's when they began. The shipments. He offered to bring in—some would say 'smuggle in' but I prefer to call it 'transport in'—a variety of luxurious fabrics he had access to throughout the Middle East, fabrics which he'd sell to me at a hefty discount. I would then incorporate those fabrics into many of the tailoring projects on my docket and . . . I would continue to tailor Mr. Fakhoury's clothing, pro bono, on the side."

At this point, his gaze shifted to Armando, who was glowering at him from the corner. He responded to the shop manager with a look of resignation. "Armando, no one complains about a suit feeling more luxurious than it felt when they first tried it on." He returned his attention to the rest of the group. "Mr. Fakhoury's wardrobe, and the demand for my services as an outfitter, both benefited from the arrangement. So did this shop, now that I think about it." He turned toward Armando and smirked. "You didn't think that uptick in tailoring projects we've had of late was due to a reputation for stellar customer service, did you?" The tailor paused, turned back to the group, seemed to reflect on all he had said, and nodded a couple of times. "It was a very tidy arrangement, if I do say so myself."

"Where is Mr. Fakhoury now?" C. J. asked. "When we last saw him, the trunk of his car was full of suitcases. Do you know anything about that?" After Malcolm Hensleigh had ended his lengthy story, her tone had taken on a softer edge, indicating she'd dismounted her high horse.

The tailor went sad once again, looked a bit befuddled.

"I wish I did know where he is," he replied. "Oh, how I wish I knew. A couple of weeks ago, I finished a sizable amount of tailoring for him, probably the largest job I've undertaken for him at one time. Suits and shirts and slacks that belonged to him, to a few brothers of his, to an uncle, and some of his friends. He came to my flat to collect them, and I went ahead and extended an advance—quite a large advance, I might add—for the next bolts of fabric he was to bring me."

Here, the tailor's body sagged, his eyes darted across the lower half of the room. "But he's gone. Vanished. Hasn't responded to a single voice mail or text message."

The tailor licked his lips quickly before continuing. "That's why I went to Egypt. To track him down, if possible. To try to secure the fabric he owed me, or at least recoup some of my money. Then I discovered he wasn't in Egypt after all, even though that's what his assistant had told me . . ."

He shook his head a couple of times, then slowly gave the group a sheepish smile. "But why am I wasting your time with all of this background? You already know most of it, I presume. I mean, that's why you came here, isn't it? To arrest me? To take me in? For smuggling, or transporting contraband across national borders, or whatever it is the police call it these days?"

Everyone in the room cast a discreet look at someone nearby.

"Because that's what we do in this country nowadays, isn't it?" he continued. "Handcuff and march out the door a person whose only crime was falling for the sales pitch of some clever charlatan."

Standing just opposite the tailor, Lara wore an expression of sorrow as she shifted uncomfortably from one foot to the other.

45

Roberto knew exactly what he planned to do.

There was little time to lose, so he was going to ask Isabela right from the start to give him some meaningful detail that would help him determine when they were going to move her to Evin Prison. If she even knew.

No messing around. No small talk. He'd just come right out and—using the game as a cover—let her know the opportunity to rescue her was now.

Or never.

He'd spent more than an hour writing down words in different sequences to get the request just right. Something that would sound relaxed and casual to anyone who might be eavesdropping (*Of course someone is eavesdropping,* he told himself.) But a sentence that, through every other word, would communicate to Isabela the importance of their conversation.

A conversation he hoped would be their last before someone found her and brought her back to him, to Puerto Rico, to Mama Minga, and Tio Santos.

Back where she belonged.

He didn't really need to go to Hanover Square, but he felt compelled to anyway. The Wi-Fi signal on his phone was particularly strong there, and for some reason he found the cozy intimacy of the surroundings comforting. Besides, it wouldn't hurt to explore the area again. Even though more than a week had passed since Antonio Tinti's murder, he thought it was still possible he might spot something they all had overlooked.

He believed that was *very* possible.

When he arrived at the square, the mime was at his usual location, leaning back, ankles crossed. This time, however, the entertainer was dressed entirely in white. A large white carnation was pinned to the left lapel of his very white suit, and both his top hat and the felt band encircling its brim were as white as whipped cream. He seemed to be in lighthearted spirits, smiling at passing pedestrians and doffing his hat at those who took the time to acknowledge him.

"Ah, you again," he said as Roberto approached. Although his voice was deep, the tone he struck was as upbeat as his demeanor.

Roberto nodded, but said nothing. Quickly though, he moved in close to the entertainer, so close it caused the mime to raise his eyebrows.

"Good to see you, too, buddy," Roberto said, patting the clown on the lapel. He shot a half-smile toward the comedian, and as he did, slid a fifty-pound note into his breast pocket.

The mime's expression changed from good-natured to intrigued as his eyes followed the designer's hand down into his pocket, then back up to Roberto's face. "Let's just cut the crap, shall we, pal?" Roberto whispered in as nonthreatening a tone as he could muster. "I'm pretty sure you know something about the murder that took place here. Give me *something* helpful. Tell me what you know."

Roberto widened his smile, but his tone became more menacing. "Or, I'll turn around and tell one of those bobbies over there that I saw you fondling one of those kiddies in the park."

The mime rolled his eyes but seemed to retreat under Roberto's threat. "Yeah, okay, no need for that," he said, his voice quivering. "I'll give you something. My reputation at the precincts is already more established than I care to admit. I don't need you to cause me any more trouble." Roberto gave the busker a genuine smile and moved his head back several inches.

His new informant glanced in both directions, put the back of one of his white-gloved hands to the side of his mouth.

"I was here that night, but don't ask me for any details as to why," he said quietly. "I'd been here about twenty minutes when this shorter gentleman—you did say he was short, right?" Roberto nodded rapidly. "All right, so I saw this short gentleman, dark hair, come here just before midnight with a much taller guy. I thought it peculiar because, well, they just strolled right up to the fence and hopped over it. The shorter man got all entangled in the shrubbery, so the taller guy had to help him out. That's all I saw. Except, maybe five minutes later, I heard gunshots."

"How many?"

The mime made an exaggerated "thinking face" then shrugged his shoulders. "Hard to remember. Not many. Two, maybe three? I thought maybe some hooligan nearby was shooting off firecrackers. Anyway, a few minutes later, here comes the taller guy, rampaging through the shrubs like Tarzan in the jungle. He climbed back over the fence and off he went. That way."

"What about the shorter guy?"

The mime shook his head. "Curiously enough, I didn't see him again."

Roberto leaned his head back to look at the section of fence the busker said the pair had scaled. "I don't really see how they could have made it through there," he said. "It would take some doing to scale that fence and the shrubs there are pretty dense."

The clown shrugged his shoulders once again but said nothing more.

Roberto glanced back over one shoulder, leaned back in. "The tall guy . . . do you remember anything else about him? Like, what he was wearing. Or if he had some sort of accent."

The mime tilted his head toward the sky, blew out some air and extended his left palm. The Puerto Rican rolled his eyes, dove into his wallet, and slapped another fifty-pound note into the entertainer's hand. Once his informant had secured the bill into a pants pocket, he flashed a quick smile at Roberto.

"He had a mac on. A very dapper one, I must say. Snagged one end of it on the fence while he was climbing over, I remember that. His complexion was darker. I thought maybe he was Spanish or Italian. Or maybe Portuguese." He shrugged and turned both palms upward. "Sorry, guvnor," he said, dropping any hint of an act. "I don't recall anything else of note."

Roberto scrutinized his contact's face for a few moments, then nodded rapidly. "Okay, thanks." He pulled his phone out and started when he noticed the time. "*¡Me cago en ná!*" he exclaimed. "It's past time!"

He swiveled away and jogged toward one of the side streets jutting off the square, so he'd have more privacy for the conversation. Once he had found a less trafficked space, he jabbed the icon of his messaging app to open it and was instantly confronted by the large red X he had seen before, an indication that the obnoxious intro video had already finished. Frantic, he punched the symbol and waited.

Nothing.

A cursor showed he could send a message if he wanted to, but the protocol called for Isabela to always start a conversation. His right heel began to rapidly tap the pavement.

Still nothing.

The clock at the top of his screen showed it was two minutes past the appointed time. *Surely, they're not going to punish me for being a minute or two late,* he told himself.

Only, he wasn't so sure.

To hell with protocol, he thought. He painstakingly typed the sentence he'd spent so much time constructing over the previous couple of days.

I know when the last day you can go over to see Evan!

Which was really intended to ask her *Know the day you go to Evan?*

He sent the message. Completely stopped breathing. Hoped she'd figure out that by "Evan," he meant the prison, Evin.

Come on, Isabela, he intoned. *Write something.*

His phone pinged. A reply.

What did you say?

He frowned and decided she hadn't caught on that he had already started the game. Again, he typed as fast as he could.

I know when the last day is you can go over to see Evan!

He pressed the send button and glanced at a young couple holding hands as they strolled past. He wondered what it must be like to feel that carefree. He couldn't recall the last time he'd felt that comfortable, that relaxed.

She still hadn't responded. Then suddenly his screen went black and the phone began to vibrate.

What the hell . . .

The vibrating intensified, then stopped. A message in a clean white font appeared on the black background.

**WE ARE ALSO VERY ADEPT
WHEN IT COMES TO
PLAYING "EVERY OTHER," MR. BERMUDEZ.
IN FACT, WE'RE WORLD CHAMPIONS AT IT.
WE'RE SUCH EXPERTS, WE'RE MANIPULATING THE RULES
TO WHERE YOU CAN ONLY CONTACT YOUR SISTER
EVERY OTHER MONTH NOW.
"EVERY OTHER" MONTH . . . GET IT, YOU BOBO?**

Gradually, derisive laughter emanated from the phone. It was soft at first but turned grating, then hideous, as it escalated in volume. The screen sputtered a few times before the cackle was replaced by a familiar, sneering face.

But, it wasn't the face of the skinny young man with a curled-up mustache who'd appeared in the video before Roberto's first communication with his sister.

It was the face of the mime, waving at him from the Hanover Square fence.

46

"I don't know what to think, Dalton. Normally, my instincts in situations like this are spot-on. But to be quite frank, I'm more than a little befuddled." C. J. was standing at the bottom of the stairs that led to the townhouse The Lee Group was staying in. Her satchel hung limply by her side, her gaze seemed fixed upon the phone box near the end of the block. Since Lee was standing on the second step from the bottom, she had to turn and look up at him as she completed her thought.

"I mean, perhaps Fakhoury and Hensleigh are as innocent as newborn babies," she said. "But if this sordid business has taught me anything, it's that the guilty are usually the people most adept at convincing you they are anything but."

Lee nodded but didn't know how to respond except to say, "I'm confused too, C. J. Do you want to come inside?"

The commander leaned her body an inch or two toward the staircase, then snapped it back. "Thanks ever so, Dalton," she replied. She turned and began to trudge her way down the pavement. "But I really do need to spend time tonight swabbing my horn." Lee watched the commander galumph her way toward the Tube stop at the end of the crescent.

He couldn't remember seeing a person look more tired and forlorn.

He trotted up the stairs and through the entryway of the townhouse. He hoped to get in a quick workout at the gym. But on his way to changing clothes, he got sidetracked by two, back-to-back interruptions. "If you have a sec, Dalton . . ." It was Liam, who had bounded down the stairwell the minute he heard Lee enter the building.

"Sure, Liam, what's on your . . ." Then his phone vibrated. With a ferocity that meant only one thing.

Need to see you ASAP.
Want to share some information with you
before your father completes his initiation.
How about the Old Operating Theatre Museum
in St. Thomas Street? Seems like a fitting place,
given your father is "severing" his ties to his
former life, yes? Shall we say, 11 pm?

Lee breathed in through his nostrils. "Sorry, Liam, I need to take this. Let me catch up with you in a half hour or so."

His youngest employee nodded but didn't move. "No worries, Dalton," he said meekly. "But it's pretty important."

His boss glanced up at him with concern. "Okay, give me fifteen minutes then," he responded.

Once Liam was upstairs, the architect refocused his attention on the text. He was torn as to whether to respond at all, and if he did, just what he wanted to say. On one hand, he relished another opportunity to squeeze some information out of this person who knew so much about what The Organization was up to, yet usually revealed so little. On the other, he'd meant it when he had said he was sick of the games, tired of being paged, tired of always being expected to jump when it was least convenient for him to do so.

He stared at the keyboard on his phone, bounced among numerous options of what to say. Finally, he lifted one finger and typed out the word

No

The response came swiftly.

Why not?

He didn't have the time or patience to go into all the particulars. Plus, he wasn't sure it was really in his best interest to help this person realize that he knew his father's "defection" was actually a clever act of deception. So he just typed back

Because

A few excruciating moments ticked by before the next response arrived.

You're not being serious, are you?
How do you think your father will react?

At that, the world's most prominent architect let out a hearty belly laugh. His fingers flitted across the keyboard in response. When he finished, he read his reply one more time, and grinning ear to ear punched the SEND button. Across the internet . . . the cloud . . . the whatever it's being called now, flew his message:

Tell my father I said I've never been
so serious about anything in my entire life

***

"Please, Liam. Don't say anything to Dalton. Please. I had every intention of reimbursing the company out of my personal funds in a week or so." Lara sat at the end of Liam's bed, both hands in her lap, one hand cradling the other.

"I just wanted to . . . shield my whereabouts from Delfina Delgado for a while. So I used the group's account as a cover. But it was only going to be for a few days. I swear."

"Lara, there is *no* Delfina Delgado. You know that, right? That woman was an actress. From Serbia, or maybe Montenegro. A former porn actress, as I understand it."

Lara stared up at Liam, who was towering above her, hands on his hips. Her mouth sagged a bit, her eyes had a dim glaze to them. "But . . . she . . ." She shook her head and then dropped her face into her hands. "Oh, how I could I be so ridiculously foolish!"

Liam remained quiet, waiting for her to reach a place of calm.

"Dalton's put me off for a little while, but eventually I'm going to have to talk to him about this. He'd notice the transaction at some point, Lara. I think it's better that someone other than you plead your case."

He stepped closer, then repositioned his hands on his hips. "What you did wasn't very wise, Lara. Let's just be glad I noticed the transaction and stopped it before it went through, shall we?"

She smiled up at him and nodded. "Yes. I'm very grateful for that, Liam. *Very, very* grateful."

He reached out, brushed several strands of hair off her forehead, then bent down and gave her a gentle kiss.

"You were very lucky this time, my dear," he whispered. "But you've got to realize, I won't always be around to look out for you when it comes to these sorts of things."

***

With such an important annual summit of world leaders beginning in the next few days, all eyes are on London. Especially those who are hoping those heads of state in attendance will make meaningful headway on nuclear disarmament.

Lee settled into the armchair in his suite and took a sip of the jie tea Margarida had brought him. His mind was whirling after the conversation he'd just had with Liam, so he had turned to the tea, and a little world news, for comfort.

The leaders of seven nations begin their negotiations here this week on how best to respond to the growing threat posed by rogue nations equipped with nuclear warheads.

He was still unclear as to how he should handle the unsettling news. He knew, of course, that Lara had not planned to embezzle the company. Her family legacy and her stake in the company would both have been ruined if she had.

Still, it was a lapse of ethics he couldn't ignore. Yes, Liam had kept the transaction from going through, but Lee couldn't be certain there wasn't embarrassing information dangling out there, lingering out there, just waiting to be exploited. By an important client. By a competitor.

By . . . *them.*

The leaders of Japan, Germany, the United States, France, Italy, Canada and the U.K. are meeting in London as a show of unity. But also to share confidential information about their nuclear arsenals and any redeployments of warheads they may be making at this time.

Lee took a large slurp of tea, tilted his head against the back of the chair. He wondered if his father had received his insider joke, then decided they probably hadn't taken the time to send it along. He wondered if he had lost for good the one person within The Organization he could rely on for direction. He wondered how much longer he could tolerate this schizoid life of designing the world's most spectacular buildings and preventing the world's most horrific crimes . . . at the same time.

He decided he needed to go back to Hanover Square one last time to test the idea that was spinning in his head. He was too exhausted to do it that night, and he had an important appointment the next day. But he needed to be fleet, for meteorologists were forecasting another downturn in the weather.

Scotland Yard says it is beefing up security throughout London in advance of the important summit. Therefore, commuters should expect delays on the motorways and the Underground.

Lee took a longer, slower sip of the tea this time, swirled it around in his palate. He thought this might possibly be the best pot of jie tea he'd ever had, and that he should tip Margarida extra when this assignment came to an end.

He softly drummed his fingertips on the table next to his chair and fantasized about that cottage in the Lake District he wanted to retire to. Lee pictured himself horizontal in a hammock behind his favorite cottage, then navigating a canoe along the lake called Buttermere. He was drifting . . . gliding . . .

This is Adam Harper, reporting from The Connaught Hotel.

He jolted awake and shook himself, sure he must have misheard. And yet knew he had not. C. J. had told him during their stroll through Mayfair that the identity of The Connaught Hotel as the site for the summit was confidential. That the public was to be told the meeting was taking place at The Grosvenor House.

In his sleepy haze, Lee also thought he'd heard the cadence and tone of the news reporter's voice before. Then the architect finally looked directly at the television, and what he saw took his breath away.

It was the older man he'd encountered in their first visit to the tailor shop. His tam sat slightly askew on his head; his left eye gleamed a deep emerald green.

47

With Lee planning to be away for much of the day on yet another of his "unexplained absences." Lara took over as The Lee Group's primary contact. So it was she, not Lee, who took the urgent phone call from C. J.

"We think we've got him," C. J. said. She was out of breath, as if she had just trotted up several flights of stairs.

"That's fantastic," Lara responded. "Who is the *he* we're talking about?"

C. J., still huffing, managed to sputter, "Omar. Fakhoury. Tinti's client at the tailor shop."

Lara pulled her phone away from her ear for a moment and looked at it, incredulous.

"That's wonderful! Where on earth did you find him? *How* did you find him?"

"Medfanfurl," C. J. replied.

Lara frowned. "I'm sorry, C. J. What did you say? I didn't catch that."

"I said, 'Edinburgh.'" The commander was panting even more substantially than when Lara had first taken the call.

"Is something going on there, C. J. Are you in need of some

assistance?" Lara thought she heard a steady pounding in the background, like someone pounding a nail into a wall.

The pounding stopped, but several seconds went by without C. J. saying anything. Still out of breath, but in a more measured voice, she eventually replied, "I'm not really sure. I mean, I'm not really sure these treadmill workouts are something I'm cut out for."

Lara flashed a quick smile, followed by a look of confusion. "Wait. There's a treadmill now . . . in *your office?*"

There was a chuckle on C. J.'s end, followed by a loud, deep sigh. "Yes, there is, and you should see the swath of destruction caused by the workers who brought it in here. I dare say this office looks like the Luftwaffe just paid it a visit." She breathed heavily a few times, but each breath was deeper than the one before it. "I need to shed a stone or two if I want to stay on this job for a few more years." The line went quiet for a moment, then she returned. "All right, maybe three stones."

Lara smiled. She found the Scotland Yard commander quirky, to say the least. But, she also had to admire the girl for having so much spunk. "So, what was Mr. Fakhoury doing in Edinburgh, of all places? I thought he was in France. Or Egypt. And how did you apprehend him?"

"Funny story, that is," C. J. replied. "Seems he was planning to board a train destined for some tiny burg along the North Sea where he has a luxuriously furnished estate house he's recently purchased. Under an assumed name and with falsified credentials, of course. He hadn't even informed his office about the vanishing act he was planning, which is why they told me and Mr. Hensleigh that Fakhoury was headed to Egypt. That was the destination he gave them as he headed out the door."

Lara heard C. J. settle into her wobbly chair, which reminded her just how amazing it was that the commander's minuscule office was somehow accommodating a chair, and a desk, and file cabinets, *and* the treadmill.

"Anyway, a chum of Fakhoury who was in school with him in Lebanon happened to be on that very same train platform, at the very same time by complete coincidence. The school chum called out to him—using the name he knew Fakhoury by, of course. We'd alerted everyone at British Rail that we were looking for Fakhoury, of course, so when a security guard on the platform heard Fakhoury's name called out, he arrested him on the spot."

C. J. emitted an extended chortle. "People live under some fantastic assumption that those of us who work for Scotland Yard are like the detectives on *Midsomer Murders,* and that we all solve crimes the way Miss Marple or Father Brown does." Her chortle wound down, and the chair creaked again, only at a higher pitch than before. "The truth is, we often stumble upon a murder weapon, or some suspect who's gone missing, the same way a Collyhurst housewife finds a genuine Van Gogh in the village antique shop."

Lara smiled again, but it was a smile born more from melancholy than amusement. She only wished the cases The Lee Group investigated resolved themselves so easily. "When are we to expect Mr. Fakhoury back in London?" she asked. "Do you want Dalton to be there when you interview him?"

"Well . . ." (C. J. was panting again) ". . . so long as the Edinburgh police cooperate with us, he should be here in a day or so." Behind the commander's voice, Lara could hear the treadmill cranking up once again. "It would be ideal if Dalton could be here when we talk to him, of course." A high-pitched wheeze entered her voice. "But . . . it's really not required." Her panting became more pronounced. "By the way . . . where is . . . Dalton?"

Lara shook her head and looked toward the ceiling, contemplating how best to answer C. J.'s query. Then the most appropriate response slowly came to her.

Shaking her head, she replied, "One only knows, C. J. One only knows."

***

Lee didn't feel anywhere near as claustrophobic in the MRI machine as he thought he would. In fact, the world's most prominent architect felt rather cozy. The machine did make quite a racket, produced a variety of chirps, clanks, and clicks he could hear despite the earphones the medical staff had provided.

His first inclination had been to bring one of his operatic soundtracks to the procedure—*Così fan tutte,* maybe, or (more appropriate, but perhaps a little too ironic) *Visitations,* a pair of one-act chamber operas that explore the theme of auditory hallucinations from the perspectives of those who experience them.

Then his better instincts took hold and he opted for the simple earphones. The color white, to match the machine he was lying prone in at this very moment.

The medical interview had gone well, he thought. Any history of heart palpitations? No. Any artificial joint or limb? No. Any body piercings, tattoos, or permanent makeup? None. (*Really? There's such a thing as permanent makeup?*)

He brushed some lint off one leg of the corduroy slacks he was wearing, waited for the long interrogation to come to an end. But then the nurse asked him whether he'd ever had a penile implant. Lee flinched (then berated himself for having taken an extra couple of beats to respond).

"Absolutely not," he'd replied, much too defensively.

Inside the examination room, the technologist had him remove the wallet, keys and coins in his pockets, as well as the Baume & Mercier watch on his wrist, a frivolous purchase he had made in Switzerland the previous winter while on a ski trip with friends. Soon enough, he was lying on the bed of the machine and considering whether he might want to incorporate its design into a train terminal he was designing for a suburb of Milan.

An assistant—a winsome blonde he guessed to be in her midthirties—loomed above him, slightly bent at the waist. She was wearing a floral perfume that Lee thought made her both a little bit maternal, and a little bit sexy.

"Do you have any final questions, Mr. Lee?" she asked.

His body went rigid. "What do you mean, 'final'?"

She smiled, tilted her head to the right. "I'm very sorry, I should have asked whether you have any *further* questions?"

He relaxed and allowed his mind to drift as he entertained a host of questions on his mind. Had she noticed what he considered to be a colossal opening in the back of his gown? Had she had ever undergone an MRI and, if so, had it affected her vision, her speech, or her sex life?

But he suspected those were *not* the types of questions she was referring to.

Then an important question he really did want to ask but had completely forgotten popped into his mind.

"A few months ago, I read that someone got sucked into an MRI machine and died when they brought an oxygen cylinder into the room," he said. "Nothing like that's going to happen here, is it? You *are going to* lock the door, aren't you?"

The nurse crinkled her brow and squinted at him for a moment, but then broke out in a broad smile. She patted him once, lightly, on the chest and then turned away. "You're quite the little prankster, aren't you, Dalton?" she tossed over her shoulder as she headed for the door.

Lee returned her smile but knew she hadn't seen it since the upper half of his torso was already moving toward the machine's inner chamber. He chuckled to himself.

She called me Dalton, he thought, as the whirs and whistles began in earnest. *She finds me attractive. I just knew it.*

***

"C. J. said she expects Omar Fakhoury to be returned to London either tomorrow or the day after. And I received an update from Anisa about thirty minutes ago that said the Scottish police have agreed to expedite his return, so that timeline now seems confirmed. Interestingly, his phone doesn't show him having any recent communication with Malcolm Hensleigh. Or anyone here in London, for that matter."

Lara wore a sober expression as she consulted the steno pad on her lap. She was wearing a black turtleneck, a black and gray houndstooth skirt, and black high heels. The only nod to vibrancy in her ensemble was the pendant necklace with an irregularly shaped, violet-colored stone.

She didn't take her eyes off the steno pad to look at Lee, even when he spoke to her.

"That's great to hear," he replied. He was sitting in a chair opposite the love seat she occupied, his torso bent forward, forearms on his thighs, fingers entwined.

"I've also followed up with the detectives at Scotland Yard who've been reviewing the paltry amount of video footage that London Transport and London Buses sent over," she continued. "They include feeds captured in the area between eleven in the evening and half past one in the morning, but neither Mr. Hensleigh, Mr. Fakhoury or anyone else we've spoken to shows up on them. Mr. Tinti is seen boarding a car around half past nine in the morning at the stop nearest his flat. But that's all."

Lee nodded, continued to listen intently to his second-in-command.

"Meanwhile, I've checked in with Bree, Roberto, and Warren. Bree has not heard any more from the waitress she's knitted with, so nothing to report there. Roberto apparently returned to Hanover Square for one more canvass of the crime scene but says he found nothing of significance. Warren has been monitoring the passenger lists of air flights coming into Heathrow, and all the other major airports in the U.K., and has been helping me catch up on the firm's client emails."

With her pen, she drew an emphatic line along the bottom of the steno pad but still did not look at Lee. "Oh, emails. That reminds me, the City of Montreal contacted us to say they'd like us to submit a proposal for a performing arts center they plan to construct."

A small clock on the table between them ticked methodically. No one said anything for almost a full minute.

"It's okay, Lara," Lee finally said.

For the first time, her eyes met his. "Dalton, I'll resign my post and relinquish my stake in the firm, if you think that's best," she replied.

The architect shook his head. "I just said it was okay. There's no need for you to relinquish your stake in the firm and I do not want you to resign." He paused, focused on the carpet for a few seconds. "You know this firm could not go on without you." He looked back at her, drilled his gaze into her eyes. "You know *I* could not go on without you."

Her mouth twitched, and she turned her head to one side as her eyes filled with tears. She placed the back of her right hand against her mouth. She pressed her hand firmly against her face and then reached for a tissue from the box on the table between them. From behind the tissue, she sniffed, "I was going to reimburse the firm within a few days, Dalton."

He nodded. "I know that."

She continued to wipe at her nose with the tissue. "I just feel so stupid . . . and so ashamed."

Lee nodded some more. "I understand," he replied. "But no one here is going to shame you. No one here wants to."

She crumpled the tissue into a tight ball and reached for her purse on the floor. Once she closed it, she sat back up in the love seat and gave him a quizzical look.

"Aren't you going to ask me why? Not that I have a particularly good answer."

Lee rose from his chair, made his way around the table separating them, and sat beside her. He encircled one arm around her shoulders, the other around her torso, and pulled her in toward him. She then violated all the protocols she had ever followed regarding expressions of affection in the workplace by allowing her head to rest on his chest.

"Seriously, Lara," he said in the softest tone possible, "after all the years we've been together and everything we've been through, do you honestly think there's any answer to that question that would make me think less of you?"

48

If it's an urban myth that London is still foggy, Lee asked himself as he made his way along the edge of Hanover Square, *then why can't I see my shoes?* A morning of abundant sunshine had given way to an evening of murky gloom. Lee had read somewhere that researchers believed pollution levels in the city had recently spiked after many years of steady decline.

Tonight, Lee was hard-pressed to argue with them.

This shroud was far more murky than the one he'd encountered the night he met his confidant in the Greenwich Foot Tunnel. Not only was the moon undetectable, so were all the branches of most nearby trees. As a test, the architect stuck one hand out at full-arm's length. He could not see it. He glanced over at an illuminated business sign across the way. He could not read it. He sensed that, on this evening, he would have benefited greatly from the services of one of the linklighter boys who, in Victorian times, would hold aloft lighted torches as they escorted residents throughout the city. To steady his way, Lee held fast to the rails of the fence bordering the square's perimeter and realized this was how it might always feel should he survive into his eighties or nineties.

Lee realized it was just an urban myth that fog amplified the sound of nearby footsteps. In fact, it did the opposite—deadening most sounds so he felt like he was wearing noise-canceling earphones . . . which Lee found beneficial in an airplane or in those ridiculous cafés that insist on describing themselves as "upscale" despite their lack of any sound-absorbing amenities like carpets, drapes or cotton tablecloths. But he did not find the silence delightful at midnight, in a quarter bereft of humanity, with a fog shrouding everything in sight.

Most of all, he worried the fog might interfere with what he saw as a critical step in the investigation. *Ha, "step" in the investigation,* he chuckled to himself. *How appropriate.*

When he thought he had reached the place he wanted to explore, he faded away from the fence and walked carefully to the left until his shoe discovered the slope of the curb toward the street. Then he bent low and scanned the concrete until he rediscovered the scuff marks that had intrigued him earlier.

He studied them more closely from this angle and that. Took out the tape C. J. had loaned him to measure their width and length. Rose from the pavement and squinted through the haze to find the metal fence beyond. Put both feet together and walked toward the ironwork, counting as he did. Rotated his body, did the same in reverse. Placed both hands on his knees, stooped very low, and sprinted toward the fence, counting once more. Hiked his left leg in the air and attempted (in vain) to position his foot on the fence's highest point. Added a few inches to his formula, subtracted them instead. Strolled back to the curb, continued beyond it, crossed the lane to the other curb, turned around once more, strolled yet again toward the fence but, this time, stopped at the curb. Dropped on all fours and viewed the scuffs up close. Struggled mightily as he tried to stand up.

Reminded himself to work out in the gym the next day.

As Lee stood on the pavement, surveying the scene, the fog thickened to where even the fence disappeared. The air became damper and dingier; droplets began to form on his shoes. But Lee, satisfied and certain, delivered a congratulatory smirk. He thrust his hands onto his hips, arched his elbows outward, and spread his feet as far as he could.

Not far away, but sounding muffled and hoarse, a crow delivered a raspy caw.

"Well," he announced, to no one in particular, "I would say that solves that."

49

Malcolm Hensleigh still wasn't talking.

"That isn't entirely true," C. J. backtracked in a phone conversation with Lee. "He's talking. But he hasn't said anything of merit. He continues to profess that he's the victim here. Continues to claim this is all about illegally imported fabrics. Insists he had no idea that Fakhoury was starting to use an alias or planned to flee to the north of Scotland."

The architect was about to pour boiling water into a cup that contained a bag of tea, then decided instead to set the kettle down.

"And we don't have a shred of evidence that he's lying, do we?" he finally replied.

C. J. waited a few moments before she gave her answer. "That is correct."

"And when will Mr. Fakhoury be arriving?"

The first part of the answer he received was a belabored sigh. "Well, Police Scotland was to escort him down here by train first thing this morning."

"And?"

"They missed the train, apparently."

"What?!" Lee had begun once again to pour the cup of tea. When he barked his surprise at C. J.'s comment, he sent the boiling water sloshing over one side of the cup and onto the floor. "Dammit!" he exclaimed.

"I know. Apparently, there was a smash-up on the motorway leading to the station. But, still."

"No, C. J., I cursed because I spilled some hot water on the floor."

"I see," the commander replied. A pause. "You sort of enjoy getting yourself into hot water, don't you Dalton?"

Lee stood back up, tossed the dish towel onto a nearby counter. Rolled his eyes.

"Back to Fakhoury . . ."

"Yes. Well, he should get here sometime this afternoon. So long as the train doesn't derail, or get hit by an asteroid, that is."

"Excellent. I'll get myself together and come over to your office as soon as I can."

"Brilliant," she replied. She paused again, then added, "I do have *some* encouraging news."

Lee had given up on the tea and moved over to the nearby dining table.

"Go on," he said as he took a chair.

"Thanks to your leaning on some of those VIPs you know in California, the manufacturer of Antonio Tinti's phone has finally agreed to unlock it for us. Our analysts are combing through the lists of voice and text messages as we speak. Hopefully, they'll turn up something relevant."

Lee was craving a cup of tea again. He stood up to make his way back to the counter.

"That *is* encouraging news, C. J." He tried to sound upbeat, but his pessimistic mood quickly took over. "They're going to have to hurry, though," he added. "I have this dreadful feeling we're not 'running out of time,' but 'out of time.' Period."

Once again, C. J.'s presence seemed to fade away and then return, more somber than when it had left.

"*Moi, aussi,*" was her curt reply.

50

The season's splendor was making a grand appearance across London that day. So, although Dalton Lee had fully intended to walk directly to C. J.'s offices in Scotland Yard, he decided to take a boat tour of the Thames, instead.

I need to think about this case, he told himself. *Or, not think about the case. Let everything I've seen and heard seep in. Or push it all out, so the answer has room to enter.*

The gate. The hedges. The suitcases. The gun. They were all swirling in his mind. Sometimes forming a clear impression. Sometimes blurring into a muddy, murky mess.

He strolled over to Westminster and purchased a ticket for one of the hop-on, hop-off boat tours that exited from its pier. When he clambered up the sightseeing deck, he was pleasantly surprised to see hardly any tourists there. That would give him even more time to think. To calculate. To consider.

As the boat chugged off, Lee peered over his shoulder at Big Ben, inside the Elizabeth Tower that rose above the north end of the Palace of Westminster. The Prince of Timekeepers showed it to be about twenty minutes before eleven; Lee couldn't help but wonder how many minutes the clock had left to strike, how many chimes the bell had left to resound, before . . .

He chose to pay little attention to the tourist attraction known as The London Eye, which was approaching quickly on his right. Lee had never been fond of observation wheels, and in his mind this one—with its spaceship-looking passenger capsules and garish, LED lighting—was the cheesiest among the cheesy. He waited, instead, for a tonier venue to appear. The Royal Festival Hall, home of the London Philharmonic and the Philharmonia Orchestra soon delivered. Built in 1951, the performing arts venue stood out—Lee thought beautifully so—in its presentation of a bright-white exterior, accented by large panels of glass. The white exterior helped the concrete building pop that much more in a neighborhood that otherwise was sooty and dark, and the glass allowed filtered sunlight to bathe the building's interior and at night allowed the colors of the interior to reflect against the water.

If only the activities of The Organization were that transparent, he said to himself.

The boat next approached Waterloo Bridge, which Lee had always found quite sad, although he wasn't sure why. Perhaps it was because it was more of an engineering marvel than an architectural masterpiece. Or maybe it was because it (and its predecessor) were so linked with endings. The original Waterloo Bridge was a site that hosted numerous suicide attempts in the midnineteenth century, and in 1841, an American daredevil was killed while hanging from a rope that dangled from one of the bridge's scaffolds. Meanwhile, the current version of the bridge was the only one along the Thames that suffered damage from German bombers during World War II. It also had served as the inspiration for numerous poems and plays that focused on lovers meeting and then parting on a bridge.

Not much to put a smile on one's face, Lee told himself.

As if on cue, the sun retreated behind several wispy clouds that had slunk in from the west.

Lee leaned back and cast an admiring look at Somerset House as it arrived on the boat's port side. Since the 1700s, the neoclassical and Victorian complex had taken on so many personalities that it was hard even for Lee to recall them all. He was just glad it had finally become a cultural center of sorts, hosting galleries, musical performances, film events, and more.

Over time, it had been the home of Queen Elizabeth the First when she was still a princess, Anne of Denmark, Henrietta Maria of France, and even the body of Oliver Cromwell when it lay in state. Architects and designers ranging from Sir William Chambers to Christopher Wren to Inigo Jones to James Wyatt to Sir Albert Richardson had lent a hand in its evolving design. Lee wondered how they would all feel to know that today, one of the complex's most popular uses was that of a movie set and a Christmastime ice skating rink.

Less sprawling, and far more architecturally interesting to Lee, was Two Temple Place, which rose just beyond Somerset House. Built by William Waldorf Astor (the richest man in the world at the time), the extraordinary mansion offered not just opulent interiors that showcased a frieze by Thomas Nicholls with scenes from *Rip Van Winkle* and *The Last of the Mohicans,* but also the largest strong room in Europe. You couldn't see them from the boat, but Lee had always been charmed by the bronze lamp standards on either side of the mansion's front door, standards that featured small mischievous boys who were, alternately, holding up a globe and talking on a telephone, a new technology for the day.

That got Lee thinking about Tinti's phone and the analysis of the call and message logs currently underway. There was no guarantee the murderer had summoned Tinti to Hanover Square by phone. But these days, it was certainly the most convenient method. The question was whether the murderer had coded the message somehow or shielded his (or her) identity. Or both.

He quickly checked his phone to see if he had a message yet from C. J. But nothing had arrived, so he returned his attention to the gently flowing river and the interesting structures coming into view.

The OXO Tower on the Thames south bank began to appear. Built in the late 1800s as a power station designed to generate electricity for the Royal Mail Post Office, the structure had been restyled into its Art Deco design in 1929.

Lee found it humorous that the government refused to allow OXO (a maker of beef-stock cubes) to construct a tower with advertisements for its products. So the developer built the tower with four sets of three vertically aligned windows, each of which "coincidentally" formed from top to bottom the shapes of a circle, an X, and another circle.

In the 1990s, the tower was refurbished once again, this time to include housing, a restaurant, shops, and exhibition space. Lee marveled that, despite the tower's historical importance and the numerous awards won by its refurbishment, the structure to this day was not classed in England as a listed building.

From seemingly nowhere, a small flock of skuas approached the boat from the back, flying in a jagged line. As they neared the tourists on the upper deck, the birds suddenly lifted and soared high above the passengers, then returned to their original flight path after they had cleared the ship's bow. Lee wondered how they knew the timing for making that move, and the altitude needed to clear the boat, as well as the timing for descending back close to the water.

Animal instinct fascinated the architect. How animals—or people, for that matter—knew precisely when to fade left, or curve right, had a regular influence on how he designed buildings. And, often, on how he solved murders.

Lee jumped up and sauntered over to the other side of the vessel, for they were nearing two of his favorite buildings in London on the south bank of the river. Lee thought the firm Herzog & de Meuron had done an outstanding job converting the old Bankside Power Station into one of the premier art museums in the world. With the Tate Modern, they somehow had managed to find a way to preserve the cavernous main turbine hall and its overhead traveling crane. He also was glad they chose the brick latticework used on the exterior of the ten-story Switch House Tower erected in 2016 rather than the glass-stepped pyramid shape originally suggested. The brick paid homage, he thought, to the power station's historic personality. And its irregularly shaped façade was, he believed, perfect for a temple dedicated to the most contemporary of art.

However, the next significant building to arrive, Shakespeare's Globe, was as un-contemporary a structure as one could find. Although Lee viewed it mostly to be a tourist's lark, he gave the architects credit for having completed, in 1997, a sterling recreation of Shakespeare's original theatre on the site, right down to the English-oak construction with mortise and tenon joints and the only thatched roof allowed in London since the city's Great Fire of 1666.

Lee thought it would be a kick to perform on that stage one day. Perhaps as Oberon, from *A Midsummer Night's Dream?* He chuckled. *And C. J. could be my Puck,* he thought.

His phone vibrated. It was a text from C. J., marked urgent. *Did she know I was casting her in a Shakespeare play,* he wondered. He opened the message:

We've found something.
A message to Tinti the day before
his murder that says
'Meet me tomorrow night at Hanover Square.
Want to get right with you because
I'm leaving London the next day.'

Also told him to leave his phone
in his wall safe and they'd explain
why when he arrived at Hanover Square

Sender used anonymous text service to
spoof their outgoing phone number.
Working on tracing it to the phone that sent it.

His heart was galloping. If he could have jumped off the boat and swum to shore, he would have. His mind was galloping as well. *Everyone seems to have had a good reason to get right with Tinti,* he told himself. *And whoever sent the text didn't leave town, of course. That's not how The Organization works. So that comment is of no use to us.*

He decided his best option now was to enjoy the rest of the tour and exit the boat as soon as it reached the Greenwich Pier.

The boat chugged forward, and Southwark Cathedral next appeared on the river's south bank. Its towering spires caused Lee to wonder whether Antonio Tinti had been a religious man . . . whether he had issued some silent prayer for forgiveness when he saw the assailant's gun pointed at his chest. Nothing they had uncovered during the investigation seemed to indicate he was particularly spiritual, but Lee knew people often keep their faith far closer to their chest than one might realize.

Had Tinti attended services anytime recently, he wondered. *Had he bequeathed any of his estate to a religious organization in need? Probably not,* he quickly surmised.

He returned to his seat on the boat's port side. Suddenly, another question came to Lee's mind. *Given Tinti's love of disco music, did he start to hum the song "I Will Survive" when he saw the gun pointed at his chest?*

He shook his head twice. *Stop it, Dalton,* he admonished himself. *That was entirely uncalled for.*

Just then, a round, bald man plodded up to him from the opposite side of the boat.

"Hey, is that the Tower of London?" he bellowed, pointing to a series of structures appearing on the northern shore of the river.

Lee glimpsed over his left shoulder. "I . . . I believe it is," he replied.

The man was wearing a green-and-maroon Hawaiian shirt, jeans, a blue ball cap with a large, red C on it, black socks, and white athletic shoes.

"Well, why isn't there something in front of it, telling us that?" he said. "Why do we have to fucking guess? I mean, there should be a big, tall banner in front of it that says, 'This is THE historic Tower of London you've always heard about!' Something like that." He looked pointedly at the architect. "Do we make people guess whether they're standing in front of Wrigley Field when they come to Chicago? NO. It says it right there, WRIGLEY FIELD. HOME OF CHICAGO CUBS. Big as life. Plain as day. So there's no fucking confusion whatsoever."

Lee looked back across the water, then back at the tourist, whose face was now a fiery red. "I guess . . . they never thought of that," he conceded. "Perhaps you should write them a letter and share your idea with them."

The tourist looked at Lee again, but with a less bellicose expression. "You know, you're right!" he said, jabbing an index finger toward the architect's face. "You are absofuckinglutely right! That's *exactly* what I'm gonna do!" His bluster exhausted, he whirled around and trudged back across the boat to his brown-haired wife who—seemingly serene and only casually interested in the passing landmarks—was strumming "A Whiter Shade of Pale" on a large guitar she had cradled in her lap.

Lee turned around again to consider the venerable prison. Although he admired the tourist's typically American zeal, he chuckled some as he imagined the person from Chicago struggling without success to escape the prison's walls.

What most intrigued Lee about the complex was the White Tower, its least-bastardized section. Initiated by William the Conqueror in the 1080s, that tower quickly became not just a royal residence but also a symbol of might to anyone traveling along the Thames. Its Kentish ragstone exterior with Caen stone details mirrored the exteriors of keeps built in Northern France as far back as the 800s. But the inclusion in the northeast corner of a round tower containing a spiral staircase was a modern touch.

Lee appreciated how the architects made sure the structure exuded security by terracing it into the side of a large mound. As a result, the northern end of the basement was partially below ground and the entrance was above ground level, accessed only by a wooden staircase that sympathizers could quickly remove in the event of an attack.

And yet, the complex's renown as a place of imprisonment and death had been overblown over time. It never had a permanent torture chamber, as rumored, and up to the First World War, only seven people had been executed inside the tower. It had, however, served as a reliable place of captivity for many celebrated people—like Sir Walter Raleigh, and Elizabeth the First before she ascended to the throne—and others who had somehow invoked the ire of some sitting monarch. People like Edward Lewkenor who at thirty-four left behind a wife and ten children after being imprisoned in the tower for high treason against the rights of ascension of Mary, Queen of Scots.

Lee wondered how the renowned ravens now held captive in the tower were doing. For hundreds of years, the ravens were a source of tourist mirth and had become superficial symbols of the alleged death and doom associated with the tower. As a result, Lee worried whether they were truly being taken care of.

"We're doing just fine, Dalton," he heard a voice croak nearby. "But you might want to check your phone. There's a message there about *your* condition you need to read."

He took his phone out of his pocket. Sure enough, he had received a text:

**Mr. Lee: This is the Thames Valley Medical Centre.
We need you to make an appointment with us
at your earliest convenience regarding the
results of your tests with us.**

Lee glanced back at the ravens in the hopes they had more insights or advice regarding the text. If they did, they chose to keep those insights to themselves. He chewed the inside of one cheek and decided he didn't like the tone of the message and would ignore it for the time being. Perhaps, for some time to come.

The Greenwich Pier was only a few minutes away. But before the vessel would arrive there, it would carry him past one more building of note. City Hall had suffered much derision from locals not particularly keen to modern architecture, but Lee loved its creativity and play. Its look had been compared to Darth Vader's helmet, an onion, a woodlouse, and less genteelly, a "glass gonad." In fact, it was a modified sphere with no obvious front or back – a perfect metaphor, Lee thought, for most city governments on the planet. He also liked the fact that the 500-meter helical walkway that ascends ten stories to the structure's top floor provides citizens with unobstructed views of the council chambers below, a nod toward governmental transparency.

Opened in 2002, the building featured triple-paned glass shaped to minimize the amount of sun that would warm its exterior. Lee shared the skepticism of most other architects who believed the energy consumed by so much glass being stretched across a double façade negated whatever energy efficiency the shape might have provided. Still, he loved the building's whimsy, and preferred a building that delighted the eye (while using a bit more energy) over one that was energy-consummate (but dull as could be).

About ten minutes later, Lee was disembarking at the Greenwich Pier. He decided the tour had provided a lot of entertainment, but not as much enlightenment into Tinti's murder as he had hoped. With Fakhoury and Hensleigh expected at Scotland Yard any minute, and the source of an incriminating text soon to be revealed, Lee wished he had resisted his impulse to board the boat and had headed instead straight to C. J.'s office.

The couple from Chicago was immediately behind him, strolling up the exit ramp. At one point, Lee heard the man say to his wife, "That was only an okay tour. They should have served us some champagne. Or, at least something local, like a good Scotch."

The architect thought about saying something, decided it wasn't worth the effort.

His plan was to summon a car to take him back to Scotland Yard. But he first wanted to dash over to Greenwich Park. The green space had been the site of the equestrian matches during the 2012 Olympic Summer Games, and Lee had spent more than one afternoon during those games admiring the majesty of the horses as they surmounted the gates, ditches, oxers, and walls used in the competition.

The weather back then had been fair, the breeze had been gentle, the companionship was sweet and flirtatious. It was one of his happiest moments of late, and he didn't mind revisiting the location that had provided him such profound, if fleeting, contentment.

Later, as he relaxed in the back seat of a car that was taking him back toward Westminster, he turned to survey the cityscape speeding by. The buildings and the fences and the gates and the pedestrians flooded past, merging and congealing into one gelatinous form of motion. All the images from the boat tour—from the London Eye carrying tourists high into the sky, to the birds soaring above the boat, to the designs of the Royal Festival Hall and Two Temple Place, to the equestrian grounds in Greenwich Park, to the antiquity of the White Tower and the modernity of City Hall, to staircases removable, to staircases helical—joined the mélange, accelerating the visual slideshow even more.

Then, as if someone had punched a pause button, there was a lurch, and the merry-go-round of images came to a sudden, jagged stop. Gradually, a coolness began to seep throughout Dalton Lee's entire body.

Something he had seen or heard or thought about that day began to deliberately chew at him. It was a detail that connected back to something else that someone had said a few days earlier.

Lee pulled out his phone, opened a search engine, and entered first one name, then another. Checked one website, then another, and then a third. Toggled from one browser window to another until he had confirmed what he had suspected.

What had come back to mind was a comment that seemed unconnected and random at the time, but now seemed deeply connected and incredibly, *massively,* relevant. A comment that explained so much that had been unexplainable to him until now. How Tinti and his assailant had gotten into the park at Hanover Square after the gates had been locked.

And exactly who it was that had murdered the tailor at point-blank range.

51

One might think a group finalizing the details for the annihilation of millions of people would be somewhat somber at the proceedings. But those members of The Organization who convened in Room 1101 of the Ivy Palace Hotel on the first Thursday of October were anything but that. Genial didn't come close to accurately describing their mood. Neither did cheery, chipper, nor even, convivial.

What they were, was gleeful. Giddy. Ecstatic.

Jubilant.

"HA, HA, Charlotte, room 1101, is it?" bellowed the oldest man in the room. "I see what you did there, you cunning old crone!" He raked his thick hair back with the stubby fingers of one hand and proceeded to bounce on his palm the Malteser he'd been balancing in the other. "1101. As in November 1, the day the Ivy Mike test took place. HA HA!! That's sterling, milady. Absolutely sterling."

A soft smile formed on Charlotte's lips as she arranged three cocoa-brown-colored suitcases side by side on the double bed next to her. Four more lay scattered on the floor of the hotel room. "It's been my experience, George, that the most successful revolutionaries are those who maintain some semblance of irony."

"A *wicked* sense of irony," joked Nigel, who stood attentive by her left shoulder.

She chuckled once, stopped, and turned to the person who was standing in a distant corner of the room. "Oh, I meant to ask, how are the acid burns coming along? Still feeling much pain?"

The person paused a beat before answering, "I'm not sure 'nicely' is the word I would use, but yes, they are coming along."

Nigel nudged Charlotte in the ribs and pointed to a square box resting on the floor next to her feet. "What's that?" he asked.

"Good heavens, my pie!" she exulted, bending over to bring the box to bed level. "I'd almost forgotten about it! Thank you, Nigel, for the reminder. Yes, I brought a little banoffee pie for us to enjoy as we unpack our gifts."

"Charlotte, I'm really getting worried about your eating habits," Nigel replied, with an exaggerated look of concern on his face. "First, it was chocolate and pizza in the grocery store, today it's banoffee pie." However, when she turned and gave him a sour look, he sent her a childish grin in return and thrust both arms toward the box. "But banoffee is my absolute favorite, so I say, 'The devil take order now, let's scoff this down!'"

Charlotte chortled at Nigel's outburst and swatted him lightly on one arm. "Now, you're going to have to share, Nigel. It's only polite."

A trio of young men stood near the other bed, grinning as they watched the frivolity in front of them. They were all slight variations on a theme of "sporty young bloke with brownish hair and solid frame." All three looked like they might be experienced lacrosse players or apprentices in the House of Lords.

"When do we get to open the suitcases?" asked the one in the middle.

"Oh, my yes, when can we open them?" asked the one to his left.

"Which one should we open first?" asked the one to his right.

George ambled over to the open pie box and slid his left hand beneath a slice. Slowly, he folded the pie into his mouth, licked his fingers, and once he had swallowed the creamy dessert, turned and looked at Charlotte.

"I don't see any reason why we can't get started, do you?" he said.

She nodded her head some, licked her lips, rubbed her hands

together as if she were washing them, then replied, "Not really." Gently, she placed a palm on Nigel's forearm. "Will you help us, luv?"

Simultaneously, they leaned over the bed and inserted small keys into the locks of the suitcases in front of them. George queued up beside them and did the same with the third suitcase beside theirs. As the locks went snap, the athletes pressed forward like gamblers at a craps table, eager to watch the roll of the dice.

Charlotte was the first to open a suitcase, followed by George, then Nigel (whose bag was acting more contrary than the others). Once the very last lock gave way, Charlotte thrust both hands deep into the luggage. George did the same . . . followed by Nigel.

"This is exciting," said the athlete in the middle.

"I can't wait," said the one to his left.

"I'm pissing my pants," said the one to his right.

As if she were withdrawing a crystal vase, Charlotte elevated the item inside with excruciating care. George was but a half step behind her; Nigel one half step after that.

What they all now held aloft over the unlocked suitcases were leather briefcases of varying designs. Charlotte's was tan and made of cowhide leather; George held a burgundy version with a retractable handle. Nigel's was mahogany in color and featured several pockets and snaps. The three athletes craned their necks closer as their colleague in the corner strolled over to look.

"Who knew that items so incredibly beautiful could also be a part of something so lethal?" someone said.

One of the athletes crouched low and heaved a suitcase from the floor onto the bed beside him. "What about the others?" he asked, letting go of the handle. "Can we open them now? Take out what's inside?"

Charlotte and George nodded in sync, and a whirlwind ensued as suitcases shifted on bedspreads and locks clicked left and right. A hush fell over the anarchists as they admired all the valises the suitcases had revealed.

"Which is the one that will contain the bomb?" asked one of the athletes.

Charlotte took on a puzzled look as she surveyed all the cases before her. "Let's see . . . this one looks like the German's bag, and this is the one intended for the American," she said, raising each briefcase a few inches off the bedspread. "I think this is the replica of the Frenchman's valise and . . . ah, here's the one that will contain the explosives. Its framework is flimsier, so the nails and glass will inflict more harm."

She strolled over to one of the young athletes and thrust it toward his chest. "Here you go, luv," she said with a subtle smile. "Make certain you pack it the way we instructed you to."

Her gaze narrowed as she clutched his chin between a thumb and index finger. "Lovely job the cosmetic surgeons did on you, Patrick," she said, turning his head first one way, then another. "Why, the scars are almost undetectable. I trust they've made you look identical to . . . which official is it you're to be impersonating?"

"The one from Canada," he replied dutifully.

"Ah, yes, Canada," Charlotte replied, her smile fading. "I detest Canada, actually. All the people there are so damned . . . *genteel*. So, a good choice I'd say. An excellent choice. And I think it's probably for the best that the first chap who accepted this assignment got smooshed by that automobile. A Lamborghini was it? Or an Alfa Romeo, I can't remember. Anyway, good thing we discovered through the grapevine . . ." At this point, she pivoted and flashed a quick grin at the person in bandages. ". . . That before he died, he'd shared most of the details about our plan with his father. What a messy, unexpected complication *that* turned out to be for us." She chuckled once, then made an exaggerate frown. "Messier for the father, though, I would say."

She kept the artificially sad look on her face for just the appropriate amount of time before replacing it with a perky smile and patting the athlete several times on the chest.

"So, what do you have to say, luv, now that your martyrdom is near?" Everyone turned to Patrick, whose mouth flickered some from all the attention. The room went quiet for a second or two, which became several seconds, and just when the pause became almost too long, Patrick let out a breath and murmured, "Power to the cause."

"Power to the cause," whispered the boy to his left.

"Power . . . cause," said the third, almost inaudibly.

Their pledges hung in the air for several moments before Charlotte brought a stark, sudden end to the silence.

"Anyone in the mood for another slice of pie?" she asked.

52

Omar Fakhoury and Malcolm Hensleigh sat side by side on a small wooden bench just outside the office of Scotland Yard commander Clara Josephine Digby. Only a few short inches separated the two men, but one would never have guessed that. For both men sat with their hands in their laps, staring impassively ahead of them. Fakhoury may have thought himself an international bon vivant, but he looked more than a little crumpled and even more peeved. Hensleigh appeared stone-faced and into his thoughts, as if he were trying to compute the square root of a six-digit number.

They said nothing to one another, acted unaware of the other's existence.

"Who do *you* think did it?" Bree looked inquisitively at Warren, who was squinting at the pair, his head cocked to one side. At that moment, he thought they resembled primary students waiting for their headmistress to give them a talking-to.

"I'm not sure," he finally replied. "My money's on the Lebanese guy. The tailor just doesn't seem to me to have the revolutionary fervor inside him to a pull a trigger multiple times. Then again . . ."

"Then again," Bree added quietly, "those are the ones who often have the most rage to unleash."

The two senior members of The Lee Group were stationed in an office directly adjacent to C. J.'s. From their vantage point, they could clearly see the two suspects through the glass windows in front of them. And through the glass windows on their right, they could clearly see C. J. at her desk, waiting for a phone call that would tell her the names of everyone who had called or texted Antonio Tinti in the seventy-two hours before his murder.

"Why isn't Dalton here?" Warren shot out.

Bree shook her head, shrugged her shoulders. "That's a very good question. You'd think he'd want to be here for this."

Warren nodded and smirked a bit.

"Probably had to go off on one of those secret adventures he thinks we don't know about. When he talks to the trees . . . or some statue, or something."

Bree studied her co-worker for a moment but said nothing.

As if instructed by some offstage director, the tailor and the Middle Eastern businessman both lifted their left legs and crossed them over their right knees. Neither gave a hint they had noticed the other do the same thing; they continued to stare straight ahead, as if watching a video screen.

"Okay, that was weird," Bree whispered. "It's like they're zombie twins, or something."

Warren nodded silently. "Only, they're not even *close* to being twins, zombie or otherwise."

They could hear "Ride of the Valkyries" playing somewhere nearby, muted but insistent. Turning to their right, they saw C. J. glance up from her paperwork and stare at the cell phone on her desk. The music continued. The commander licked her lips once before she extended her left arm and brought the phone to her ear.

Automatically, Bree clutched Warren's nearest elbow. He placed one palm on the top of her back. "I can't believe Dalton isn't here for this," he said softly.

Bree looked to see if the phone call had altered the composure of either Malcolm Hensleigh or Omar Fakhoury. It had not. However, she noticed that the shoe positioned over Fakhoury's right knee had begun ever so slightly to bounce.

She looked back at the commander, who had risen from her chair and was bent over her desk, scribbling into a small notebook. Periodically, C. J. would nod, like one of those toy glass birds that continually dip their heads into a beaker or cup as if taking a drink.

"Can you tell anything?" Warren said, craning to look around Bree.

The senior architect shook her head. "No. She's moving her lips, but I can't read them. But it does seem like they're giving her *a lot* of data."

They waited patiently and struggled to discern what clues they could from the indirect view they had of the commander.

Who continued to nod. And continued to scribble. And continued to nod even more.

On Warren and Bree's left at one end of the vestibule, a door opened, and two muscular guards strolled into the waiting area. They appeared to just be surveying the room, but then they approached the bench where Fakhoury and Hensleigh were sitting and positioned themselves at opposite ends. Both spread their feet to shoulder's width and crossed their hands over their belt buckles.

Hensleigh flinched slightly as he glanced up at the guard standing beside him. Then, he reverted to his look of utter boredom.

"What do you want to bet C. J. summoned those guys with some hidden buzzer in her office?" Warren asked.

Bree smiled and nodded, then returned her gaze to C. J., who seemed frozen in midcomment, her mouth open, her pen in the air. Then, she broke from the dreamlike state, leaned toward her notebook, and resumed her scribbling and nodding.

Bree nudged Warren with her elbow. "I want you to know that if this does lead us to the killer, Warren, I really hope it's your wife we get to free from captivity. Your kids have been without their mum for way too long."

He didn't look at her but nodded. "You're right. They have been. But you know how this goes, Bree. We're only able to rescue the person whose whereabouts the killer knows. At the end of the day, it's a crap shoot really."

"Still," Bree replied, nudging him once more, "we can hope." He smiled but kept his eyes locked on the two men on the bench.

There was a stirring in C. J.'s office. She had moved the phone away from her ear and was holding it at arm's length, glaring at it. Then she tossed it gently onto her desk, collected the sheaf of scattered papers nearby, and stuffed them into a manila folder.

"Looks like. . ." Warren began.

"We may know something," Bree concluded.

The commander rounded her desk, folder in hand, a stern expression on her face. As she exited her office, her eyes caught those of Bree and Warren in the adjacent room, but she gave no hint to them as to what she knew, or what was about to happen.

"Should we go out there? Bree asked.

"Let's wait," Warren replied.

As C. J. approached the stoic pair on the bench, the guards became more tense and formal. She murmured a few words to the officers, which caused them to relax their stances. Once she had finished conveying what she had to say, Omar Fakhoury and Malcolm Hensleigh slowly rose from the bench, turned, and glided their way down the corridor, still looking straight ahead. As they passed the office in which Warren and Bree were standing, both broke out in broad grins. Fakhoury lifted one arm and patted the older tailor on the upper back.

"What the hell?" Warren muttered.

Through the doors at the other end of the corridor, Dalton Lee burst into the vestibule like a passenger hoping to catch a plane already leaving the gate. Bree and Warren took his arrival as permission to leave their perch of observation.

"Oh, there you are, Dalton," C. J. said matter-of-factly. "We had to let them go because neither of their phones was the one that sent the text to Tinti."

"I know," Lee stammered through breathlessness. "We need to move . . . immediately."

"Yes, we most definitely do," C. J. said as she scooted back to her office. As she made her way past Lee's two senior architects, she called out, "So, Bree my dear, it looks like all this time you've been keeping company with a femme fatale."

"What?" Bree gave the commander a quizzical look.

C. J. returned the look with a cautionary one of her own.

"It took a while, but we finally matched the text message to the phone that sent it. Turns out, it's a phone that belongs to your knitting partner, Mariam."

53

When they led her into the interrogation room, her hands and ankles shackled, Lee was surprised that she wore nowhere near as surly an expression as he had expected. She seemed to be more in shock than anything else, or possibly confused as to precisely what was going on. Although she had no good reason to be confused. They had very clearly read her rights to her. Had very clearly spelled out the charges against her. Could not possibly have made it more clear to her that confessing her connection to The Organization and providing additional details about the group's plans in London were her only hopes of receiving any leniency.

And they had stressed that, depending on which judge was handed her case, even *that* was a shot in the dark (pun intended).

One of her hands was wrapped in a loose gauze bandage, secured by tape. The other lay limp on the tabletop, palm side up.

"All right, I think we're ready to proceed," C. J. announced.

The commander sat on the opposite side of the table from the accused, along with two other officials from Scotland Yard. Lee occupied a chair in one corner of the room. Because of his expertise into how members of The Organization think and behave, he had been given the privilege of observing the interview. In a small anteroom, the rest of the team prepared to watch the proceedings through a one-way glass.

C. J. shuffled some papers, looked back at the murderer.

"So, Bridget, how long have you been a member of The Organization?"

The young waitress seemed to stare at a point just above and to the right of C. J.'s left shoulder. If Lee had not known better, he would have thought she was a feral child raised by wolves who was encountering civilization for the very first time.

She licked her lips twice, glanced at the ceiling, then seemed to compose herself and directly meet C. J.'s glare. "A year, maybe a little more, maybe a little less," she replied.

"And why did you want to join them?"

She grinned, let out a short, low scoff.

"To disrupt the status quo, of course. The reason any of us joins The Organization. To show all of you there is a glorious world beyond all the ridiculous rules, and regulations, and stipulations imposed upon you. To help everybody bask in the light. The radiant, resplendent light that comes from living a flawless life in a flawed world, from moving through this universe guided only by your free will, your own instincts, and your own natural impulses."

Her head was slightly tilted, her face now beamed pleasantness and peacefulness. But Lee was sure he detected a steeliness appear across her face just before she concluded her comments with, "Power to the cause."

C. J. was unmoved. She looked as if Bridget had just insulted her mother or had announced there was no greater abomination on the planet than saxophone jazz. "I see. Then perhaps you can explain to me how you are able to reconcile this concept of 'living a flawless life,' as you call it, with shooting, in cold blood, a man who had been kind to you, who had loaned you a sizable sum of money, who had just lost his only son in an automobile accident. You did that, Bridget. You did *all of that*, and still, you believe your life is *flawless*, do you?"

The waitress blinked a few times and looked as if she was in the middle of short-circuiting. Her face returned to that of someone lost, befuddled, trying unsuccessfully to connect one dot to any other.

The question went unanswered.

The commander leaned back in her chair and waited. Picked up her phone, flipped through a message or two. A moment later, she returned her scrutiny to Bridget. "So, after Niccolò Tinti died in the accident, The Organization planted you at the diner and taught you to play up to his father to see if he'd confide that his son had told him about their scheme. And, in time, that's exactly what he did. Since he had developed a bond with you, you won the lottery and got to be the one who murdered him."

Bridget sat impassive to the commentary, looked beleaguered and bored.

"Around the time you needed to carry out your assignment, Mariam mislaid her phone in the restaurant, as she was prone to do. So, using one of those anonymous text services that make the job of those of us in law enforcement *so delightful* these days, you sent Tinti a text telling him to meet you at Hanover Square around midnight so you could repay the money he'd loaned you so you could retire your mother's back taxes. If there ever was such a delinquency, that is."

Bridget shifted in her chair and thrust herself forward. "There was!" she bellowed.

"How much of one?" C. J. parried back.

Bridget retreated. "A few hundred pounds."

"And how much did you persuade Mr. Tinti to loan you?"

The waitress dropped her head some. "A few thousand pounds."

C. J. laughed once, looked back at her papers. "I see. And, once Mr. Tinti arrived at Hanover Square, you persuaded him to enter the park with you . . . precisely how?"

Bridget replaced her pugnacious appearance with a sly smirk. "Wouldn't you like to know?"

The commander leaned forward, set her forearms horizontal in front of her like a trench line that was not to be crossed. "Oh, we know, Bridget. We most certainly know. We just like to have our theories substantiated by the person who will spend the rest of her life in prison because of it."

The waitress's face soured. "Maybe I'll just leave you with your theories then," she replied, glowering.

For several seconds, everyone in the room remained quiet. Soon, however, C. J. decided to resume the dialogue. "After you murdered him, you tossed the gun into a dumpster near Hampstead Heath so we'd be inclined to think it was one of the bocce players there who'd committed the crime."

The waitress didn't respond, choosing to inspect her fingernails instead.

"Truly, Bridget, it was a brilliant scheme," C. J. continued. "Until it wasn't."

Lee recrossed his legs, reflecting on the disparate clues that had helped him deduce it was Bridget, not Mariam, who had used the Glock to extinguish Antonio Tinti's life:

—The use of the phrase "want to get right with you" in the text message luring Tinti to Hanover Square, which reminded Lee of the loan Tinti had made to Bridget, a loan Tinti was especially eager to have repaid since she also told him she was leaving London the next day.

—The cellophane wrapper found on Tinti's body, a wrapper identical to those used to protect the peppermints Lee had lifted more than once from the bowl near the diner's front door. Although cellophane doesn't easily yield fingerprints, C. J.'s assistants had risen to the challenge just that day and linked a partial print they found on the wrapper to the young waitress, confirming her guilt even more.

—And then there was the clue he acquired during his tour of the Thames, the clue that helped him deduce how Bridget and Tinti had entered the park . . .

C. J. shifted in her chair and cleared her throat. "Bridget, I must be frank with you. We have more than enough incriminating evidence to put you away in Foston Hall or possibly even, Bronzefield. The one thing, the *only* thing, you can do to make this situation easier on yourself is to tell us the location of someone your group is holding hostage."

The commander slid a small notebook and pen across the table, nodded first at it, then at Bridget. "The speed with which you deliver that information will determine how much mercy the court extends to you."

Bridget's jaw remained defiant. "I have no idea what you're talking about. I have no idea where we keep those people. I have no need or interest in *your mercy.*"

C. J. leaned forward once more, met Bridget's jaw and raised it one.

"It's important you understand, young lady, that we know very well that as part of one's initiation into The Organization, one must memorize the locations of all the hostages the group is keeping captive. You are tested on that. Fail that test, and you don't get in, isn't that right?"

C. J. cocked her head to one side and assumed a worried expression. "You *are* a bona fide member of The Organization, aren't you, Bridget? Or, do they still consider you just a—what is it they call that level of associate—oh, right . . . a *novice*. Is that what you are to them, Bridget? Just a novice? Does your mother know they only think of you as *a novice?* For we'd be more than happy to deliver that information, if you'd like."

Bridget flinched. "Don't you dare," she hissed.

Now it was C. J. who wore a self-satisfied smirk.

"My dear, I am the commander of Scotland Yard," she replied. "There's nothing I love to take on more than . . . a dare . . . especially one issued by someone with less than half my years and half my experience."

With that, Bridget's combativeness withered. She looked down at the notebook, then at her attorney, who indicated through the arching of her eyebrows and a tilt of her head that the waitress should probably accept the deal.

Bridget grabbed the spiral end of the notebook and yanked it toward her. It took only a few seconds for her to uncap the pen and scribble a few words.

"Legibly, please," C. J. uttered in a monotone.

When she was finished, the waitress didn't bother to replace the cap. Instead, she hurled it and the pen in C. J.'s direction, as if they were darts being tossed toward a dartboard in a tavern. Then she nudged the notebook toward the commander. Her duty completed, she looked up and shot a disgusted look toward the back of the room.

"Why is *he* here?" she huffed, flinging one arm in Lee's direction.

"Who is that guy, anyway? The poofter back there with the fetish for cheese toasties. What does he have to do with any of this?"

Before she chose to answer Bridget's questions, C. J. turned to look at the architect and flashed a broad smile his way. "He's the reason you're sitting here, Bridget. He's the one who figured you out."

Bridget went back into a daze but shot Lee a look that made him feel like a three-headed donkey.

One of the other police officials leaned in and whispered something to C. J., who nodded several times in response. The commander then scooted her chair back and gripped both of its arms to hoist herself up. "I agree, I think we're done here," she announced. She then handed the notebook to one of the superintendents beside her and quietly added, "Follow up on that if you would, *chop-chop.*"

She headed for a door at the back of the room in the corner opposite from Lee. Two female guards stepped forward and flanked Bridget as she rose to return to her cell.

But C. J. whirled around for one last parry. "By the way, Bridget, we know all about your group's plot to commit a suicide bombing tomorrow at the G7 summit meeting. I'm sorry, but I'm afraid my agents will be crashing that little party you had planned and shutting it down before it ever gets underway."

The waitress turned from the guard who was holding her most tightly and caught C. J. square in the eye.

"You think we're launching The Transformation *tomorrow?* At the summit meeting? It's not the presidents and prime ministers who carry the nuclear codes, you silly bat." She threw her head back and chortled. "Oh, isn't that smashing? Isn't that just how you people think? Well, sorry to fuck up your little raid, *commander,* but The Transformation isn't taking place *tomorrow.*

"It's taking place tonight. Where the attachés are gathering. To plan the meeting for those world leaders you've been so worried about, a meeting no one's going to give a shit about once the slaughter we have planned is discovered."

54

The rap on the door was brief but insistent. He double-checked that he had the lighting just right, that the shades were fully closed, and that the pillows on the king-size bed were immaculately fluffed.

His inventory complete, the attaché to the prime minister of Canada took a deep breath, then darted forward, pausing to take a quick look through the peephole. Just to be certain.

He really liked what he saw. Smiling broadly, he turned the knob and opened the door wide.

"Patrick, right?" he said with confidence.

"That would be me," the young athlete replied, a coy smile on his face. "I believe you called for a massage?"

"A massage. Riiight," the Canadian replied.

Hands stuffed into the pockets of his tight, acid-washed blue jeans, Patrick strolled into the expansive hotel room—a junior suite, really—scrutinizing every dark corner and piece of furniture he passed. In addition to the jeans, he wore a tight, red, short-sleeved, button-down-the-front shirt (with both sleeves rolled up to emphasize his biceps), and white sneakers. As he paraded through the room, he dropped from both of his shoulders the straps connected to the small backpack he was carrying. A bag he quickly flung onto the floor.

"You don't have to worry," his client said. "I'm cool. I'm not a cop. And I think what you're looking for is over there." He pointed at the nearest nightstand, which was topped by an alarm clock and a white envelope that was bulging at the seams. Patrick veered toward the envelope, opened it, flipped through the multiple bills it contained, and quickly secured it inside one of his backpack's zippered pockets.

"That works," he said to his client. "So, your name is . . . John?"

"Um, Sean. And let's just keep it at that. I have a government job, so I need to be extra . . ."

"Careful. Got it. Hush, hush, and all that."

Sean nodded, smiled, then strode over to Patrick, who firmed his entire body as the attaché approached.

"Wow, if I do say so myself, we sure look a lot alike," the Canadian said. "*A lot.* The resemblance is almost creepy, except you're more muscular than I am." The Canadian gripped the masseur's prominent shoulders and squeezed them hard, then buried his face into the athlete's shirt.

Patrick wrapped one arm around the attaché's waist, put the palm of his free hand on the back of his client's head, and leaned toward his ear. "Slow down, mate, we've got an entire hour," he whispered.

Sean continued to nuzzle Patrick's chest and squeeze his back. Once more, the hustler moved his lips close to the Canadian's ear. "Hey, the agency said you're a regular customer, so I know you weren't really wanting a massage, but I do give a pretty spiffy one if I say so myself. How about you let me get you completely relaxed before we get down to some serious business?"

Sean shifted his face from one part of Patrick's chest to the other. Eventually, the government employee replied, "Yes. Please."

Within moments, the Canadian envoy was naked on the bed, lying on his stomach, his arms splayed above his head like a criminal who was being arrested.

"Okay, in the interest of time, I'm going to focus just on your back and upper legs," Patrick said. "Then we'll start having some *real* fun." The masseur straddled Sean's lower torso and began to run his thumbs up either side of the attaché's spine, moving them in small, tight circles as they ascended his client's back. Quickly, he switched to the bottoms of his palms, making similar motions with them. He then transferred the pressure to his fingertips, randomly poking and prodding the Canadian at the top of the back, on both sides, and near the bottom.

The attaché grimaced a bit, ran the edge of one thumb along the top of the bedspread. *Oh, great,* he thought. *This guy doesn't have a clue as to how to give a good massage.* When he felt the weight of the masseur suddenly lift off him, he opened his eyes.

"Close your eyes! Don't move!" Patrick barked. "I'm just getting some lotion I like to use. It will help relax the knots in your back. I'll work on your back for another couple of minutes, then you can do whatever you want with me."

The Canadian started to protest but decided the moisturizer probably would make the massage more comfortable. He closed his eyes again and let himself sink a little deeper into the bedspread as he started to fantasize about the fun he'd have with this stud when the time came around for it.

That's when he felt the prick of the needle, followed by the rush of a searing-hot fluid. No more than ten seconds passed before his heart began to canter and everything went from white to brown to gray to black.

***

The queue was starting to move again. All seven of those in line were neatly attired in blazers, slacks, and bright-white dress shirts. Each wore around his neck a lanyard bearing a tag that indicated the nation he represented: the United Kingdom, the United States, Canada, France, Germany, Italy, Japan. Each gripped at his side the leather briefcase containing the whimsical set of numbers and letters that, if programmed into the right device, could launch their country's nuclear arsenal.

Except for the attaché from Canada, whose valise contained a sophisticated assembly of switches, circuits, wires, and receivers.

He had assumed a place in the middle of the line and was behaving as inconspicuously as possible. It helped that even though they undertook casual conversations with one another now and then, or called out to one another down the line, the attachés took their jobs (and especially the goals of this particular meeting) very seriously.

Ostensibly, their objective that night was to review the agenda for the following day's meeting of their nations' leaders and to smooth out any unresolved details. Surreptitiously, and more importantly, their plan was to each develop a new nuclear password for their country and then share the expired codes with one another as a declaration of their commitment to the alliance. And as a stern statement to the others that if they thought they had cracked any nation's code, that achievement was now null and void.

"Hey, Sean, how've you been? You look like you've put in a lot of time in the gym recently." It was Kasuo Sakamoto, the attaché to the prime minister of Japan. Educated at Berkeley, he spoke English as impeccably, if not more so, than the "Canadian" he was talking to.

"I have. Glad to know it's paying off. Thanks."

The Japanese envoy smiled back. And waited. When he realized nothing else was forthcoming from the Canadian, he turned back around. The person now answering to the name of Sean smiled to himself, pleased to see the instruction he had received from his compatriots had worked—the instruction to not ask questions about the other attachés so he could avoid lengthy, detailed conversations with them. Conversations that might blow his cover.

Delicately and discreetly, he traced the edge of the detonator inside his right pants pocket. *Power to the cause,* he recited to the heavens.

Silently, he went over the plan of attack. They would be seated in the hotel conference room and be served beverages and light hors d'oeuvres. To ensure that his judgment would in no way be impaired, he would, of course, decline any alcohol (although he was rethinking that part of the plan, given this would be his final night to enjoy it). They next would review the agenda for the following day's meeting and resolve any potential bumps in the carpet they had identified.

There was one question he had been programmed to ask so his participation in the meeting did not seem too removed:

Will the fact the meeting was scheduled to conclude at half past four in the afternoon in any way interfere with the planned photo opportunities making the evening news cycles in major markets around the world?

"We all know the importance optics play at summits such as this," he would add.

Following their approval of the next day's agenda, there was to be a toast to the attaché from Italy, who was soon leaving the Italian government to take a job with one of the country's biggest industrial firms. Once the toast had been made, and as the others sipped their wine or water, he would reach inside his pocket and press the detonator.

What will it feel like, he wondered. *Will there be any pain, or does life stop so quickly, there's no sense of pain whatsoever? How soon afterward will I become aware of my martyrdom? Will I instantly see my fellow revolutionaries exulting in the success of The Transformation? Or is there some sort of cooling-off period before I acquire the gift of universal sight they assured me I would have?*

For the fleetest of seconds, a doubt settled in. *Only, what if there's nothing? What if there's just a deep, infinite void?* He shook the notion away and quickly shifted his thoughts to Charlotte, Nigel, and the others, to their infectious smiles and nonstop bravado. *My comrades would never lie to me,* he reassured himself. *Never.*

The line of attachés was plodding forward now, the security protocol having turned them into silent, shuffling automatons. At the front of the line, the attaché to the prime minister of the United Kingdom placed his briefcase onto the conveyor belt, raising his arms above his head as he stepped into the body scanner. Behind him, the attaché to the US president did the same, placing his briefcase carefully on the belt, then raising his arms as he proceeded through the scanning equipment. Their valises glided into the black void of the scanner, like amusement park rides entering a fun house tunnel.

The ritual of placing the briefcases on the conveyor belt continued on and on, with no one (except the counterfeit Canadian attaché) aware that the briefcases the government officials were retrieving at the far end of the conveyor belt were not the briefcases they had placed upon it. That the security guards working the conveyor belt and the scanning equipment were not (as their badges suggested) employees of Citadel Security International but associates of The Organization instead. That the security guards who were *supposed to be* working this detail were instead lying dead in some hotel room, corporate rental, or flat, felled by the same injection of pancuronium bromide that had sent the real attaché to the prime minister of Canada off to the Great Beyond. That the briefcases being handed to the attachés at the end of the conveyor belt looked identical to the ones they had relinquished, but in fact were not, as they did not contain any nuclear codes or any details about where each country's nuclear warheads were located.

Nuclear codes and warhead information that—along with the official briefcases—were now in the hands of The Organization. For them to control. And deploy.

Wherever and whenever they wanted to deploy them.

55

"What do we know?"

C. J. raised a palm to hush Dalton Lee as she struggled to hear what was being said at the other end of the line. Less than half an hour had passed since Bridget had revealed The Organization's true intentions. In a corner of C. J.'s office, Anisa was in a chair with her legs swept up underneath her, furiously texting someone on her phone.

"I see. Yes. Where was his body discovered? In his hotel room? And . . . he died of what?" A long pause ensued before she added, "Oh, my, that is troubling. Yes, quite troubling." She paused again and began to receive what sounded to Lee like an unrelenting torrent of information. Then she pressed her ear closer to the receiver before she interrupted the person on the other end of the line with, "All I want to know is, do we have enough time to position a sniper across the street?"

Anisa stopped typing and looked up from her phone, first at C. J., then at Lee, who returned her look of concern. Slowly, the inspector shook her head, and he nodded back to let her know he agreed with her assessment that the plan being discussed was not the wisest.

"Well, I agree, I don't particularly like it either," C. J. continued into her phone, "but it does seem to be the only option we have at this point. And, if you say we can get someone on the roof of that building across the street in the next fifteen minutes, then, yes, I am authorizing it. Go!"

Lee turned again to Anisa and raised his eyebrows, but the inspector's focus had returned to her device. C. J. clicked off her phone, sighed heavily, and looked over her shoulder at Lee.

"It seems the attachés have already gone into conference," she muttered. "We're doing everything we can to alert someone there, but no one with the security company that was assigned to the meeting is responding, which makes me very uncomfortable. And, the attachés themselves are under the strictest of orders that once they have started their session, they should respond only to messages involving a family emergency.

"We have a sniper taking a position on a rooftop directly across the street from the room they're in. Fortunately, we have an excellent relationship with the chairman of the bank headquartered in that building. I realize it's a strategy that's fraught with calamity and could very likely end in disaster." She gave the architect a distressed look. "But I'm afraid it's the only reasonable strategy we have before us right now, Dalton."

Lee squeezed the commander's shoulders. "Well, if it's the best we can do, then we should most definitely do it," he intoned.

C. J. looked down at the floor, scuffed it with the bottom of one of the black court shoes she was wearing.

"God save the Queen," she uttered. Then under her breath added, "God save us *all*."

56

The Canadian attaché was much more relaxed now that the social hour was behind them. By keeping all his responses to just one, short, generic sentence, he had succeeded in not raising anyone's suspicions.

Or, it seemed that way, anyway.

He and the other attachés had taken their seats at an oval mahogany conference table with a top that gleamed from a recent polish. Out of curiosity, he scanned the arrangement—mostly to see who would likely be the first to die once he pressed the trigger in his pocket.

They had placed him at the far end of the table on the side closest to the windows. The attachés from Italy and Germany were on his right; directly across from him was the representative from Japan. *Sorry, Kasso, or whatever your name is, but given where they've placed you, it looks like you're a goner for sure,* he said to himself. *Which is really too bad, because you seem like a pretty straight-up sort of guy.* Next to the Japanese representative was the US attaché, and next to him, the attaché from France.

As the meeting's official host, the gentleman representing the UK's prime minister was seated at the head of the table and responsible for leading them through their responsibilities. They were in the middle of reviewing the agenda for the following day's meeting of world leaders, a subject he found immensely boring. But he had done a good job of feigning interest, he thought, flipping through the pages of the agenda and placing his index finger on certain lines of the text *just so,* to appear as though he were truly reading it. He would nod periodically, especially when one of the attachés expressed an opinion that seemed more than just a tad important to him.

He also believed he had articulated perfectly his question about how well the timing of the conclusion of the following day's meeting would intersect with photo opportunities. Assured it would not interfere with the world leaders getting their faces on most news programs, he smiled and went back to his role as an utterly cooperative terrorist-in-hiding.

As they began to consider the suitability of the following day's lunch menu, the Japanese attaché pushed a note toward him and gestured to him to open it.

I need to step out to take a quick call.
Pay attention for me until I get back?

Sean nodded, which prompted the Japanese envoy to rise from his chair and head for the conference room door.

"So, I think we're agreed that the agenda for tomorrow morning is fine as is, but we may want to suggest a couple of amendments to the afternoon session—is that correct?" The attaché from the United Kingdom was scanning the faces of everyone in the room, his spectacles at the far end of his nose. The others softly murmured their agreement, and the Canadian representative joined in, nodding as vigorously as he could.

But his enthusiasm was only for show.

It doesn't really matter, you fools, he thought as he regarded the others around the table. *Come tomorrow, when the extent of the destruction here is dominating the newscasts and our long-awaited Transformation is underway, the last thing anyone is going to think about is this silly, pompous agenda of yours.*

***

"Are you in position?"

"Getting there."

"What seems to be the problem?"

"Having to navigate around a lot of debris up here. Shouldn't be long."

"You're right, it shouldn't be. We have a very narrow window to operate in."

"Speaking of windows, which one am I supposed to shoot through?"

"You're joking, right?"

"Yes. I'm joking. I have it in my sights now."

"Good. Keep it there. And might I suggest we dispense with the comedy?"

A pause. Then . . .

"You know, you used to be a lot more fun to work with."

***

Their review of the following day's agenda complete, the attachés turned their attention to the logistics associated with transporting everyone from their respective hotels to the meeting site. The Japanese representative slipped back into the room, took his chair opposite his Canadian counterpart, and sent another note his way.

Did I miss anything important?

Sean picked up his pen.

No. Except, out of concern for excessive mercury, we've asked the chef to serve halibut rather than ahi tuna. ☺

He slid the note back to the Japanese attaché, who read it, looked across the table, and grinned broadly.

"So, I believe we have the security details worked out for transporting our leadership to the summit meeting," said the attaché from the United Kingdom. "Is there anything else we need to discuss?" The representative from France raised his hand.

"Have we decided who will deliver the invocation tomorrow?"

"Ah, yes. A very good question, Monsieur Dubois. We've not yet finalized that detail; however, we do have several candidates who should be able to deliver an invocation that will honor the diverse faiths represented in the room. We expect the name of the person selected for that task to be confirmed by the end of this afternoon."

The French attaché smiled and nodded his satisfaction with the answer.

"Well then, if there are no other details regarding the agenda we need to address, might I suggest that, before we proceed to that critical task before us that involves not just the security of all our homelands but every other nation as well, we stand and pay tribute to our associate from Italy, Signore Moretti. As you know, this is the last G7 summit he will be attending before he assumes a new and enviable position within the private sector."

There was a shuffle of chairs. Then, the seven attachés to the seven most important leaders in the world stood to make a toast to their soon-to-be-departed colleague.

57

"You don't have much time. You have to take the shot."

"I know that. I'm just letting you know I'm not very confident about how this is all going to turn out."

"You *need* to be confident. You need to be *very* confident. And *very* precise. You're called a *sharpshooter* for a reason."

"I'm not a sharpshooter, I'm a sniper."

"Oh, bleedin' hell! Are you gormless? This is no time to worry over names. Are you going to go through with this, or do we need to put someone else up there?"

"Okay, he's back where I need him. Ready to fire. However . . ."

"No, 'however.' Just take the bloody shot.

"NOW!"

***

Each attaché held in his hand a glass brimming with Krug champagne. They all turned to the representative from the United Kingdom, who was to deliver the laurels intended for their comrade from Italy.

"Signore Moretti, this body has been honored to have your service for . . . ten years now, I believe?" The Italian envoy nodded that the speaker's calculation was correct. "I know that I have known you for more than fifteen, and have benefited enormously from your astute counsel, your precise attention to managing details, and your commitment to building professional relationships that pass the test of time. We have been inordinately fortunate to have you as a part of this august group, and we will miss your contributions enormously, but we do wish you the very best in all your future endeavors.

"Now, will you please join me in celebrating the service of Signore Moretti, by toasting him in your native language?"

As they all raised their champagne flutes aloft, the attaché from Canada shifted his glass from his right hand to his left. Then, as discreetly as possible, he slid his free hand into the right front pocket of his slacks and wrapped his fingers around the apparatus hidden there.

Suddenly, the glass he was holding shattered in his hand and a torrent of gunshots resounded throughout the room. His thumb was on the electronic trigger . . . but as the room began to whirl in different directions, it slipped off the mechanism . . . and a dark curtain began to descend.

The last image he saw as his life drained away from him was the attaché from Japan standing directly across from him, determination on his face, a pistol in his hand.

58

"If C. J. does show up, I'm not sure all of us will fit in this office."

Bree elbowed Liam, who was crushed up against one of the commander's filing cabinets. "Well, you certainly shouldn't blame it entirely on *her*," she said with a huff. "You're no starving runway model yourself, bucko. If we do end up with some sort of overage issue, you're just as much to blame as C. J."

"Just as much to blame for what?" The commander waddled into the room with what appeared to be a lime-green pool noodle under one arm. Everyone shifted first one direction, then another, to accommodate both new arrivals.

"Are you taking a . . . swimming lesson . . . this afternoon, C. J.?" Lara gave the policewoman a look that teetered between bemusement and bewilderment.

C. J. paused. "A what? Swimming lesson?" She glanced over at the noodle, which she had just set upright against the control panel on the treadmill in the corner.

"Oh, that. No, no swimming lesson for me. I learned to swim before I learned to eat. No, I'm leaving on an Aegean cruise in the next couple of days. I'm hoping to bask in the sun and enjoy the warm breezes in Santorini before winter here gets underway in earnest. Who knows, perhaps I'll meet some dashing Don Giovanni as well."

Everyone smiled, despite the fact they were all struggling with their visions of C. J. wearing any kind of swimsuit, cavorting in the ocean with the pool noodle, or bouncing up and down inside a pool doughnut.

Bree let out a sudden shriek. "The skirt!" she blurted out. "You bought it! You're wearing it!"

The rest of the team noted for the first time that, indeed, C. J. had on the yellow country-western skirt she had admired in the shop owned by Tinti's ex-girlfriend. C. J. did a twirl for everyone, causing the fringe to swirl along with her.

"I won't be taking this on the trip, of course," she said, admiring herself. "I mean, it's not really very Mediterranean, is it? But I figured it's Friday, and we've stymied those bastards once again, so why not dress for a celebration?"

Liam leaned away from the file cabinet.

"C. J.," he began, a wide grin crinkling the area around his temples, "I promise that the blokes at a particular pub in Western Australia I sometimes frequent would find you totally irresistible." The Scotland Yard commander tilted her head to the side and offered a flirtatious smile in return.

Warren wrapped his arms around his torso to make himself skinnier and then scooted over beside his boss. "There's one detail about the case that I'm still foggy on, Dalton," he began. "How did Bridget and Tinti get into the park that night since the gates were all locked?"

Lee nodded at his employee. "Excellent question, Warren. I didn't know myself until I took that spontaneous boat trip along the Thames. Or, I should say I didn't know until *after* the boat trip. I left the boat at Greenwich Park, where the equestrian events of the Summer Olympic Games took place a few years ago."

Lara tilted her head. "Dalton, you're not going to tell us they rode jumping horses into the park, are you?"

He threw his head back and issued one loud laugh. "No, Lara, but you're not far off." He paused, scanned the room. "Anybody recall Bridget mentioning that one of the things she and Tinti had bonded over was the fact both of them had competed in track at one point?" Those who had attended the interviews in the diner nodded that they had.

"Well, I did some quick research and confirmed that they not only excelled in track . . . they both excelled in the *high hurdles.*"

Lara spoke up. "That explains the scuff marks you found, and the footprints on the other side of the fence inside the park. And probably the piece of fabric in that low-hanging tree branch."

"Exactly. Tinti may have been in his late forties but remember, he was still in excellent shape, according to Mariam. So once Bridget met up with Tinti in Hanover Square, she issued him a friendly 'Olympic' challenge to enter the park with her by hurdling the fence. Unfortunately, he chose to take her up on that challenge."

"And it unfortunately turned out not to be such a friendly challenge after all," Anisa pointed out.

"So what about the Lebanese guy?" Liam asked. "And that tailor he was in cahoots with? They seemed guilty as hell to me. I mean, the suitcases that were in the trunk of the businessman's car. I guess that was him heading off for Scotland?"

C. J. stepped forward. "Yes, that's correct. Neither Fakhoury, Hensleigh or that firebrand from the bocce court had anything to do with Tinti's murder and as best as we can tell are not in any way connected to The Organization. Of course, Fakhoury and Hensleigh *will* have to answer in court for their violations of our import-export regulations. My guess is Fakhoury will get hustled back to Lebanon when all is said and done. And Armando says that Mr. Hensleigh told Anisa he hoped to be out of the shop by Christmastime because he was planning to retire around then. But I now suspect his retirement is going to arrive a few months earlier than he had anticipated."

"What was he doing on Cyprus most of last year?" asked Warren. "Something to do with their import-export scam?"

C. J. released a long chuckle. "No, Mr. Hensleigh's sabbatical in Cyprus had absolutely nothing to do with fabric. In fact, quite the opposite." Warren gave the commander a look that indicated he wasn't following her.

"Let me put it this way," she continued. "Even though Mr. Hensleigh's profession is that of a tailor, we've learned he is one of those who subscribes to the philosophy that a beautiful body is an unclothed body. Anywhere and everywhere. And Cyprus, as it turns out, has several beaches that cater to people of his . . . persuasion."

The room fell silent and remained that way for a few moments until Bree finally uttered, "Eww."

"So I've been wondering," Bree began. "What happened to the briefcases the attachés brought to their meeting? The real ones containing the nuclear codes, the briefcases the fake guards replaced as they were going through the security machine?"

The commander nodded once emphatically. "Fortunately, we apprehended those valises a couple of kilometers away, in an unmarked van that the counterfeit guards were accelerating toward the M3. It seems none of them wanted to be near the meeting site when everything went kablooey." She sniffed a couple of times and added, "Can't say that I blame them."

"*That* would explain how the Japanese representative was able to get a pistol into the room," Warren said. "All the guards who were really members of The Organization had already left the scene."

Anisa cleared her throat. "Not . . . quite. Two of the guards were still there, so I had to send an agent in with a box of markers."

"Markers?" Lara repeated.

"Yes, I think you Americans call them magic markers? Only, there weren't really any markers in the box the agent brought to the meeting. Just the pistol Kasuo needed to take out the person posing as the attaché from Canada."

Lara shook her head, thoroughly confused.

"It was a spectacular ruse, really," Anisa explained. "See, Kasuo and I go way back. We were in grad school together at Berkeley. I've followed his career in Japan's diplomatic corps ever since.

"Anyway, when Bridget announced during her interrogation that it was the attaché meeting The Organization was targeting, not the meeting of world leaders, I knew Kasuo would probably be there.

"So I texted him from C. J.'s office to let him know what was going on. We agreed I would send one of our agents to the hotel with a box containing the gun, heavily wrapped in Teflon tape in case one of the guards insisted it go through the scanner. And we agreed that when Kasuo came out of the meeting room to meet our agent, he'd tell the guards the box just contained some markers they needed for the meeting inside. And it worked. When our agent arrived, the guards waved the box right on through without even thinking to look in it."

With an impish grin, she added, "The people who join The Organization are terribly ruthless, but they're not always terribly bright."

"And with *that*," Dalton said as he extended one arm in a grand flourish, "I am happy to introduce the newest member of The Lee Group, Anisa Nassir. It's probably inappropriate for me to say I'm delighted by this development, since it stems from the fact she's had someone close to her abducted by The Organization. However, I *am* delighted that she's joining us with C. J.'s blessings, and that she'll be bringing her special insights into the personality of The Organization, and how it thinks, to our investigations."

Lara leaned close to Lee's ear. "And what about Liam?" she whispered.

"Staying with us," Lee volleyed back as quickly as he could. Just then, the door to C. J.'s office opened.

"Roberto!" someone called out.

"And . . . Isabela!" rooted someone else. The designer sauntered in, both hands on the shoulders of the little sister who had been in captivity for almost five years.

"I can't thank you all enough for this," he said, wiping his eyes. "I never thought I'd see this day. I'd pretty much given up hope, at times."

"We hadn't, Roberto," Bree said in earnest. "And you should probably thank C. J. most of all, since she's the one who forced Bridget to reveal Isabela's whereabouts."

The designer placed one palm near his heart and nodded at C. J., who returned the gesture. "Oh, and I'm sorry we're late," he said, "but you know how I am about carbon footprints, and, well, the walk here was pretty time consuming."

"We're just glad you made it *and* that you brought Isabela with you," Lara said, beaming.

The designer whispered into his younger sibling's ear. "What do you say?"

"*Gracias,*" she replied, before she erupted into giggles and squirmed out of her older brother's grasp.

"Didn't anyone bring a bottle of champagne, or at least some prosecco, so we could make a proper toast?" Bree asked, glancing around.

Lee pivoted and reached into a leather caddy he had brought to C. J.'s office, a caddy Lara had referred to on the way as his "man purse." The architect removed a large vacuum flask, loosened the stopper on it, and extended it toward C. J.

"For you, Commander Digby," he said with a nod.

"You do realize, Dalton, we Brits rarely drink our tea from a thermos."

"It's not tea, C. J. It's drinking chocolate. And, I prepared it myself. From my own secret recipe."

The commander responded by ducking her head and blushing. "Oh, Dalton. Now that *truly* is thoughtful. I'm sure it's just . . . *magnifico.*" She took a long swig of the chocolate and her eyes widened to indicate that it was, indeed, to her liking.

"Oh, that reminds me, C. J. I also brought you something." Bree handed the commander a large, gaily wrapped package that had been sitting on the floor. "Open it."

Soon enough, the commander was holding aloft a tote bag identical to the one Bree had been sporting. Except, this bag was mauve. "I found it online and had it delivered," Bree said. "I hope you like it."

"It's exquisite, Breeze, really it is. Perfect for carting my pool noodle to the beach."

Bree considered saying something, but decided to let it go.

Dalton cleared his throat. "Given the length of our flight back to Los Angeles, and the delays involved these days with security clearances at the airport, we best be off. But before we go, I truly want to thank you, C. J., for all the work you did on this case and for keeping us all so . . . entertained . . . throughout."

The commander leaned her head to one side, indicating she had no idea what Lee meant by "entertained."

"Truly, you and Anisa and the rest of your team have been the perfect hosts. And colleagues. I hope our paths cross again, but if they do, I hope it is under entirely different circumstances."

C. J. stepped forward and raised her thermos high above her head. "I must say, I've been grappling with what to say to you and your colleagues, Dalton, when this moment arrived," she began. "After much thought, I have finally settled on this. *Και σε ανώτερα!*"

Everyone in the room nodded, exchanged glances.

"And that means?" Lee inquired.

C. J. rolled her eyes up to the ceiling and called forth one of her goofy grins.

"I have no idea," she replied. "It's something my travel agent told me to say to everybody in Greece when I'm saying goodbye to them. It has something to do with the future . . . making it better . . . something like that."

The employees of The Lee Group nodded again, only with broad, genuine smiles this time. Their leader took one step forward and offered the commander a respectful, formal bow.

"Well, Clara Josephine Digby, may whatever you said, and whatever it means, extend to you, to your career with Scotland Yard, and to all of people who call this wonderful city of London home.

Foreshadowing

The Organization may have been stopped for the time being, but it hasn't given up on its overarching strategy of helping people live flawless lives in a very flawed world. Dalton Lee and the rest of The Lee Group will realize that soon enough, when they are summoned to one of China's most exotic playgrounds and discover that *Murder Becomes Macau,* as well.

***

Please post a review of *Murder Becomes Mayfair*

We would be grateful if you would write an honest review of this book on the page of the bookseller you purchased it from. If you participate on Goodreads, we'd appreciate a review of it there as well. Your review could help other mystery lovers find the book and enjoy it as you did.

***

Get the Backstory

This is not the only time The Lee Group has solved a mysterious murder and deduced how the victim interfered with a takeover scheme planned by The Organization.

Learn more about the architects/detectives who make up The Lee Group, as well as the cult they are shadowing, in:

Murder Becomes Manhattan
murdermanhattan.com

Murder Becomes Miami
murdermiami.com

Connect with Jeffrey Eaton

Facebook
facebook.com/daltonleemysteries

Twitter
twitter.com/murderbecomes

Instagram
instagram.com/murderbecomes/

YouTube
youtube.com/channel/UCdrWC7rirBf-7cKHIIYz14g

Pinterest
pinterest.com/murderbecomes/

Get the inside scoop about the next *Murder Becomes* mystery thriller, and the other upcoming works of Jeffrey Eaton, by signing up for the Jeffrey Eaton email newsletter at **jeffreyeaton.com**

About the Publisher
The Cornet Group LLC was established in 2014 to bring forward intriguing perspectives and intelligent writing presented through the genre of fiction.

Learn more at:

thecornetgroup.com